ADMIRAL OF EARTH

Admiral of Earth

JAMES K. MCVEY

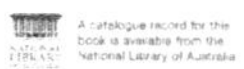
A catalogue record for this
book is available from the
National Library of Australia

For mum and dad, who gave me a love of books and writing.

ALSO BY JAMES K. MCVEY

Children of Ennaris
The Children Return
The Blood Rises
Ennarisi Unite
Children of Destiny

CONTENTS

Prologue

"Captain to the bridge. Initiate battle stations. Shield generator to full. Positive charge to the hull plates."

Lieutenant Sanfil tried to remain calm even as the sinking feeling hit her. Her voice was steady, her face showed none of the worry she was feeling. Around her, the small bridge crew responded well, as she knew they would despite being very young. As the muted tones of the battle warning echoed through the ship and the emergency lighting strips flashed alternately red and amber to ensure that the message was not missed, she ran her own checks and did not like what she saw.

Captain Mactow strode on to the bridge. Sanfil stood and made her way to her usual battle station as the captain took the command chair, nodding to his officer in thanks.

"What do we have?" Mactow asked.

"Cruiser," Sanfil replied. "Appeared off our rear port quarter without warning. Sensors didn't note it until it fired up its drive. Only one showing on screens. It's close."

Mactow nodded. The sensors on the federation fleet's ships were well below the capability of the Empire's ships and the fact had been called out repeatedly to Fleet but with little effect other than expressions of understanding. It appeared that fixing the problem was a larger exercise than it had been thought to be and was beyond the current capability of Earth's best scientists. But right now it was Mactow's problem. The enemy cruisers out-massed him greatly, outgunned him massively and were much faster. And they never operated alone.

"I've charged the hull and brought the shield generator up to full power," Sanfil told her captain, turning from her screen to look at him with a resigned tilt of her head.

Again Mactow nodded. Without reliable energy screens - effective defensive screens remained the stuff of science fiction still - the fleet had developed a method of positively charging the hull plating. The Empire ships' energy beams carried a slight positive charge and if they could manoeuvre so that they only received glancing blows the like charge may help them to withstand or even in some way repel the impact. It was a vanishingly small chance, however, for the enemy ships usually discharged much greater energy in their beams than the Union Fleet ships could handle.

"Engines?" Mactow asked.

"Standard engines are online and fully operational," Sanfil said. "I've brought them up to full power. Just got the full power indicator. We should be able to hold that for a while. Jump engines are still drained but we've started to charge them."

"Okay then," Mactow said. "Let's get out of here. Helm, steer away from the cruiser with a slight starboard lean. Lieutenant, go to full power. Aft shields to full, push the generators as far as they'll go."

Mactow knew the shields would fail as soon as the first energy beam battered against them, but it may hold them for enough time to escape. Earth ships now knew not to try to fight their larger, more capable enemies. Earth ships had yet to win a direct engagement against this enemy. Furthermore, the jump engines were for short distance use only on Fleet ships, especially the smaller patrol vessels like this one, and took forever to recharge.

The ship shook slightly as the engines exerted their full power. Inertial dampers struggled to adjust and the inhabitants of the small Earth ship suffered intermittent G-force effects. Officially rated a gunship - all aboard knew that its guns were sub-standard against the

Empire's ships - the vessel had the latest technology that could be fitted to a ship of this size, but it was inadequate against this enemy.

"They're firing," Sanfil called out urgently.

"Hard to starboard, down fifteen degrees," Mactow ordered.

Starboard and port were old directional terms and up and down were all relative, of course, but it was easier than trying to reel off spatial coordinates and vectors in this situation. The ship responded sluggishly but managed to get out of the way of the beam of energy that speared through its original course.

"Took a little wash from the energy beam," Sanfil reported. "Rear shields have failed. Engineering reports a few interior panels have dislodged. Nothing serious."

Mactow cursed bitterly. The Earth-based fleet had been so sure of themselves while they were swanning around the sector nearest to Earth for three centuries after achieving true space flight capability. Then they pushed out further and encountered the Empire ships - and found themselves out-classed completely. That was almost a hundred years ago and things were no better now. Earth's technology could not stand up to this enemy and win.

"Captain, new contact. Second Empire cruiser, ahead and above," Sanfil reported. "They're firing."

"Helm, jink hard left then hard right and dive," Mactow shouted.

The small ship rocked as the new energy beam gave it the lightest glance on the upper plating but, without shields that could deflect it, the ship suffered damage. It rocked viciously then, miraculously, righted and continued on its course.

"Dorsal sensors are offline," Sanfil reported. "Hull plating took only a touch from that one."

Mactow nodded, thinking furiously. The Empire ships had shown that they had standard tactics for a range of outcomes and did not adapt quickly to new circumstances, but two cruisers against a single gunship was unlikely to end well for the Earth ship.

"Launch all counter-measures," Mactow ordered. "And launch the recordings."

Sanfil sighed. The recordings were launched when the ship was expected to be destroyed. At least someone at Fleet headquarters might get to see some of what transpired.

"Counter-measures away," Sanfil reported.

Around the ship fifteen ports opened and an array of old-fashioned chaff was launched along with a selection of noise-makers that produced the same engine signature as the ship. The chaff formed a cloud in their wake, although travelling along with them as it dispersed, and the noise-makers dashed off in different directions.

The ensign on the helm flung the ship into a set of evasive turns, dives and lifts. Mactow and Sanfil both had to hold onto their chair arms as the dampers failed to compensate well enough. The fourth member of the bridge crew, a young ensign on his first cruise, vomited, at least with the presence of mind to aim away from his console. The sickly sweet-sour smell permeated the bridge and caused them all to feel queasy before the scrubbers quickly pulled the odours away.

"Recorder away," Sanfil reported, and then she snarled. "Captain, engine performance is dropping."

"Are we within range of either ship?" Mactow asked.

"Well out of our range," Sanfil said, "but well within both of theirs. Engine output down to ninety percent of maximum."

Mactow nodded. Again, Earth's engineering was not of the same standard as the Empire ships. Mactow cursed everyone who had a hand in the design of these ships. Supposedly, the ships were designed by the best that Earth had, but they were not good enough. It was a tale of a more advanced and aggressive Empire meeting an unprepared and technologically immature Earth. And Earth was losing. The young Union that the humans had pulled together needed to find a way to deal with this enemy from some sort of position of strength, he thought, but he had no idea how that would happen.

It was his last thought. A directed energy shot from the rearmost Empire ship slammed into the small vessel amidships. The ship was shoved sideways violently. Most of the small crew sustained serious injury as they were thrown against walls or equipment. The bridge bulkheads collapsed. One of the heavier pieces landed on Mactow, killing him instantly. Power conduits ruptured. The vessel's external plating lost its charge immediately. The engine overloaded its constraints in moments and the containment field for the relatively new ion fusion generator failed.

As the second blast of energy from the other Empire ship reached out to spear it, the small vessel exploded. The vacuum of space made it appear quite small and the volume of debris was likewise quite small. The two Empire ship commanders compared notes before returning to their patrol vectors. It had been a victory but had not been a contest, which was how they preferred it.

| **part one** |

MELLIVAR

*575 years before the events described
in <u>Children of Ennaris</u>*

| 1 |

Battle Mage

The small blinking light was the only break in the darkness of the cavern. As it blinked slowly on and off it showed, intermittently, a low couch with a single occupant apparently resting peacefully. The occupant was a woman. The brief periods of illumination showed that she was neither tall nor short for someone born on the planet of Ennaris. She had dark hair arranged such that it formed a thick halo as she rested. She was dressed in dark clothes, a tunic and loose breeches. Her feet were bare, as were her hands. The latter were folded on her abdomen. The first impression one would take from seeing her calm and relaxed expression in repose was of a gentle, tolerant and kindly person.

First impressions can be wrong.

The single light blinked faster and a ceiling light panel at one end of the cavern came to life. Slowly the volume of light increased. The single blinking light flashed faster still and was joined by a second and then a third. The console above the low couch soon showed an array of lights flashing in a peculiar pattern. A second ceiling panel lit. The whole cavern was revealed by the increased light. It was quite long with solid walls seemingly hewn from the surrounding rock. There was an arched doorway at one end. Arrayed along both of the long walls were twenty low couches with consoles above them. Only this single couch had an occupant and it was the only one whose console was active.

The woman stirred.

A panel lifted from the previously solid-looking wall and a small shelf extruded, extending a third of the way down the length of the couch, coming to a stop at the woman's shoulder. A beaker of pale-coloured liquid was on the shelf.

The woman's eyes opened. For a moment she stared at the ceiling and then placed her arms by her side. Gathering herself, the woman pushed herself into a sitting position, swivelling so she sat on the couch with her feet resting on the hard floor. She stretched, working her back and shoulder muscles, as one would when awaking from a long sleep.

"Assistant, what is the date, please?"

The woman's voice was scratchy. She grimaced and reached carefully for the beaker. With a firm grip established, she hoped, she lifted the beaker to her lips and took an initial sip as a voice responded.

"Good evening, Marjory. The date is the 82,175th cycle of sequence Dritera in the Tenth Era. You have been in stasis for five hundred cycles."

"Thank you. Please prepare the tactical displays. I will be in the control chamber shortly."

Marjory took two more sips from the beaker and then drained the remaining contents in a single draught. She endured the astringent taste without gagging - which was different to the last time she had exited stasis when she had tried to down the contents in one go - and replaced the beaker on the shelf. The shelf quietly withdrew into the wall and the panel slid down to cover the service cavity forming an apparently solid wall again. Marjory stood carefully and tested her legs. Both worked which, she thought wryly, was a good sign. Tentatively, and then with greater confidence, she walked back and forth a few times, feeling her leg muscles regain much of their tone. She then strode through the arched doorway.

She was in a passageway with several more arches branching off from its length. Marjory started to walk towards the furthest end but paused as she reached the second of the arches. Quietly she walked into the cavern and stood at the foot of the only occupied couch. A tall, lean man lay in repose on the couch, his sandy hair slightly awry. He wore similar garments to Marjory but with a green fringe to the hems of arms and legs. He would awaken in one thousand five hundred cycles, with Trabor and the twins taking their turns to check on the world and its progress after Marjory. Each would remain awake, in the world that Ennaris had become, for two hundred cycles.

She reached out to Drewflin but did not touch him. Sadly, she contemplated her life partner. He was her equal in raw power if not greater but, where she was battle trained and dealt in destruction for the most part, he was a healer of people, animals and plants. They should have been contributing to the high civilisation that had been Ennaris. Instead, they were watching over a disastrously regressed civilisation that had come close to complete annihilation, and by their own hands. Their efforts to save the planet from the final attack by the rogue Mage Goroth and his supporters had been successful, but at a terrible cost. The result had been the near total destruction of the galaxy's most advanced civilisation, casting its people back to the equivalent of the early stages of urbanisation, with strong elements of a hunter-gatherer lifestyle taking root in several parts of the planet. Shaking her head, Marjory forced her anger and sorrow aside. There was work to be done.

That work took some time. Marjory walked into the main control chamber of the facility that housed the Mages. From here she was able to control many aspects of the high technology protections that remained around Ennaris. Once again, as she had many times in the past, she considered the injunction against high technology that existed on the planet's surface. Created by the legendary old Mage Halfgar, it was almost complete to her knowledge, and yet did not halt the control systems available to her in this control centre, nor the satellite defences that shielded Ennaris from all others. She did not know how that could be the case and she could not ask Halfgar, for the legendary Mage had extended himself beyond his physical body's limitations in creating the interdiction and died in doing so. She missed him still.

It was another frustration among the many that awaited the Mages as they took their turns overseeing Ennaris life.

She reviewed the logs from the available sensors on the planet and in the space around it. A few new wars had been fought, it seemed, and the sensor arrays had provided the material from which the Assistant, the most advanced synthetic intelligence Ennaris had ever produced, had developed a briefing of events since Marjory had last been out of stasis. The twins had intervened in one of the wars, it seemed, preventing a genocide from happening when the bandit who took the title of King of Escar tried to eliminate the small towns to the west of that city. The political map of Ennaris had been redrawn several times. The new kingdom of Escar - or it had been new when the twins intervened - was one of them.

The space-based monitor logs showed that nothing had happened for the first two or three hundred cycles of her latest stasis sleep. But then they started to detect ships with a design broadly similar to come of the older ships of Ennaris, although much coarser in execution. Initially, they passed Ennaris infrequently but, in recent times, were passing more often. Those ships were probing space in the near vicinity of Ennaris. Could they be searching for the planet? The Assistant had used Ennaris' security systems to interrogate several of the ships and found them to be from a civilisation whose leader was known as Likud. Marjory frowned. Could it be? Likud had never been found and the remaining Mages had speculated that he had fled before the barrier on technology had been imposed fully. The civilisation with those ships originated in Andoreth, officially known as Nikera-7, a planet that had been subject to quite a number of uplift expeditions. Likud had been a second to Goroth on the last, controversial, expedition to Andoreth. That may also explain how the ships showed considerable similarity to old Ennari ships. If the leader *was* Likud, did the probes mean that he was seeking to re-enter Ennaris? She made a mental note to come back to that line of thinking.

With that initial review complete, Marjory took stock.

Ennaris remained in a poor state. The Ennarisi, the people of the planet, were only a few steps above barbarity in some places and were even closer to it in others. Admittedly, it seemed that the worst excesses following the devastating end of Goroth's rebellion had passed, but large areas of Ennaris were depopulated. All of Ennaris' cities, once among the wonders of the galaxy, had been destroyed completely. Some were completely obliterated, some had been drowned, while others remained but were in ruins still. One advantage of the advanced civilisation that had been Ennaris, especially when paired with Mages who could reinforce and shape those construction materials - which included the twin Mages Raglin and Ragnor - was that their buildings lasted for a very long time. Little other than the advanced Ennarisi weapons that Goroth had deployed could have destroyed them. The downside of that was that the ruins that resulted from the use of such weapons also lasted for a very long time.

Some of the more enterprising survivors had tried to re-use some of those near indestructible remnants. Most, however, merely worked around them. They tilled fields where large blocks of stone-like material jutted forth or moved the site of a dwelling to cater for ruins found when laying foundations. Many people now had no knowledge of where the blocks or shards of blocks came from. Memory faded quickly when such a near-total disaster took away all but the need to survive. Most did not care, for their lives were hard. Knowing that Ennaris has once been a shining jewel of the galaxy helped them not at all. Marjory knew that they had to be made to care, however. If the Prophesy left by Halfgar was to be believed, Goroth would return and he would have to be faced once again. This time, he would be met with a pitiful few opponents.

Marjory's face hardened as she thought about facing Goroth once again. She had defeated him once and she would do so again, assuming the fates gave her an even chance. And she had Drewflin still. Between them they could achieve almost anything, so she firmly believed. They *would* lift Ennaris once again. The Ennarisi *would* take their place in the life of the galaxy, as they had once before.

Meanwhile, it was time for her to do her patrol, as she thought of it. For this purpose, the Mages often became travelling Tellers, storytellers who roamed far and wide across Ennaris, keeping as many memories alive as they could via oral tradition. It was not a role that Marjory felt in any way suited to, but it allowed them to talk to the people, to remind them of their past and to forewarn them of the battles that were prophesied to come. It was a constant struggle though, because with one of the Mages awake for two hundred cycles at a time, and then a gap of three hundred cycles before another would awaken, the stories stagnated and became legends. Legends became fairy tales. Fairy tales then were forgotten, even though non-Mage Tellers were trained to maintain the tales. The stories needed to be refreshed, the Tellers needed to be reinvigorated. Perhaps, Marjory mused as she ate a simple meal prepared by the technology that for some reason continued to operate within the Council Chambers, it was time to remain awake. Perhaps the Mages needed to make their presence known again.

Her meal complete, Marjory nar Drewflin, last Battle Mage of Ennaris, donned her disguise as a travelling Teller and made her way through the passages of the Council Chamber. It was time to see what had happened during the time that she had been in stasis.

| 2 |

Village

"What in the name of every Guardian?" Marjory muttered as she heard the commotion ahead.

There were loud shouts and curses punctuated by shrill shrieks of fear or rage, the latter likely to be women, Marjory thought as she moved from a walk to a brisk jog. As she approached the crest of the small hill that she had been climbing, a scream rang out, followed by a stentorian bellow.

"Stay in line there, all of you. Get that one!"

Over the crest of the hill came a young woman, panic making her run in a slight crouch. She was looking back over her shoulder as she almost ran through Marjory. Realising at the last moment that someone else was ahead of her, the woman gave a squeak of dismay and slid to a stop in Marjory's outstretched arms. A few moments later, three men in mismatched leather armour over some sort of uniform crested the hill and charged towards the two women.

"Stop her!" one of the men shouted.

Marjory pushed the woman behind her and faced the oncoming men. The three pulled up when they saw the robe and walking staff, the usual signs of a Teller.

"Hold," Marjory said firmly. "What goes on here?"

"None of your business, old woman," the same speaker snarled. "We're takin' her so we can deal with her and her type once and for all. Out o' the way or you get taken with 'er."

"And by 'deal with' I assume you mean to kill this young woman? And her type I guess are her family?" Marjory asked calmly.

"Not just family, all of 'em. The whole bunch are gettin' what they deserve."

"Ah, and who determines what they deserve?"

"The Lord Goodfin, o' course. He needs this land and these ones won't move."

"Ah, so this Lord Goodfin decides he wants the land that is owned by these people, so he kills them all? Is that how it goes in these parts?" Marjory maintained a calm mien, but inside she boiled. *This* is what Ennaris had become? "Let's go have a chat with this so-called 'Lord', shall we?"

"You be careful what you say, old woman. The Lord ain't too 'appy 'bout bein' talked back to," the speaker of the three men snapped as he gestured the other two to move behind Marjory and the young woman. "But you can 'ave yer say and get what ever comes to you. Come 'long with us now."

The young woman whimpered as Marjory regarded the speaker and then nodded.

"It's okay," Marjory said to the young woman. "Things will be fine. What is your name?"

"My, my name is Marjey," the young woman said, haltingly.

"Marjey?" Marjory said as the small party started to walk toward the crest of the hill. "That's an unusual name."

"I was named for Marjey, the greatest ever Mage," Marjey replied.

"Huh, Mages! Ain't no Mages, never 'ave bin. All stories, nothin' more," the speaker of the three men said.

Marjory was stunned. Was this woman named after her? Not quite correctly, but still. Her emotions caught up with her in that moment. This woman was to be killed for some petty warlord to build one of the interminable temporary empires, which at best would last until he was killed in some meaningless skirmish, after which another one would rise to do the same.

They reached the crest and Marjory saw the cause of the commotion. A small village stood to the side of the road that she had been following. A clutch of around twenty cottages occupied a small dell, with a small orchard and some fields that stretched up another hill behind the cottages. Standing on the road in front of the cottages, a line of around fifty people, mostly men and women with a small number of children, were facing a mounted man, with a row of ten guards behind them holding spears and swords. A man in a grubby pale-coloured robe stood beside the mounted man. The mounted man was pointing.

"That one and that one," he said.

Two young women were pushed forward at spear point to stand in front of the others.

"Lord Goodfin, we 'ave 'er," the speaker shouted, causing the mounted man, now identified as the Lord, to turn.

"Good, she can join these two. They'll make a warm bed for the next few nights. What's this other one? A Teller?" Goodfin laughed. "I've no need for a Teller. She can join the others unless there's somethin' worthwhile under the robe."

"And the others will all be executed to satisfy your greed, I take it?" Marjory said evenly, as the group continued to walk towards the scene.

"Fancy speakin'," Goodfin snarled. "I don't need yer words, woman. I don't need even to see what yer hidin' under that robe. You can join that lot and get what they get. Bring the younger over with these two."

"Oh, I think you do need to see what I have under these robes," Marjory said evenly.

She dropped her travel pack from her left shoulder and let go of her staff. The pack thudded to the road surface, while the staff remained standing without her holding it, as though waiting for her to reclaim it. In a single fluid movement, Marjory shrugged out of the Teller's cloak, revealing the black tunic and fitted trousers of the Battle Mage. The trousers had short scabbards built into them that extended down each thigh, with stubby hilts protruding. The mounted man laughed again.

"That's a nice trick but yer still nothin' I need," he said harshly.

"No, but I am what they need," Marjory said, gesturing to the line of villagers. "You should rethink your policy of exterminating those who have what you want."

"And who are you to make me do that?" Goodfin waved to the three men. "Kill her now."

"Ah, Lord," the trio's speaker said. "She's wearin' swords!"

"Is she?" Goodfin said, uninterested. "Well then, take them from her an' then kill her."

"I am the one who'll stop you, Goodfin," Marjory said, in answer to the Lord's question. "My name is Marjory."

"Well, Marjory, you can hand over them fancy swords, or knives more like, and join the others or we'll make yours a painful one."

"I think not," Marjory said.

With a single fluid movement she grasped both hilts and pulled then away from the short scabbards built into her trousers, taking quick steps to reach an open part of the roadway, well away from Marjey. Turning, Marjory smiled grimly and waited, arms held out at forty-five degrees to each side.

Goodfin snorted.

"What are they? You wanta hit us with those little knives?"

Marjory smiled.

"Well, what are you waitin' for," Goodfin shouted. "Get 'er!"

The trio of men who had chased Marjey rushed at Marjory, shouting inarticulate battle cries that may have been meant to intimidate their intended target. They died quickly. Marjory pivoted in place as the twin Battle Mage swords flared into life and quickly extended to form thin blades. The razor sharp edges slashed two torsos open as the first two men reached her, slicing through the boiled leather armoured breastplates like they did not exist. She danced backwards and held her ground, crossing the swords to catch the strike of the third with no apparent effort. She pushed him away easily and waited while he raised his sword again in what he thought was a killing stroke. Both swords pierced him. Holding him upright for a moment while he stared at Marjory, she watched the light go from his eyes. A gout of blood issued from his mouth as Marjory withdrew her swords.

She returned to stand still, flicking the few spots of blood from her swords disdainfully before extinguishing the energy blades and slapping the sword nubs back into their sheaths. She stared at Goodfin, an unspoken challenge to take her on himself. Instead, the self-proclaimed Lord gestured to the men standing behind the villagers.

"Get 'er! Kill 'er!"

Half of the men pushed through the line of villagers, thrusting them aside rudely as they did so. The others followed a moment later. Marjory waited until they were all charging at her. Her hands blurred as she pulled throwing knives from various places - two held on thin thongs hanging down behind her back, two more from the narrow belt around her waist, another two from the inner lining of her boots - and as fast as she drew them she threw them. Six men stumbled and fell, each with a knife placed exactly where Marjory had aimed. Then she leapt from a standing start, somersaulting over the remaining men to land lightly on her feet. The men skidded to a halt and turned.

The four surviving men spread out and started to move in an arc towards her. Marjory drew and activated her Mage swords once again and charged the right-most two, slipping past their ineffective sword strokes and slicing each across their necks. Blood spouted as they fell. The other two stopped and stared.

"I suggest the two of you will be better served by going somewhere else," Marjory said conversationally, showing no signs of exertion as she sheathed her now inactive sword hilts again. "I suggest you also choose a new line of work. If I find you causing any trouble anywhere else I will deal with you."

She stretched out one hand and the staff floated across to her.

The two men glanced to each other and, as one, backed away. Goodfin shouted at them in rage as they turned and started to run up and over the hills. Marjory watched them go. Once they had run over the hill crest she turned back to Goodfin.

"Deal with her, you idiot," Goodfin roared to the man standing by his side.

"Yes, my lord," the man nodded before turning to face Marjory.

He started to make strange shapes in the air in front of him. Marjory recognised the shapes that were inexpertly being drawn. Where had this one learnt to do that?

"That's not a great idea," Marjory said to the robed man.

"I am Heblis, famed wizard of the northern plains," the man replied haughtily, even as he continued to weave his pattern. "I warn you to leave now before I complete this conjure and bring damnation on you."

"All you'll do with that load of arm waving is to kill yourself," Marjory replied, while she watched for any of the supposed lord's men returning. "Where did you learn that, anyway?"

"I am privy to the secrets of the lost Mages," Heblis replied. "It is my task to re-establish the civilisation that was lost."

"And you chose Goodfin as the one to do that?" Marjory asked ironically. "He's one of the causes of the loss of civilisation. And the Mages are not lost."

"I will work with what I have," Heblis replied, ignoring Marjory's last words.

"You missed a bit," Marjory said, helpfully.

"What?" Heblis asked, startled so that he paused his arm waving for a moment, enough for the conjuration to break down.

"At the third movement of the second periodic containment you missed a bit. It's a fairly easy one to miss but most student Mages get away with it. But you tried to combine it with a call to fire and it would have resulted in you being burnt to a crisp." Marjory shrugged. "If you really want to help to bring back Ennaris' civilisation then come with me and I can show you how. Better yet, one of my friends can show you how to make that mess you were doing into something that actually works."

"I need no help from you," Heblis snarled.

He restarted his conjure, waving his hands faster than before, muttering under his breath as he did so. Marjory listened intently and as he progressed her eyes opened wide.

"No," she ordered. "Do not complete that."

Too late. With a triumphant laugh the supposed wizard - to be fair, he did have gifts but no real training - clapped his hands together in front of his face. The air swirled in front of him, creating a vortex. A tiny hole appeared in the air before him and through that hole a hand extended.

"Come, I command you," Heblis shouted.

"Fool!" Marjory shouted, drawing her considerable power in readiness to combat what this idiot unknowingly had brought forth.

The hand extended to reveal an arm, coloured in such a dark red as to be almost black, with claws at the end of the hand rather than fingers. Veins the colour of hot lava throbbed along the arm as though the skin cracked and healed over immediately, only for the effect to repeat elsewhere.

"Yes, come to me, my beauty," Heblis shouted as though in ecstasy.

Marjory gripped her staff. Heblis was bringing forth one of the Kindred, a type of demon that Marjory had fought before. The hand extended further as the tiny hole grew, reaching towards Heblis. He stood and trembled in excitement, continuing to push his own power into the conjure. He did have some power, Marjory thought absently. He could have helped. The arm reached Heblis, who leaned towards it. In a single movement the claws at the end of the arm gripped Heblis by the throat and in another movement broke his neck. Heblis' lifeless body slumped into an untidy heap at the feet of Goodfin's hrss. The power died and the hole to the Kindred's dimension, wherever it was, disappeared with a pop. The portion of the Kindred's arm that had extended through the hole dropped to the ground where it sizzled for a few moments and then withered into dust. Marjory quietly sighed in relief. Goodfin stared at his wizard's body.

"You have lost," Marjory said to the warlord. "I assume these were your best men?"

Goodfin came back from wherever his shock had taken him to glare at Marjory.

"I got plenty more of 'em. When they get through with you -"

He stopped as Marjory's walking staff transformed. The gnarled crown was now a smooth clasp and gripped a milky white stone which was lit by an inner silver light that slowly roiled. The stone looked like it was alive. Marjory walked - stalked - toward the self-styled lord, who tried to kick his hrss into motion. Marjory did not have the facility with animals that Drewflin had, so she merely held the animal in place with a peremptory mental command. Goodfin grew panicked as she drew near. Finally, the Mage stopped no more than two spans from the hrss and glared. For more than a hundred cycles during this time out of stasis she had walked or at times ridden around Ennaris and seen many things she disliked, some that she hated. Of them all, the worst were the greedy, self-centred petty criminals masquerading as warlords, and with this particular specimen in front of her, the frustrations and anger at what Ennaris had become boiled over.

"You are nothing more than a common thief," Marjory ground out. "You're no lord of anything or anyone. You should not even be on that animal. He's better than you are."

Marjory gestured and the erstwhile lord was lifted straight up. His eyes were wild but he reached for his sword and a belt knife. Both were wrenched from his grasp and tossed to the road side by another thought.

"You feel you can take what you want. You have no concern for your fellow Ennarisi. You care only for yourself. There are too many of your type on Ennaris and I'm sick of you."

Another thought ripped Goodfin's leather breastplate open, front and back, and dropped it to the ground. Next followed his blousy shirt and the belt that held the now empty scabbard and knife sheath. His boots were peeled off his feet and deposited with the growing pile alongside the hrss. Finally, his strides were torn from him, leaving only his small clothes. Hanging in the air now was a thoroughly cowed, quivering and markedly over-weight man. His olive-brown skin had a pasty overtone, his eyes were wide and threatened to pop from his face, and his hands waved impotently.

"I have no doubt that you have killed many to get what you want, but I'm not going to do the same to you. But hear me well, Goodfin, lord of nothing. I am Marjory nar Drewflin, Mage of the Council of Mages, Battle Mage of Ennaris. I will be aware of what you do and if I hear of you doing anything to anyone in the future I will track you down and hang your entrails from the five nearest trees."

Goodfin was flung with a final thought, landing with a solid thud and skidding on his face and stomach. He scrambled to his feet, panic etching new lines on his doughy face.

"Go, and do not return," Marjory commanded, gesturing along the road. "Move!" she barked sharply when he made no attempt to leave.

Goodfin started to run down the road, stopping every so often, panting hard. Each time he would turn to see Marjory watching him still. Finally, he reached the point where the road rounded a bend and he was hidden from view by the earthen bank that edged the road at that point. Marjory turned to find the villagers staring at her still.

"The hrss is yours, use it for the good of the village. And for the Guardians' sake find someone trustworthy who can fight and who can teach you to fight. Goodfin was only one of many who will take whatever they can get."

Marjey stepped forward and bowed deeply.

"We - we thank you, my Lady," she said carefully. "I think you for rescuing me and my family and friends. How can we repay you?"

Marjory smiled, allowing the tension to fade away. "You have no need to thank me. My service is and has always been to Ennaris and its people, even if we have not always succeeded in protecting you. Live your lives in peace, but be prepared to fight against such as Goodfin."

"You are a Mage, my Lady?" Marjey asked. "You said your name is Marjory."

"I am a Mage, Marjey, and my name is Marjory. I stood with Drewflin to defeat Goroth. I am who you were named after."

Marjey gasped, as did most of the villagers behind her. Many of them huddled together in fear, and some made signs to ward off evil, for many stories were told of the Mages committing atrocities. Marjory was aware of them and had sought to counter their effects for much of this time out of stasis. She wanted very much to find out who was spreading those particular tales.

"You need have no fear of me," Marjory said to the villagers. "The stories you have heard about the Council Mages killing and maiming ordinary people are untrue." She could see that many were unconvinced and sighed in regret. "Still, I will leave you to your lives. Live them well."

None asked her to stay. Marjey bowed deeply once again and stood back.

| 3 |

Mission Accepted

Marjory was still mulling over the conflict with Goodfin and his crew of ruffians as she rounded a bend in the road late on the following day. Standing in the centre of the road was an old woman, dressed in a dizzying array of different coloured swathes of material worn over what may have been an old tunic. The woman turned when Marjory rounded the corner, as though awaiting her arrival. Marjory slowed her pace and looked around, suspicious. To one side of the road was an old cottage backed into a huge stone the size of a small hill. Marjory had walked or ridden this road several times in the more than a hundred cycles she had been out of stasis and had never seen this cottage or the huge stone. It was one she would have noted.

The old woman waited patiently.

Marjory was unable to sense anything abnormal in the surrounding area, which was a problem because that cottage and great rock should not be there. She continued to walk towards the woman, seeking to maintain the air of an ordinary Teller just going about her business.

"Well met Marjory, Battle Mage of Ennaris," the old woman said as Marjory was still a short distance away.

Well, so much for trying to look like an ordinary Teller.

"Good day," Marjory replied. "I don't recall meeting you and I have a good memory for people. How do you know who I am?"

"Ah, I represent those who know much. They certainly know and honour one of those who stood against the rebels and prevailed."

"Prevailed?" Marjory asked with a twist of her lips. "It doesn't feel as though we prevailed. It feels more like we lost."

"And yet Goroth has been imprisoned and Ennaris continues to exist," the old woman stated. "You of all people know how much power was released that day. You stood against a planetary attack weapon and held its worst effects at bay, ultimately destroying the attacking vessel itself." The old woman smiled gently. "We all lost that day, but you ensured that we were not annihilated. You had help, of course, but your efforts will mean that you are always held in the highest esteem."

Something strange was happening, Marjory thought. This old woman should not be able to speak with any sort of knowledge about the weapons the rebels unleashed against the Council Mages.

"I had Drewflin and a small number of Council Mages to help, and one or two of the rebels returned when they realised what Goroth and Likud were trying to do." Marjory gestured around. "It was not enough."

"You were also assisted by the Guardians, Battle Mage."

"Guardians?" Marjory asked, shaking her head. "There are no Guardians. Why have they never revealed themselves or provided their aid during those darkest days."

"But they did aid you," the woman replied. "Think back to that time when you and your Council Mages were failing under the onslaught."

Marjory was about to refute the statement but paused. She did recall getting a boost from somewhere at a critical time, an influx of power that she thought must have been one or two of the Mages who gave their life force entirely. But maybe not. The power influx was of great size. It allowed her to hold and then push back on the power beam from the capital ship that had broken orbit to attack them. Could that have been the Guardians taking part?

"You should know that in opposing the damage done that day, three of the Guardians lost their own lives in protection of Ennaris and its people," the old woman said softly, sadly.

Three Guardians died? Marjory, like Drewflin and many of the Mages of the past, had never been sure if the Guardians were real or not, and erred toward the latter. Halfgar had assured her repeatedly that they did, and Marjory knew that the twins believed in them. But, if they were real, then the thought that they could die was shocking.

"Yes, the Guardians are not all-powerful. They can die in extreme circumstances. Appanu, Angkor and Zang. Remember their names and honour them, Battle Mage, for they were the ones who absorbed so much of that destructive energy that was turned on you that they perished. Had they not done so, then you would have been destroyed and Ennaris lost."

Marjory was stunned. She replayed that day in her memory once again, using her training to unpick the events from several angles, thinking about the progression of actions and reactions that had occurred, leading up to the climax when they had all been rendered senseless from the effort involved. Yes, it fitted. The attacking ship should have exerted much greater destructive power. She knew that because she was one of the designers of its latest upgrades. It all fitted. She felt overwhelmed at the new understanding. She needed Drewflin. He had helped her to remain grounded in the face of the overwhelming odds they had faced that day, and he would help her to process this discovered knowledge. But Drewflin was not here. Marjory forced herself to come back to the moment.

"Who are you to know of such things? Are you a Guardian?" Marjory asked, a little more sharply than intended.

"I am not one of the Guardians," the old woman said. "I have been asked to intercede, however. There is a need for you to leave Ennaris. That need is real and immediate."

"Leave? Why would I leave? There is so much work to do and so few of us already. If I leave the others will have to do even more. And if the Prophecy comes to pass then I am needed here."

"The final events of the Prophecy are coming closer, it appears," the old woman replied, nodding. "That is one of the reasons for you to leave."

"And go where, do what?" Marjory demanded, her anger rising. "What could be more important than trying to rebuild Ennaris?"

"The Children," the woman replied.

Marjory stared and her anger deflated. *The Children?* The Prophecy spoke of the Children of Ennaris returning to fight with them against Goroth and his rebuilt forces. She and Drewflin had discussed the obscure passages many times. The identities of the Children were masked and opaque. Everyone had assumed that the Children were Ennarisi who rediscovered lost powers and would stand with Marjory, Drewflin and the other remaining Mages. Drewflin had raised the thought they may not be Ennarisi at all, but Marjory had been unconvinced.

"The Children? Are the Children not of Ennaris, then? And they need help?"

"The Children are of Ennaris but not *from* Ennaris," the old woman confirmed. "At least, that is the conclusion reached by Fernis and others."

Marjory closed her eyes for a long moment and took a deep breath. Fernis! A Guardian who legend said was second only to Odruf. A name from myth, as Drewflin had come to believe in his increasing despair and anger, an anger that Marjory could see and feel building even where others continued to see a forever calm mien. It was a lack of belief that Marjory shared most times, one that she wished - hoped - was incorrect at others. A legendary figure from the time of Ennaris' earliest days.

"Are you acting at Fernis' request?"

"I am, and that of Odruf."

Odruf, the equally legendary leader of the Guardians.

"What of the others?" Marjory asked.

"The others are prepared to allow those who stayed on Ennaris to guide them in this," the old woman replied.

"Stayed?"

"Most of the Guardians were forced to leave Ennaris after the rebellion was ended," the woman explained. "Odruf and Fernis remained to maintain Ennaris as far as they were able. And they need your help."

"Why did they leave?" Marjory asked, still not sure what to believe.

"The Prophecy made it clear that, if the Guardians remained on Ennaris, then Goroth would be victorious. Why is not stated, merely the fact. Knowing who was inspired to write the Prophecy, the Guardians decided not to invoke the risk. They have dispersed across the galaxy to assist other planets and peoples, as has been done by individual Guardians at times in the past. They will return when the time is right."

Marjory looked around her. The road ran through a section of what had been neatly tended farmland but had become overgrown by shrubs and trees. The land had reverted to the wild quickly after the farms were abandoned in the wake of the destruction, disease and breakdown of civilisation that had occurred after the rebellion's destructive climax. This road was a poorly kept, dusty path that traversed the sector, running from one struggling town to another struggling town, both of which were in the grip of warlords who sought to extend their grasp. Goodfin's base was far enough away that he was not involved in this particular conflict. Marjory had intended to try to stop what she was sure would become a bloody war shortly. Now she was standing in this road with an old woman speaking of disastrous events of long ago, of legendary beings, of the Prophecy that few remembered or cared about in the hardship and pain of daily life.

"Who are you," Marjory asked for the third time. "And what do you want of me?"

"It is not I who ask this of you, Battle Mage," the old woman said formally, ignoring the first question again. "Are you prepared to listen to the request?"

Marjory paused for a moment. Doubt and uncertainly warred with her desire to understand more, to know more. For whatever reason, she believed this woman. But she did not want to leave Ennaris. She did not want to leave Drewflin. Or the others, but Drewflin was her beating heart, he was the one who kept her centred. And yet…

"I will listen," Marjory replied. "What is it you would have me do?"

"Not I," the woman replied. "But Fernis."

"I do you honour, Battle Mage of Ennaris," a deep voice said from behind Marjory.

Marjory yelped, startled. She spun around. Walking toward her was a tall man. Long flowing dark hair was tied neatly at the nape of his neck and hung down his back. He wore what seemed to be a homespun robe of forest green. He exuded a young-old feel. Marjory stared as she opened her Mage sight to view the newcomer's aura, which nearly blinded her. Belief followed in a rush. Almost without volition she knelt before this being.

"Guardian," she whispered in awe, staring to the ground.

"Nay, Marjory, you need never abase yourself to me or any of us Guardians," Fernis replied, lifting her to her feet.

"I believe my job is done, Fernis?" the old woman asked from behind Marjory.

"Indeed it is," Fernis replied. "As always, you have my thanks and the thanks of the Guardians, Dharmoney."

Dharmoney!

Marjory swung around again to stare at the old woman, who gave her a kind smile. Another legend!

"I'm afraid I must ask you for your staff, Battle Mage," Dharmoney replied.

"M - m - my staff?" Marjory stammered, overwhelmed for one of the very few times in her life. "But - but - I need it."

"And I will hold it for you," Dharmoney replied, "or your successor. You will have no need of it where you will be going, but it may be of use here."

Marjory turned to Fernis who merely smiled and nodded. She looked to the Mage staff that she still held, now back in the passive guise of a walking staff. She weighed the staff in her hand and then, with a sigh of resignation, handed it to Dharmoney. The staff flared into life and was muted quickly, before shrinking to little more than the nub of a staff.

"I hope to see you again, Battle Mage," Dharmoney said. "May the hunting be good and the enemy worthy."

"And the victory sweet," Marjory replied automatically to the old, in fact ancient, warrior farewell.

Dharmoney turned and walked to the cottage, entered and closed the door. Marjory turned back to Fernis - she had turned her back on a Guardian! - and opened her mouth to speak when there was a huge *crash* from behind her. She spun back and was stunned anew. The cottage and its huge stone backing were gone.

"Dharmoney has her own way of doing things, does she not?" Fernis said.

"Um, I'm feeling a little out of my depth right now," Marjory replied as she turned once again to face Fernis. "Dharmoney" - she closed her eyes and took a deep centring breath at the thought of having met the legendary saviour of Ennaris - "Dharmoney said you want me to leave Ennaris. Where and why?"

"What do you know of the Prophecy?" Fernis asked.

"Probably not as much as I should. Drewflin is the one who spends time examining it." She paused and her eyes opened wide. "Drewflin! He has lost so much belief in the Guardians. Will you reveal yourself to him also?"

"When the time is right," Fernis replied. "For now it's not."

"But he needs to know you exist, even if we have been left to fend for ourselves," Marjory objected. "I'm afraid of what he may do when he finds I am gone. He has so much anger, so much *rage* being held inside."

"You have been allowed to fend for yourself but you have never been alone," Fernis said kindly. "One of us has been with you in one way or another for a very, very long time, even before the rebellion. However, to answer your first questions, we want you to go to Ordoreth to help the people of that planet. They have recently achieved space travel but have fallen into the path of an implacable foe from Andoreth."

"Likud!" Marjory spat out, recalling her briefing from the Assistant. "I would very much like to find Likud."

Fernis laughed at the Battle Mage's change of demeanour from confused Mage to angered warrior.

"You may or may not meet him," Fernis replied, confirming Marjory's thought that the Likud who was leader of Andoreth was the same one who fled when Goroth was defeated. "But we want you to help the people of Ordoreth to stand against Likud and his empire."

"Why?" Marjory demanded. "What is there about Ordoreth that is so important?"

"Ordoreth is very like Ennaris in many ways, not least in its people. As you know, it was seeded by Ennaris long ago, and as a result the people of Ordoreth are very closely related to the Ennari. The Prophesy states that the Children of Ennaris will return. Both Ordoreth and Andoreth were uplifted by Ennaris, and both received significant genetic material from the Ennarisi teams to assist them to do so. We believe Ordoreth to be the source of the Children."

Marjory nodded slowly. "So not from Ennaris but of Ennaris - one of the colonised uplifts," she said. "Drewflin and I discussed that possibility often. But could it not apply to Andoreth also?"

"Indeed, and we hope that is not the case for Andoreth has been subdued almost completely by Likud. If the Children come from Andoreth then we fear that Ennaris may be lost, for they would side with Goroth."

"But the Prophecy -" Marjory said, and than paused, thinking.

Fernis nodded. "The Prophecy does not say that the Children will fight with the Council Mages, but that they will be at the final battle and will lead the way to victory. It does not say on which side."

Marjory nodded. "But at the moment those of Ordoreth are outmatched by Likud's forces? If I know him he will be using crude but overwhelming force." She thought. "The sensors noted the passage of ships from Andoreth and their design is heavily based on those of Ennaris from a time long before the rebellion, only more massive and less capable."

"Likud was never interested in the design of those ships and has little subtlety," Fernis replied with a wry tone. "Power in quantity appears to be his mantra. However, the people of Ordoreth have a different philosophy, one that is more in accord with what Ennaris was. But they are in great danger. They need someone to help them to survive and then to hold their own against Andoreth. But you will have to work subtly and not seek an abiding leadership role yourself, although you may find yourself occupying one at times. For at the right time you will be needed here."

"If I survive," Marjory said with a slight smile, thinking back to Dharmoney's words.

"If you survive," Fernis acknowledged with a tilt of his head.

"How do I get there?" Marjory asked after a resigned sigh, acquiescing to Fernis' request.

"I will take you to the moon base and you will take a ship. The base has everything you will need and it remains intact. It is outside the interdict on technology."

"Very well, Guardian," Marjory said with a slight bow, taking a look around at the surface of Ennaris, hopefully not for the last time. "To Ordoreth."

"I will give you more information at the moon base. And the people of Ordoreth do not call it by that name."

"Oh? What is their own name for the planet?"

"Earth!"

| 4 |

The Plan

Escantil - an ancient Ennarisi word that referred to that odd stage that occurs during almost any battle between attack and defence - was the name of the moon base. It was exactly as Marjory remembered it, only without the bustle of people moving around the corridors or riding the shuttles between the levels and the different stations. It had an eerie feel to it, she thought to herself. This base had housed over five thousand personnel, military and other. It was not meant to be empty.

Fernis had taken her to one of the hanger bays and left her there after giving her a deeper briefing. How he knew which one to go to she had no idea - he was a Guardian, after all. But this was the one that held the advanced experimental ship that she had been working on when the rebellion broke out - 'exploded' was a better word - and when Marjory had been called back to the surface by the Archmage. Everything was as she had left it, down to the mostly completed schematic that popped up once she had scanned her DNA into the security system.

Of course, given that she was officially now the ranking - and only - Battle Mage of Ennaris, there were a huge number of alerts to work her way through, and not a few requests by the various subordinate synthetic intelligences for approval of various repairs, changes and updates. She spent almost a day working her way through the minutiae of the moon base's operational requirements. As ranking Battle

Mage this now was part of her domain, a fact that caused a moment of deep introspection. She could not neglect the base's requirements, however. When the rebellion broke out she was a shooting star in the Mage circles, along with Drewflin, destined for great things, but far in the future. No matter how great were her gifts and how bright her star, there had been dozens of trained Battle Mages ahead of her in the hierarchy of the various stations around Ennaris and the many sectors of the galaxy that Ennaris claimed as its area of interest. Now there were none and the responsibility fell to her.

There were several requests for upgrades to the repair facilities to cater for vessels that were not yet designed, let alone built, but the requests were accompanied by suggestions for design improvements of ships that would use those facilities. Marjory examined them closely. The proposed improvements were impressive. In fact, some of them were inspired. Thinking back to the several Andoreth vessels that she had seen, with their crude but powerful designs based on older Ennari ships, Marjory knew that she would have to get better ships built for Ordoreth - Earth, she reminded herself. The designs proposed were improvements on existing designs, some of which she had worked on. Several of those she had designed from the start. As a rule, they were sleek, fast and would pack a serious but unexpected punch. Exactly what may be needed against Likud.

She approved the modifications for the facilities to support such ships, and then ordered the designs to be downloaded to the experimental ship. Then she thought further and ordered the manufacturing facility to start to build a new class of single seat fighter craft based on some of the evolved designs. Why should Ordoreth get the benefit, she thought, when Ennaris may have the same need at some stage. She ordered the hundreds of older fighters to be recycled or, if possible, upgraded to the revised specification. The system popped up a budget approval request, which Marjory approved with a rueful smile. Some things did not change. Then she reviewed various other designs, metallurgical studies and energy generation designs. Once she had cleared the mundane requests and worked through the more esoteric ones, she spent half a day looking through records from many branches of the military, exploratory and defence establishments that Ennaris had once had. She ordered various records, design sheets and process documents to be downloaded to the ship.

She may be gone for some time, she realised. That may mean that she would not be back at the exact time when Goroth emerged from stasis. She needed to set in place a means of being informed when events started to move forward. But what would they be? How could she make sure that she would be able to get notified when those events occurred? Then she realised it would have to be one of two things - either something about Goroth or something about the one person who would take the right action, no matter what. Drewflin! She thought through the various scenarios that she could envisage, made a few updates and then entered several commands into the security system. On the surface of the moon a small slot opened and a series of sensors were launched. Several took station around Ennaris. The rest set out on various journeys to multiple locations that would allow for her to be notified of happenings, if her nascent plans came off.

The experimental ship, which was the size of a overlarge shuttle or a small frigate, was prepared for a long journey. 'Shuttle' and 'frigate' were poor descriptions for the vessel. Marjory had been working on a relatively small ship that was able to traverse enormous distances and that had a potent combination of defensive and offensive capabilities that would not be expected of a vessel of its size. A large number of experimental technologies had been planned for the ship, and most had been installed already. Marjory made adjustments based on the design AIs' suggested upgrades - they had had thousands of cycles to consider improvements - and then decided to wait for the improved systems to be installed. This ship would be a mini-destroyer, a pocket destroyer as she had always thought of it, in the guise of a larger shuttle or even a personal transport.

Finally, she felt that she was ready, or as ready as she was likely to be. Five tendays had passed since Fernis had left her at Escantil. She had downloaded everything that had been gleaned from a single Ordoreth - Earth - ship that had passed one of the closer farstations, including star charts, language files and various history narratives. She would work her way through them on the journey. However, she had reviewed some of the records from the Earth ship. After long thought, Marjory decided not to go to Earth after all, but to one of the outer sectors where they likely would have immediate need of her assistance. Earth was losing each and every battle with the Andoreth ships, for their vessels were no match in speed, fighting capability or defensive capability, and those weaknesses had to be halted quickly.

It was shortly before her planned departure that Dharmoney walked onto the bridge where Marjory was making final preparations. There had been no indication of a ship approaching, no sign of any kind of power surge, no sensor readings. The old woman - or, Marjory corrected herself, one who *looked* like an old woman - was just there. In her hands she carried a small box which she placed on the command console.

"Fernis and Odruf thought you may need this, Battle Mage," she said conversationally without any preamble.

"What is it?" Marjory asked as she gave this legendary, nay mythical, figure her full attention.

"It is called Shakar," Dharmoney replied.

Dharmoney touched the box and the sides folded back onto themselves and then laid flat. Inside, floating as though on a repulsion field, was what looked like a rock.

"It looks like a rock," Marjory said, with a querying look to Dharmoney.

"It is a rock," Dharmoney confirmed. "But Shakar is a very special rock. Shakar has agreed to assist you with your task. It is a sentient being. It is able to establish a kind of rapport or connection with whoever holds it. The result can be … difficult for some. You see, Shakar strips away any illusions you may have about yourself. It feeds back to you that which is you, unfiltered by your own self-image, self-doubts or self-delusions. For some it can be shattering. For others it can be empowering and affirming."

"Have you held it?" Marjory asked, curious.

"I have," Dharmoney smiled. "It was … intense."

"And did you learn anything about yourself?" Marjory asked.

"Oh yes, quite a bit. It can be confronting to see yourself as others see you. It can be even more confronting to have your own self-image shaken and shifted." Dharmoney paused. "Your mission is of the utmost importance to Ennaris, Battle Mage. Unless you have clear self-belief I suggest you only use Shakar to help find those of the character you require, those who may become a champion for your battle with Goroth and his minions, but you may wish not to undertake the trial yourself."

Marjory stared at the stone, floating above the base of the box. She glanced to Dharmoney thoughtfully.

"I have never asked others to do that which I am not prepared to undertake myself," she said quietly.

Dharmoney smiled briefly.

"Nor have I," she replied. "Think on it and be sure in yourself before taking the challenge, for there is no undoing what Shakar will reveal."

"Will Shakar speak or communicate with me in any way?" Marjory asked.

"Not in a way you can understand or replicate, I'm afraid," Dharmoney said with a shrug. "Fernis was aware of the existence of Shakar and its kind and requested their assistance. I have had no contact with it other than my own experience. And, it seems that once you have had that experience it will not be repeated. I tried."

"And when the mission is completed, I just bring Shakar back with me?"

"I think that would be best," Dharmoney replied. "I'm sure one of the Guardians could retrieve it but, to my knowledge, Shakar does not move on its own volition. Despite its ability to levitate itself, it cannot move through space."

"Thank you," Marjory said after a moment of thought. "I will consider how best to use Shakar's assistance."

Dharmoney nodded and walked from the bridge without any ceremony or leave taking. She never appeared on the ship's sensors in the hangar. No ship launched from the moon base. She just disappeared. Marjory sat and looked at Shakar for a long time, turning over possibilities and options. Finally, she sighed and returned to the tasks involved in preparing to leave, occasionally glancing to the console where Shakar floated gently as though it was a leaf lifting and falling on the tiny swells of a pond.

Finally, she was ready to depart. One last thing was needed. Marjory had thought long and hard about a name for her vessel, and finally had hit upon the name 'Fendaristil', which combined the twin concepts of critical mission, 'fendar', and rescue, 'aristil', both words from one of the old Ennarisi tongues that had been maintained over many millennia. She made the necessary adjustments to Escantil's records - and then authorised the change, which was highly irregular but the only avenue available for the supervisor system given that Marjory was the sole remaining authorising official - and entered the coordinates to the navigation system. Finally, she settled herself in the command chair on the small bridge and opened a channel to the launch control synthetic intelligence.

"Escantil Control, this is mission vessel *Fendaristil*, requesting release and launch."

"Mission vessel *Fendaristil*, release and launch approved. Good hunting, Battle Mage."

"Acknowledged, Escantil Control."

Fendaristil launched via an iris that opened in a small crater on the surface of the moon. Marjory knew there were much larger portals that could be opened into the launch bays, but the tiny one that she used would not be seen unless a vessel was on top of it, and none were. The ship's intelligent agent (IA) engaged the vessel's stealth capabilities. She was on her way.

The trip to the area of space that was controlled by the Union - as it seemed the Earth-led confederation called itself - took Marjory almost fifteen tendays. She could have made it in much less time but she had a lot of research and planning to do.

Part of the time was spent familiarising herself with the various dialects that had been detected. *Fendaristil* continued to scan the available frequencies, establishing a relatively narrow band that the Earth-led coalition used almost all the time. The encryption used was fairly rudimentary and no match for any Ennarisi IA, let alone *Fendaristil*. Marjory obtained a fairly clear idea of what she was facing. It was not good!

In terms of language there were only three or four crucial dialects but dozens of less used and understood ones. She chose the dialect spoken on Brelobat, a planet in the outer reaches of the Union's territory, in the opposite direction to Ennaris, as the one that she would use in the event there was a problem with word choice or pronunciation. It had enough variations from the normal versions as to appear to be a different language. That was an easy problem to solve. The extensive lexicon that *Fendaristil* developed was loaded into Marjory's translation implant, a technology that all Ennarisi had embedded when young, or at least had until the rebellion.

Of more concern was the military capability. From transmissions intercepted by farstations and passed to *Fendaristil*, Marjory could piece together the position. The Union ships were far behind those of Andoreth. They were outgunned, out-massed, out-numbered and the ships had almost no true defensive options but to run - and they were much slower than the Andoreth ships. Marjory monitored four engagements between Union and Andoreth ships and they all ended the same way - the Union ships were destroyed quickly. In two of those engagements, the Union vessels seemed to have made it away from the pursuing Andoreth ship, only to find that they had been herded into the path of another Andoreth ship. In a third, the ship did not sense the Andoreth ship until it was too late and it was destroyed with minimal resistance. The fourth Union vessel decided to attack rather than defend and was lost before it could even get within range to launch its own weapons.

So, add to the list that the Union vessels had poor sensor technology and poor tactics, the latter probably because the commanders of the ships did not survive long enough to learn, adapt and improve those tactics that they did have. It was obvious that the order of priority had to be to make the Union ships hard to kill and only then could they be made hard to beat.

That led to the next problem. The hierarchy of the Union space fleet, based on intercepted communications, resisted external assistance, which meant Marjory would have to become an insider to make any change. She could not just walk into the military and be heard. Joining at a junior level, if she could do so, would mean that she had to work through the ranks. She was not sure if she had the time, at least for the initial phases. Also, there was something odd about the consistent refusals to meet with people who were offering upgraded sensors, better plating for the ships, stronger drives. That stubborn resistance to new ideas would bear some consideration. So, she needed to work her way into the establishment, but from the outside.

After making and discarding plan after plan she hit on what she believed would be the logical best plan - to make a compelling case for the better technologies to be adopted by forcing the decision-makers to make that decision. How? By a demonstration of the outcomes. That led to a second plan. In order to demonstrate the outcomes she would have to be able to produce at least one and maybe two or three better ships. And she thought she knew just how to accomplish that.

First, however, was Shakar. Despite what she told Dharmoney, Marjory had been uncertain as to whether she would undertake what could be a difficult experience that had the potential to damage her mission. Still, as she *had* told Dharmoney, she truly believed that she should ask others to do only that which she was prepared to do herself. She was three days away from Union space. Surely the trial would not take that long.

Shakar continued to float above the base of the box. Marjory stood before the console and regarded the rock. There was no indication of sentience, no indication that Shakar was anything but a rock, a little larger than Marjory's hand, except that it was levitating. Marjory twisted her lips wryly. *Either do it or don't,* she though to herself. She reached out and gripped Shakar in one hand. Oddly, the rock now fitted the palm of her hand perfectly.

For a brief moment nothing happened. Then Marjory was turned inside out, or so it felt. With a blast of raw power, Shakar gripped her whole psyche and for what seemed like hours tore it apart and examined every bit of it. She could feel her memories being sifted and sorted, weighed and evaluated. Time dilated. The feeling of her innermost self being *reamed* became her whole being. The sense of helplessness threatened to overwhelm her but, at that thought, the innate strength of the Battle Mage came to the fore and she held firm against the onslaught. She endured. The intense examination of her inner self slowed and finally came to a halt. Marjory breathed a short sigh of relief. Dharmoney had been right - it was intense.

Then the playback began.

Marjory was flooded with wave after wave of sensations, an immediate sensory overload that threatened to sweep away all that she was. Back through time she went as she saw her earliest failures with her gifts, then jumping forward to her triumphs in the academy for design, and back again to the time she met Drewflin, the lean stripling who she would claim as her own. Forward to the acclamation she received as one of the two youngest ever additions to the Council of Mages, along with Drewflin. Forward further to the point where they both realised that Goroth needed to be stopped. Forward again to the anguished moment when she knew that her son had been killed and then her single-handed attack on the rebel encampment. Back again to the time of the attack by the extra-galactic Grel, when Marjory had led the defence of the outer quadrant and routed the attackers. Forward to the joyous time when she could tell Drewflin that she was with child. Back, forward, back, forward, forward again. The flood of images continued unabated.

Through it all Marjory was aware of the sense of failure or triumph at each point, and equally aware of the feelings of others at those same junctures. She was shocked when she realised that Goroth's rebellion was as much because he saw her as usurping what he saw as his own rightful place in the Battle Mage community. Was she ultimately responsible for the rebellion that devastated Ennaris? She *felt* the disdain towards her by some Mages who were many thousands of cycles older than she was, when she was raised to the Council ahead of them. She experienced the odd mixture of fear, awe and hatred held by Likud to such an extent that she had never been consciously aware of before. Likud, who became irrational at the idea of Marjory sitting on the Council and having any sort of influence over his own fate. But then she felt the love that Drewflin *exuded* when she gave birth to Marflin, their only child. And the high regard with which she was held by many others in the Mage community. The celebrations when she and Drewflin were raised to the Council was in stark opposition to the Goroth and Likud camp.

Back and forth Shakar took her, switching topics, timelines, perspectives and sentiments in a seemingly unending river of sensations and feelings. She felt battered and shaken, exhilarated and shattered. No pattern repeated itself as she was flung across the course of her own life and the events that she had experienced. Her sense of self was stretching, becoming thin, and yet underneath it all was the knowledge that almost everything that she did was for the people of Ennaris. She acknowledged her mistakes and missteps, she recognised times when she could have done things better, she sorrowed at the times when she had caused physical hurt or emotional pain because of error or lack of empathy with those she said she wanted to help.

The questioning, the doubts, the uncertainty about whether she truly had their interests at heart or was seeking self-aggrandisement - all assailed her relentlessly. Yes, she thought, she was proud that she had been the youngest ever to be appointed to the Council, although barely because Drewflin was not much older. Yes, she had sought advancement through both the hierarchy of the Battle Mage community and the design division of Ennaris' military machine. Yes, she was a hard task master and had only become harder since the rebellion. Yes, she suffered incompetence or fools not at all. All of those could be failings but she held her own thoughts against Shakar's insinuations and tendrils of doubt.

For she also found that she had been the source of strength to those who sought her assistance. She was gratified and a little surprised to find that she recalled times when her team members had been pleased to be on the receiving end of a lesson in advanced design or aeronautics, weapons or tactics, all of which came so readily, so intuitively, to her but that she learned over time did not do so for many - most - others. She held firm against Shakar and pushed back. There were wins and losses, successes and failures and she relived them all over again in depth. But she refused to give in to the sly innuendo of those failures, or the *felt* hatred of those who had considered her to be some sort of enemy long before the rebellion.

She held her identity. She was Marjory nar Drewflin, Battle Mage of Ennaris! The last Battle Mage of Ennaris. Her *life* had been dedicated to the service of her people, even if she did despise many of the lowest elements that had crawled out from their hiding places in the many long cycles since the rebellion. She had lost her own son to the fight, as had so many others. She would not crumble! She would not wilt! Not now, not *ever*! She *would* see Ennaris safe once again!

Shakar released its grip on her and Marjory staggered away from the console, almost dropping the stone. She went to one knee, hanging her head as the physical effects were felt now. She was shocked to see that mere moments had passed, almost no time at all, during which she had lived and relived her life, her choices and their outcomes. She hauled herself to her feet again and reached out to place Shakar above his box once again. But, as she did so, she felt the being who was Shakar deliver its verdict. A warmth extended from the sentient rock, reaching her heart, suffusing her with a sense of love, of acceptance, of inner peace, of honour given. And with it came a single word, a word that she felt in her very core rather than heard.

Worthy!

| 5 |

Mellivar Arrives

"**M**ister Drummel, there's someone to see you," the industrialist's pretty young assistant announced. "She says she has something you need."

"What I need is some damned common sense to prevail in the Fleet supply arm," replied Arn Drummel. "But right now I'm not doing anything worthwhile so why not have a chat with someone new. Who is it?"

"She says her name is Mellivar."

"Who does she represent?"

"No-one, I think," the assistant said cheerfully. "She said she's all by herself."

"Fine," Drummel sighed. "Send her in."

Marjory strode through the doorway of Drummel's office, situated above the manufacturing floor of a high technology plant in the city of New Greph, the third largest city on the planet Keplas. From her research, Marjory knew that Keplas was a relative backwater in Union space, being largely agrarian. It had limited industry, and what there was mostly was situated on a series of orbital platforms. The people of Keplas had decided not to repeat the mistakes made with the home world and countless others since the people of Earth had industrialised. Drummel's small factory on the surface was an anomaly, although she knew that he also had a much larger facility on a small orbital.

But Keplas also was close to the frontier where Likud's empire met Earth's Union space, and so was an ideal location for the first phase of her plan.

"Mister Drummel," Marjory said as she entered, "thank you for seeing me."

"Well, it's not as though I have a huge amount to do," Drummel replied sourly, gesturing to a seat near his work station. "Business has almost stopped recently, as you can see, Ms Mellivar."

In fact, Marjory had selected Drummel in part because his contracts had dried up and his factory was standing idle. That and the fact that he had been one who had pushed hard against the decisions not to purchase what he claimed were more advanced materials that would provide better protection for the Union's vessels. As a result, he had been blocked from further work and it appeared that other customers had been warned away. That was behaviour that Marjory thought merited further investigation, but it could come later. *Fendaristil* was already on it, though.

"Just Mellivar. That's what I wanted to speak to you about," Marjory said. "I need a manufacturing facility, but one capable of turning out advanced alloys and materials. You have one that is largely idle."

"What sort of advanced alloys and materials? And for what purpose?" Drummel asked without apparent interest. "And it probably doesn't matter, anyway. My credit has run dry as punishment for fighting against the Fleet's procurement division, my materials suppliers have refused to deal with me and I probably will be losing the orbital any day now."

"You owe money?" Marjory asked.

"Up to my ears," Drummel replied sadly.

"And what about the new plating you tried to sell to the Union Fleet? Is that real or theoretical?" Marjory eyed Drummel uncertainly, the air of defeat about him having grown as the conversation lengthened.

"How do you know about that?" Drummel's interest levels lifted at Marjory's question. "That was rated highly classified. I'm not supposed to talk about any part of it. Is this some sort of test?"

"If it was," Marjory said with a smirk, "you just failed. No, no test. But I am interested and I may have a proposition that could ease your money worries."

"What sort of proposition?"

"As I said, I need a manufactory, one able to turn out and shape advanced materials. But I want it to be operational already, with relatively minor retooling needed. So, was your supposed new plating real or just plans? According to the proposal you put forward it had better ablating capabilities, would be able to resist the - ah - enemy's energy weapons for longer, and was lighter than the existing material."

Drummel regarded Marjory steadily for a long moment.

"How do you know that? Even most of my staff don't know those details," Drummel stated.

"Not quite true," Marjory replied evenly. "By the way, what is the name of your quite lovely assistant?"

"Um, what?" Drummel fumbled under the abrupt change of direction. "Yes she is. Lovely, that is. Her name is Margey."

"Another one," Marjory muttered.

"Sorry, what was that?" Drummel queried.

Marjory shook her head, waving away the question with one hand.

"Margey, please come in," Marjory said conversationally.

There was a gasp from outside the office and the sound of someone - Margey - slapping the door open control in the outer office, and then slapping it again. And again. The door stayed closed.

"It won't work," Marjory said in the same conversational tone.

"What won't work," Drummel asked, puzzled.

"Your outer door," Marjory said. "I sealed it after I entered."

"Why?" Drummel was starting to become alarmed. "What are you after?"

Drummel's door slid back into its wall housing and Margey rushed into Drummel's office. Her pleasant, cheerful expression had been replaced with a snarl. She gestured with the small gun held in her right hand.

"Get up and go around behind Drummel," Margey ordered Marjory.

"What, what … huh?" Drummel tried to speak but could find no words.

"Margey is not who you thought her to be," Marjory said gently to Drummel before looking to Margey. "Fleet security?"

"Fleet security?" Margey snorted her disdain. "They have no idea. Now get up, like I told you."

"No, I like it here," Marjory replied, apparently unconcerned as she looked at the weapon.

"This is not some sort of stungun," Margey spat. "*This* gun is a projectile weapon, one of the old ones. It fires a slug of metal that causes serious damage."

"No," Marjory said. "*That* gun does not work. In fact, *that* gun is getting quite hot and the projectile accelerant is about to explode." Marjory increased the rate of heating she was applying to the weapon's metal components, using one of the lower order techniques that some Mages learned at a young age. "Is it not?"

With a yelp, Margey dropped the gun. Marjory pushed a shield around it just in time. The powder inside the bullet casings exploded as it hit the floor and tore the ancient gun apart, but the shield held the metal fragments bound as they lost their energy. There was a clatter of shattered metal as the shards and fragments hit the floor. Margey and Drummel stared at the remains of the gun.

"What's happening?" Drummel said, bewildered.

"Margey, here, is not an assistant, at least not for you. She has been in frequent communication with a Captain Jonsil from your Fleet headquarters," Marjory replied.

"Jonsil?" Drummel looked from Marjory to Margey and then to the ruined gun, still unable to take in the recent events. "But he's the head of the section that refused to deal with me. Why?"

"Indeed, why? I think that's an excellent question. I believe I know, but how about we let Jonsil's spy tell us." Marjory raised an eyebrow to Margey. "Margey?"

"That's Ensign Petarson," Margey replied, standing straight and facing Marjory. "And how do you know that?"

"I intercepted some of your communications," Marjory replied with a frown. "Margey - sorry, Ensign Petarson - was sending Captain Jonsil information about your new material, the results of the testing, what was happening with your business position. Pretty much anything that came her way, I expect."

"But I still don't understand. Why would Fleet want to spy on me?" Drummel asked.

"Because you're an agent of the Empire," Ensign Petarsen snarled, pointing at Drummel.

"I'm a what?"

"Don't play that game," Petarsen laughed bitterly. "Captain Jonsil told me all about it, how you developed some supposedly new ideas and offered them to the Empire when Fleet wouldn't buy. Now what? You space me and continue on your merry way, I suppose?"

Drummel looked at Marjory with a lost expression. Marjory, in her turn, regarded Petarsen for some time, long enough to make the spy uncomfortable.

"What are you staring at?"

"Why, at you, of course," Marjory replied. "I think you truly believe Drummel is an agent. Well, I am sorry to have to inform you but you are wrong. Looking at the pattern of behaviour and the results of that behaviour, I expect Jonsil is the agent."

Petarsen blinked in astonishment.

"Captain Jonsil? How can you say that?"

"It's pretty simple. Jonsil has been refusing any and all requests to supply new materials and technologies for quite some time now. I was able to trace back some four to five cycles - er, years - and the pattern is clear. In addition, he has used his position to ensure that those same suppliers went out of business. And, it seems, Jonsil has been buying up the remains of those businesses when he did so, which means he has those technologies." Marjory smiled at Petarsen. "And, without intending to be offensive, why would a fairly senior officer in the Fleet employ an untrained ensign as a spy in a situation like this? It should have been handed to a security division. But the results are clear. Union ships are failing in their engagements with your enemy, time after time, because they have substandard ship construction, sensor technology, materials and weaponry. Jonsil has held back advances in all of those areas."

"But, but he wanted to maintain total security," Petarsen replied with a troubled expression.

"Yes he did, but not for the reason he gave you. It was so that his operation did not raise flags. You may be interested to know that you are part of a relatively long line of spies he has employed. All of the others are dead, based on your Fleet records." Marjory sat and waited.

"How can you know that?" Petarsen asked, looking askance at Marjory. "Fleet security is the strongest there is."

"No, it's not," Marjory stated simply. "But don't take my words for it. I downloaded my findings into Drummel's system. Take a look and see. The names are all there. I'm sure you can access the Fleet records from here."

Petarsen went back into the reception area wearing a troubled look, while Marjory remained seated. She smiled at Drummel's obvious discomfort.

"Do not be worried," she said in a matter-of-fact tone, "the evidence I found is pretty clear."

"Who are you?" Drummel asked, frowning. "How can you break into the strongest security system around? What is it you want?"

"What I want is a factory capable of producing advanced materials and forming them into suitable shapes. You have such a factory. What I want is a partner who will take the advances I am bringing and use them for the good of the Union. You have proven that you have sought to do so and I expect will do so again. What I want is someone who is able to front for me in manufacturing and selling those materials and the finished goods I plan on making. You seem to be able to do that also." Marjory shrugged. "There are others who I considered, but your unique circumstances are a better fit."

"What circumstances are they?" Drummel asked.

"Why your financial position, of course. Jonsil has effectively crippled you as a business. You said that you have almost no credit, no suppliers and no customers because of his efforts. So, I want to buy half of your business, and I want you to make the materials to the specifications I have developed, and then to make the machinery and parts that I have designed." Marjory gazed at Drummel calmly and waited.

Drummel stared at Marjory.

"You want me to sell you half my business? This is all I have," he said numbly.

"And you won't have it if you don't partner with someone else," Marjory stated in as kindly a manner as she could. A Battle Mage is not a kindly soul, however, and it still sounded like an ultimatum. "Let me put that another way. You still run the business. After a defined period, you can sell the technology advances we make to other parties, but the first supply will be going to the Union forces. After another defined period, I will leave and the company will revert to being fully owned by you or your heirs again." She raised an eyebrow. "How does that sound?"

"Why?"

"Why what?" Marjory returned.

"Why do this? You buy in, provide what you tell me is advanced technologies and then leave it all with me? Why? What's in it for you?" Drummel wanted to believe but this sounded too good to be true. "Convince me."

"This is not for me, Drummel," Marjory replied. "This is to save Earth and its people, and I represent those who want that to happen very much. Let's just say it's for the children."

"You speak as though Earth is not your planet?"

Marjory considered for a moment. She had met Drummel mere moments before and knew very little about the man as opposed to his business and its dire straits. She looked at him. Everything she had seen about the state of Earth and the Union told her that she needed to trust someone for her to make the advances needed, but was this too early? Once revealed, her identify could not be hidden again without actions that she had no desire to take. She gave a mental shrug. Trust, it was.

"That's because it is not my home," she said quietly. "I am not of Earth or any of its colonies. But Earth is of me and mine."

"I don't understand," Drummel replied, exasperated. "But I don't have many choices, do I?"

"You don't have to understand. And no, you have very few options available to you." Marjory stood. "Do we have a deal? If we do, I want to start immediately."

"I found it," Petarsen shouted from the outer office area.

Marjory looked to Drummel and smiled. "Let's see what our spy has found."

Petarsen pointed to the flat screen on her workstation. A list of almost twenty names was displayed.

"All of them were on special assignment for Jonsil. All of the assignments resulted in high tech companies folding up and a shell company bought all their assets. All of them died in one form or another shortly after returning to Fleet Procurement," Petarsen said flatly, her lips pursed in anger. "Jonsil has to be the missing link."

"What do you do now?" Marjory asked.

"I have a contact or two in security," Petarsen said. "I may not be very experienced but I'm from a Fleet family. I'll make a few calls and get a proper investigation going."

"Don't make the calls from your own communication devices," Marjory advised.

Petarsen nodded. "I'll make sure of that." She turned to Drummel. "Mr Drummel, I apologise for the distress I have caused you, and for accusing you of being an enemy agent."

Drummel nodded, staring at the screen. "So many! So many advances held back," he whispered. "It's no wonder we've not been able to make headway."

"Well, let's see if we can fix some of that," Marjory replied.

| **6** |

Sandpiper

"**I** don't understand," Drummel said, staring at the shattered gear mechanism. "This should have stood up to those forces easily."

Drummel and Marjory were standing beside an advanced milling machine. Drummel held the remnants of a gear housing in one hand and the matching remnants of an equally destroyed gearing assembly in the other.

"These were made by one of the external companies, were they not?" Marjory asked him.

"Yes, but it's one that has extensive contracts with the Fleet and has held them for a long time."

Marjory nodded, pensively. One Earth year, almost exactly an Ennaris cycle, had passed since the day when she entered Drummel's office, and a lot had happened in that time. Petarsen had been as good as her word. Jonsil had been investigated and found to be an agent of the Empire - it seemed Likud had made himself Emperor, which had made Marjory snort when she first heard it. Drummel's credit had been restored but Marjory had brought with her significant sums of precious metals and jewels that still funded the work that she had started immediately on entering the partnership.

Initially sceptical, Drummel had examined the schematics and specifications for the first of the technologies that Marjory had brought with her. These were sensors, capable of detecting almost any vessel whether lying in wait or not. They were so far in advance of the

Fleet's current capabilities that Drummel could barely work through the specifications. When he did, however, he stared at Marjory in astonishment.

"Did you design these?" he asked.

"No, not these ones," Marjory replied with a small smile. "These are an old design but very reliable."

"How old?" Drummel queried, curiosity winning over the engineer.

"Older than you can ever imagine." Marjory smiled again as she made the reply.

"Who are you, Mellivar? Where do you come from," Drummel had asked.

"I am a friend to Earth and the Union," Marjory replied seriously. "You will have to take that on trust. Where I come from is not information that I can provide, I am afraid. But it is far from here and under threat from some of the same forces that endanger the Union."

Drummel had asked similar questions over the year since Mellivar had arrived but had come to accept that he would get no reply. Instead, he had concentrated on restarting his business, with Marjory's material and technical designs to the fore.

Materials were the first sticking point. The alloys Marjory specified were not known to the Union or its few allies, mostly human worlds. Drummel wanted to contract the manufacture of the alloy to a second party but was over-ruled. Instead, they had found an orbital foundry that was another of Jonsil's victims and Drummel Industrial purchased it. The equipment was near new and was capable of producing the more advanced metals that Marjory needed. Initially, they would provide upgrades to its own equipment, then they would develop the high grade alloys needed for the sensors and finally to produce the finished castings. The foundry was moved to close proximity with Drummel's orbital.

Against her better judgement, Marjory had agreed to having some of the simpler mechanisms manufactured by a separate company, one with a good reputation and that was a regular supplier to the Fleet.

This simple gear mechanism, produced by that factory from base materials provided by Drummel's new foundry, had failed under a fraction of the stresses Marjory expected it to tolerate.

Without a word, Marjory turned to a storage carton standing nearby and pulled from it another gear mechanism. This one she examined closely, allowing a tendril of her metal sense to stretch across the surface. There! A minute fracture - no, more like an infinitesimal weakness than a defined fracture. She checked another and a third. All had the same weakness in the same place. Either the process had failed or the weakness had been introduced deliberately.

"Did we get all of the tailings back, as I asked?" Marjory asked Drummel.

"Yes, within the usual margin of loss," Drummel replied. "Why? Do you think this was deliberate?"

"If I had to make a bet, it would be that your trusted manufacturer has kept samples of the alloy and added an imperfection to this batch. I would be prepared to wager that they will be trying to replicate the alloy and then will offer the same gear mechanism to the Fleet." Marjory considered that statement. "Or it could be another example of being suborned by the Empire."

"But this gear has no use outside your full design," Drummel said.

"They don't know that," Marjory said after a moment. "You told them this was just a new design for one of the Fleet items, so they may well believe the new material will give them an edge."

"Will it?"

"No. The manufacture of that alloy needs the strictest quality control, but even more it needs the process that you have established. If each and every part does not go to plan then it won't work."

"So we don't do anything?"

"Oh, you complain about the stress fractures and get our money back, but we bring this back in-house and watch that company. What is its name, again?"

"Advanced Metals and Milling. It's an old company, very old. It's now part of the Census Corporation, bought around eight years ago.

I've used them before when I had overflows from orders. Back when I had orders."

"Even so," Marjory said, "we keep an eye on them and deal with this ourselves from now on."

The first batch of gear mechanisms produced by Drummel's own orbital factory rolled off the line eight months later. while causing some delays to the schedule, these parts had no such weaknesses and passed all stress tests easily, which deepened Marjory's suspicions about Advanced Metals and Milling. She instructed *Fendaristil's* AI to monitor communications to and from the company and its executives, and then turned her attention back to the work at hand.

All of the components she needed were now available to her. While Drummel Industrial now had over a hundred staff once again, the new assembly line was completely automated, so it was anti-climactic in one sense when she issued the instruction to start and the machinery gave a quiet chirp and nothing else. A few indicator lights blinked on and off to show which elements were active. Less than thirty minutes after starting the assembly process Marjory held the first of the new sensors.

A simple examination showed no flaws. Marjory nodded to herself in satisfaction.

"Let's see how this works," she said to Drummel, who watched with a blend of excitement and apprehension.

"How do you want to test it?"

"I think a simple test flight will do the trick," Marjory replied. "I need a few more of these and then I'll replace the forward sensor array in *Fendaristil* with these new ones. Then," she continued with an oddly predatory grin, "we go hunting."

The new sensors, despite being a very old Ennaris design, fitted into the mountings on *Fendaristil* without issue. They should do, Marjory thought absently, as the mountings had not changed for millenia before the rebellion. Marjory and Drummel boarded the sleek vessel.

Marjory slipped into the pilot's chair, ran a cursory check that the ship was ready and took it out of the factory's docking bay.

"*Fendaristil*, run diagnostics on the forward sensor array," Marjory said.

"The array is functioning correctly," *Fendaristil* replied after a minute or two.

"Estimated sensor range?"

"Sensor range on the forward array is estimated to be two point nine seven three million kilometres," the ship stated. "Sensor range on the dorsal sensor array…"

"Never mind," Marjory broke in. "Concentrate on performance of the forward array only for this flight."

Drummel glanced to Marjory. "What is the range of your other sensors?" he asked, curious.

"A bit further," was all Marjory said in response. "No questions about *Fendaristil*, remember?"

"I'm going to regret agreeing to that, I think," Drummel grumbled.

"A deal is a deal," Marjory laughed. "But let us run those tests. *Fendaristil*, where is the closest Union vessel?"

"The Union patrol gunboat *Sandpiper* is patrolling the outer reaches of the system. Approximate range is nine hundred million kilometres. Intercept time at best speed is three point seven Earth minutes."

"What? Three point seven minutes? Our fastest ships would take more than twenty minutes and this is only a shuttle." Drummel stared at Marjory. "I've asked this before. Who are you?"

"I am as I have said, a friend representing other friends. Our interest is in ensuring that Earth and the Union will survive." Marjory held up one hand. "Enough! We can discuss that later. We need to complete this test. *Fendaristil*, get us to within five million kilometres at best speed. Show the forward view on the main screen."

The blank wall in front of the bridge changed from being a vague off-white wall to a wall-size viewscreen. Drummel gasped. The scene blurred as *Fendaristil* accelerated, and blurred further as the ship performed a micro-jump. After three minutes, the scene settled again. Centred on the screen was the unmistakable shape of a Union gunship set against a backdrop of a large asteroid, with smaller asteroids ranged across the width of the screen behind the large one. As per the current defensive doctrine, *Sandpiper* was prepared to duck behind the asteroid if an Empire ship was sighted.

"Five million kilometres from *Sandpiper*," *Fendaristil* said.

"Very well. Start moving towards her, but at an angle as though we are just passing and she happens to be in the same part of space," Marjory directed the ship.

"You're not going to fly the ship yourself?" Drummel asked, puzzled.

"*Fendaristil* will respond to threats faster than I could in some circumstances," Marjory replied. "Anyway, it allows me to do other things."

"Four million kilometres," *Fendaristil* reported.

Marjory concentrated on the screen. She touched a stud on her armrest and the display changed slightly. At the bottom left the sector was now displayed, with *Sandpiper* shown in the centre as a red diamond and *Fendaristil* shown as a small blue dot.

Drummel stared at the display.

"How are you getting all of that information?"

"From the sector sensors, such as they are. We are using *Fendaristil's* sensors and, um, we may have seeded this area with our own sensors," Marjory replied.

"How many of your own sensors?" Drummel asked. "There are over two hundred orbital sensors in this region but they can't give that sort of information."

"Twenty," Marjory replied.

"Three million kilometres," *Fendaristil* reported, then, "forward sensors are picking up *Sandpiper*."

The main screen now showed a sensor trace, with a ship detected at two point nine nine million kilometres distance.

"Not bad, slightly better than expected," Marjory said, nodding.

"Does *Sandpiper* see us yet?" Drummel asked.

"No," *Fendaristil* replied. "Closing to two million kilometres."

Marjory and Drummel watched the main screen. Drummel was staggered as the sensors resolved an increasingly detailed picture of *Sandpiper*. Marjory was frowning and shaking her head.

"One million kilometres," *Fendaristil* reported.

Still *Sandpiper* showed no sign of sensing their presence.

"If we were an empire vessel we would have her lined up and ready to fire," Marjory said flatly. "The only reason the Empire ships don't fire at this point will be to make sure they understand the capabilities of the Union vessels. *Sandpiper* is dead and just does not know it."

"Five hundred thousand kilometres. Sandpiper sensors have registered our presence," *Fendaristil* reported.

"Unidentified ship, this is Union Starship *Sandpiper*. Identify yourself or be fired upon," came a peremptory demand over the enforcement channel.

"Good day *Sandpiper*. This is *Fendaristil*, private vessel based in Keplas, Captain Mellivar speaking," Marjory replied in a calm, matter-of-fact voice.

"*Fendaristil*, Acting Captain Wallis speaking. Be advised we have reports of Empire activity in this region." Sandpiper's acting captain sounded tense and his voice strained.

"Understood, Captain. We appreciate the warning. We will be returning to Keplas momentarily."

"Empire vessel identified," *Fendaristil* broke in. "Range four million kilometres. Approach vector two three one point nine five."

"Scan for the second ship," Marjory responded crisply.

"Second Empire vessel identified, range six million kilometres, approach vector four nine seven point three three," *Fendaristil* reported immediately.

"Six million?" Drummel was stunned.

"I told you my designs were old. I never said I used them," Marjory said. "Strap yourself in, Drummel. This will get busy fast."

"You can't be going to stay here," Drummel objected. "This is a classic pincer. *Sandpiper* has no chance and we'll be just a side show."

"Not if I have any say in it," Marjory muttered. "It's time to start to fight back. *Fendaristil*, send the scans to *Sandpiper*." She touched a spot on her command pad. "*Sandpiper*, we have two Empire vessels inbound in a pincer formation, sending you the scan information now. Don't ask how, we can discuss that later."

"Er, receiving the scans. You must be mistaken, this is showing four and six million kilometres distance," Acting Captain Wallis sent.

"These are experimental sensors. Just believe me," Marjory replied. "You need to get out of here, and now. You can't match them. Both are light cruisers."

"Our job is to protect this region," Wallis replied, and Marjory could imagine his jaw jutting out belligerently. "Leave this region, *Fendaristil*, and let us do our job."

"I like this guy," Marjory said to no-one in particular, before re-opening the channel to Sandpiper. "Affirmative, *Sandpiper*. May the hunting be good and the opponent worthy."

"So we're leaving," Drummel breathed. "Thank god for that."

"Not likely," Marjory replied. "*Fendaristil*, shields up, active scans, engage the cloak, open weapons ports, all weapons hot."

"Wh - wh - what?" Drummel stammered. "Shields! *Cloak!* WEAPONS!" His voice rose with each exclamation.

"Calm down, Drummel, and make sure that you are strapped in. There's only two of them and Likud can't design a warship that's worth any one of my ships anyway. *Fendaristil*, manual control. Prepare to extend the shield around *Sandpiper* when we are close enough."

Marjory placed her right hand on a small pad that rose from the arm of her chair. The pad formed around her hand, presenting touch points beneath each finger. *Fendaristil* swooped away from its approach vector to *Sandpiper*, to come in from the rear of the Union ship.

"*Fendaristil*, provide *Sandpiper* with a track showing us departing the area," Marjory directed. "We don't want Wallis thinking we are still here," she explained to Drummel.

"Track provided. The first Empire vessel is within range," *Fendaristil* replied.

"Hold fire. Establish a stable position above and behind *Sandpiper*. Can we extend our shields that far?"

"Affirmative," *Fendaristil* replied. "Secondary power grid coming on line. Shield extended."

"Let's stay just here for a bit. Let me know when Wallis is going tactical."

"Tapping into *Sandpiper's* communication systems," *Fendaristil* responded. "On speaker."

"Captain," a disembodied voice called urgently. "If those scans were right the cruisers will be ahead and above and behind and below. Also, I'm getting some strange energy readings, almost like there's an energy source nearby."

"Initiating a dampening field on our emissions," *Fendaristil* reported.

"See if you can identify it. I'm not sure about this ship that suddenly has sensors that can see fifteen times further than ours." Wallis' voice still sounded strained. "But I'm not about to ignore the chance that she's right. Charge the hull, charge the cannon and all torpedoes."

"Sir, if we do that and get hit we'll go up like a -"

"I'm well aware of what may happen, Ensign," Wallis replied sharply. "But we need to be able to respond. We'll head towards the closest of the targets and try to put some angle between us and the further one. It's the only chance we'll have. Ahead full. Prepare a spread of torpedoes."

"Staying with *Sandpiper*," *Fendaristil* reported. "It's hull has taken a mild positive charge. Altering the shield resonance to compensate. Accelerating to point one light speed."

"That's its fastest," Drummel said. "They don't have anything else."

"The Empire ships are much faster than that," Marjory replied. "They don't have a chance of escaping. That may be next on the list, I think."

"Next?" Drummel asked, watching the viewscreen nervously.

"Sensors first so they can see what's coming. Engines next so they can evade as necessary." Marjory smiled. "We can't do everything at once."

"And after that?"

"Shields so they can survive an encounter, and weapons so they can stand and fight if necessary." Marjory stared at nothing, her eyes narrowing as she thought. "Better ship designs come after that, I think."

"Within range of the Empire cruiser," *Fendaristil* commented. "Designated as Empire One. The vessel coming up from behind designated as Empire Two."

"Has *Sandpiper* acquired Empire One yet?" Drummel asked.

"Not yet," Marjory replied.

"Empire One has fired its main energy weapon," *Fendaristil* reported.

"Strengthen the front shield, just in case," Marjory ordered.

"Captain, energy discharge," *Sandpiper's* ensign called out across the still monitored connection. "We've been fired upon."

"Damn it!" Wallis shouted. "Evade. At least let us get within firing range."

Sandpiper dropped and twisted, but it was too slow. The energy bolt appeared to hit the small Union vessel on its top quarter. In fact, the bolt was deflected by *Fendaristil's* extended shield.

"What happened?" Wallis demanded.

"No idea, sir," the ensign's panicky voice replied. "It must have missed."

"Whatever, we'll worry later. I want all four tubes to fire in a ripple shot, one second apart. Target the source of that energy shot, proximity trigger. Track back along its path." A pause while his orders were carried. "Fire all tubes!"

"Firing one, two, three, four," a third voice reported, drier and calmer than the ensign. "Tracking along the return vector. Hope something's there."

In a piece of exquisite control, *Fendaristil* opened and closed slots in the shield to allow each of the four Union torpedoes to launch on their way unimpeded, reinstating the shield fully after the fourth had passed the shield edge.

"Are they on track?" Marjory asked.

"They are," *Fendaristil* replied. "The Empire vessel has not changed position after firing. It is reacting to the weapons fire now."

"Arrogant of them. Let's give them a headache," Marjory grinned. "Fire a broad beam extended Seema pulse. Send it so that it envelopes the four torpedoes before Empire One knocks them down."

"Firing," *Fendaristil* reported. "Empire One and Empire Two will have detected that."

"I know. Now send a narrow beam plasma shot so that it hits Empire One's shield just ahead of the first torpedo."

"Seema pulse? Plasma shots? What does this shuttle carry?" Drummel looked around the small ship in wonder.

"Captain, picking up the Empire ship," the ensign's voice came over the link. "Torpedoes are tracking towards it."

"Seema was a weapons engineer," Marjory replied to Drummel's question. "She designed a specific type of pulse that would expand through an area of space and act as a sort of shield before dissipating, although it can be used as a weapon against energy shields, too. We should be able to use it to ensure at least some of the torpedoes get to their target. And *Fendaristil* is not a shuttle." She ignored the question about plasma shots.

Empire One sent bolt after bolt from smaller pulse cannons. The first pulse hit and destroyed the first of the torpedoes, to a groan from *Sandpiper's* ensign. The next bolts were repulsed by the Seema pulse, the odd energy pattern arriving just in time to act like a protective bubble around the remaining three torpedoes.

"Firing," *Fendaristil* reported again.

A new beam lanced out from the Ennari ship, a shifting ball of plasma forming and speeding off through space.

"What was that?" Wallis asked.

"No idea, Captain," the laconic voice replied. "Came from somewhere near, though. And it's not targeting us."

"Find the source," Wallis ordered. "Where are the torpedoes?"

"Still tracking," the same voice said in response. "Lost that one to some sort of cannon fire, I expect. But the other three show still moving forward. No idea how, Captain. I don't think anyone has managed to get a torpedo this close to an Empire ship before."

"I think we may have some help," Wallis replied. "Stay on course. Ready another spread of torpedoes."

"Empire Two is closing," *Fendaristil* reported. "Within range in three minutes. Empire One is firing its main energy weapon again."

"Torpedoes ready," the laconic voice reported.

"Wait," Wallis ordered. "Let's see if our hidden friend can shield us from this lot first. That energy burst would destroy the torpedoes."

Marjory nodded her approval.

The energy bolt from Empire One struck the shield and dissipated again. Both ships shook. *Fendaristil* weathered it easily, but a small plume rose from *Sandpiper's* rear quarter.

"Fire!" Wallis commanded. "And find that leak and close it."

A second spread of four torpedoes leapt from their tubes on *Sandpiper*. Once again *Fendaristil* opened gaps in the shield to allow them to launch unhindered.

"I would say the Empire ships are getting worried. The plasma?" Marjory was studying the plot on the screen carefully.

"The plasma shot will hit the screens in twelve seconds, one second ahead of the first torpedo," *Fendaristil* said. "I estimate it will take point six of a second to breach the shield. The Empire shields are quite old in design."

The front screen showed the moment the plasma shot hit the shield. A huge flare erupted around the nose of Empire One. A gasp of astonishment could be heard from the Union ship, probably the ensign, Marjory thought. The front shield of Empire One died. A fraction of a second later the three remaining torpedoes flew through the gap in the shields and detonated using their proximity triggers close to the skin of the cruiser. The results were anti-climactic.

Plumes of gases and flame billowed from the site of each explosion, the flame being short-lived in the vacuum of space. Empire One carried on as though nothing had occurred. But the Union scientists had studied the Empire ships as far as they were able and knew the armour they faced was thick and strong. Within each torpedo was a super-toughened bullet of an advanced uranium-ceramic hybrid material that was shaped for deep penetration. Each exploding torpedo flung these bullets at the armour skin of Empire One with enormous force. The bullets penetrated the thick armour of the ship and then a further charge buried within the bullet detonated, tearing gashes in the skin of Empire One.

"Impressive," Marjory said as cheers were heard from *Sandpiper*. "I'll need to examine the log of that. Meanwhile, let's give them another assist. Fire a two second burst from the main cannon, target the damaged region. Narrow spread, maximum force."

"Firing," *Fendaristil* acknowledged.

"Captain, another discharge of … something," was reported over the link by the laconic voice.

"Something what?" Wallis asked.

"I have no idea, but whatever it is I want one," came the dry reply. "It was a short burst of some sort of massive energy discharge. Not really visible to us but it shows as a short stream heading for the enemy ship."

"Empire Two is within range. Firing main weapon." *Fendaristil* waited a moment. "Reinforcing rear shield. Impact in five seconds. Our cannon burst will reach Empire One in thirteen seconds."

Once again the two vessels shook from the impact. Once again *Fendaristil* came through unscathed. *Sandpiper* took more damage.

"Captain, that came from behind. Must be the second cruiser. Main weapons system is offline," came the dry voice. "We've lost the positive charge to the armour. Engine room reports one of the plates is buckled, which is where we're venting."

"But somehow we're still alive. Bring the chief and his crew up here and close the engine room bulkheads," Wallis ordered. "We'll have to hope she holds together. I want all of that action saved and made ready for dispatch. I don't think any ship has survived one direct hit let alone two, so we really don't know what to expect."

"Captain, look!" the ensign called, excited.

On the main screen Empire One took the brunt of *Fendaristil's* main weapon exactly where the three torpedoes had split the armour plates. The front of Empire One blew out as the spear of energy struck. A gaping hole expelled gases, objects and debris in a doughnut shape. Of the four new torpedoes only two made it to within striking distance. This time, however, one of them sailed through the breach and exploded within the ship while the second added to the armour's damage. Secondary explosions punched more holes in the armour. The ship started to turn away.

"They're running," Marjory said. "*Fendaristil*, bring us about. Target Empire Two. Plasma shot followed by main cannon for five seconds and then a second plasma shot. Hit the bow. Fire!"

"Captain, another discharge from whatever we have near us. Heading behind us."

"The second cruiser!" Wallis exclaimed. "Do you have it on sensors?"

"No, but it has to be there," the laconic voice replied.

"Impact," *Fendaristil* reported a few seconds later.

Drummel stared at the high resolution image on the screen in front of him. The first plasma burst struck the front screen of Empire Two just as it fired its main weapon a second time. The plasma erupted as the two forms of energy met and Empire Two was enveloped in a huge ball of light. All of its defensive screens failed and the front of the vessel was flung aside, presenting its length instead of its bow to the approaching cannon burst. Through the centre of the explosion drove the five second burst from *Fendaristil's* main cannon.

It impacted behind the bow and sliced down the side of Empire Two as it continued to swing. The armour was cut open like a tin can. Secondary explosions could be seen clearly. Then the second plasma bolt hit the ship. To Drummel, it appeared that the plasma was chewing through the entire width of the vessel, spreading as it did so. Empire Two exploded, casting fragments large and small in every direction.

"Keep an eye on the debris," Marjory ordered calmly. "What of Empire One?"

"Some of the debris may come close. I recommend we depart the vicinity. Empire One has turned away. It is listing heavily. Inertial dampers may have failed." *Fendaristil's* unemotional voice was a counterpoint to the excited chatter from the Union ship.

"Quiet," Captain Wallis ordered and the hubbub subsided.

Marjory examined the main screen as Empire One limped away. The expanding ball of debris was definitely moving towards the two ships.

"Whoever you are," Captain Wallis said into the quiet, "on behalf of the Union Fleet I offer our thanks."

Marjory smiled wryly and touched the communication control on her command pad.

"Captain, you have an expanding debris field from the second ship coming in this direction. I suggest you get away as fast as you can," Marjory said.

"Debris field? The ship is damaged?"

"It has been destroyed," Marjory replied without inflexion.

A moment of stunned silence followed as the crew of *Sandpiper* considered that news.

"We'll head back for base, as advised. I recognise that voice," Wallis continued. "Is that invitation to discuss sensors still open? And perhaps weapon upgrades?"

"It is, Captain. I look forward to the discussion."

Marjory cut communications. "Pull the shields back. Close all ports. Power down the weapons. Set course for Keplas. Maximum sublight speed." She glanced to where Drummel was watching the viewscreen, which still displayed the expanding debris field. "Drummel, are you okay?"

"I'm not too sure of that, Mellivar," Drummel replied. "Tell me, if a vessel this size can do that, what would your larger vessels do?"

"Whatever they wanted," Marjory said. "But we no longer have those larger vessels. They were destroyed."

"What?" Drummel gasped. "Who beat you? With such advanced technology, who could beat you? And where are they?"

"It was a long time ago, Drummel, and you have no need to fear any new enemy." Marjory sighed. "But we ran up against our worst foe, Drummel. We destroyed ourselves."

| 7 |

Engines and Shields

Marjory stood beside Drummel on the bridge of *Fendaristil* and surveyed the damaged facility, floating in a destabilised orbit as a result of the attacks. One day earlier, this had been a research facility, with fifty dedicated technicians and engineers working to turn Marjory's advanced component designs into working prototypes. Most of the fifty had escaped the attack in escape pods and had been recovered by rescue craft, but nine had died.

"We have no idea who did this?" Marjory asked quietly.

"No," Drummel replied. "The ships appeared on the edge of sensor range and before anyone knew they were under attack the station had been hit by several missiles."

"Did we have the new sensors installed?"

"Not yet," Drummel sighed. "They were going in this week. This was the last of our orbitals to get them."

"So maybe someone knew that. Are there any missile residues or engine traces we can use?"

"Nothing so far. The missiles appear to be standard issue for the Union Fleet, based on descriptions of the attack, and it's well known that they go missing at times," Drummel replied, "and we're unable to do much about engine residues as yet. We don't have the ability to do detailed scans of those things. Can you?"

"Maybe," Marjory nodded. "*Fendaristil*, start a scan of the region up to half a million kilometres away from the orbital. Look for any engine residues or traces, anything that may give us the type of vessel and a track."

"Starting the scan," *Fendaristil* reported. "This will take approximately four hours."

Drummel shook his head. "Four hours. To do something that remains in our science fiction books."

"It is only fiction until someone invents it," Marjory smiled, before her expression turned grim again. "I will find who did this. I will find out why. And I will stop them."

Slightly more than four hours later, Marjory was seated in her cabin, reading one of the science fiction books that Drummel had mentioned. She found it both amusing and enlightening. Amusing because the author, lauded as one of the giants of Earth science fiction from the middle of the twentieth century, made assumptions about the universe that were in some ways remarkably prescient and in other ways completely naive. It was enlightening because the society that was described in the book had been deemed to be quite radical because of characteristics included in the story such as equality of gender and non-conflict over skin colour. She wondered what she would find when she left for another part of the Union.

A soft chime sounded.

"*Fendaristil?* You have the scan results?"

"Yes," the ship AI replied. "There were two vessels. They were identically powered but have slightly different engine emission signatures. I have traced the engines to Apex Industries, one of several manufacturers of weaponry, engine and control systems for Earth. The damage to the orbital facility showed residual traces of X15-2, a high explosive manufactured by Apex Industries."

"On the face of it that does not prove anything, though," Marjory mused. "Those ships could have been from anywhere and just happened to have those engines installed, and the missiles may have been stolen."

"Yes," *Fendaristil* agreed. "I have also found reports of several attacks in the sector by two pirate ships, working together. There is nothing to indicate that these are the same ships and there are no descriptions of the vessels from those attacks. In each case, either the attacked vessels were destroyed or a facility was attacked using stand-off missiles."

"That sounds familiar," Marjory said.

"I conducted further research and found that two ships had been stolen from a research facility owned by Apex Industries several years ago. The engines were experimental and the material used matches the residues. It seems there was a breakdown in security protocols, making the thefts quite simple. I also gathered as much information about the attacks as I could find. There have been five that definitely fit the pattern of two ships attacking in a coordinated manner, and another two that may have the same pattern. Three were against orbital facilities. All were owned by companies who either competed against or were associated with competitors of Apex Industries. The vessels attacked were all transporting items manufactured by other competitors of Apex Industries or companies related to them." *Fendaristil* sounded very pleased with itself.

"That is very good work," Marjory commented approvingly. "It's quite a case you have built up. I wonder why no one else has thought of that?"

"First, the Union is unable to conduct the residue tests I can," *Fendaristil* replied. "Second, pirate attacks are surprisingly common in Union space. Third, there are suspicions in Union security that Apex has been behind several attacks, but they have been unable to find proof."

"You tapped into Union security's systems again?"

"Yes. I suggest that better encryption techniques should be one of your targets for capability lift. The current ones are woefully inadequate."

Marjory was sure that, if it could sniff in disdain, *Fendaristil* would have done so.

"Consider it on the list," Marjory nodded. "Meanwhile, let's see what we can do about Apex Industries. It looks like we have two targets - the two pirate ships and then whoever is directing them."

"I have started to build a profile of Apex Industries. It will take more time yet. I have plotted the locations of the attacks by the two ships, both confirmed and suspected. I did find a possible track away from this attack and have included that on the chart."

"How confident are you about that track?"

"Very confident of the direction, but that may only have been the first of a set of evasive manoeuvres."

"Agreed. Do you need to stay here for any more time?"

"No. I have what I can get," *Fendaristil* replied.

"Good. Then set a course for Keplas. We have to push harder on the new shields."

"The new sensors have been installed in more than fifty Union ships so far," Drummel told Marjory with satisfaction, two years after the first new sensor was produced.

They were sitting in Drummel's office on Keplas.

"And," added the young woman seated in the third seat around the low table, "we have had the first report of the new sensors allowing a ship to evade an Empire pincer."

The young woman was a new addition to Drummel's staff, vetted by both Marjory and *Fendaristil*. Besnil Barjen had been a post-doctoral researcher in exotic materials engineering who had examined one of the new sensors when aboard a Union ship for a Fleet contract. Immediately after the contract was completed, she located Drummel and asked for an interview. Five days later, with Marjory's blessing, she had joined Drummel's staff. That was three months ago. In that short time, Besnil had established herself as a gifted materials engineer. She had even started to tinker with the alloy used for the sensors, believing she could improve on it, and *Fendaristil* reported to Marjory that the work was promising.

"What happened?" Marjory asked, interested.

"USS Sandpiper was patrolling the Reaches when they picked up the signal and hid behind an asteroid."

"Sandpiper?"

Marjory was delighted that the first ship to get value from the new sensors was Captain Wallis' vessel. The Captain had delayed his report until after meeting with Marjory following the mission that saw them survive an encounter with two Empire vessels because of Marjory's intervention. During the meeting, Marjorie had convinced Wallis that her ship's capabilities had to be kept secret for her to be effective in her efforts to improve the Union Fleet's capabilities. Thus, Wallis became the second person that Marjory entrusted with confidential information.

After that meeting, and with some initial misgivings, Wallis had altered his report to remove the assistance of a second ship. Instead he stated that, after *Sandpiper* had evaded the attacking ships for some time, the first Empire ship had suffered multiple failures for an unknown reason, but that had allowed his torpedoes to impact and enough damage that it limped from the scene of the action. At roughly the same time, the second Empire ship had exploded for an unknown reason, but that he had not stayed for any length of time in the area to investigate.

Wallis was aware that the report was being looked at with some scepticism, but he had kept enough presence of mind to collect several pieces of debris from the destroyed ship to back up his claims of a battle. There was no sign of *Fendaristil* on Sandpiper's sensor traces. Despite the sceptics, *Sandpiper's* crew had received citations and were the toast of the sector. Wallis was confirmed as captain of *Sandpiper*. He also had become a regular visitor with Marjory.

"Yes. Captain Wallis maintained an active log of the entire encounter, if hiding and watching the Empire ships go past is an encounter. The new sensors apparently allowed him to identify the Empire ships before they could identify him."

"As they should do," Marjory replied. "And yes, hiding and watching is a very valid form of encounter when you are outgunned and have no shields worth the name."

"And if your ship is so much slower than the enemy's ships," Drummel added.

"Yes, especially that," Marjory concurred. "Running or hiding are excellent tactics when the alternative is destruction."

"And yet Captain Wallis was able to damage an Empire ship in the past," Besnil commented. "Could he not do so again?"

"I think you'll find that *Sandpiper* was very lucky on that occasion. I also doubt that Empire captains will be as complacent in future as that one may have been. I expect that captain is no longer in command of his or her ship."

"So will the new engines have any chance of helping with any of that?" Besnil asked. "I've looked at the specifications and they seem to be quite different to the orthodox Union engines."

"Well, hopefully the engines allow Union ships to have a chance to run and evade a bit more when they come across Empire ships. Better engines also generate more usable power, which means more energy available for use in the future. And our design will build much smaller and lighter engines, and yet produce two or three times the power. That also allows us to make ships that run longer, and then we also are able to redesign the hulls. It will be a vital step forward." Marjory thought for a moment. "We also need to make sure we can retrofit the new engines to older hulls."

"How far are we from building a prototype?" Besnil asked.

Marjory smiled, and Drummel grinned widely.

"What?" Besnil demanded. "What did I say that's so funny?"

"We have had a prototype being tested for several weeks now," Marjory told the materials engineer. "So far it has passed all of the tests. We have been planning to put it into a test ship but need to locate one. Any ideas?"

"As a matter of fact," Besnil said slowly as she thought furiously, "I do know of one or two. What sort of ship would be needed?"

"Something about *Sandpiper's* size or a bit larger," Drummel replied. "The Mark 1 engine is smaller than those installed in that class of vessel, but it uses very different fuel. That's going to be something else we need to consider. The fuel can be made much more readily than the current exotic mix. It'll reduce the poisonous emissions of the current engines, too, so the engine compartments become simpler to build. But it will have to have a separate production facility."

"What do we need to do to make that happen?" Besnil asked.

"That will be one of the most important bits," Marjory said. "We will release the formula and method to whoever wants to manufacture the fuel. That should help. It means the existing manufacturers can re-tool and compete, and hopefully that reduces the impact."

"Won't that also make it available to the Empire?" Besnil asked.

"It will," Marjory agreed. "So we need to protect the engine designs. Without them the fuel is useless."

Silence fell for a short time. Marjory watched the newest member of the team as she stared at the wall of Drummel's office.

"I may be able to get that ship for you," Besnil stated finally. "One of the Fleet teams I worked with had a patrol ship assigned to them for a range of experiments. The recent budget cuts have left it mothballed. But I might be able to get it reassigned. Are you prepared to bring the advanced research team in on this?"

Marjory and Drummel shared a look. Besnil was not to know that they had been discussing how to get a path into the Fleet research and design arm. This may be the way, and the engines were destined for the Fleet anyway.

"If they are prepared to make that ship available to us, then yes, I believe we will be prepared to reveal the new engines to them," Marjory said carefully. "But they will have to discuss it with no-one else. If they will do that, then we will agree."

Only five weeks later Marjory, Drummel and Besnil stood with Commander Alicia Mengral of the Union Fleet's research and design section on an observation deck of the orbital platform known as

OB12. While nominally intended to be a Union research base, OB12 (Orbital Base 12) had several non-military levels that formed a small ship service and transit facility.

Agreement to use the patrol vessel that had been intended to be a test bed for various new initiatives had taken a few days to be obtained, and was sealed finally when Captain Wallis had weighed in on Marjory's side. Once the specifications had been examined by a Union engine expert, however, excitement started to build. Now, with the patrol ship *USS Serene* sitting in the space dock, with the new engines installed and, for completeness, a full suite of the new sensors, tension was rising. The test flight would occur in less than twelve hours.

"All is ready, Commander," Besnil said as the group of four looked at *Serene* floating in the dock.

Umbilicals remained attached to the ship, and several maintenance people moved around the vessel making sure there were no last minute issues.

"Who'll be going with us?" Mengral asked.

"We all will," Marjory replied.

"Is that wise?" Mengral said with a frown. "If anything goes wrong then your company loses its entire senior management."

"We have the greatest confidence," Drummel replied. "Besides, if we're not prepared to ride in the ship with our engines, why should we ask someone else to do so?"

"Well I didn't exactly ask the Fleet team to take the trip," Mengral said drily.

"But you did allow for concerns to be raised, and for people to make sure they could find no little thing out of place. Had they found anything I doubt that you would have ordered them along," Drummel rejoined.

"True. Very well, then let's get on with this."

The attack came as Marjory and Drummel walked across the main passageway of OB12's highest non-military level. This level had been intended, optimistically as it turned out, to be a shopping mall servicing military and civilian populations alike. While there were a small number of retail and service businesses on the strip, most of the units remained unoccupied. As a result, the lighting of the section was muted to conserve power, especially during OB12's "night" period when the few businesses were closed. It also offered a short-cut of sorts for those moving from the Union Fleet's research facility to the civilian accommodation levels below. Marjory and Drummel were taking the short-cut, deep in a muted conversation about the day's events.

A whisper of sound alerted Marjory and she spun to confront three men who were attempting to move up behind them stealthily. Surprise lost, the three charged. Two carried pistols and the third a wicked looking vibro-knife, designed so that even a simple nick would cause significant damage by the minute but very rapid vibrations of the blade.

Marjory swept Drummel behind her with enough force that he stumbled across the wide passage. Then, rather than retreating as many would in similar circumstances, she moved to meet them at an angle. The first of the pistol-wielding pair was pitched into the knife man and both tumbled to the deck, freeing Marjory to deal with the second gunman. He stopped and took aim, only to find that Marjory was now above him and descending fast. Drummel stood against the further wall with his mouth open as he watched Marjory's leap. She kicked the gunman squarely in his chest and then landed lithely on both feet. The gunman flew across the passageway and hit the opposite wall with sickening force. As he slumped to the ground, Marjory turned back to the other two.

A shot rang out, loud in the confines of the strip, and Marjory felt the tug as the bullet grazed the arm of her shirt before ricocheting off the metal wall and being lost down a nearby side service alley. But her immediate target was the knife-man. He held the vibro-knife with a poise and confidence that spoke of long experience. Marjory watched carefully as he moved towards her.

"What do you want, and why?" Marjory asked as she manoeuvred to stay on the man's left side.

No answer. Marjory had not really expected one but she had hoped that the question might cause a moment's hesitation. The knife-man held her gaze with steely intensity. There was no hint of emotion on his face, nothing that gave away his immediate intent. This one was a true professional.

Another shot, this one aimed at Drummel, also missed as the factory owner dodged behind a crate. A third hit the crate but failed to penetrate its tough skin. Marjory glanced towards the gunman for a brief moment. She stepped backwards suddenly, quickly enough to surprise the knife-man who was about to use what he thought was a momentary distraction to advantage.

Marjory reached up behind to grasp the tiny throwing knife slung down her back and, in a single fluid motion, drew the knife and flung it at the gunman. The knife flew with unerring accuracy to slice into the gunman's neck, spraying blood in an arc but, more importantly, removing the threat. Marjory moved back towards the knife-man, locking eyes again. Now, however, she saw doubt and uncertainty. She had dealt with two of the assailants easily, and now prepared to take on a vibro-knife wielding opponent with bare hands despite obviously having weapons available to her.

Marjory was almost within his reach when he made his attack. Darting forward, he wove an odd pattern with the vibro-knife, creating a weave in the air that, he knew from experience, mesmerised his victims and allowed him to get close enough to strike. Marjory was not mesmerised. She allowed him to close and then stepped left in the moment he struck. His movements were fast. The Battle Mage's were faster. She grasped his arm and used his own slight momentum to pull him off balance before delivering a sharp jab to the back of his neck. Nerves and muscles succumbed to the jab. The knife hit the deck as his arm and hand lost strength. Marjory gave the knife a quick kick and then unceremoniously snapped the hardened heel of her palm against his temple. Her assailant collapsed in an untidy heap.

Marjory glanced around warily. The action had taken only a minute or so and it seemed that, despite the noises involved in a Fleet facility, especially the three gunshots, no one was interested. She found *that* interesting, but it would keep. Swiftly, she retrieved her knife and wiped it against the second gunman's tunic. She checked the first gunman to make sure that he was dead, then examined their guns carefully, without touching them. There was nothing special about them to her eyes and she surmised that they probably would have been disposed of immediately after the assault. She left them where they had fallen.

Drummel was rising from behind the crate as Marjory moved back to the knife-man. She crouched and turned him over, then grimaced at the green foam that coated his teeth and lips. Grelis! *Fendaristil* had surveyed the types of drugs used in the Union, and grelis was one often associated with rapid death by poison. There was no known antidote and it killed within seconds. The knife-man must have had some sort of release mechanism in his mouth, perhaps tied into his neural system to activate should he be rendered unconscious. She did not bother with any sort of search. These were professionals and would have nothing to identify them or their employers. With a frown, Marjory stood. She would learn nothing here and they still had a test to conduct.

"You've done that before," Drummel said as he moved to stand with Marjory, despite being shaken badly by being so close to his own death.

"A time or two," Marjory replied as she looked around.

"I don't understand how you can be so calm," Drummel continued. "I'm shaking so hard I can barely stand."

"It comes with time and experience, and I have both." Marjory glanced to Drummel. "And you are standing up to more shocks than I thought you would be able to. Which is good. We won't find anything here. These were experts, professionals. And we have a test to run and that won't wait. But it is obvious that someone knows and is trying to stop us."

"The Empire?"

"Perhaps, or a competitor. Maybe both. Whoever it is probably won't stop so we need to be careful." One more glance around to make sure they had left nothing of their own here and Marjory indicated with a nod of her head towards the far end of the strip, away from the small intersection where the encounter had occurred. "Say nothing about this to anyone for now. Let us go."

USS Serene floated in the space dock. The umbilicals that provided station power had been retracted. The shuttle that had delivered the last of the participants for the test had retreated to the station's internal bay. All was in readiness.

"Mellivar, all stations show ready," Besnil reported from her console alongside the captain's chair.

"Very well," Marjory replied from the command chair. "Pilot, move us out slow and steady. Thruster jets only until we are outside the station's limits."

"Aye, captain," the Fleet pilot assigned to the test replied. "Thrusters only."

The ship moved slowly but steadily through the array of retracted docking clamps until it cleared the immediate vicinity of the station. Several spectator ships were clustered to one side. They were, largely, from Fleet but a few were from rival organisations to Drummel Industrial. There were always observers of the test range, no matter the security measures that were put in place, which pointed to security holes that Marjory found to be disturbing. Perhaps demonstrating the scale of the problem, Fleet had decided years before that there was little point in chasing every observer away when the test range was so large.

Marjory and Commander Mengral watched the main screen intently but there was nothing of note to see.

"Captain, we're outside the station's declared boundary," the pilot reported.

"Very well, bring the main engine on line, prepare for main drive thrust."

"Main engine on line," the pilot announced a few moments later.

"Power profile is looking good," Besnil reported. "If anything, it's a little better than the last test indicated."

Marjory nodded. She expected nothing less, but risk management demanded taking things carefully.

"One third thrust," Marjory ordered.

The pilot repeated the order and moved the slider just past the third of the ten notches on his control screen. *Serene* built speed and moved away from the station, followed by the the gaggle of spectator ships. Shadowing them all was the unmanned and cloaked *Fendaristil*.

"At zero point one light speed and climbing," Besnil reported.

"I thought you ordered one third power," Mengral said, frowning.

"I did," Marjory confirmed, pointing to the readout on the screen. "We are resting on one third. We will stay here for a short time to make sure there are no anomalies before increasing power."

"Our best ships make point three light at the moment," Mengral said. "But they can't hold it for very long. Point one is the maximum cruise speed."

"Yes, which is one reason why they are so vulnerable," Marjory replied carefully lest she upset the Fleet representative. "The new sensors will allow them to see the Empire ships before they are within weapons range. These engines will allow them to get away once sighted."

"How fast do you think we will be able to go?" Mengral asked.

"*Serene* is a small and light ship, but the engine we have fitted is a smaller version. We should be able to get up to point six of light speed. You get more time dilation as we go higher and stresses start to build, so that's probably the limit with the current ship design."

"You mean we could go faster?"

"A little faster. You will need what are popularly called faster-than-light engines to really get anywhere though. Your ship designs are not suitable for them as yet." Marjory smiled at the thoughtful look on

Mengral's face. "But that's a little further away. For now, we should be able to allow you to survive an encounter."

"And surviving a fight?" Mengral glanced at Marjory. "Do you have something for that also?"

"Perhaps," Marjory replied. "Besnil, are we ready to increase?"

"Yes," Besnil replied. "Everything is reading green, the sensors are picking up nothing except the following ships. A couple of them have dropped off, by the way. The rest are falling behind."

"Probably saw what they needed to see," Mengral said wryly, looking to where Drummel stood to one side, watching the screen intently. "Your competitors will be getting worried."

"They should be," Marjory snorted. "They've been holding you back with their outmoded technologies for too long. Okay, let's show them the real show. Pilot, engine to two-thirds."

"Aye, captain, two-thirds," the pilot replied before taking a deep breath and pushing the slider to a point between the sixth and seventh notches. "Showing two-thirds engine power."

Serene leapt away from the spectator ships, quickly putting a significant gap between them. The Fleet ships powered down to await the outcome, as planned. Two of the spectator craft started to pursue but both gave up the chase quickly.

"Zero point four light speed," Besnil reported. "Climbing to zero point five."

"At two thirds power!" Mengral breathed.

"You will find that the operating limit for *Serene* and her sister ships in this patrol class will be around seventy-five percent of the available power. We have allowed a large margin for error in case the ship needs to get out of danger quickly, but these ship designs will not survive that thrust or speed for very long." Marjory paused while she examined the readouts on the main screen. "Drummel, I can feel a very slight vibration that should not be there. Can you?"

Drummel nodded, holding his head on an angle in concentration, as though he could hear the vibration.

"I expect it's the problem we discussed. The ships have been built with wider structural tolerances than they will need to have with these engines. If we had to go much faster than this it'd get fairly uncomfortable."

"Let's see," Marjory nodded. "Take her to seventy percent and hold there."

The vibration increased as the ship built speed, rapidly becoming uncomfortable for all concerned.

"Zero point six light speed," Besnil reported, beaming a smile to both Marjory and Drummel. "But it's a bit bumpy."

"Yes, bring her back down to half power, please, pilot," Marjory ordered. "Set course for the station. We'll make some modifications to the ship and try again in a couple of weeks. Then we can see about sustained running."

| 8 |

Engagement

"So, tell me about these shields again?" Captain Wallis made the request over the mug of tea he held ready to sip.

"What part do you want me to repeat?" Marjory asked.

"The part about not having to rely on a low level charge to the hull plating when our shield fails at the slightest sneeze," Wallis said. "That's never worked to my knowledge and yet for some reason whoever's in charge seems to think it's the peak of technical brilliance."

Marjory smiled at the complete disdain in the *USS Sandpiper's* captain's voice. In the nearly eight years that she had been involved with Earth's Union, she had heard the same disparaging tone used by almost every fighter when discussing administrators, echoing the same she had in the Ennari protective force all that time ago.

"A positive charge can deflect a positively charged particle energy bolt," Marjory said reasonably, "if the positive charge carries the same potential as the energy bolt. Which is impossible to do when applied against a metal skin of a low-powered space vessel. You just can't carry the level of charge needed. Even if you could, the impact would still knock you around a lot and the current ships would be likely to suffer some sort of failure from the effects, probably catastrophic. No, you need to spin the deflecting charge out from the ship, project it a sufficient distance so that those charges are caught and negated without the impact being felt, at least not as much."

"And what sort of power requirement is there for that?" Wallis asked, watching Marjory over the rim of his mug.

"Pretty large, certainly larger than your ships are capable of producing at the moment," Marjory said.

"But what about with your new engines? They seem to produce more than enough power to drive the ship. Could they be used?" Wallis kept his voice steady, but Marjory could see the gleam in his eyes. "Or is that why they're so much more powerful than they need to be?"

"The new main engine can provide the power well enough," Marjory nodded, "but it would be better to add a secondary power source for the shield generator. They are slaved together and can support each other as a form of redundant capability."

"And in the future this secondary power source can provide weapons also?"

"Perhaps. But we will have to redesign your ships first, either partly or totally. The more powerful energy weapons would tear them apart were you to fire them. The energy recoil can be pretty harsh and needs to be handled."

"What sort of changes will we need?"

"They will be quite extensive. We can do some of the changes when we upgrade the build to handle the engine stresses. It is a similar process in some ways, but we need to change the shape of the hulls, give them a less blocky profile, sleeker and smoother so that projectiles that get through the active systems have a chance to glance off rather than dig in." Marjory rocked her hand slightly. "That's a different prospect and much more expensive."

"If I gave you *Sandpiper* would you be able to use her as a guinea pig?"

"Guinea pig?" Marjory asked puzzled. "What is a guinea pig?"

"A small rodent from Earth. They were used to test various pharmaceuticals and other medical treatments. It just became part of the language to mean a test subject." Wallis looked at Marjory. "Most people have at least heard that term."

"I'm from a small place far away and never took much notice of such things," Marjory replied easily. "I was concentrating on designing ships and bits of ships."

"Like sensors, engines, controls systems, shields and weapons," Wallis said drily. "All of them?"

"Yes, like all of them," Marjory agreed, refusing to rise to the implied challenge. "And how will you 'give' me *Sandpiper*? Don't you need her to do your patrols? What will you and your crew do, just float through space waving your arms?"

"She's due for a complete refit for your uprated sensors and your new engine. The engine compartment requires major structural changes anyway, not to mention giving the ship the finer tolerances to operate effectively with the power plant. I think we can probably look at that as a chance to include your new changes to her skin also. And perhaps that secondary power unit?"

"And when Commander Mengral finds out?"

"I've already spoken about it with Alicia," Wallis said, smiling at Marjory's raised eyebrow, which was about as surprised a reaction as he had seen from her. "She trusts you pretty much completely, you know. *Serene* isn't suitable for the latest changes but *Sandpiper* may well be, from what you told me last time we discussed this. She'll swing the additional funding."

"Well, I *have* been using *Sandpiper* to adjust the designs to the current set of vessels," Marjory mused. "Maybe we can use your ship as this test pig."

"Guinea pig. And you need to adjust the designs?" Wallis asked, an amused smile breaking out as he did so. "Does that mean you've designed a whole new ship?"

"No," Marjory said seriously, before looking to face Wallis fully. "I have designs for five classes of ship, from a patrol ship to what you would call a dreadnought."

Marjory smiled at Wallis' stunned expression.

"*Fendaristil*, are we ready?" Marjory asked.

"Yes, all is ready," the ship AI pronounced. "*Sandpiper* has exited the dock and is moving towards the rendezvous point. She will meet up with *Serene* and *Tranquil* and head to the test site as a full patrol."

"*Tranquil!*" Marjory snorted. "Whoever names the Union's warships needs to have a reality check."

"I believe the idea was to project an air of calm and reassurance," Drummel replied from his place on *Fendaristil's* command deck. "Especially given the number of ships that were being lost to the enemy interceptors. Thankfully, with your sensors, and especially the newer versions that Besnil worked on, those losses have been reduced. But it also means they have to come up with new name series, so this one is drawn from forms of meditation."

"Meditation? That works very well in preparing for a fight," Marjory stated, "but is fairly useless once the fight actually starts. Fighting ships should be named for their purpose, or for something of significance."

Drummel chuckled. Every so often Marjory's carefully concealed pugnacious character shone through, especially when she was with Drummel. But he had been with her in several fights over the nearly ten years they had worked together and he knew her true character. *No*, he thought to himself with a wry mental shrug, *I only know another aspect that she allows me to see.*

"The three ships are powering their main drives," *Fendaristil* reported. "We are cloaked and have shields raised. I have set a safe distance of fifty thousand kilometres between us and the closest of the three ships."

"Very well," Marjory replied, settling in her chair. "We follow them and watch what happens."

"Were you disappointed that Commander, sorry Captain now, Mengral refused permission for you to be aboard *Sandpiper?*" Drummel asked.

"No, I had no real wish to be there for this test," Marjory said in response. "We can tap into their control systems from here and read their progress, but I wanted to be able to provide additional protection."

The three patrol ships all had the new engines and moved together, gathering speed. *Fendaristil* matched them with ease. Marjory watched the status reports into which *Fendaristil* had tapped and noted that the vibration appeared to have been solved for each ship with the latest revisions to their hulls and bracing components. The ships reached point six light speed and ran at that speed for thirty minutes, achieving their first test objective, before backing down as they approached the shield test zone.

"You believe those reports of Empire activity in the area?" Drummel asked, worriedly. "We've not seen too many of them close to Keplas for quite a while."

"You always have to expect enemies to be where you don't want them to be," Marjory replied as she tapped instructions into her command pad. "That's how you survive. And in this case I expect the last thing the Empire wants will be for the Union to get better engines, so I expect them to try to stop us." She stopped to frown as she stared at the screen. "*Fendaristil*, prepare to set up a tight beam to *Sandpiper*."

"Something?" Drummel asked, watching Marjory stare at her screen.

"Maybe. More like something missing," Marjory muttered.

"Link to *Sandpiper* is ready," *Fendaristil* reported.

"Very well. Bring the weapons on line. Extend the sensor reach as far as they will go. Bring secondary power to full." Marjory tapped on her screen. "*Sandpiper*, be aware that Battery One is not in place."

Battery One was a minimally manned specially built platform with a prototype laser weapon mounted on it. It was to play the role of an attacking space craft to test the shields.

"Ah, our guardian angel is back," Captain Wallis replied with amusement rich in his voice. "Can you see anything else?"

"Two ships are running quiet at four million kilometres," *Fendaristil* reported. "Sensor returns indicate they are Empire cruisers."

"Keep scanning," Marjory ordered, although she knew it was unnecessary to do so. "*Sandpiper*, two Empire cruisers are running dark at four million kilometres."

"The cruisers are powering up, moving towards *Sandpiper*," *Fendaristil* noted.

"They're coming towards you," Marjory told Wallis.

"We have them on the edge of our sensor range now," Wallis reported. "We'll abort the test and return to Keplas."

"Make it a fast turn. These ships should be able to out-run you," Marjory noted, even as the three patrol ships started a wide swing away from the oncoming Empire ships. "*Fendaristil*, take a position above and behind *Sandpiper* by ten thousand kilometres. Strengthen the rear shields."

The three Union vessels settled on their course for Keplas and increased their speed. *Fendaristil* shadowed them, maintaining separation as ordered. As Marjory had feared, the Empire vessels could better their speed and closed the gap inexorably.

"Close to one hundred kilometres. Prepare for shield interlock," Marjory ordered.

"Closing," *Fendaristil* replied. "Interlock is ready."

"Wallis, you are going to be caught," Marjory transmitted.

"Agreed, will these shields hold up?" Wallis replied calmly.

"On your ship, they should. But the other two don't have those shields."

"So, what do you suggest?"

"I want you to drop behind *Serene* and *Tranquil*. Use your shield to protect them. The Empire ships are both coming up from behind with this vector."

Marjory continued to monitor the oncoming vessels, almost grinding her teeth at the need to wait.

"We have dropped back into a rear guard position. I'm not sure we can protect both ships and ourselves," Wallis noted almost conversationally.

"You won't have to," Marjory said. "Remember that blue button I told you not to press?"

"Yep," Wallis replied drily. "All sorts of strange things happen if that button is pressed. Something about the world ending, if I remember correctly."

"I did not say the world would end," Marjory retorted. "I did say that we have yet to prove that it worked with this design."

"And?"

"And now we get to see if it does," Marjory said crisply. "Press the button and hold it for three seconds." Three seconds later Marjory spoke again. "*Fendaristil*, initiate interlock."

"What just happened?" Wallis asked, concerned.

"We just interlocked our shields to yours," Marjory replied. "This should give us the time needed to get back into our own space."

"The first Empire ship is in firing range," *Fendaristil* reported. "They are firing."

The energy bolt reached across space and struck the combined shield and dissipated, followed by a second and then a third.

"Shields are down to eighty-seven percent. The second Empire ship is in range and firing," *Fendaristil* reported.

"Mellivar, all three of those ships have the new engines in them," Drummel said. "Can they sustain emergency speed for long enough to get closer to Keplas?"

"Yes, but *Sandpiper* would have to reduce its shield diameter," Marjory nodded, as the second Empire ship's energy blasts were dispersed by the linked shields.

"Shields to seventy-two percent," *Fendaristil* noted.

"And the shields are dropping rapidly. However, I think we may be able to do something." Marjory tapped her console for a moment, lips pursed in concentration, before touching the communication button. "Wallis, I need you to drop back a little further. We will close on you. We will send all excess power to the rear shields and reconfigure them to a wider spread."

"And how does that help us?"

"Once we have the shields configured, send *Serene* and *Tranquil* on emergency boost. They'll need to make sure we are between them and the Empire ships at all times."

"On full boost those boats are gonna be a little uncomfortable," Wallis noted.

"Yes, but they should be able to get away from the Empire ships if we stay between them," Marjory replied as the combined shield took another blast.

"Okay, dropping back. Are you controlling this?"

"We will take control," Marjory confirmed. "*Fendaristil*, all secondary power to rear shields. I want a Seema burst followed by a plasma burst two seconds later. Set the Seema burst to expand to its widest perimeter. Target the plasma burst at the closest Empire vessel."

"We are unlikely to do any damage at this range," *Fendaristil* reported.

"I know, but it may take some attention and buy extra time. Wallis, get the two ships running in five seconds."

Fendaristil fired its twin weapons in sequence two seconds apart. At the five second mark *Serene* and *Tranquil* leapt forward, angling to keep *Sandpiper* and *Fendaristil* between themselves and the oncoming Empire ships. Of course, they were not aware that Fendaristil was with them.

"So far so good," Drummel commented.

"Extending the shields," *Fendaristil* reported.

"Wallis, we'll let *Serene* and *Tranquil* get as far away as we can and then I want you to follow them," Marjory directed.

"Does it seem strange to anyone that a civilian craft is protecting Fleet ships?" Wallis pondered aloud. "Mellivar, this is not the way things are meant to go."

"We'll make that change soon," Marjory assured him. "For now, though, this is about making sure you can survive long enough to help make the change happen. As a matter of record, though, at least the shields worked."

"That they did," Wallis chuckled. "And the new engines do, too, although we remain a little too slow still."

"That will change also," Marjory promised. "The others are far enough away now, I believe. On my mark, go to full forward thrust. *Fendaristil* will take rear guard position. Ready, ready. Mark!"

On *Sandpiper*, Wallis pushed the engine setting to the red line and the vessel moved smoothly ahead of *Fendaristil*. The Ennari craft slid into the rear guard position, angling its shields to form a protective funnel. Two blasts from the Empire ships were diverted by the shields. Fifteen seconds later *Fendaristil* accelerated.

"The Empire ships are turning away," Marjory said, looking to Drummel.

"You have that look," Drummel replied nervously. "That usually ends up with me being shot at."

"Not this time," Marjory smiled. "But it does make me wonder who informed the Empire of the test."

"Well, we made it out of another one," Drummel said with satisfaction.

"Not everyone," Marjory replied bleakly. "We lost Battery One and a handful of Fleet personnel."

Drummel's mood soured as he nodded agreement. The Empire spies were everywhere, it seemed. Were they in his company as well?

| **9** |

Farstation 105

"**I** am going to be gone for a short while," Marjory announced.

She and Drummel were sitting over coffee in his office. They had just agreed the specifications for the latest engine improvements designed to allow Fleet vessels to match the sublight speed of the Empire's cruisers, both light and heavy versions. The redesign would require additional work on some of the ships that already had Marjory's engine installed, but promised to allow them to escape the clutches of the Empire pincer traps more readily. Some ships could not take the upgrades and would be either assigned to less taxing work or would be retired.

"I don't believe you've taken any sort of holiday for the whole time I've known you," Drummel nodded. "And that's been, what, twenty-three years now."

"I will not be on holiday," Marjory replied. "I am going to find out who has been informing on our plans, and then I will be purchasing a weapons manufacturer. There are a small number that are in need of financial assistance."

"Weapons?" Drummel asked. "Why not build them here?"

"Our manufacturing capability is stretched very thin at the moment. We have Besnil's sensor improvements, the revised engines and the shield components that all need to be accelerated to get the Union ships up to the level needed. Then there is the new hull being laid down for the first of the medium cruiser-class ships we designed. But those new ships need far better weapons than are available now, and weapons manufacture is a very different business to making ships, engines and components."

Marjory glanced out the window to where the old orbital manufactory had been joined by three others. In the distance she could see the new space dock where the new cruiser had started construction. It was nothing more than a collection of spars at the moment, but that would change rapidly as the uprated construction bots swung into gear.

"So," she continued as she turned back to Drummel, "the best bet will be to buy an existing business and use it for the purpose."

"The same as you did with my company," Drummel noted.

"Yes," Marjory agreed. "I believe this has worked out well so far."

"Well, we've both become very rich," Drummel replied, "although we could be much more so if we didn't hold our prices down."

"I'm not here to be rich," Marjory responded impatiently. "And I know you don't feel the need to have more, either. But the profits can be put to good use."

"And the spies?"

"They are a priority. Fleet security has found a few, but there are many more, I have no doubt," Marjory said. "And every time there is a test we seem to find Empire vessels lurking about. And not just us. Last week Centaur Industries' test ships were chased by two Empire ships when they were testing their new targeting system. And a few months ago Integrated Systems lost a test ship when they were in final trials of their new communications array. You know there have been others. Too many of them. So, I will do my own investigation. It should not take too long."

"What will you do?"

"I will set out some bait and see who takes it," Marjory said, giving that by now well-known feral grin.

"And the bait will be?" Drummel asked, knowing the answer.

"Why me, of course."

Fendaristil hung against a backdrop of a green-tinged planet, uninhabited as far as anyone knew and uninhabitable by humans without massive initial and ongoing cost. Early survey teams, long ago, had been enthusiastic about the planet on first glance, until they tested the atmosphere and found that it was largely comprised of a previously unknown caustic gas. That may have been a minor problem had the soil of the planet not been riddled with the same main element. The scans had shown no lifeforms, or none that were able to be sensed through the atmosphere or via an automated lander gathering samples. The planet received the designation Lepta-5, but was generally called Jade. It was well off the usual travel lanes, and the system was isolated somewhat from other systems in this arm of the cluster. It made Jade perfect for Marjory's purpose.

"Nothing on long-range sensors," *Fendaristil* reported.

"Are all of the remotes out and operating?" Marjory asked after swallowing a mouthful of coffee.

"Yes," the ship replied. "The five repeaters are in a slow orbit around Lepta-5 while the ten long-range sensors are seeded through the approaches to this location. The five platforms are cloaked and are in place."

"Very well. I doubt we will have long to wait. However, just to allay suspicion, let's run some tests," Marjory said.

"What sort of tests would you like?"

"Something showy. Is there anything we can shoot at?"

"I could launch a couple of drones and then shoot them," *Fendaristil* suggested.

"That should work. Set the drones to be at, say, five thousand kilometres and then wait until we have an audience before we put on a show."

Two drones shot from the launch tube that emerged below the bow of the ship and sped to designated locations where they hovered. Marjory leaned back in the chair and contemplated her current position.

She had been gone from Ennaris for almost twenty-five years now - cycles in Ennari terms. There remained over one hundred cycles before Trabor would be awakened, and another five hundred after that before Drewflin would be awakened. She hoped that she could return by then. She had succeeded in getting the Union forces well on their way to being a more capable defensive force, but she knew that it was not enough against any civilisation that had Likud as its leader. But she also knew that her time with Drummel was coming to an end. She had added some grey to her hair and changed her appearance slightly to look older but that would only last for a short time. In reality, she had one more thing to do with this phase of her plan, which was to get the weapons program started. She could finish some of that later.

Her thoughts were interrupted by a gentle *tweep* from one of the consoles.

"We have three ships running in what passes for stealth mode approaching from our forward quarter," *Fendaristil* reported.

Marjory smiled at the disdain that the ship AI could project at times. It was as though the ship was offended that its opponents were sloppy, like they were not paying the level of respect that it deserved. In reality, of course, the technology employed was immature.

"Very well, give them a show," Marjory ordered.

Fendaristil deployed one of the small defensive cannons and fired a single shot at one of the drones. A few seconds later the drone exploded in a spray of alloys, ceramics and plastics.

"Good shot," Marjory commented.

"I thought a kinetic round would give a more impressive result," *Fendaristil* replied.

"Let's see what -" Marjory's comment was interrupted by an incoming signal.

"Stand to and prepare to be boarded," was the peremptory command.

"A little abrupt," Marjory noted. "Do you have a read on who they are yet?"

"The signal came from the rear-most ship. All three appear to be similar to the pirates that were causing trouble in this sector five or more years ago. None of the ships carry identifying beacons, which is not a surprise. Each has a crew complement of eight. Similar weapons spread, minor beam weapons, some kinetic cannon and two torpedo tubes each. No shields. Two of them are carrying the experimental engines made by Apex Industries."

"We never did take the time to find them, did we?" Marjory mused. "Seems they found us. Convenient."

"I repeat, stand to and prepare to be boarded!" the demand came for a second time. "This is your last chance. Next time we destroy you."

"Impatient, aren't they?" Marjory commented. "Very well, let's welcome our visitors. Open the bay door and let them come in that way. I will meet them in the cargo hold. That should hold down the damage."

"Understood. Should I leave shields down?"

"No. Once the boarding party is inside raise them again and secure against communications. Jam the ships' communications too. Keep scanning. These three may be all that were sent, or there may be others coming."

Marjory stood effortlessly. She was wearing the black tunic and well-fitted breeches of the Battle Mage. The twin sword hilts were visible in their places on the thigh sheaths. Deftly, she swung her throwing knife harness over her shoulders and settled it in place. *Better,* she thought. *That feels better.* Action was coming and she was ready.

The five pirates made their way into the cargo bay by way of the rear loading bay. All wore body armour designed for use in the vacuum of space. Most were patched and mismatched. One was complete and in pristine condition. The leader, Marjory surmised. Two carried blaster rifles and the others pulled blaster pistols from holsters strapped to their legs. The five quickly looked around the largely empty but fully pressurised cargo bay, one of the rifle bearers tapping the arm of the one who Marjory took to be leader and gestured to where Marjory stood, unsuited.

"We're taking this vessel," the leader said in slightly accented Standard.

"No," Marjory stated.

There was a moment of silence as the invaders processed that single word.

"You have no ability to tell us yes or no," the leader said impatiently.

He gestured to the two on his right, who moved forward confidently, arrogantly. As they approached Marjory she slapped her hands to her sword hilts and, in a coordinated movement, extracted both of them, holding them as extensions of her arms that were held out at forty-five degrees on each side of her body. The ready stance she had been taught long ago remained her staple to initiate both defence and attack.

"I said no," Marjory said without inflexion.

The two advancing towards her stopped as though they had hit a wall. They stared at the swords, then at the face of the woman who held them. With a thought, Marjory activated the sword blades, which blazed into life and then settled to a dull sheen. Uncertainly, one half-turned to ask a question, while the other allowed the muzzle of his blaster rifle to waver slightly. It was all Marjory needed. She changed from being as still as a statue to a whirl of movement, *shifting* between the two men. Each sword flashed, once. She quickly stepped back into the ready stance. On the deck in front her her were two lifeless bundles.

"I said no," Marjory repeated.

The leader of the five invaders hesitated, while the other two standing with him just stared at the tableau. Both men had taken a single thrust through their throats. The movement had been like lightning.

"Kill her," the leader snarled, levelling his pistol at Marjory.

His action was met by a single small bolt of Mage fire from Marjory. The Mage fire enveloped the leader's right hand, melting armour, flesh and blaster at the same time. He screamed in agony and then stared as the two swords suddenly were floating in air and the two hands that had held them a moment before now held throwing knives. A split second later both of his companions collapsed with a knife each through their chests.

"Now, while you can still speak, who are you and where are you from?" Marjory asked conversationally as she walked forward to retrieve the knives.

"You will be destroyed for this," the leader gasped in reply, trying to hold his arm steady. His right hand was little more than a misshapen lump.

"No, I won't," Marjory said. "Who are you and where are you from?"

The leader struggled to reach a device attached to the left side of his body armour with his left hand, finally managing to tap it.

"Skarl," he growled. "Kill this ship."

With no acknowledgement he repeated his command. "Skarl, kill this ship."

"Skarl cannot hear you," Marjory told him. "*Fendaristil*, status of the three ships?"

"All three are holding station," the ship AI replied immediately. "Weapons are active and targeted at us. I have been able to break into their systems and have found the point of origin for the last several flights. It is in the Origel system, about thirteen light years away. Oh, and this one's name is Krelis Orvis."

The injured man was swaying, sweating profusely as the reaction to his injury took hold. "Skarl," he shouted.

"As I said, Krelis Orvis, Skarl cannot hear you,' Marjory repeated. "Your best bet will be to tell us how many vessels there are in the Origel system. I will then take you for medical treatment."

"You - you - will - die," the man managed to get out. "When I - do not report - they will - open - fire."

"Ah," Marjory said. "A sensible precaution. *Fendaristil*, target their weapons systems. As soon as they show signs of using them, destroy them."

The invader was on one knee, then both knees. He was swaying from side to side, eyes closed. Marjory watched him for a moment. She walked to a small hatch near the main entry, tapped a code and removed a pack once the hatch cover slid up. From the pack she took a small cylinder. She walked to the collapsing man and placed the cylinder against his neck. A quick press of her thumb to the dimple in the side and a strong anaesthetic was injected. The man crumpled to the floor alongside his dead comrades.

"The three ships are preparing to fire," *Fendaristil* reported. "Targeting the torpedo tubes."

Three small ports opened in *Fendaristil's* side. Thin beams speared from the three ports, one to each of the ships. A moment later the beams switched off, the first torpedo tube of each vessel having been damaged beyond use. A moment later again and the beams repeated, targeting the second torpedo tube of each vessel. One of the two vessels with the Apex Industries engines exploded as the beam met an emerging torpedo. The second and third vessels turned away from *Fendaristil*. Marjory decided to let them go.

"Thirteen light years is beyond the range of these ships to stage a raid, so there must be closer bases," Marjory mused aloud as she watched the two vessels move away on diverging courses.

"I have analysed the last ten journeys for each ship. There are three common points where the ships stopped at different times to each other. They are broadly spread but each is within striking distance of this region of space. They may be rendezvous and re-supply points." *Fendaristil* paused. "Awaiting orders, Battle Mage."

The form of address caught Marjory by surprise. *Fendaristil* was not as close to being a sentient AI as the Council Assistant was. However, the ship was the most advanced of its kind ever produced on Ennaris and the ship AI approached the Council Assistant's capability. To bluntly remind Marjory of her position and role in protecting and advancing the Union's interests from the Empire indicated that *Fendaristil* had identified something that she may have missed. Marjory was never one to give flippant replies in most circumstances, but she gave deeper thought to her answer.

"What do you recommend?" Marjory asked.

"There are two key considerations," the ship answered without hesitation. "On one hand, you are not expendable in this mission, and proceeding without adequate reinforcements may leave you vulnerable. Such reinforcements are unlikely to be available to you, certainly not in time to assist. The counter argument is that you are here to help the Union to grow and expand. These pirates have made that task difficult, not the least because in order to counter them you may have to improve the Union capabilities faster than is wise. However, I have much greater capabilities than either the Union vessels or the raiders, based on what we have seen to date. I recommend that we proceed to the first rendezvous point and make a decision about action once we have seen what that location has to tell us."

That accorded with Marjory's natural inclination. She turned the counter argument over in her mind but could find no reason to play safe at this time.

"Agreed," Marjory said. "Plot the course and show it on screen, please. Then take us there at best speed. We should be able to outrun the two survivors of this encounter."

Four hours later, after a series of micro-jumps, *Fendaristil* slid into the Krisbor system, with a muddy yellow sun in the far distance. Three rocky planets orbited the sun and a broken ring of asteroids gave mute evidence of one or more collisions in the distant past. The ship's cloak was active and passive sensors were extended to their maximum extent.

"Anything?" Marjory asked.

"There is a very faint energy signature coming from the third planet, or close to it. I am trying to identify the signature. There is a familiar pattern but identifying it is proving to be elusive." *Fendaristil* managed to sound annoyed at the setback even while keeping its normal impassive tone. "I have identified the signature. It is not a Union signature. It is an Empire one but with some differences to those of the warships that we have encountered."

"That makes sense if it's a fixed base or an orbital station."

"Yes, and I believe this one is built on an older source still. This is an Ennari installation. I have identified the underlying system. Shall I attempt communication?"

Fendaristil waited while Marjory ran through the possibilities. If it was an Ennari facility then getting access to the system would be simple, as she had all of the command codes by virtue of being the lead Battle Mage of Ennaris. But this facility had been taken over, somehow, by the Empire. Did they have any sort of trigger to send notification to Likud if it was compromised? That was what she would do - had done, in fact. But first things first.

"Are there any ships in the vicinity?" Marjory asked.

"None show on sensors, and none show as power sources," the ship replied. "Either they are shielded or are running quiet, or -."

"Or are not here," Marjory concluded. "Which station is this and when was its last report?"

"This is Farstation One-Oh-Five," Fendaristil responded after a brief pause. "Records show that it last reported its status as online and functional one thousand three hundred and seventy four cycles ago. On receiving no acknowledgement it went into solitary mode."

"About one thousand four hundred Earth years," Marjorie nodded. "That was about three hundred cycles before the Empire started its expansion push."

"Should I attempt to contact the station?"

"Why not? You have the command codes from the time when it last made contact?"

"Yes, trying them now. The station has responded."

"And?"

"It is awaiting orders, Battle Mage," *Fendaristil* replied.

"Order the station to dump its logs to you," Marjory said after a thoughtful pause. "Then I want you to analyse the logs and see if you can identify how many ships are using the station."

"I have also asked if there are ships due to arrive," the ship stated. "There are five due to arrive within the next three days."

"Good thinking," Marjory replied. "I should have thought of that. One of them is likely to be the ship we destroyed, the other two are likely headed here. That means there is another raiding party heading this way."

"The station is sending its logs. I have instructed it to purge the logs once I have them," *Fendaristil* reported. "The logs are extensive. It will take some time to process them for unique ship signatures."

"Estimate?"

"Three point oh two Earth hours," *Fendaristil* said. "The early entries indicate this was an Empire facility, and the power signature built on top of the Ennari one is an Empire signature."

"Which may indicate an existing active link or may just be because of the pirate takeover. Is it still an Empire outpost? For all we know these raiders found the station abandoned and just moved in. Or maybe not." Marjory stared at the viewscreen for a few moments, idly tapping her teeth with her middle finger as she thought. "As soon as you have the logs stored let's move out of range of the station's sensors. But drop a relay drone and instruct the station to send all sensor traffic through it."

Just over three hours later, *Fendaristil* placed a schematic of Farstation One-Oh-Five on the main viewscreen. It looked like a stubby cylinder with three rings of five spikes, which were the hard docking points, extending from the cylinder.

"The station is a type twelve farstation, equipped to handle twenty ships simultaneously, although only fifteen can hard dock at one time. Soft dock umbilical tubes are available from the ends of the station for a further five vessels. One thousand and ninety two cycles ago an Empire vessel docked, using the correct command codes. It landed a contingent of thirty personnel and departed. Over the next fifty cycles seven unique vessel signatures were recorded. At the end of that period a secondary power source was added to the station and the Ennari power source was relegated to maintenance tasks only." *Fendaristil* changed the display to show a sequence of ships arriving and departing in rapid time. Each individual ship signature was placed as an icon to the left side of the display.

"The same seven Empire vessels visited the station over the next three hundred and twenty-seven cycles. From that time until now there were an additional sixty-eight Empire vessels. The last of the original vessels departed the station for the final time approximately eight hundred and thirty-one cycles ago. The last Empire vessel to dock at the station was seventy-three cycles ago." The screen changed to show an array of the seventy-five Empire vessel icons. "Approximately ninety cycles ago the first ship with a Union signature docked at the station. There were three Empire vessels docked at the time. In the last ninety cycles there have been a total of twelve vessels with Union power signatures, including the two experimental Apex engines."

"So, it's pretty clear that these raiders are in league with the Empire, then," Marjory said with a frown. "What I find surprising is that they continue to run the older style Union power plants. If Likud is outfitting them to disrupt Union activities then why not upgrade the ships." She thought a moment longer. "Of course, that could lead to the Empire technology falling into the wrong hands - the Union Fleet, for example. So, use them but don't give them any of the advances the Empire would have from Likud's knowledge of Ennari technology. Luckily, he was not on any of the design and research teams."

"They do have Apex Industries' engines," *Fendaristil* reminded Marjory.

"Yes, and that may be a pointer to the source of their intelligence. But it may just as easily be that Apex were testing better engines and the Empire decided to take them. Time will tell in that regard."

"The twelve ships have been in and out of the base at increasingly frequent intervals during the ninety cycles. It would appear that they were paying more attention to this sector in recent times."

"Since we have been here and started to improve the Fleet's capabilities," Marjory said, nodding as though in affirmation. "Well, at least we managed to get their attention. So, now we need to dispose of them."

"We know that one of the ships has been destroyed and that a further four will dock shortly." *Fendaristil* made the observation and waited.

"Right," Marjory agreed. "Which means we can take almost half of them off the table if those four go down."

"Every farstation was equipped with basic defensive weapons," *Fendaristil* prompted. "The Battle Mage over-ride codes will allow them to be used."

"If they remain intact and operational," Marjory replied. "While they were built to last, they also needed constant maintenance. We can't rely on them to be usable. No, my memory of the type twelve farstations is that they also had one more feature that I can use."

Forty three hours later *Fendaristil* reported ships entering the system.

"Engine signatures match the two we encountered several days ago," the ship reported. "One vessel running the Apex engine, the larger vessel appears to be acting as escort."

"They probably will have to dock there for some time to make repairs," Marjory replied. "Let's wait and see if we get the rest."

"The schedule held by the station indicated two further ships should arrive within hours," *Fendaristil* noted.

"Okay. While we're waiting, try to get a lock on how many of the farstations in this sector remain active," Marjory ordered. "I feel that it is more likely that the Empire will be using similar tactics elsewhere. I expect them to be slightly outside the Union sphere of influence, like One-Oh-Five."

Slightly over four hours later, two more ships entered the system, moving steadily towards the farstation. *Fendaristil* took note of the engine signatures and matched them against the station's records.

"Confirmed the two ships entering the system have docked at the farstation numerous times," the ship AI said.

"Very well. We let them dock. Then we take them off the board."

"Will you give them an opportunity to surrender?" *Fendaristil* asked.

Marjory's face hardened as the implacable warrior came to the fore.

"They showed no mercy for their victims," she growled. "They get none."

A short time later, *Fendaristil* reported that the ships had made a hard dock at the station.

"Connect me to the station, please," Marjory directed.

"Connection has been established, Battle Mage," *Fendaristil* reported formally.

"Farstation One-Oh-Five, this is Marjory nar Drewflin, Battle Mage of Ennaris, transmitting command codes. Acknowledge," Marjory transmitted.

"Farstation One-Oh-Five, acknowledge Marjory nar Drewflin, Battle Mage," came the reply several seconds later.

Marjory nodded, letting out a breath she had not realised she was holding.

"One-Oh-Five, enter silent mode," Marjory directed.

"Silent mode active."

"One-Oh-Five, initiate self-destruct immediately."

"Self-destruct initiated. Countdown commenced. Silent mode does not allow for occupants of this station to be notified. Please confirm."

"Understood and confirmed," Marjory said. "Continue."

Three minutes later the Ennari weapons system of the station overloaded and exploded. Around the end rims of the station, on each docking spike and in a band around the centre of the cylinder, the defensive weapons held stores of energy and munitions. They detonated simultaneously. The station was cut in two around the centre while at the same time the ends blew out into space. Each of the spikes disappeared into the rapidly expanding halo of debris. None of the four docked ships emerged, except as part of the debris cloud.

"The station has been destroyed," *Fendaristil* reported unnecessarily.

"Note in the log that Battle Mage Marjory nar Drewflin ordered Farstation One-Oh-Five to initiate self-destruct as it had been compromised by an enemy force. Add a note of commendation for the station AI."

"The log has been so noted," *Fendaristil* acknowledged.

"Now, did you get the locations of other compromised stations?"

"I have done so, Battle Mage. There are two other farstations that demonstrate similar activity to One-Oh-Five. I have them plotted."

"Do you have other farstations identified that have not been compromised as yet?"

"I have identified a further fourteen farstations in this sector," *Fendaristil* replied. "None appear to have been occupied or visited by Empire vessels."

"Very well. Send to each of the fourteen farstations to initiate full lock down on my authorisation. And take us to the next closest occupied station."

| 10 |

Departure

Twenty-seven days later, *Fendaristil* docked at the home office for Drummel Industrial. Awaiting Marjory as she disembarked, apart from Drummel and Besnil, were Captains Wallis and Mengral with a contingent of Fleet security. Krelis Orvis had been placed in stasis and was released to be arrested. Marjorie gave an abbreviated version of the encounter with the pirates, putting the capture of the pirate leader down to luck, which neither Wallis nor Mengral believed for a moment although neither objected.

"The pirates had taken over an old space station," Marjory told Drummel later that day over a fresh coffee. "The station was more advanced than they knew, but it also had been altered by the Empire. Luckily, I do not believe they knew about some aspects of the station. The station self-destructed while the pirates were docked."

"It just self-destructed, this super advanced, abandoned, Empire-occupied space station," Drummel said flatly. "Just like that? You did nothing to make it self-destruct?"

Marjory looked at Drummel over the rim of her coffee mug. Their relationship had grown to the point where he was the only one Marjory fully trusted away from Ennaris, and there were very few she trusted on Ennaris. He knew that she was not from the Union territories. Wallis and Mengral suspected that there was something different about Marjory but Drummel *knew* there was.

"I ordered the station to self-destruct," Marjory said, locking eyes with Drummel.

"With the ships docked?"

"With the pirate ships hard docked," Marjory confirmed. "I did the same a few days later with a second station. All of the Empire-aligned pirates that have been using those stations have been dealt with."

"Mellivar, who are you to order such a station to self-destruct?" Drummel asked gravely. "I believe I now need to know. Your ship is so much more advanced than anything we or the Empire have, your knowledge of engineering and weapons are greater than anyone I know, and your fighting skills are superior to anything I have seen, not that I am an expert on fighting. But who am I helping? Is this an attempt to make the Union into a puppet, beholden to a different empire? We have been building this out for more than two decades now, and I believe I can trust you, but you need to trust me, too."

"I do trust you, Drummel," Marjory said. "But... The problem is that if anyone discovers where I am from or what I am doing then Likud and his Empire will stop at nothing to destroy both the Union and my home world. And that I cannot have."

"You speak of Likud as though you know him." Drummel replied with a wry twist of his lips.

"We have history, I think is the expression used on Earth. He cannot know of my existence in this place, or my mission will fail and both of our civilisations, and the galaxy itself, will be doomed."

"Your mission! So, you were sent here? By whom?"

"Yes, I was sent. Those who sent me are as far above us as we are to the lowest creatures of any planet. In our earliest days, they were near to being our gods. For most of my people, they are no more than legend, myths used to entertain or to scare or to uplift spirits. That is what they were to me until I was given this task. But they are real and they are trying to ensure that the civilisation they spent eons lifting to greatness survives."

"That civilisation is not Earth or the Union, is it?" Drummel asked quietly.

"No, it is not," Marjory replied. "I am sorry for all those who see the Union and Earth as the centre, but my goal is to protect a far older world and its civilisation from what we brought upon ourselves. We nearly destroyed our own world and I refuse to allow that to happen again. And that is why I am here."

"So why *are* you here, then? If you are so far advanced, why do you need to help us? What do we have that you need."

"That I don't really know. There is a prophecy, a very old one in your terms, on my world that tells that the evil that befell our civilisation will rise again and will be confronted by us and our children in a final battle. I am here to make sure our children are able to assist." Marjory shrugged. "And the first order of business is to make sure you survive."

"The people of Earth are your children? How?"

"It was my predecessors who lifted your predecessors from their prehistoric lives and helped them make the jump towards civilisation. Then we helped you to evolve your own forms of civilisation before we left you to your own devices."

Drummel stared at Marjory, stunned. "Your people were the progenitors of mine?"

"In a way. The basic genetic material was so similar that we believe our origin and your own were tied together somehow. We did add some of our genetic material to your own as we helped your ancestors. As the Guardians lifted us so we lifted you. The Guardians believe that Earth will provide the children to help us in our battle to survive what is coming. They tasked me to assist."

"So those plans you brought with you, the ones you have devised since being here, the tools and advances made - all of them were from your own history?"

"Yes, but older, less capable than the latest we had. Frankly, the Union would not be able to deal with the jump from the basic technology you have had to the cutting edge. And make no mistake, Drummel, what we had all that time ago is well in advance of the cutting edge of the Union and others today. Even the Empire from what I have seen."

Drummel considered.

"But Likud - who's a person not just a title? He," Drummel continued on receiving Marjorie's nod of assent, "must have knowledge of your technologies also? You have history, you say, but I'm guessing he's from your own planet also?"

"Yes," Marjorie smiled without humour, "I'm a large part of the reason he had to leave. I was one of the group that broke up the rebellion and captured the leader. He may believe that I am dead, but I don't want him to discover that I am helping the Union to build strength."

"Yes, but if you can do this for us why can't he for his Empire?"

"I think he is trying to do so," Marjory replied, "but he was not part of any of the design and research teams, unlike me. He was never trained to develop the ships, tools and weapons as I was. Yes, these designs are from my world, but I had a hand in designing or updating many of them. He did not. So, he is working from memory of using the older ships and weapons, and he only had a small ship when he fled. Effectively, he had to start over again."

"So where do we go from here?" Drummel asked, absently rubbing his hand through his thinning and greying hair.

"Weapons, as I said before setting the trap. We need to get the Union to near parity with the Empire's weapons. I estimate that will take almost ten years." Marjorie considered her words. "And then I will be disappearing."

"What? Why?" Drummel's confusion and distress shone through.

"My friend," Marjorie replied sadly. "We have been doing this for almost twenty-five years. You have aged considerably in that time, while I have not. While I can change my appearance there remains the risk of being discovered. I will return at a future time for the second phase of my plan."

"You are not really ageing, then?"

"No, not as you are."

"How old are you, Mellivar?"

"I have lived for more than fifteen thousand of your years," Marjory replied softly.

"Fifteen…" Drummel stared. "But that's…"

"Impossible?" Marjory smiled. "Not so, my friend. Merely not known on your world."

Drummel paused to process what he had been told. Over fifteen thousand years! That meant that Mellivar was alive when humans were in the earliest stages of civilising themselves. But then, they were helped in that by Mellivar's people. The idea that this woman was so old took time to work its way into Drummel, and when it did he found himself with questions, so many questions. But he settled on one.

"Mellivar, who are you?"

Sighing, Marjory shook her head. She had crafted a blend of grey and dark hair, almost black, and had added a small number of age lines to her face. Her figure had thickened slightly, although she did not bother to change her style of walk or speech. Lithely, belying all visual evidence of age, she stood and seemed to blur. Where there had been a woman in the middle stages of middle age, now there was a young and vibrant woman, standing tall and proud.

"My name is Marjory nar Drewflin, and I am the last Battle Mage of Ennaris, a world far from here. Once we were the light of this galaxy but we fell and, in falling, have been diminished greatly. However, we must once again face the evil that caused us to fall. Our own brand of evil. If we fail then the galaxy will fall also, for our foe, whose name is Goroth, will assume control of all sentient beings. The outcome will be terrible, I believe."

"And you need humans to help?" Drummel asked, eyeing Marjory askance. "You've seen how our technology compares to the Empire's. You've seen how easy it is for humans to fall victim to our own fears and prejudices. You've seen how venal many of our supposed leaders are. In which universe do we look like someone who can help the likes of you?"

"Why, in this universe," Marjory replied, shrugging her appearance back into character. "Not yet, admittedly, but I have been given a little time."

"How long?" Drummel asked.

"About five hundred Earth years, give or take a decade or two," Marjory replied off-handedly. "It gives me enough time to establish the Union as a viable alternative force. At least, that is the idea."

"Five hundred years," Drummel sighed. "So, not something I'll be seeing. I trust you Mellivar - Marjory - but I truly hope you're not taking advantage of my trust. I'll never know, of course, but I don't want to be the cause of the Union and Earth being destroyed."

"I can only point to the work we have done together to provide you with some confidence in my motives, my friend. To be honest, had I wished to damage the Union I could have done so without doing any of the things I have done. *Fendaristil* was and remains far in advance of anything the Union can defend against. But I believe you raise a good point about longevity," she mused. "I must remain Mellivar for the time being. And I will need to remain invested in this company, even after I am gone. Or at least, after I change identity. I will have to remain away long enough for memory of Mellivar to fade away. I will need to change identity regularly."

"Make each of your identities descendants of Mellivar," Drummel replied. "We can restructure Drummel Industrial so that you have something to come back to when you need to do so. Some sort of trust with our descendants having equal share. I'll have my lawyer draw up something that should last. You will have to make sure that your future selves are descendants of Mellivar. I have no direct descendants but you can be sure that distant relatives will come out of the ground to grab a share once I'm gone. So, we'll add a rider that your descendants get first offer should my side want to sell."

Only a year later, Drummel Industrial purchased a startup company with designs for a revolutionary new form of weapon, a high-powered rail gun, which was a markedly new take on a old concept.

The weapon's design called for more power than was available at the time in most ships, and needed larger vessels than the Union had available, but it promised to be considerably more accurate and faster to recharge. The prototype had been shown to military representatives and had failed in spectacular fashion during the demonstration. Not only did it need enormous power, but it also overheated as soon as the first slug was fired and then exploded as a result. Consequently, and not too surprisingly, the value of the company was reduced to almost zero. All investors except the founder were happy to be bought out at a number somewhat greater than zero. The founder was convinced that his designs would work and refused to sell his minority holding.

Marjory met with the owner, a young engineer named Jamison Dart, with the intention of brow-beating him into submission. Instead, she found a brilliant, although slightly erratic man, whose ideas were far in advance of the technical capabilities of the Union at the time. Impressed at what she saw and heard, and given Drummel Industrial now owned those designs, Marjory decided to spend time examining them. She loaded the specifications to *Fendaristil* while she looked them over. Together, Battle Mage and ship AI drew up a list of subtle design failures and deep technical limitations that meant the weapon as devised by Jamison Dart would not, *could* not, work.

Dart was crest-fallen as he paged through the list during a second meeting. He muttered harshly to himself as he saw how each of the flaws in his design fitted together with the technology limitations.

"I don't understand," he complained to Marjory. "Each of the component tests passed. Even the initial full test passed before we ran the demonstration. Everything was fine. The design and technicals were fine. Why did it fail at that point?"

"Because when you ran your internal tests you used your own power supply, which was shielded and fully regulated. But you ran your demonstration at the Fleet testing facility, and that power supply is closer to a real world supply, with minor variations and fluctuations that your design could not handle. In any event, if your railgun had passed that test you would have found it had stress fractures. Had you fired it another two or three times the couplings would have disintegrated and the end result would have been the same." Marjory pointed to three points on the diagram that was displayed on the main viewscreen in the conference room. "These highlights are three key stress points. We can't see the weapon of course, but I have no doubt of those stresses. Then here," and she tapped the screen in two different places, "and here, there are couplings that would have buckled."

Dart was shaking his head as he reviewed the calculations.

"I never realised the power profile was so different," he said, dismayed. "It's a complete failure. I'll never get another job. I'll sign over my shares to you if your offer remains? At least I can get some money to live for a while."

"The offer remains," Marjory replied. "But I have a fresh condition."

"What?" Dart asked dispiritedly. "Taking advantage? Kick me while I'm down?"

"Not at all," Drummel replied. "We will purchase those shares at the price offered. And then you will join us at Drummel Industrial as head of weapons research."

Dart's head shot up and he stared at Drummel, then at Marjory, and then again at Drummel.

"What? Head of … Why would you want that?"

"Because your design was not completely wrong," Marjory said crisply. "Yes, there are design flaws but we can get around those."

"But given all of the technical problems you've pointed out, there's no way I can build a rail-gun that will work!" Dart exclaimed.

"No," Marjory agreed with a decisive nod of her head. "You cannot make it work with the current level of technical capability of the Union, or with those flaws in your design." She paused and shared a secret smile with Drummel while Dart looked on, perplexed. "But I can."

"I don't understand," Dart told Drummel. "Where did that ship come from?"

"That is one of Mellivar's designs," Drummel replied without looking away from the scene outside the viewing window of the Fleet test centre. "We have five of them being built. This is the prototype."

"You're using a prototype to test the new weapon?" Dart asked. "Is that wise?"

"This is Mellivar's prototype," Besnil Barjen replied, as though that were all the explanation required. "They don't break."

"Never? That's … that's …" Dart stopped speaking.

"That's Mellivar," Besnil finished for him.

Outside the window, a sleek vessel emerged from the shrouded space dock. In itself, the shroud was something different. Fleet security had already fended off two attempts by rival companies to penetrate the shroud to see what was being built. No scanner could penetrate the strange material employed, another Mellivar design adapted from Ennari technology. Production of the shroud material required yet another step in manufacturing techniques and material design. Already Drummel was in discussion with several companies whose executives had witnessed or been told of the failed attempts to see through the new material and had started to think up additional uses for it. But the ship that emerged had silenced everyone.

Union ships were not especially pretty. Relying on the fact that space was almost completely vacuum and the old rule of thumb that said that a ship could be a cube and still be effective in space, most Union ships were designed for function, with the skin applied largely, it appeared, to hold everything inside. But the *Sunseeker* was different. This ship was twice the length of *Sandpiper* but it was only slightly wider and deeper. The bow was slightly flattened and the bridge sat behind an actual window - more advances had been made in hardened silicate polymers to make that happen - which was set into the front third of the vessel. Behind the bridge, the ship's upper edge levelled for the middle third and then tapered sightly towards the tail. A single stubby fin protruded from the centre of the ship's top surface and ran down its length, tapering until it merged with the body of the vessel near the tail, which flared out once again and held the single engine. The ship's skin was smooth, with no protuberances breaking its lines. However, bulges protruded from left and right below the bridge, giving the impression of elbows. Drummel heard speculation from those around him that the bulges were landing gear, or sensors, and there was confusion about the new weapon and its whereabouts.

Sunseeker worked out of the space dock and presented itself side-on to the watchers. Spurts of white gas were emitted from points along the side nearest the onlookers as manoeuvring thrusters moved the ship laterally away from the shroud and the station. At ten kilometres, the opposite thrusters were engaged and the ship came to a stop. Marjory's voice came over the loudspeakers.

"Brevil base, this is *Sunseeker*. In position at ten kilometres distance, target acquired, all systems green."

"Affirmative *Sunseeker*," came the dry reply. "Clear to commence the test."

The watchers had been briefed that this would be a stable test, with both ship and target remaining in place. *Sunseeker* would send a single pellet from the new railgun at the small target asteroid that had been pulled into place ten kilometres away from it. The watchers should be able to see the strike of the pellet, assuming it worked. The kinetic energy discharged when the pellet struck the asteroid would release enough energy to lift a good sized cloud of debris.

"Acknowledged Brevil base, clear to test. Deploying kinetic weapon."

Mellivar's voice was matter of fact, as though she had done this a thousand times. *Which*, Drummel thought with a touch of awe intruding on his thoughts, *she may well have done.*

A hushed silence in the viewing area was broken as the bulges split open to reveal not one but two larger than expected railguns, one in each pod. The ship's skin folded back into its fuselage, leaving the railguns hanging from a single support pylon each. The railguns swung down and around on a gimbal, swinging to left and right and then in a complete circle. Excited commentary broke out as the onlookers realised that they were looking at a weapon larger than any that had been seen before, and one that could fire in any direction.

The firing of the two guns was missed by many, and almost missed by Drummel. While he had seen the tests leading up to this test, actually seeing it in the ship induced a tenseness in the joint owner of Drummel Industrial that he could not recall feeling for quite a long time. A few seconds later the first puff of dust was seen, followed a moment later by the second. The guns had fired a second apart to make sure the energy load was spread more evenly. Drummel turned to where Jamison Dart stood, watching a perfect demonstration of a railgun where seven years ago his own demonstration had failed spectacularly. Dart was smiling broadly.

The excited commentary changed to confusion as *Sunseeker* started to move. The ship accelerated smoothly, swinging away from the station. Drummel, who knew what was coming, felt the tightness come again. This was very much a make or break move. While it had been agreed with Fleet, it had not been practiced. Over the loudspeaker Marjory sounded sure and in command.

"Brevil base, initiating phase two. Helm, make your course one eight zero degrees relative. Accelerate to point zero one. Steady, steady. Reverse course. Accelerate to point zero two. Weapons, clear to acquire target. On my mark, wait, wait. Fire one, fire two."

Sunseeker swung on a tight racetrack course moving up the range before turning sharply and increasing speed as it came back towards the target. When it was almost alongside the viewing area the guns fired in sequence and the ship swung away again, Marjory's commands ignored by the watching group. Again, a few seconds later, one and then a second puff of dust was raised from the asteroid. The watchers applauded and turned to each other in excitement. It took a moment for several to realise that *Sunseeker* was coming around once again.

"Brevil base, initiating phase three. Weapons, deploy main gun."

All comment stopped again as the leading edge of the topside fin peeled back and a single muzzle poked out. A couple of hushed exclamations of awe were all that broke the silence.

"Weapons, clear to acquire target, set sequence alpha. Fire!"

A rapid series of four energy pulses were spat from the gun as *Sunseeker* swung past the station again. All eyes swung to the asteroid in time to see the energy pulses hit the asteroid in a spread. At the second strike a small part of the asteroid broke off, followed by more pieces from the third and fourth pulse.

Drummel felt the tightness in his chest release and he smiled, only to grimace as it returned with greater force. Even as Marjory reported that the test was complete, Drummel collapsed.

"So, upstaging my moment, were you?" Marjory joked as she entered the hospital room.

"Couldn't have you hogging all of the limelight," Drummel replied from the hospital bed.

Monitors displayed his vitals from above his head. Medical sensors were attached to his forehead, chest and both arms. Marjory glanced at them and frowned. *Drewflin, I could use you now,* she thought.

"Yep, not good," Drummel said. "Oh, I'll live for a while longer, so I'm told, although it'll be a bit of a struggle. I'll have a whole lot of nanites running around inside me to keep things running, but my days of running the show are numbered. Looks like we'll have to initiate that hand over sooner than we planned."

"Well, Fleet was impressed by the demonstration and have already agreed to commence refitting any ships that can handle the railgun or the pulse cannon. That's not many. There will be plenty for Besnil to look after." Marjory paused for a moment, momentarily lost for words. "I was supposed to leave before you," she said quietly.

"The legals are all done, so hopefully you'll have sufficient funding for whatever comes in the future."

"I will stay until the first of the ships are outfitted. Besnil will have designs for new ships, sensors and weapons available at regular intervals. Of course, she is improving on many of them already. I feel that Drummel Industrial will be in good hands."

"I'll be in the office from time to time," Drummel said, "so you can update me."

The two stared at each other for a moment.

"You did it, Marjory, Battle Mage of Ennaris," Drummel said, loud enough that she, and only she, could hear.

"*We* did it," Marjory replied. "There remains much to do yet, but the Union Fleet now has the basic tools they need to fight. They will be improved over the centuries to come, but the start is made."

"I envy the people of your world that they have one such as yourself to stand for them," Drummel said.

"There is one greater than I," Marjory replied, straightening and allowing the illusion of age to drop away for Drummels' benefit. "He may not yet truly realise it, but he will prove to be the best of us. He is Drewflin, my life partner."

"Then he would be someone I would like to meet," Drummel said sadly. "My life has been so much richer for your presence in it. To meet the one you have chosen as a partner would be truly amazing."

"Relax and get as well as you can," Marjory replied as she shrugged back on the illusion of age. "I will bring you updates regularly."

Fourteen months, two weeks and four days later Marjory stepped into the passenger lock of *Fendaristil.* Turning, she gazed at Drummel and Besnil. All three struggled with their emotions. Much had happened since the weapons test. *Sunseeker* had been commissioned as the first Star class light cruiser for the Union fleet, three more ships of the design had been completed and commissioned, and seven more hulls laid down. Twelve of the modified attack boats, including *Sandpiper,* now had the new pulse cannons. None could handle the vibrations or power requirements of the powerful railguns, so Jamison Dart had started a design exercise to develop a smaller version. The engine design had been uprated again and retrofits were under way.

Two months before had come the stunning news that *Andromeda*, one of the new Star class cruisers, had met and successfully fought off two Empire cruisers. True, it had taken some damage, the crew was shaken and there had been some injuries, but the ship had withstood multiple energy blasts and had even managed to fire both railguns and pulse cannon before escaping. The news came as great relief to many people, but to Marjory most of all. It meant that she could move to the next stage of her plan.

Already Marjory had established the Fernis Foundation, a charitable organisation dedicated to enhancing the lives of those who were deemed to require it. There was no indication in any of the Foundation's literature, legal materials or documentation that told how beneficiaries were selected. The Foundation would bring together its beneficiaries on a regular basis to undertake self-improvement activities, receive training in various life skills and, without being aware, to be tested for nascent gifts. For the beneficiaries' primary qualifying attribute was that they carried the Ennaris gene. The first such gatherings had already been held, with Marjory on hand to welcome those who accepted the invitation. She had found it surprisingly emotional to realise that she may be interacting with the Children, or those who may bear the Children. The Foundation would be managed by *Fendaristil* while Marjory was involved with other elements of the long term plan. It was another piece of the puzzle.

And so it was time to leave. For thirty-three years, Marjory had laboured to get the Fleet better equipped, while dealing with moles, traitors and enemy agents who all tried to hold back or destroy the advances made. The change in the Union Fleet's capability was astounding.

"I understand that you or one of your descendants will remain in touch from time to time," Besnil said. "However, I wish it were you staying."

"It is time I departed," Marjory said. "I have much to do and time is limited."

Besnil looked slightly puzzled at the choice of words. However, she merely nodded and looked to Drummel. The latter's emotions were clearly visible, his distress at Marjory's departure causing her to have a momentary thought of staying longer. That passed, however. With scant ceremony, the two nodded to each other. Leave taking had taken place over the weeks since *Andromeda's* escape, and little more was to be said.

As Marjory started to turn, however, Drummel spoke.

"There was something you have said to crews that have taken delivery of our technology, our ships," he said. "The way you say it, I believe it must be a warrior's benediction. So, may the hunting be good and the enemy worthy and the victory sweet, Battle Mage."

Tears sprung to Marjory's eyes. She stepped from *Fendaristil's* passenger lock once again and walked down the small ramp and back to where Drummel stood. Besnil gasped as Marjory allowed the illusion of age to fade away. Gently, Marjory reached out and placed her hand over Drummel's heart.

"Drewflin is the healer of the family, but he taught me a thing or two," Marjory said, as a tear ran down her cheek unheeded.

Besnil gasped again as Marjory's hand glowed a muted green. Drummel's eyes opened wide and his dry, waxy skin smoothed just slightly and then regained some of the colour of old. Besnil looked from Drummel to Marjory as though seeing a ghost.

"That should hold you for a few more years, old friend," Marjory smiled.

Then she turned and deliberately walked through the passenger lock. The ramp concertinaed into the lock and the hatch slid into place. Immediately, *Fendaristil* gently lifted from the deck and floated through the landing bay where it had been parked for much of the last three decades. It moved into the airlock and then out the spaceward side, and accelerated away from the station.

Mellivar was never seen or heard from again.

But her descendants were!

| part two |

WARRIORS

475 years before the events described in <u>Children of Ennaris</u>

| 11 |

Warriors of the Light

"Sir, may I present General Maneril Selvis."

Fleet Admiral Terrance Lester gestured to the door where the general was waiting. Nodding, General Selvis approached the old-fashioned desk behind which sat Karuta ben Grill, the Chair of the Union's Council of Member Worlds, the leader of the Union. Flanking ben Grill were the two Deputy Chairs and a number of advisors, all senior in their fields of finance, logistics, security and several other disciplines. Selvis stood to attention, snapped a crisp salute, and stood beside Lester at parade rest with hands clasped in the small of her back.

"As you know, sir," Lester continued, "General Selvis is the youngest flag level officer in the Union's history. She has proven herself in several major encounters with Empire forces, and led the successful defence of Brolgus Nine when the military leadership was suborned and subsequently revealed to be Empire collaborators. She has proven to be one of, if not *the*, finest strategic thinker the Union has produced. General Selvis has been studying patterns of Empire sympathiser incursions, security breaches and insurrections, as well as our responses to them. She has what I believe is a worthwhile proposal to put before you as a means of combating the increasing difficulties we have in dealing with these events via our usual military or special forces methods."

Ben Grill regarded the woman standing in front of him. She looked to be around forty Earth years of age, with long dark hair swept back and held in place by a simple clasp at the nape of her neck. She was slightly taller than average with a trim figure. She wore no decorations beyond her general's stars in a neat row on the raised collar of her tunic. Ben Grill recalled from the briefing notes that she spurned to display her array of medals, including the Cross of Valour and the Green Star, two of the highest military decorations. And they were earned in the field, he knew. For such a young officer, she had been involved in many difficult and dangerous situations and had succeeded in each of them. That was worth celebrating in and of itself, but she had done so with small loss of Union forces. Her stated ethos was that the armed personnel who fought under her command were not mere resources to be expended, but valuable women and men who deserved to be seen as such. Sentiment surveys among the military consistently showed that she received the highest satisfaction scores from her subordinates, which was important to the Union's military management.

It was her eyes, however, that held ben Grill's attention. He had met the general several times at functions and briefings and he always came back to her eyes. He would describe them as a smoky gray-blue colour, which implied calm, but that was somewhat misleading. The general had a way of looking at one that gave the impression that she was peeling back the layers that everyone built over themselves. It was as though she had seen so much, knew so much of people and their reactions, that she could uncover secrets merely by gazing at them. It was a very direct gaze, which could intensify to a very sharp and uncomfortably piercing stare when she wished to challenge or berate. Her eyes also told of pain and loss, things that were not in her dossier and, at their back, the Chair felt that he recognised steely resolve. They were, he thought not for the first time, old eyes.

"Good morning, General," ben Grill said. "It's a pleasure to meet you again. Please tell us of your proposal."

"Sir," General Selvis nodded. "I have a short presentation I would like to show before speaking to the proposal?"

Ben Grill nodded agreement and Selvis waved a hand across the desk panel. A segment of the desk turned a darker shade. She then tapped her command pad. The darker segment on the desk flared to life. Above it a holographic image showed a frozen moment. Ben Grill recognised it as the moment when Brolgus Nine's representative leader was assassinated by the military cabal that sought to stage a coup. It was one of the events that defined Selvis' career to date.

"This is Brolgus Nine. I am not going to take you through that event in detail. You all know that the military leaders sought to take over the planet and present it to the Empire, and that we managed to thwart that plan. What few people are aware of is that on Brolgus Nine we uncovered evidence of similar efforts on other worlds. Subsequently, Union military intelligence was able to foil plots on Croilip, Helpernia, Verilian and Prostellor, some by military personnel, some by civilians who had achieved levels of influence and, thereby, may have had credible opportunities to take power in various ways."

Selvis paused as the murmur among the advisors quieted. The Chair and his security advisors were aware of those events, but others were not.

"In addition, we have evidence of a buildup of Empire military and logistics bases in an arc across the region of space where its control intersects with areas over which we claim influence. As a rule, and this goes back a long time now, the Empire uses agents of various kinds - pirates, others posing as merchants, industrialists who work for them voluntarily or involuntarily - to staff and supply those bases. However, we have also identified bases occupied by Empire citizens."

More murmurs went around the gathered advisors.

"The problem," Selvis continued once she had the room's attention again, "is that when we use standard Union military personnel to arrest, remove or quell unrest caused by these agents we tend to find ourselves with very blunt instruments. Increasingly, there is resentment building in the populations of these planets about 'invasions' by Union forces from outside their space. As you will know, Union garrisons tend to be staffed by personnel not from the planet on which they are stationed, largely to ensure we do not create conflicts of interest for our force members. Also, on several occasions the need to direct a military response has been identified and the delay involved gave time for ring leaders to escape. We were left with lesser participants or scapegoats."

The holo-emitter worked through a series of images and snippets of media coverage of arrests, injuries to uprising participants and civilians caught in the violence, and then protests against military actions. The final image shown was of a Union flag being burned in a city square, with hundreds of people watching and cheering.

"These types of protests have been increasing. Already we have movements on several worlds demanding their authorities block off-world troops from being deployed on the planet. Every transgression by a member of the military is given prominent coverage on certain media channels. There are elements of the media that we know are in the pay of the Empire, knowingly or otherwise. Others just see it as a means of expanding viewer numbers. Nonetheless, the result is a growing chorus against what are seen as heavy-handed tactics and the resultant outcomes in injuries, damage and additional unrest."

"And your proposal?" ben Grill asked.

"I propose to establish an elite unit, within the Union military but on the periphery and staffed with suitable military and non-military members, tasked with adopting a much quieter, more methodical but less predictable method of identifying and dealing with the drivers behind various events we have been encountering. While traditional military forces will continue to be needed, the new unit will take a far more strategic approach."

"Special forces and elite units have been tried in the past," Asper Krendis, one of the Deputy Chairs commented. "They have not always been as successful at these operations as were hoped. How will this new one be any different?"

"Yes, ma'am, I agree." Selvis stopped speaking for a moment, gathering her thoughts before continuing. "Special and elite units in the past have been more the sharp tip of the spear to go into difficult situations ahead of the main military force or for such things as surgical strikes. Likewise, there have been law and intelligence task forces that have targeted specific crimes, criminal figures or organisations. All of them took the elite in their fields and made them into better and less blunt instruments. But all were still from those branches of military, law enforcement or intelligence. The proposed unit will bring together all of those skills, supported by a range of analysts and support teams. We don't intend for the unit to be staffed merely by elite Fleet or other military personnel. They will have to be able to act with discretion, independence and tact, but have the skills to intercept and address whatever is found. We will look for motivated individuals less interested in pure fighting and more in ensuring that motives are understood, and that true subversives are identified and captured without collateral damage or injuries."

"That sounds similar to any number of other elite units, I must say," Krendis said. "I do agree that we need to make some headway against what is becoming a pattern of both subversion and incursion. I'm concerned about units such as the one proposed taking their own decisions, acting unilaterally. You may have the best of intentions for this unit and your own record shows that you are one who believes in balancing the military and civilian objectives. How can you be certain that your team members will live those values?"

General Selvis was ready for that question, but gave the impression of deep thought before answering.

"We intend to have deep profiling of any candidates for inclusion," Selvis said carefully. "That is both military and non-military alike. There are tools we can use for the purpose. Military personnel will need to be highly skilled, of course, but the non-military personnel will also need to be able to acquire adequate skills should they need to accompany teams in the field. Likewise, strategy, tactics and political skills will need to be acquired by the military members, more so than is normal. Support staff will be as important as field teams. They must all share the values, the aspirations, the intent that will be core to the unit. I expect there to be some missteps but we must continue to assess those who join the unit and make sure that those values are held closely." She paused and swiped a hand through the hologram that had been locked on the burning flag. "There can never be guarantees, however. All we can do is the best we can do and then remain vigilant."

"And how will the unit be named?" ben Grill asked.

Selvis relaxed slightly. If they were asking about more inconsequential details then there was a good chance of approval. But to Selvis the unit's name was important because it would send a signal about the values that the unit's members represented. So she looked from face to face before answering the question.

"I feel that it is necessary for the identity to be established early. For that reason we want the name to tell at least something of the ethos under which the unit will operate, even though their existence will be hidden from most. They will be engaged in a fight for the Union, to protect the Union from the darkness that our enemies seek to bring on us." Selvis held her head high as she looked to ben Grill, the fierceness of her gaze almost pushing him back in his chair. "I propose that this new unit will be the Warriors of the Light."

"That went well," *Fendaristil's* AI commented as Marjory walked onto the bridge.

"It did," Marjory agreed, unbuttoning her general's tunic. "I'm confident that we will get approval. Do you have that list of tests ready? We will need to be ready to move quickly."

"Yes. There are a range of the usual aptitude tests, the skills tests and personality tests. The blood tests are normal, as are DNA tests. However, I included an additional DNA test for any Ennari genetic material. I have also established a routine that will push that test into the civilian population's DNA tests. While there are gaps, there is almost seventy percent of the population tested before and at birth for health issues."

Marjory nodded. "That is a little intrusive but may be the best method for us to adopt. And can we be sure that we will get adequate visibility of the results, once General Selvis has departed?"

"Yes. I inserted a very subtle instruction for matching results to be held and transmitted to a specific node that we can monitor, no matter which role you are playing at the time."

"Very well. I hope our assumption that the Children are more likely to come via a military background is right. If we could come up with a way to screen the whole general population it would be useful. That would make the likelihood of identifying suitable candidates simpler. But, seventy percent is a good proportion. Meanwhile, I need to make a start on setting up the unit, whether I get the job or not. I want to make sure this team is set up and ready to go, with the right approach laid out."

"I have the profiles you asked for," the AI said. "I have based them on the Ennari colonisation team profiles, but with the addition of some of the security and social attributes that we discussed. Analysis says that if you can set a standard team size of three then you should be able to have a spread of skills to suit a range of different situations."

"Three? We used five on Ennaris, although that was very conservative. Please put together a template for a team. The spread of skills needed, personality types, the usual stuff. What about weapons? As a rule the teams should carry standard weapon loads, with specialists able to take their own choices. We need to make sure we cater for situations where we deal with different societal types. These teams will go into places where they may not be able to carry advanced weaponry, so we will need them to be trained in a wide range of weaponry. Already there are planets that eschew modern tools and weapons for more rudimentary ones, some even going back to medieval lifestyles, as though that will help."

The AI ran through thousands of scenarios in the quarter second before responding. "I will analyse the types of societies that are in the

Union or within the Union's sphere of influence. We can extrapolate the types of weaponry that may need to be used from that. One of the aptitude tests will be the ability to pick up new weapons and tools."

"Search out suitable locations for the headquarters and training facilities. Perhaps they should be separated and isolated, able to be defended readily and with good communication capabilities." Marjory thought a little further. "The ideal location would be an orphan planet in a stable enough orbit, well away from asteroid belts that could obscure approaches."

"I will start a survey immediately. The locations will have to be away from frontier zones also," *Fendaristil* noted. "I will have a list for you some time tomorrow morning. One question remains, though."

"Yes?"

"What about Shakar? Do you propose to use it also?"

"I plan to do so," Marjory nodded. "But not for this basic selection process. I feel we will need to establish strong candidates for the children, or at least some of them. I feel Shakar may be of use in determining the most elite. They are the ones that I expect will be the champions we seek."

"I understand," *Fendaristil* replied. "Shakar can be used to identify the cream. I will weave that into the plan also."

"Thank you. Meanwhile, I have to get back to the base. Admiral Lester expects a decision within the hour."

| 12 |

Headquarters

The next six months passed in a swirl of logistical arrangements, slicing through red tape and planning. The Chair and both Deputy Chairs had been unanimous in approving the new unit, but for a trial period and on a limited basis. That was not a surprise to Marjory. What was a surprise was that the Chair directed that the unit would be outside the normal military hierarchy. Rather than reporting to either the space fleet or land forces leadership, the new unit would report directly to the Union executive officers. The rationale was obvious - often problems were found to be within the military hierarchy, so having this new unit targeted at those subversive elements and potentially subject to the authority of one or more subversives made little sense.

The decision left several military leaders angry, but not Admiral Lester.

"This makes good strategic sense," he told Marjory when they were alone. "Anyone who objects to it needs to step back and think about what we're trying to do. This will be the best way to make it happen."

"Yes, but we need the military leaders to come in behind us on this, too," Marjory replied. "If we alienate them then we may find ourselves without ground or air support. Of course, those who object may need to be assessed for other motives, but we need to be careful. This could just be inter-service rivalry. We risk sliding down a deep hole if we are not careful."

"I agree, as does the Chair, which is why he wants you to lead the unit," Lester said. "It's your choice. But you need to be aware that this may damage your career. It's no secret that you're considered a candidate for my chair in the future. This may put a crimp in any such aspirations."

"I have enough to worry about without your responsibilities," Marjory replied. "I feel no great need to run the whole of the Union military. And I am passionate about this unit being established and made useful. I will take the lead."

"What are your estimates for kickoff? I've seen your team profile templates. I must admit, I hadn't considered some of those aspects, but the more I reflect, the more I like the idea of having a combination of hard military and less edgy strategic and societal skills. It'll be tough finding the right people."

Marjory nodded. "We only need to find a dozen initially, and that from the entire military forces at our disposal plus some targeted non-military occupations. I expect the vast majority will come from human ranks. We only have two or three non-human members of the Union that could play a part and I am working them into my plans. But it will be humans first as they will be easiest to deal with, and almost all of our problems have come from the human populations. Suitable locations for command, logistics and training facilities are top of the list, alongside building a command and support team. The parameters for suitable bases are in the briefing pack I sent over."

Lester nodded. "Yes, I reviewed them. Makes sense not to have them all together. But I think this becomes something for you to locate for yourself rather than using regular military channels. It will allow tighter security in the long run. For now, you sit under my command, but separated from your old duties. Once we're comfortable with the arrangements you'll transition to one of the Chairs." He paused as Marjory nodded. "Oh, and one other thing. You've been promoted to Lieutenant General, by order of the Chair. Congratulations!"

"That's not needed," Marjory objected. "It may make things harder to put me above those we need to use for support."

"Maybe, but it may make it easier, too. For the record, I recommended the promotion and it was agreed without hesitation. I think you'll need the rank, Maneril, whether within the regular military or not."

Marjory considered. The promotion would cause even more resentment from those who felt that she was being promoted too quickly. She was thought to be too young for the rank. *If they only knew*, she thought with a quirk of the lips, one that was noted by the Fleet Admiral.

"Thought of something funny?" Lester queried.

"Ah," Marjory replied, thinking furiously. "Just thinking of the comments that will be made in certain quarters when this becomes known."

Lester shrugged. "They'll get over it. Meanwhile, go find your team and then your bases, in whatever order you decide. You have been allocated somewhat more in funding than you asked for, again on the Chair's orders. But don't go spending it all at once. You'll have to justify it at some stage."

"Understood. I will provide a monthly update to you in person," Marjory said. "We can work out what gets written down and what is left out of the written record for now. I will have complete notes held securely off-system so we can back-fill anything needed."

Marjory had a short list of people who she wanted to come on board to help start the Warriors of the Light but she had to make sure the unit would start before she could ask them to give up current positions, and possibly whole careers. She fed the names into the limited AI available to her on the base before opening a channel to *Fendaristil*.

"Have you been able to locate potential sites for the base?"

"I have a list of twelve ideal sites," *Fendaristil* replied, "at least from what I have been able to gather from various reports. Several of them have had surveys, others have not. There are a further hundred and eighteen possible locations, factoring isolation and security as two of the most important attributes."

"Can we visit the most likely ones and get back in a day or two?" Marjory asked.

"Not all of them," the ship replied. "However, we could divide them into two expeditions of two days each. Do you want me to transmit the list of likely sites to you?"

"No, let's keep this off the official systems for now. Prepare for the first of the two expeditions. I will take a look at each site when I get on board this evening."

The rest of the day was spent reviewing personal, service and career records and setting meetings in diaries for three days hence. One of the meetings she arranged was with Harrisil Vance, the current CEO of Drummel Industrial. As usual, *Fendaristil* had maintained a watch on the doings of the corporation while Marjory put herself into stasis for the time between leaving as Mellivar and returning as Maneril Selvis. Financially, the company had gone from strength to strength, while development of the ships, sensors and weaponry from plans left by Marjory had progressed rapidly. As expected, Besnil had improved several of the designs, and the Union vessels were being built largely using Marjory's designs. Now, Marjory had an idea about how to outfit the Warriors without going through Fleet procurement, at least for some items.

Fendaristil left its hard dock almost as soon as Marjory boarded. The ship cleared the environs of the shipyard around which the Fleet facility was located and accelerated to the maximum speed that would be expected of a small ship of its size. Once out of effective sensor range of the station and any ships in the vicinity, *Fendaristil* jumped to light speed.

"The first site is a dwarf planet orbiting a yellow star in the Krel system. There is a small asteroid field but it should not be a problem.

No moons, no additional planets. Surveyed for colonisation seventy-three years ago but rejected. The soil is too poor and the planet's gravity is only zero point seven Earth standard."

"We can make that work," Marjory said. "We don't need good soils and we can rig artificial gravity fields. In fact, we probably need to do that to prepare for the different environments the Warriors will face. Anything else?"

"Krel One has several small caverns that may prove to be of use as secure docking facilities. There are clear fields of fire through the system. This is my most promising planetary site. No-one has laid claim to it, given the survey rejected it."

"Yes, no-one would get funding for any sort of project if the surveyors rejected it as unsuitable," Marjory replied. "Have you looked up who the licensing authority is for Krel One?"

"I have. It is the ninth sector Fleet logistics office."

"That makes it easier. We can just have it taken off the available list and transferred to us."

Fendaristil dropped from FTL on the edge of the system and commenced its own survey. The asteroid field was thin and composed of small asteroids and lots of small rocks and dust. Otherwise, the system was empty of anything other than the sun, Krel, and its single dwarf planet. *Fendaristil* moved close to the planet. The atmosphere was almost non-existent, which would not be a problem, and the scan of the planet showed the two shallow caverns beneath the surface as reported by the Union scan but also a larger, deeper cavern that the Union scan with its lesser equipment had missed. Marjory spent several hours poring over the reports, charts and readings that *Fendaristil* produced before declaring herself satisfied.

"This will be ideal as the training facility," she declared, sitting back in her command chair. "We will have to establish a good line of supply, but that will not be hard. Drop a sensor to the planet surface and leave two or three others around the planet so we can see if anyone else takes an interest in Krel now that we have."

"Sensors deployed," *Fendaristil* reported minutes later. "I have set a probe to monitor any seismic activity also. There are three shielded sensors around the planet. They will report to the probe which will report to me."

"Very well. What is your second site?"

"This one is what I envisage as your administrative centre," *Fendaristil* replied. "It has several key advantages. First, it is off any regular routes and is on the edge of a diffuse nebula. The infra-red emissions are very low and easily shielded. Second, it has good access and departure paths, with the nebula offering some small assistance. Third, it is defensible. Fourth, it is an intact facility and you have the command codes."

"A farstation?" Marjory asked, amused at *Fendaristil's* meandering reasoning.

"Farstation One-Three-Two," *Fendaristil* confirmed.

"An older one?"

"Farstation One-Three-Two was built approximately sixty-four thousand Earth years ago. It was to provide logistical support for colonisation expeditions in what the Union defines as the ninth sector. It requires some repairs, and expended its available materials slightly more than a thousand Union years ago. There are no suitable sources of materials within reach. Its defensive suite is mostly intact and it has a sensor web through the approach lanes, although some have failed and could not be replaced. The station has not been discovered by Union vessels to date, and it is well inside Union territory so the Empire has never located it either."

"But how do we explain the existence of the farstation and the fact that we could access it?" Marjory mused. "I do like the idea of bringing some of these bases back on line and into use."

"The fact that they represent an older civilisation will not cause as much shock as it may have done when Earth people were not aware that other people existed. The Union has its first non-human members, after all. It may cause some consternation in some quarters and the academics will want to crawl all over it, of course."

Fendaristil displayed an image of the farstation on the screen. It was a tall, slim cylinder with something resembling an ancient water-based aircraft carrier's superstructure emerging from each end of the cylinder. A small band of spokes ran around the waist of the cylinder. The specifications for the cylinder were displayed alongside its image.

"Only about a hundred personnel," Marjory read. "That's a small contingent. And only able to handle eight vessels in hard dock at a time."

"For your command base you call for no more than thirty people on site permanently. You also will not need to have many vessels docking. Farstation One-Three-Two is a viable option."

"Agreed. We can leave it as an option. How many other farstations do you have on your list?"

"Three," *Fendaristil* replied. "There are quite a number that we could use, but the three I have chosen share many of the factors you seek in terms of isolation, approaches and size. After all, your requirements were similar to those defined when the monitoring farstations were planned. But I also have a further seven sites that may be suitable. They are on screen now."

"I don't think we will need to visit the farstations," Marjory said as she pulled the list of sites toward her. "But find out from their AIs what their repair needs are. We can get Drummel Industrial to manufacture the materials and then we can deliver them."

"Done," Fendaristil replied moments later. "I expect replies within an hour. Each of the farstations reported similar concerns, largely for replacement alloy sheets and various components such as couplings and conduits. They don't have raw materials within range of their automated units and so were unable to make their own replacements. Drummel Industrial will need to be supplied with the material specifications and designs. I can have them ready within two hours."

"Very well," Marjory replied. "I think we will skip the first, third and sixth of these options. The second and fourth are options for the training facility so let's visit them. Then we can have a look at the fifth and seventh as headquarters possibilities."

Marjory returned to her Fleet office two days later. After a morning spent dealing with the usual administrative tasks that her subordinates were unable to complete without her authorisation, she arranged a meeting with the Fleet Admiral.

"I have identified locations for logistics, training and a headquarters," Marjory said.

She tapped her pad and Lester's holo-emitter came to life. Krel One was displayed as a rotating image.

"This is Krel One," Marjory explained after allowing Lester time to examine it. "It is a dwarf planet, around two-thirds Earth gravity, isolated and distant. It has two caverns suitable for conversion to storage facilities. More important, it has another deep cavern that would be ideal for a backup headquarters. The deep cavern is not easily scanned and we can add some blockers. With a relatively small amount of work, Krel One would be usable."

She tapped her pad again. A second planet was displayed, a gas giant. A third tap and the view zoomed into a moon that started as a speck before expanding to occupy the holo, spinning slowly.

"The planet is Viris, a gas giant in the Arnos system in the eighth sector. The moon is one of thirteen orbiting Viris. The others are too close to Viris itself to be of use, but this one, Viris Nine, has the right size at around point nine of Earth, is composed of volcanic materials but is stable of seismic activity, has a stable orbit and near Earth gravity. There is no usable atmosphere, but we would use domes and internal chambers. Again, it is well away from normal shipping channels. Viris is composed of standard gasses that are found in many more accessible systems, so we would not expect mining to take place for quite a long time to come. Approaches are readily monitored using the new Drummel ultra-long-range sensors."

Lester examined the image for a moment, zooming out again to see the size of the moon against the planet.

"That's a large planet. All one will see from the moon is that thing hanging over your head. How will that go?"

"Well," Marjory shrugged, "we will be looking for people who are not fazed by things like that, so it may be the first test. I don't think that will be a problem once training starts. They should be too busy. The permanent staff may need to be rotated out fairly regularly to give them a break. But we have other stations near gas giants and most people don't seem to experience difficulties."

"Okay," Lester nodded. "And your HQ?"

"A story first," Marjory said. "You know that we have only found a small number of non-human civilisations so far, with the Empire being the one that caused most shock and most concern." She waited while Lester nodded. "A long time ago there was another civilisation, one that spanned most of the galaxy. This was before Earth developed space capabilities. In fact, the civilisation existed long before the people of either Earth or the Empire went into the trees let alone came down from them. When I say this civilisation was ancient, I am talking in time scales beyond a million years."

Lester stared. "How do you know this? Why haven't we heard about it before."

"The civilisation collapsed," Marjory said in reply, with her tone even. "They left behind a small number of space stations scattered across the galaxy. I found one of them during my survey and was able to access it. The AI running the station was able to use my ship's AI to learn our language. And it has been monitoring our ships that passed close enough. I spent some time on the station recently, determining if we can use it. I believe we can."

"You want to use an unknown and alien space station for your headquarters? That's crazy!" Lester said, standing in his agitation. "What makes you think you can trust that AI? What makes you think this station is in any way safe? Just how old is it, anyway?"

"It's sixty-four thousand years old, Admiral," Marjory replied evenly. "And I believe we will be able to use it. The station even gave me its command codes."

"Sixty-four thousand years?" Lester flopped back into his chair in shock. "Sixty-four thousand years old? It has to be a piece of junk," he gasped.

"Not at all," Marjory said with a smile. "Much of the station is in pristine condition. Its power supply is online and operational. There are repairs needed and the AI provided me with a list of the materials it needs to fabricate parts and make repairs. It will require an up-rated alloy to be produced. I contacted Drummel Industrial and they are ready to help us."

"Drummel, eh? They're the best at that sort of thing, but they usually don't take any call. How did you get onto that?"

"They like a challenge, apparently. And their founders made sure that the Union would get their best efforts any time necessary. I called them on that. And, of course, I am of Clan Mellivar." Marjory shook her head, as though clearing it of the inconsequential discussion. "Anyway, I am prepared to take you to the station, if you wish to come. It will be a two day round trip, probably."

"On a Fleet ship or your own?" Lester asked with a grin.

"We'll take mine, I think," Marjory replied. "We'll have better security than on a Fleet vessel. Too many people have access to the ships' logs."

"I agree. And the food's better on your boat. You're a Mellivar?" he asked with a side glance to Marjory. "I wasn't aware of that, although I should have been. I think we need to discuss that, too."

Lester watched the station come closer. The huge cylinder with the strange end structures hung in space, vaguely lit by the light of the distant sun. As *Fendaristil* approached, a single light illuminated at the end of one of the spokes. Marjory piloted the ship to the hard docking point - *Fendaristil's* AI was reduced to menial tasks while humans were aboard - but allowed the ship and station to set the final sequence and establish the lock.

The two senior officers walked from *Fendaristil* to the station. There was no noticeable difference in gravity or atmosphere, nor was there any indication of wear and tear that Lester could see. The corridor along which they walked was clean and without a scratch. There were no rusted components, nor leaking pipes such as human space stations exhibited after a scant fifty years in operation.

"How can this be?" he asked aloud.

"The station was built to last, Admiral," Marjory replied. "The materials are not like our own. They are not ferrous metal like we use as a base, and thus they do not rust. The material is harder than anything we have, and yet the station is able to take a block of this material and shape it into whatever it needs."

"It's remarkable," Lester breathed.

"It was built to house about one hundred people, with room to dock eight vessels at once. There are a range of function rooms, speciality facilities like gymnasiums, even a shopping precinct of sorts. No shops though." Marjory pointed to the front. "We are going to the command position, Admiral. This would be where the station was managed."

They reached a set of double doors that whispered open, presenting a two-level deck. In the centre was a broad pit, occupying roughly half of the floor space. Four chairs occupied the space close to the outer edge, arranged as four points of a square. The raised level surrounding the pit had eight chairs. Otherwise, the decks were bare. Marjory moved to one of the chairs and sat. Immediately a screen shimmered to life in front of her. She gestured Lester to take another chair. When he did so, moving carefully and looking all around as he did so, another screen flared into being ahead of him.

"These are holo screens," Marjory explained. "Most of the station's controls are accessible via these screens. Each station has a slightly different screen, so there was some specialisation involved. But we can also put the display on a main screen." She glanced to Lester, smiling slightly at his dumb-founded expression. "One-Three-Two, display my console on the main viewer."

Immediately, a new display winked into view, seeming to drop into the centre of the deck. The display mirrored Marjory's.

"One-Three-Two, display a schematic of the station," Marjory directed.

The smaller display in front of Marjory and the large display changed to show the space station and its different levels as a schematic. Marjory pointed out key points to Lester, reaching into the holograph and highlighting sections with a touch.

"Living quarters are spread out across several levels. The access level we entered on is here, and there are logistics and support sections above and below it. Engineering, life support, medical, stores - all are in that space. There are several observation stations at the top and bottom in those structures that seem to be tacked to the ends. But also in those sections are weapons systems that we cannot access. The station's AI informs me that it was ordered to be locked down and it will not change that position."

She looked to where Lester was staring at the schematic and a faint smile played across her face. Lester had been one who believed that the Union, and Earth in particular, was a leader in space, notwithstanding the evidence over the last three centuries that told them that the Empire, for one, was more advanced. Of course, Marjory had provided a lot of the technology to allow the gap between the Empire and Union capabilities to be reduced. Now she was showing him that the Union was far behind a civilisation so ancient that he could not comprehend it. Perhaps, she mused, this was needed to allow them to make the next jump, that understanding that no matter how far you feel you have managed to grow, you may always come upon someone who is ahead of you.

"The AI controls almost everything about the station. It has sensors everywhere and some of these options allow command staff to access them. It is not hidden, just that the AI is far more efficient so the command staff concentrated on other things. That's why there were so few staff, I imagine. This station appeared to be a re-supply and sector command station. It has limited propulsion abilities but can move if needed."

"Maneril, I'm staggered at the state of this station," Lester said. "I want to see more of it, but I can see why you feel it's suitable. I'm not sure I understand just why the controlling AI allowed you to have access."

"Why don't we let the AI explain," Marjory said. "While not sentient, this AI is far in advance of our own in the Union. One-Three-Two, please explain why you agreed to the Union using this station."

"When I received the request by the general for access I communicated with the other AIs in this sector," the station AI said in a low female voice speaking accentless Standard, the sound issuing from several hidden speakers at once. "We agreed that the Union represented the best chance for us to support people closest to our own, but that we would allow a single station only to be used at this time. Farstation One-Three-Two was selected. All facilities of this station are available with the exception of weapons."

"How many other … um, farstations are there?" Lester asked.

"There were thirty-six farstation AIs in the conference."

"Thirty-six?" Lester repeated, stunned. "Can you show me where they are in the sector?"

"For security reasons I am unable to do that, Admiral. On reaching agreement that I would allow access we also agreed that the other stations would implement the security protocols directed by the Battle Mage. All other farstations in the sector have cloaked."

"Cloaked? You can cloak a space station? How is that possible? And what's a Battle Mage?"

"Cloaking technology is not available to share," the farstation's AI replied. "The Battle Mage is the leader of the defence services. The last Battle Mage gave instructions to the farstation fleet that remain in force."

"But this Battle Mage must be dead," Lester objected. "That must cause you to allow exceptions."

"I am sorry Admiral. The Battle Mage lives. Her instructions stand."

"The Battle Mage lives?" Lester repeated in a whisper after taking a moment to wrap his head around that simple statement. "The leader of the defensive forces for this advanced civilisation remains alive? But we have never come across anything of it before now, nor heard of it before now." He turned to Marjory. "General, were you aware of this?"

"Yes, Admiral, which is why I wanted you to come out here. You, as the leader of the Union's military, need to be aware that this civilisation that predates Earth and the Empire by eons, and that once claimed most of the galaxy, continues to exist."

"But are they friends or foes?" Lester asked.

Marjory was not sure if it was a rhetorical question or not, but she answered anyway.

"For now, Admiral, I suggest that we treat them as friends. I also suggest that their existence must be kept secret. Knowledge of their existence will spark both a form of panic among many people and also something like a gold rush among those who will see the opportunity to exploit what may seem to be a technology treasure trove somewhere. You should know, Admiral, that three farstations were compromised by the Empire several hundred years ago and handed to pirates in the third sector. They were preying on Union vessels, especially experimental ships in the time when many technical advances were being made. They were destroyed. Each of the stations self-destructed." She turned to face Lester. "We must ensure their existence is not known, and that this station's origins are not known."

Lester nodded thoughtfully.

"For now, I agree," he replied slowly. "We will have a trusted team examine this station but purely to see what we can understand about its construction and materials. I agree that you should use it as your headquarters for the Warriors. If nothing else it ensures knowledge of its existence will be secured to an extent. Everything about this civilisation and this network of stations will be held at the highest security level." He rubbed his hand across his head, the stubbly hair rasping as he made the gesture that Marjory recognised from other stressful situations. "Let's get this one occupied as soon as possible."

"Yes, sir," Marjory replied.

| **13** |

First Warriors

"Welcome to Headquarters station," Marjory said. "I am General Maneril Selvis. This is where you will spend the next two weeks before shipping off to the training facility. Initial training will take three months, although your training will continue from time to time as missions allow. At the end of initial training you will be assigned to your duties as Warriors of the Light. You are the first cadre to come through this station. You are rated as the best in the Union, whether that be for hard combat skills, weapons, tactics or for individual or mass profiling, political and social assessments or intelligence. All of you have several of these skills. None of you have them all. Your training will seek to fill in enough of the gaps so that you can be effective in the field. Any questions?"

Marjory stopped pacing back and forth in front of the ten men and women standing at parade rest in a single line. Several of them appeared to be ill at ease, while others held the stance rigidly with eyes only moving to follow Marjory.

"Yes, er, General," one of the ill at ease men called. "Does this mean we are joining the military? That's not what I thought was the case."

"Yes and no, Mr Horwin. You are joining a form of the military but not as most people see it. The Warriors are not subject to the same military hierarchy as regular forces, for example, and we will operate independently of the regular military forces, at least for now and for the foreseeable future. That may change over the long term, of course.

However, we will require the military for support services from time to time, and some of the assignments may require military outcomes. You will be taught as many of the skills that the military are taught as we can teach you in a short time. Those that we feel you may need, at least. We expect that you will need the improved stamina and fitness that come with military training. Even if you don't have to take part in full-blown combat missions you will need to know how to handle weapons to some extent."

She turned to survey the line of candidates. "And those of you who come from the military are going to learn other, non-combat skills. You all volunteered, you all have been highly recommended, even if those who recommended you did not understand what you were heading into. As of now, you do not speak about this facility, or the training facility. As Warriors, you will be sent into situations that require either tact or directed action, or both at different times. In most of those cases, we will not want anyone to be aware that a Union presence was in place. We do not want most people to even be aware of the existence of the Warriors. We will take you through all of this in detail as part of your orientation. Any more questions before we get started?"

Marjory waited a moment before nodding.

"Excellent. Flight-Colonel Excalis will give you your billet assignments. This station is old but fully functional. Do not go into restricted areas as there may be live defensive weapons within them. If you have any questions you ask Flight-Colonel Excalis or me. For the military among you, military protocols are relaxed as of now. You will not acknowledge senior officers as you normally would. We cannot have that identify you as Union military in the field. You will wear civilian clothing suited to the training being undertaken. Allow your hair to grow out but be aware that you will be training in EV suits, so nothing that will interfere with that. I think that's all. Flight-Colonel?"

Excalis stepped up and nodded to Marjory.

"On that table over there are new personal infopads," Excalis said. "Each has been keyed to you and only you. Your billet allocations have been sent to your pads, along with instructions about how to reach them, locations of exercise facilities, mess hall, break rooms and such. Restricted areas are marked on the station schematic. In some of those spaces weapons are hot. This is your only warning! You have the rest of today to settle in. Orientation commences tomorrow. Schedule and locations are on your infopads. Each of you will be assigned a military rank. That is to ensure that we have no issues with support services, which will be provided by the Union military. Within the base those ranks have no meaning. We will describe team makeup as part of orientation. For now, grab your infopads, find your bunks and get organised."

He nodded and turned away, joining Marjory as both left the briefing room. The men and women in the line looked momentarily nonplussed. The military personnel were unused to informal dismissals and the non-military were unsure of just what they should do. After a few moments, one of the women wearing military fatigues shrugged and walked to the table. She found the infopad marked with her name, tapped it and placed her thumb on the reader where it was marked and started to read the screen that was provided. Her action sparked a general move to follow suit.

Orientation and induction into the new Warriors of the Light resulted in two of the candidates leaving the program. There now were eight remaining. Horwin, one of those who departed, explained that he had not wanted to join a military organisation and, while he appreciated that the Warriors were not regular military, it still felt like it was. Marjory nodded thoughtfully as Excalis repeated Horwin's words.

"Maybe we need to describe the Warriors in other terms," Excalis said. "Horwin is exactly the type we want, but his type just don't want to be soldiers."

"It may be that we just have a small group who will fit," Marjory mused. "Or we may find ourselves with more military and fewer non-military. After all, the Warriors are, strictly speaking, a military unit. I feel that will be the position at some stage. Time will tell."

"We don't have a lot of time, though," Excalis replied.

"There is enough. We have eight remaining candidates. I expect one or two more to drop out as we progress. Hopefully that will not be the other non-military ones."

Marjory cast her mind back to the teams that were employed for similar purposes in the wide-spread Ennari confederation. Admittedly, those were not dealing with subversion or rebellion, at least not as a normal task, but they did have to deal with the differences between the military establishment and the civilian population. When she thought about it, however, the ex-military members of that force usually out-numbered the others significantly.

"I would not be too worried about it at the moment," she said to Excalis. "But I do think we may need to support the non-military candidates somewhat. As I said, this is not meant to be normal military, but it will tend towards it from time to time."

"We can also look to some of the induction procedures," Excalis said after a moment of further reflection. "As a matter of course we had them all lined up at attention, as one example. That shouts military. We should have just brought them together in a conference room or something like that."

Marjory raised an eyebrow and smiled. Excalis was showing how invested he was in making this work. This highly decorated military man had proven to be one of the finest brains the Union Fleet had produced in recent times, and his service record showed that he had the courage and tenacity required. He was especially renowned for his actions when he was one of a small team that had survived when their patrol ship had been severely damaged in an Empire ambush and had crash landed on a nearby planet. For three weeks the team had survived, largely due to Excalis' own efforts. Two of the team had succumbed to wounds, and the planet had shown its own teeth in some of the predators that seemed to thrive in the near-jungle environs in which the team found themselves. But they had survived, malnourished and battered as they were, until they stumbled upon a crew from a nearby planet that were harvesting particular plants from the same near-jungle.

"Then let's make those changes for the next batch, and during the training for this lot. We can drop the regimental aspects but try to retain the disciplinary elements somehow. This is *our* opportunity to learn also," Marjory said.

The training program drew on several elements of the Union military's elite teams training, including a survival course that Excalis led, but it also included several topics drawn from softer skills that most military programs did not cover.

Weapons was an easy one to include. Each of the six ex-military personnel had favoured weapons, even those whose service was mostly spent in space, while one of the civilian recruits had experience in several weapons from hunting on his home planet. The eighth struggled to do much more than aim and fire the most basic of weapons. However, it was made clear that the weapons experts would be the ones to wield those in the main, while the less capable needed to understand enough to protect themselves as well as they could.

Strategy and tactics proved to be a more even affair. The former military members of the group tended to be more rigorous in their planning, but the two remaining civilians displayed a flare for establishing imaginative and often unorthodox solutions to the problems with which they were presented. The reluctance of the soldiers and spacers of the group to accept those unorthodox solutions faded slowly. The trainers, who were from military and non-military backgrounds themselves, encouraged the unorthodox.

It was a former asteroid miner named Hidal Rodrig who showed the way in this regard. She sat and watched as the team debated potential approaches to the problems presented. As Major Will Brechis, one of the tactical trainers, put it, she seemed to just absorb the problem and the ideas and then let them stew for a bit. He swore that he could see her turning the whole problem, first one way and then the other, in her mind, shifting perspectives and peering into alternatives. Once options had been presented and conversation died down, then the quietly spoken Rodrig would lay out a plan that relied on the range of skills that the Warriors had or would be trained in and blended solid preparation with daring and imagination. Inevitably, the simulations showed that this plan would have the best chance of succeeding, whether the objective was to overturn a revolt led by an Empire agent or to thwart a subversive incursion or even merely to swing public opinion from one path to another.

When queried, Rodrig explained that she often had to come up with unusual solutions to problems faced when undertaking surveys of asteroids or establishing mining ventures. She was often working with a very small team well away from support systems where a mistake could have catastrophic consequences, and so she had learned to examine potential solutions from all angles and not to discard any option.

Marjory was pleased at the outcome. Rodrig was a graduate of the Fernis Foundation and had been invited to join the Warriors. To find someone with a true knack for tactical planning amongst the first cohort was a bonus, for she had not expected that to occur. She had the Ennaris gene, so perhaps this was the emergence of a gift. Marjory shrugged. Time might tell. Rodrig was poor in firearms skills and at this stage lacked the acceptance that was usual among the military team members that casualties may be taken. Oddly, perhaps, that seemed to make the bond between the miner and the other team members stronger as it became evident in short order that she would be the planner for their missions. Any mission she planned would have a better than even chance that they would return.

The team worked through a range of subjects that were thought to have application to the sorts of missions they would have. Economics lessons taught them about the interactions of a society's financial system and how to spot oddities that could lead them to uncover plots or agents. Communications experts showed them how skilled operators could use the public media, which was so important on so many worlds that needed to stay in touch with happenings across the Union, to sway opinion in ways that may not be obvious. Half-truths blended skilfully with fabrications often led those who lacked the ability to think critically into thought patterns that could then be exploited to serve the interests of other parties.

Psychologists spoke to them about a raft of topics ranging from reading body language to identify people who might be lying to methods of exposing motivations via subtle manipulation of queries and responses, and on to the re-emergent field of psionics. The latter was an area that took Marjory's attention when one of the trainers, a member of a university research team that was investigating the mental workings of high-intelligence individuals, was adamant that psychic abilities were real and could point to events where psychic influences could have been at play. While the trainee Warriors scoffed, as did most people of the time, Marjory decided to dig deeper. After all, Ennari Mages' gifts usually involved manipulation of the physical world by the power of the mind, and even the physical side of those gifts would use the Mage's mind power to enhance physical capabilities. Marjory herself, one of the most gifted Battle Mages ever seen, was aware that she used her mind strength to help her to perform physical feats that were beyond most others. Drewflin, Marjory's life partner, described what he did as channelling the power around him through his mind and will, and thus to the object of his attention, be it animal, plant or person.

It was after several long discussions with the trainers that Marjory decided to include psionics in the list of subjects taught in the Warrior Academy. Perhaps this was another avenue to take to identify the Children, those scions of this sliver of Ennaris who may play a large role in the future of her home planet. Perhaps those mind powers were pointers to the Ennari blood showing through. When tested, none of the initial cohort of Warriors showed psionic skills, including Rodrig, although Marjory doubted that the tests used would give meaningful results. Still, her goal was to try to identify good candidates for the Children, and this was a valid potential path to take.

The short training period on the headquarters station was followed by a longer period on Viris Nine. Here they were trained in the various methods of handling different environments, in higher and lower gravity than that to which they were accustomed, the far more advanced use of environmental suits and, of course, continued instruction in tactics and defensive techniques. Unsurprisingly, Rodrig excelled in the elements of training that revolved around non-standard environments. As she said at one stage, most of her adult life had been spent in what many would consider to be non-standard environments. She still could not fire any sort of weapon accurately, though.

At Viris Nine, the team also studied the various outposts of human civilisation through the sector, and those known of the Empire. While they had been told of the parameters of the Warrior missions during their introduction on the headquarters station, it was during this phase of their training that the true mission started to dawn on the team members. This would be a blend of intelligence gathering, subtle activities to support the Union where Empire activities were identified, and military-style action where necessary, but as a last resort.

The large moon was a confronting place when they first arrived. A standard Fleet domed facility had been built, almost literally dropped onto the surface and anchored to the bedrock of the moon. There was a single large dome with enough space for a small administration block, tiny living quarters for each team member and instructor that had been modelled on a crew cabin of a small corvette, and a single open space that would serve as both common area and learning zone. The usual 'net facilities were available with the added layers of security that already were the norm for the Warriors. A landing pad was a short distance away from the dome, with a walkway umbilical stretching across the surface of the moon between the two. All of it was fairly normal for a startup facility.

What was not normal was the parent planet that loomed overhead, occupying almost two-thirds of the sky at some points but never completely out of sight. And loom the planet did. The dome was largely transparent, with the ability to darken parts for privacy and to allow sleep in the accommodation cubicles. Otherwise, when one looked up it was to see the enormous mass of Viris seemingly ready to fall on them. All the time. Already, two of the administration staff had been transferred back to headquarters station because they found the sight to be overly confronting. A rotation roster had been established for the others to provide a break.

The Warriors were expected to be of sterner material but there was no mistaking the fact that this was a test. Once again Rodrig took it in her stride. She reminded the team that simple physics kept the moon where it was relative to the planet and, as long as the laws of physics remained intact, then so would the moon's orbit. The former military members of the team had mixed reactions, ranging from the phlegmatic to the ragged edge of nerves. The training regime on Viris Nine used a second dome that was dropped and anchored away from the main dome. This dome contained adjustable gravity plates and generators to simulate anything from a quarter of Earth gravity to the equivalent of Earth's gravity, which remained the human norm, and on to twice Earth's gravity should it be required. For zero gravity, training would take place in space.

The variable gravity allowed them to understand how changes in gravity affected them, in myriad ways large and small. Simple things like using sanitary facilities were standard training aspects for anyone likely to head into space, although the availability of artificial gravity on ships had rendered most of those difficulties a thing of the past. Still, projectiles behaved differently with different levels of gravity, as did individuals when in combat. Techniques that worked perfectly well in Earth standard gravity became almost unusable in a quarter of Earth's gravity. The emphasis in this aspect, while continuing to train the team in defensive and offensive techniques, was to understand tactically what changes may be needed to their plans for many situations. It was true that no occupied planets had less than four-fifths of Earth gravity and no more than one and a quarter of Earth gravity, but the Warriors were expected to go into any place where humans went.

Weapons training continued, as did the briefings about events and happenings around the Union. The Warriors were expected to know at least the basics about each and every planet that formed the Union, and the main outposts that tended to be separate from but ultimately dependant on their nearest planets. Inevitably, these outposts were mining or exploration facilities and tended to be transient, lasting at most a hundred years or so before being abandoned. A small but growing number of these facilities were used for off-the-grid living once the miners left. Inevitably, also, while part of the appeal of such living was moving beyond the direct influence of a planet and its government, there remained the expectation that they would be protected by the Union. Where the military authorities in each sector grumbled about wasting resources on protecting those who did not wish to partake of Union society, the Union's politicians were more easily influenced to ensure that such protection was extended to the isolationists. After all, many of those isolationists were very wealthy.

The training program was difficult. The stresses encountered were constant, deliberately so. All of the members of the Warriors suffered in one way or another. In fact, several of the instructors were showing strain also. However, the Warriors would find themselves in highly stressful situations when they were isolated, so being able to make decisions under such pressure was one of the outcomes sought.

It was twelve weeks into the training on Viris Nine when Harl Xavis, a former special forces space marine, cracked. Pressure had been building as the team underwent near constant simulations of a range of scenarios. Xavis struggled to maintain the overall standard that the others managed to achieve, including the remaining two civilian members. With the exception of weapons, where he was close to the best of the group and where Rodrig maintained her record as the outright worst, his performance slowly slid down the charts. The instructors maintained a monitor and a counsellor met with him every second day, but the slide seemingly was inexorable. He was unable to explain why that was the case, and his frustration levels mounted. Finally, while undergoing an EV training session on the surface of the moon, he made a small error. In itself, the error had little bearing on the training session. However, for someone who had held himself to very high standards through his career, it was the final straw. The camel's back broke.

The first inkling anyone had was when Xavis gave an inarticulate cry of anguish and rage over the team channel, following a minor mishap when he stumbled on a small piece of surface rock. Rodrig, she who had been in many stress-filled situations in her life to date, heard the tone and swung around to stare to where her team-mate was unslinging his carbine. Xavis took aim at the offending rock and pressed the firing stud repeatedly.

"Harl!" Rodrig shouted across the team channel. "Harl! Stop!"

Her shouts alerted the other members of the team and the instructor, who was monitoring from within the control centre. All started shouting, creating a cacophony over the channel that only served to take Xavis further over the edge.

"Quiet!" Rodrig snarled, and then louder. "Quiet! All of you! Stand still!"

The noise coming over the channel died away. The team members, scattered as they were around the training site, stood still and watched, stunned. Rodrig turned back to Xavis and gasped. Through the large helmet visor Xavis' eyes were huge. A fixed stare was directed towards her and the carbine was being lifted.

"Harl!" Rodrig said, trying to remain calm. "Harl, listen to me! Put the gun down!"

Xavis gave a small shudder and turned away from Rodrig, focusing instead on Kresta. The former soldier immediately lifted his own carbine in response, but held his fire. Around the large training ground, the other team members also raised their weapons, varying between carbines, laser rifles and pulse pistols, depending on personal preference. Rodrig stood without a weapon, hands raised and held apart to make that fact obvious.

"Everyone, don't fire," Rodrig said clearly and slowly. "Do not fire. Harl, I want you to put the gun down and sit down," she continued. "No-one wants to get hurt here, no-one wants to hurt you. You're doing fine. Just put down the carbine and come with me."

Xavis appeared not to hear her. He continued to stare, looking from Rodrig to Kresta and then to Jaster, the three who were within easy view from where he stood, and then back to Rodrig. His carbine remained raised but not aimed. Its muzzle wavered as he swung his head drunkenly in a repeating circuit between the three team members standing within his view. In her head up display, Rodrig could see the other team members' positions, all of whom were still except one. Anders, another special forces member in his military life, was edging towards Xavis.

"Harl, listen to me, look at me," Rodrig said calmly, evenly.

If she could hold Xavis' attention then perhaps Anders would be able to overpower him. She trusted the former special services soldier to do so without hurting Xavis.

Instead, Xavis twisted suddenly, having seen the moving dot in his own HUD. He raised his carbine and fired in a single movement. Rodrig shouted.

"Harl, no!"

But the damage was done. Having started to fire Xavis did not stop. Anders had been ready and made a shallow, ungainly dive behind a rocky outcrop nearby as soon as Xavis started to swing around. Other team members took whatever cover they could find, all while Rodrig shouted at everyone not to return fire. The Mark 17 Carbine was a small-bore, short-barrel percussion weapon, capable of rapid-firing small pellets of a hardened ceramic thinly coated by a ferrous metal composite which allowed them to be accelerated in a manner similar to a magnetic railgun. Its stock and barrel magazine held two hundred pellets when fully loaded. In the hands of a skilled operative, the Mark

17 Carbine was accurate over short and long range and could cause significant injury. Xavis was a skilled operator.

A steady stream of pellets swept around the training ground as Xavis held the firing stud down and looked for his fellow Warriors. The leading edge moved towards Rodrig as she stood exposed, still talking to Xavis, pleading with him to stop firing and put the weapon down. With a sense of the inevitable, Rodrig saw the former space marine move his sights towards her, all while keeping the firing stud depressed. A quick glance around her showed no cover of any kind. With a resigned sigh she started to back away. She would not be able to get far enough away, but perhaps greater distance would allow her to survive the injuries she would suffer.

In a sort of daze, Rodrig saw Xavis' muzzle move to settle on her. She fancied that she could see the pellets emerge from the barrel of the Mark 17 Carbine and speed towards her. But none reached her. Shocked, wide-eyed, Rodrig saw the pellets hit what seemed to be a solid wall. They seemed to hover, aimed at her heart as it seemed to her, waiting to speed towards her again.

A figure walked past Rodrig. Stunned, she saw that it was General Selvis, walking across the training field without an environment suit. Pellets continued to surge from Xavis' carbine and they continued to hit the invisible wall. Dozens now hovered in place. Selvis raised her right hand and Xavis' gun fell silent. The hovering pellets fell to the ground, landing softly with a series of light thuds. Xavis continued to hold down the firing stud, shaking the carbine when it failed to function. Selvis walked up to Xavis and plucked the carbine from him, dropping it to the rocky surface of the moon. She quickly reached out and pressed her hand to Xavis' arm. Xavis suddenly went limp and collapsed. As Rodrig continued to stare, the general gently picked up the unconscious Xavis, much more easily than would be expected, and carried him off the training ground.

"I don't understand," Rodrig said, bewildered. "How did you survive without an environment suit? The atmosphere of Viris Nine is almost non-existent, and what does exist is lethal. And why did Xavis' pellets just stop? I was right in their line of fire and they just seemed to hit a wall. And then Harl just collapsed when you touched him. Why did that happen?"

Marjory smiled. The team members were in Marjory's ready room, off the main command centre of the Warrior complex on Viris Nine. None of them were quite sure of what had occurred as all had sought cover away from the withering hail of high velocity pellets emerging from Xavis' carbine. All knew that something had stopped Xavis' attack on his team and that Rodrig had been saved from serious harm by the sudden appearance of General Selvis.

"I was wearing an experimental environment suit," Marjory said with a confident smile. "No, I can't tell you anything about it, before you ask. It may make its way to the standard equipment list or not. There are some bugs to iron out." She paused, thinking that the main bug was that there was no such suit, although *Fendaristil* had a design ready to be tested. "I also used a personal shield to stop the slugs from the carbine. Another experimental item." This one was real, although the experiment had commenced on Ennaris thousands of Earth years earlier. Marjory had decided to make it available to selected Warriors, at some stage in the future. However, it had been Marjory's Battle Mage gifts that stopped the pellets in their tracks. "As for Xavis collapsing, I think that was coincidence from the strain. He will recover, just for your information. It will take time but our medical team seems to believe he will be alright. He will not be returning, of course, either to the Warriors or the marines, unfortunately."

Rodrig remained sceptical but the rest of the team seemed to take it on trust. Only she had seen General Selvis touch Harl just before he collapsed. Oddly, all recording instruments had failed at the same time. She was smart enough to know not to pursue it though. Shrugging to herself, Rodrig nodded and waited for the general to speak.

"You need to put that behind you," Marjory said, "hard though that will be. You have all been in situations where team members have been lost or hurt. This is no different. We have our first mission. Which is the reason I am here at all."

The remaining team members all looked at each other before all looked to Rodrig, something Marjory did not fail to notice. It seemed that the former miner's leadership was tacitly acknowledged, even by the military members of the team. In some ways that was a surprise, but not in others. The trainers had reported consistently that Rodrig had the highest levels of team interaction. She always looked to make her plans as safe for the team as possible while achieving their targets. She was known to have had real world experience dealing with many difficult space-borne problems and was prepared to share her experiences with her fellow team members as a means of helping them learn about what they faced in space beyond their own experiences. In fact, most of the team had not experienced pure space to the extent that she had. And, as the episode with Xavis had just shown, she remained calm under extreme pressure, at least outwardly.

"Are we ready for a mission, general?" Rodrig asked. "You saw what happened with Harl. We could do little in that situation."

"Incorrect," Marjory said crisply. "You had several options and you chose one. It may have seen you dead, and you need to learn from that. You could have all opened fire on him and killed him. You could have all retreated as fast as possible. You could have tried to outflank him while one held his attention." She nodded to Anders as she said that. "What you chose to do was to talk him down. The only problem with that tactic was that you tried for too long. One of you should have taken a disabling shot at Xavis when it became obvious that Rodrig would not stop him. Learn from that. Situations change." She looked around the team members, several of whom nodded while others winced at the criticism. "But that is a situation that is rare. What we have here is one that is becoming more common. Gather around."

Marjory moved to stand behind a holotable. The team gathered around her and the table. With a swipe she pulled a series of images onto the table from a holding tab. The images organised themselves into a three by three grid. Marjory touched each as she spoke, opening them into a larger view above the grid before each shrank back for the next to expand.

"This is Helios, a human-occupied planet well inside Union territory." The planet zoomed out of the grid, showing as a blue-green ball slowly spinning with two satellites moving with it. "Helios is at threat of leaving the Union. Your task will be find out why and to stop it if possible."

Helios

On the face of it, the mission was a textbook example of misinformation on a planet-wide scale, combined with subversion of the planet's political leadership. Helios had been settled only two hundred years earlier. It had been populated, largely, by members of a breakaway group of environmental activists hailing from a much longer settled planet named Verdis. The breakaways objected to the mining of Verdis' mineral wealth and what they saw as the resulting environmental degradation, although all were wealthy as a result of it. The Helios Environmental Corporation had been formed and in short order had raised the funds necessary to lay claim to Helios. Surveys undertaken about one hundred years before that time had shown that Helios would sustain human life without atmospheric assistance, and had land suitable for agriculture. There were many minerals listed on the survey, but few were of any note at that time.

However, very soon after the colonists arrived, Helios was found to have indications of archorite deposits. Archorite was a relatively new and rare heavy metal that had demonstrable benefits as an ingredient in modern space vessels' engine fuel, especially that used for Fleet vessels. Ironically, Marjory had thought as she reviewed the mission profile, it was her more advanced fuel that would use the mineral, although she had specified that synthetic alternatives should be used, as the Ennari had synthesised the mineral for use in their fuels. The synthetic element had been developed long in the past to replace the heavy metal that was to be found on Ennaris and nearby planets, moons and asteroids. Human industrialists who licensed the formula from Drummel Industrial had sought out the heavy metal following its recent discovery by mineral explorers. Mining, it seemed, was cheaper than synthesis, especially if it could be obtained cheaply.

Five already-settled human planets and several moons and asteroids had been found to carry deposits of archorite, and were being exploited at a rapid rate. Miners were always looking for further sources of minerals, and the old survey of Helios, when examined anew, showed indications of archorite. Helios, therefore, became the object of unscrupulous ambitions by several mining conglomerates. It was the Union, upholding the rights of the settlers of the planet, that blocked attempts to perform deep surveys and then to mine the archorite. The solution to that problem appeared to be to remove the Union from the equation and the way to do that was to have a two-thirds majority of Helios' citizens vote to break away from the Union.

"So there are no Empire agents involved, then?" Kresta asked. "I thought our job was to stop the Empire?"

"There *appear* to be no Empire agents involved, but we cannot be sure of that," Marjory replied. "In any event, your job is to protect the Union from all threats to its existence, not just those from the Empire. This situation may be caused by unscrupulous business people taking advantage. However, there may well be more to this. Archorite is an important mineral for the latest fuel advances. While it can, and probably should, be synthesised it can be mined and refined more cheaply if circumstances are right. Should the Union lose access to deposits of archorite then it is possible for the Empire to gain them. The new engines fed by this new fuel gives us an advantage over the Empire, the first true advantage we have ever had. The method by which archorite is synthesised is a closely held secret. Long range plans by the Empire could be to obtain sources of archorite and then try to replicate the new, more advanced power units that use it. Your job will be to establish whether this is, in fact, a form of swindling against the planet's population or a form of subversion by Empire agents. In either case, your job is to stop it."

"So," Rodrig said into the silence that followed Marjory's lengthy reply, "how many of us go and when? And do you have in mind any suspects for us to start with?"

"You as a team will decide how many go," Marjory said with a short smile. "Our optimum team size is expected to be three, with a range of specialities being represented. However, this is the first mission so we should use it to see what works. You may decide to divide into two teams and have different angles in play at the same time, or you may decide to have a single team. That will be up to you to plan out and present to me. You have three days to plan the mission. I will be back then to hear the plan and decide whether I agree with it or not."

Rodrig looked around the Warriors, receiving nods from each.

"Very well," Rodrig said to Marjory. "In three days we will have our plan ready for review."

Three days was a short time to put a plan together, especially for the first mission of a new team. Marjory expected little in the way of detail and so she was prepared to extend the time or provide her own flavour to it. Flight-Colonel Excalis, who had been with the team for some of the time while they explored avenues of investigation and response and put the plan together, remained noncommittal. He refused to be drawn on any details or the team's approach, merely saying with a sly smile that it was not his plan and he would leave it to the team.

"Good afternoon, general," Rodrig said as the team assembled around the briefing table. "We are prepared to take you through our plan."

"Very well," Marjory replied. "I have been looking forward to this. First, some developments. The President is worried about Helios, as it seems the outcome is being watched by other planets that may also be at risk of leaving the Union. We have discovered inconclusive evidence that this is being fomented by the Empire, possibly more as a means of disrupting the Union than to get access to the archorite. We hope that you can confirm or disprove that as part of the mission."

"Yes, general, that was one of the scenarios we discussed," Rodrig replied, sharing a smile with Excalis. "We can put greater emphasis on that as we go through the plan. The plan calls for two teams of three members each. We considered what you said about optimal team size and agree that it allows for a spread of skills and some flexibility in team capabilities. For this mission, given there are seven of us, I will act as coordinator on planet while the teams are in place.

"Team one has Kresta as lead, with Justine and Orest as members. Team two is Jasper as lead with Ulfis and Randall as members. Each team has what we consider to be suitable hard and soft skills for the respective team tasks. Our research has provided us with initial indicators to be investigated. Team one will concentrate on the representatives of the mining cartels that are seeking to influence the planet's leadership. Team two will investigate the leaders themselves. Each of the team leads will provide a summary of their own plans. Overall, we expect to spend up to four weeks on Helios, but we're flexible and will re-evaluate as we uncover evidence or otherwise."

Rodrig paused, glancing to Marjory and Excalis in turn. Marjory gave a short nod to continue.

"From what we've been able to determine, there are two mining organisations that are trying to gain an advantage. We intend to use that competition to get an opening. Likewise, there seem to be three key figures among the political leadership. The most likely leader of that group is the deputy premier, who has been on Helios only five years. Kresta and Jasper will take you through their plans in more detail."

Kresta stepped forward and touched a stud on the table's controls. A holograph of Helios appeared above the table, spinning slowly in place. Two spots were highlighted.

"General," Kresta said in acknowledgement. "I'll brief you on team one's plan. First though, some context that we found. Twelve years ago there was an unofficial survey of Helios. It was unsanctioned and was conducted without the knowledge of the Helios community. This survey identified two significant deposits of archorite, shown on this holo. The survey was funded by Henders Resources, one of the mid-level mining corporations. Henders has a history of somewhat shady activities and has been subject to many fines in a few sectors. Several of their mines have caused significant damage to their surrounding environments. Probably the worst one, the Planar mine on Frisus Three, rendered a large part of the planet's only continent uninhabitable following a toxic dam breach. The same incident caused marine damage which impacted the food supply for Frisus Three. Henders has a strong advocate in Senator Griffith and walked away with a hefty fine but no further legal ramifications. Other Henders mines have caused lesser damage but enough for complaints to be lodged. There is a pattern of not cleaning up or remediating mining sites as Union law requires. Each time they pay a fine and move on. Team one will target Henders in the first instance. We believe this is likely to be unscrupulous business tactics more than anything else."

"Sounds like a lovely company," Marjory said drily.

"Yes, general," Kresta replied with a shake of his head. "Not a great advertisement for miners, that's for sure, although they're not alone in some of their practices. We'll use that in our work. The second miner we believe may be a different proposition. Junos Global is more of a conglomerate with mining as one of its activities. It's a young corporation, only around fifty years old, and was formed by bringing together a series of old companies that compete in several different fields. Apart from mining, Junos includes companies that deal with ship design, weapons manufacture and construction of terrestrial and orbital facilities. There's a technology arm and a small publishing and marketing house. The mining arm has a history of applying political pressure to obtain benefit on planets where their mines are built or that controls the surrounding space where moons or asteroids can be exploited. The marketing house takes care of much of the public information produced. Lots of bias, of course. Still, there's nothing too different there when you look at the miners overall. However, the ship design and weapons companies over the years have had a number of security breaches that have raised eyebrows in Fleet Security. Some of their designs were leaked along with weapon specifications for some of the Fleet's ancillary ships. As you know, Drummel Industrial have a near lock on the main capital ships, but there are many more smaller vessels used than those that Drummel builds and Junos delivers weapons systems for some of them. Empire agents are known to have obtained the leaked ship and weapons specifications and there is an ongoing investigation into Junos as a result. We will be looking into potential links with the Empire for Junos Mines."

"That sounds promising," Marjory said. "Is this your most promising avenue, do you feel?"

"We feel that it's likely that both teams will find something," Rodrig said from the side. "Our research shows that the political leadership has ties to the two mining concerns. The general population remains unaware that a survey was, in fact, conducted and that new deposits of archorite were found. Most of the reaction so far stems from concerns that the Union will allow such a survey to be undertaken, using historical examples of similar actions elsewhere."

"Your research appears to have found information that is not readily known," Marjory said mildly, eyeing the team members.

"Yes, general," Rodrig replied. "We took advantage of an opportunity that arose to obtain intelligence on the players in this situation."

"And that opportunity?"

"Well," Rodrig said with a half-grin, "Justine just happens to be a wiz at data systems. It seems she can break through most firewalls and encryption with the right tools, and not be found out. And the Fleet has the right tools."

"And so you asked the Fleet for their help?" Marjory held her tone steady, while her own concern level rose.

"Not exactly," Rodrig replied.

"I accessed the Fleet network and then used its dark net access," Justine said with a shrug. "It was easy from that point."

"Just like that? You 'accessed' the most secure network in the Union?"

"Yes, general. I have an account on the Fleet network, so I can come and go easily. And I have security clearance, as I'm sure you know. That's what I did before I joined the Warriors, on contract with Fleet. I created that one almost five years ago."

"An account in the Fleet network," Marjory said deadpan, looking to Excalis, who looked mystified. "Five years ago?"

"Yes, general. I had a friend in Fleet procurement who found something strange. He asked me to help him track it down. He managed to get me into the network and I traced down the problem. Someone had dropped a back door into a very old security routine and used it to monitor the workings of Drummel Industrial. I found it and disabled it. Then I added my own entry point so I could keep an eye on whoever did that, but I've never found a trace of them." Justine smiled again. "Or they're good enough that I've not seen a trace of them when they returned. I never closed it down."

Marjory recalled *Fendaristil* telling her that she had to activate a backup routine to maintain a watch on Drummel's activities but Marjory had not asked why.

"I'm good enough," Marjory heard from *Fendaristil* in her auditory implant. "But she was very good. I'm surprised anyone found that."

"Any other illegal accesses to secure facilities you feel we should know about?" Excalis asked with a frown.

"No, Colonel," Justine replied.

"No, there are no other illegal access points, or no there are none you feel we should know about?" Marjory asked with a straight face.

Justine considered for a moment before her response. "None you should know about," she replied. "But you never know when they may be useful."

Marjory stared evenly at Justine for a moment, and stayed that way as she spoke next, only then looking away with a tiny quirk of her lips.

"Team two's plan?" Marjory asked.

"Ah, I probably should state that Justine helped us, too," Jasper said.

"Fleet access again?" Marjory asked, resigned to the answer.

"Ah, no, general," Justine replied carefully, despite smirking. "The Union Criminal Intelligence Bureau. I came across a hack some time ago when I was tracking down a potential leaker. I fixed it but again left myself an entry port. I've not used it since but it remained available. It allowed us to see what was being said about a few people."

"So," Jasper said, taking control of the session, "team two will look at the political leadership. Justine found some interesting information from the bureau that we probably should have been given for this mission. The deputy premier was under investigation several years ago for a range of activities. Most of them were low level stuff. Things like missing tax returns, false statements during election campaigns, associating with some criminal elements, using influence to get out of fines. That sort of thing. Nothing much out of the ordinary for political types. But the investigation threw up possible links to the Explorer Guild."

"Explorer Guild?" Marjorie asked with a tilt of her head. "Interesting. We've never been able to prove the Guild has links to the Empire but it remains a strong likelihood."

"Yes, Admiral," Jasper nodded. "The UCIB lead investigator suggested that the possible links should be investigated further but it seems nothing was done. There is a note in the file that such an effort was not required and that thread was closed." Jasper touched an icon on the screen. "I have sent the file to your private inbox, general. You may wish to consider it further."

"I have the file," *Fendaristil* said to Marjory. "I will attempt to locate any links."

"Thank you," Marjory replied to Jasper. "I will do exactly that and let you know if we find anything."

"So, team two will be following up on anything like those other activities UCIB uncovered, and will stay awake to potential Guild or Empire activities. There also seems to be some sort of underground paramilitary organisation being established by the deputy premier. There are unconfirmed reports of stand-over tactics being employed and people disappearing who opposed the deputy premier. That will be another avenue. We're pretty sure that such an organisation exists, so we must be prepared for some form of conflict should we manage to bring them out into the open."

"That will be the key tactic here, general," Rodrig said, taking up the lead position again. "We want to see if the movement to leave the Union is being fomented externally to the population and, if it is, then we intend to make it very public. If it's not, then we have something else to consider. Should we interfere? The Union has always said that membership is voluntary. If this truly is a valid movement away from the Union then the Warriors probably should not interfere and we will recommend that the situation is handed back to the Union leadership to address by political means."

Marjory considered, nodding slowly.

"And do you believe this is merely a local movement, started by widespread discontent on the planet?" Marjory asked Rodrig, glancing around the team members.

"From what we can uncover so far, it's a possibility we need to evaluate," Rodrig replied. "But on balance we feel there's something else happening. As Kresta said, the existence of the survey results is very tightly held, so the population is unaware that Helios has two large deposits. The previous survey was more cursory and only found indications that archorite may exist. Nothing confirmed." She pointed to the two highlighted regions on the holo. "We can use that to advantage, but you may have to make the Union leaders aware of the situation. As soon as we advertise that it exists the other miners will try to crowd in. Even if this is an Empire scheme, and assuming we can eliminate it, that news will cause further problems."

"Leave that to me," Marjory replied. "I'll discuss it with the right people when it is the time to do so." She looked to Excalis with one eyebrow raised, receiving a shake of his head in response to say that he had nothing to add. "Very well, then. I'm not too sure about where this will lead but it is our first mission and something without a full military flavour will be a good one to get started with. Still, take care of each other, and make sure you remain in touch with command. Anything more?"

Marjory nodded as there were head shakes around the team.

"If there are any queries pass them through Flight-Colonel Excalis or send them directly to me. I may be briefing the Union and Fleet leadership so the Flight-Colonel should be your first contact point where possible."

"Encrypted relays have been dropped around the planet," Excalis said. "They're shielded using some experimental technology and should escape detection by all but the more advanced Union ships, and they won't interfere. Only the Warriors will be able to decrypt it. Your personal communicators have the details embedded already. This will be a standard protocol for Warrior missions and we'll test it on this mission. It will allow communication within the team and with command. Don't hesitate to use it."

| 15 |

Militia

Seventeen days later, Marjory was reviewing Rodrig's latest report. As planned, the former asteroid miner had established herself in the main city of Helios and was acting as the teams' coordinator on site. She received frequent updates from the two teams and put the results together, building a picture of the events leading to the situation found on Helios. The two avenues of investigation had both paid off.

Team one, by a mix of covert surveillance and smart deduction, had uncovered incontrovertible evidence of collusion between both Henders Resources and Junos Global and the Helios deputy premier, Markus Oreal. At the same time Justine, the team's hacker, found signs of communication by Junos Global with the Explorer Guild. Meanwhile, team two had tracked several of the premier's political cadre to in-person meetings with others who turned out to be known Explorer Guild soldiers. These, in turn, had been tracked to several locations where there were groups of visitors to the planet. The groups were explained as being there for birthday parties, business conferences, extreme sports competitions and a number of other reasonable purposes. The team identified more soldiers among the groups and speculated that they all were Explorer Guild soldiers.

The political situation had started to boil. The media of the planet, all but one outlet of which was firmly under the control of Markus Oreal and his associates, ran story after story of supposed outrages by Union officials against planets that wanted to leave the Union, or that sought to protect themselves from the ravages of miners, or against those with principles that differed from the planetary citizenship. Oddly, in an age when information flowed freely and was available to all, these tactics flourished. When a population is primed to believe that they are being targeted for their beliefs or principles, it can be easy to drive them towards more extreme versions of the same concerns. The Oreal-controlled media did that very effectively via a range of channels from supposedly independent news, through various social avenues and even into the sphere of entertainment. Avatars of popular entertainers were used to reinforce the fears and concerns of the populace that they were about to be abandoned or, worse, forced to accept the practices that they and their forebears sought to avoid. The echo chamber so formed drove the rising ill-feeling towards what, inevitably, would soon be a crescendo.

Some of the lies being told were easily refuted, if someone were to make the attempt. The sole media outlet that was not dominated by the deputy premier and his allies was trying to do just that. They maintained a constant stream of refutations against the lies, half-lies and innuendo of the Oreal camp. It was obvious, however, that they were fighting a losing battle. Several reporters had met with accidents that resulted in deaths or serious injuries, publication systems failed unexpectedly, and a campaign of mud-slinging against the few remaining reporters was taking a toll.

"So, you feel this is mass manipulation?" Marjory asked as she sat across a small table from Rodrig.

"Yes," the Warrior planner replied. "Definitely. Justine was able to trace the hacks that took down Veritas Media's ability to publish their news and commentary. We also managed to obtain video surveillance of Explorer Guild thugs attacking Veritas' staff. I think we have enough for them to be charged."

"Do the local police force have the ability to do that?"

"No," Rodrig responded with a shake of her head. "We're fairly sure that, if they tried, then it would cause something like a coup to occur. We estimate that there are at least fifty Explorer Guild members on the planet, probably all soldiers. They'd be enough to stage that coup given the light police force in place. If nothing else, the police force would be seriously damaged. At the right time we'll involve them. The planetary police appear to have been penetrated anyway."

"And if we bring in Union forces to do the arrest we play into the hands of Oreal and his cronies."

"That's another thing," Rodrig said, looking up from her tablet to Marjory. "Oreal is a puppet for the Guild, which likely means for the Empire, but we think he's going to try to take the planet out from under them. Some of his actions don't stack up. He's trying to build his own militia, for example. It's very quiet and he's using the true believers from the original settling families as his core. Perhaps we can use them to blunt any coup attempt if we can get the right leverage."

"How do you intend to do that?" Marjory asked, impressed at the depth of the team's thinking.

"We play them off against each other," Rodrig replied with a grimace. "I can't see us doing that without casualties, though. So I plan on the Warriors playing a part also. I'm sorry, General, but this first case will have to include a military component also."

Marjory nodded slowly, turning the idea over. The plan had been to make this a non-military exercise but the analysis seemed sound enough. In some ways it could even be better for the non-military effort to be handed over to the military side of things for a limited joint engagement, demonstrating both judgement and restraint in getting results. But the correct results would be needed.

"We've made some contacts in the militia already," Rodrig continued after watching Marjory for a few moments and getting no immediate objections. "Kresta has established himself as ex-military using one of the covers he was issued. That cover included time as an instructor. We allowed them to find that out themselves. That was when he was asked if *he* could help *them*. He told them he also had a friend who could help. That's when he took Randall with him. So far, they've been accepted, although warily. It was Oreal who ran the idents. Justine traced that. The data has been sent to you for your attention. There's an exposure in Union security and that may point to an Empire cell if the tie-up with the Guild is right."

Marjory nodded again, pleased and impressed. Rodrig was showing much greater insight than expected, and the team to date had met all expectations and hopes. Now the dangerous phase would start. The team would engage what were now being treated as subversive elements. As always, plans were made but became little more than directions of travel once the engagement occurred. The first element of the plan was to make public the tie up of the Explorers Guild with the Empire. This would have two key impacts, or so it was hoped. The first was to blunt the effect of the propaganda that would follow, inevitably, once pressure went onto the planet's leadership. The second was broader. The Guild operated in many places and this was the first time the link to the Empire would be aired publicly. Marjory had briefed and obtained clearance from Fleet Intelligence, who were making their own preparations in various locations around Union space to react to, or take advantage of, any outcomes to the revelations.

Two days later the plans went into effect. First came the revelation of the illicit survey by the mining consortium. Rather than rely on the already subverted news media to make the findings public, the team fell back on a very old-fashioned means. Weather-proof posters were plastered over public spaces and paper leaflets were strewn wherever the Warriors could gain access. A day later, a carefully worded and anonymous message was delivered to every citizen's personal device, with links to sites on the Hypernet Web that provided details of the surveys, the names of the organisations involved, and the links to the planetary leadership. The survey results showing the deposits of archorite were included in full.

The news hit like a thunderclap.

Outrage spread like wildfire as the citizens realised they had been hoodwinked. Even the more moderate citizens demanded that Oreal stand down while investigations were undertaken. Stunned and shaken at the sudden and unexpected turn of events, Oreal and his inner circle took refuge in the Council headquarters, activating security protocols that effectively isolated the building from outside access. Helios News, one arm of Oreal's media supporters, ran immediate rebuttals, slamming the reports as fake news and the Hypernet Web sites as contrived and false. However, without knowing who they were fighting against, Helios News floundered and the message became muddied accusations against unspecified parties. Finally, they settled on the Union as being to blame but, without specific targets, the refutation was blunted.

Veritas Media, on the other hand, picked up the stories and ran them with every bit of detail they could find, adding some guesses that were not too far from the truth, and re-running older stories about Oreal's behaviour that had failed to achieve cut-through previously.

After two days, the Warriors released security video of Alist Bredic, Oreal's chief of security, meeting with Explorer Guild members. Audio of the meeting was poor but it was clear enough to hear Bredic arrange for Veritas Media's staff to be harassed. When asked what level of force was required Bredic clearly replied that he would not be worried over a few deaths. Veritas leapt on that revelation and detailed each and every attack that had occurred on reporters and other Veritas staff, including in one case grainy video of the killers of a junior reporter, several of whom resembled members of the Guild Explorer delegation.

The pressure quickly built on Oreal and his associates. Rodrig decided to move the schedule forward so, on the day following release of the Bredic video, all of the evidence that Justine had obtained of the links between the Explorers Guild and the Empire were posted to various information distributors. The new revelations caused a furore around Union space. On Helios, they were linked back to the meetings of Oreal's henchman with those who were now shown to be Guild Explorer members. Those reports, delivered by the once again trusted Veritas Media, very clearly drew the connections between corrupt miners, the Explorers Guild and the Empire, and showed how the people of Helios had been played for fools by Oreal and his cohort.

The Premier of Helios, who had not been aware of what was transpiring and was not part of the conspiracy, called for calm and to allow the Helios police to do their jobs. Unfortunately for her, it was less than an hour later that Justine's recently compiled list of police who were in the pay of Oreal's cabal was released. That the chief of police was involved was no longer any sort of surprise, as he was known to be one of Oreal's close friends and was holed up with him in the Council headquarters. The real blow was evidence that all three deputies and almost one quarter of the rank and file police were also accomplices. There was no way the Helios police force could be relied on for this job.

The lid blew off!

The Council headquarters was besieged by hundreds of extremely angry Helios citizens, the same ones who had cheered for Oreal's platform of leaving the Union and taking back control of Helios by the people of Helios. All demanded action against Oreal, ranging from incarceration to various forms of punishment both banal and inventive.

While the pressure was being raised by the series of escalating revelations, Kresta and Randall were playing on the concerns of the militia members. Planned by Oreal to be his own private army, the members of the militia were worried. Would they now be targeted as associates of Oreal? Would they be blamed for any part of what had occurred, especially when it was discovered that several of their number were, in fact, Explorer Guild plants?

Kresta had little sympathy for the militia members. These people had been prepared to undermine or overthrow the legal government at Oreal's instigation. Most of them were quite comfortable with the idea of others being hurt so long as they were not affected. Standard issue for the militia was full face masks to reduce the chance of members being identified, along with nondescript, low quality armour and uniforms. So, now the question was how to bring these people on board as an auxiliary force to work with the remaining police force and the Warriors if - although Kresta thought *when* was more likely - they faced the Guild's fighters.

The answer, of course, was to play to their own self-interests. Kresta and Randall had provided identities of the small number of militia who they had been able to befriend. Then, Justine identified additional militia members using advanced data mining techniques that established links with the known members. The resultant list of names, with some additional incriminating data, was placed on a secure site that, supposedly, Kresta could access because of his reserve status. Kresta then showed the list of names to his militia contacts and watched as panic ensued.

Rather than being part of something that they believed would further their own self-interests once free of the restrictions imposed by the Union, the militia members now found themselves reported as known associates of criminals and probable Empire agents. Kresta and Randall, acting the part of loyal Union military personnel, albeit retired, made loud noises to distance themselves from the militia, all while delivering dire warnings of what happened to Empire agents and collaborators.

As pressure mounted and the situation spiralled towards an uncertain outcome, the Premier of Helios appealed for assistance from the Union. The sector governor expressed surprise that Helios would want Union help and was reassured repeatedly that such was the case. The Council had discussed the matter. Evidence was made available to them by Rodrig, anonymously, that showed how many of the reports of Union atrocities had been fabricated or exaggerated. In the absence of Oreal and his supporters, and worried about retaining their own well-paid sinecures as much as, or perhaps more than, the welfare of the people of Helios, the Council had agreed to seek closer ties with the Union. The governor agreed to consider the matter and terminated the call just in time to prevent his broad grin from showing on screen.

The level of concern had already hit panic levels for some of the militia when reports about the Union being asked to intervene started to make the rounds. Rodrig gave Kresta a prearranged signal. Gathering four of the more nervous founding members of the militia in an impromptu meeting, Kresta proposed a method of salvaging something for the members. He laid it out bluntly.

"I've been in touch with one of the Union's sector intelligence people who I worked with in the past. He told me they're preparing a list of charges for Oreal and his accomplices. The plan is to deal with them as Empire agents. That includes the militia, given that you were planning to help Oreal overthrow the government."

"But we were just protecting ourselves from the Union," complained Killian Ritter, a grandson of one of the founders of Helios and previously a loud supporter of Oreal.

"I tried to tell the commander that you were not really agents of the Empire or revolutionaries and had been self-interested fools taken in by Oreal," Kresta said as though agreeing with Ritter. The others exchanged glances at being characterised as fools even as Kresta continued, "but he wasn't overly inclined to offer any leniency. It seems there have been a raft of planets where something similar has been tried and the citizens had cottoned onto it and taken action to protect the planet and its place in the union. Helios has not shown that sort of smarts." Kresta paused again as he looked around the gathered group. "It's a shame there isn't some way to show that you're actually loyal and not really Guild and thus Empire sympathisers."

"Well," Mas Jukking, grand-daughter of another founder said as she glanced to Ritter, "we did get a message from Ventix to be ready to take action. Orders to follow, the message said. Maybe we could pass that along to the authorities."

Ventix was the Explorers Guild soldier charged with being the militia contact. Justine had intercepted that message and passed it on. Therefore, Kresta knew that its contents had not been that vague. The message called on the militia to rescue Oreal and his inner circle of Empire agents before the Union forces arrived. Unsaid in the message but clear to the Warriors was that the militia would be left to their own devices after that. The Guild was cutting its losses and preparing to run.

"Just passing on the message would not have any real effect," Kresta replied in a commiserating manner before raising his head sharply as though he had just thought of something. "However, if you actively opposed the Guild's actions that may very well allow some leeway to be given. Do you know where and when this action is to take place?"

"Yes, in around two hours. We're to be at the usual place then. I think the plan is to go to the Council building and get Oreal out and safely away."

"Well, okay then," Kresta said thoughtfully. "Perhaps we can use that." He glanced to Randall who was trying out his own thoughtful expression and nodding as though in agreement. "Maybe if you were instrumental in capturing Oreal and the Guild soldiers that will give enough reason for charges to be dropped."

"But, but we're just citizen militia," Jukking said with a slight whine.

"We were going to be led by Ventix and others of his team," Ritter chimed in. "None of us know how to lead anything like that. We've had minimal training with the weapons they gave us."

Randall snorted. "Then you're in trouble, aren't you?" He sighed theatrically and shook his head, before glancing to Kresta. "What d'you think?"

Kresta shrugged, deciding it was time to finish the discussion before he and Randall overplayed their hand. "How about if we helped?" he asked Randall.

"What, you and me? We've been out of the game for a while now," Randall replied, frowning.

"Not that long," Kresta demurred. "And I'd kind of like to get these guys off the hook. They've been duped, that's obvious. I think they've learnt their lesson with this."

The four militia exchanged speculative glances. Jukking and Ritter nodded, taking the decision for the small group. Kresta could see the calculations starting already in the minds of the militia. How could they lay the blame on the newcomers? He decided to scotch that line of thought immediately.

"Okay then. You get the others to agree and we can bring one or two others in also. And in case you get any silly ideas, this discussion has been recorded and will be sent to Fleet Security if you don't follow through."

Chagrined, the militia stood as a group and watched as the two Warriors walked away.

16

Marines and Mayhem

As Kresta and Randall set the trap for the erstwhile militia, the position became more complicated for Rodrig as she prepared the final touches to her plan. With the expectation being raised that some form of direct action would occur, the Fleet Marine Corps decided that it was their domain and made that position clear to the sector governor. The latter, not aware of the existence of the Warriors of the Light or their role in the events unfolding, agreed and ordered the Marines to deal with the Guild force, estimated to be around fifty to sixty members. Colonel Westin Black, the ambitious leader of the Marines force on the Union heavy cruiser *Kaiser*, rapidly put his plan together. He and twenty of his Marines were strapped into their drop ship in short order.

Rodrig's objections, passed via Marjory, were over-ruled, despite Marjory's forceful statement of prior operational status. Rodrig could do little except meet Black and provide a situation update for the Marines. That went poorly.

"Ms Rodrig, I have no idea who you are or what you're doin' here but this is my operation and I'll run it the same way I always do," Black growled when confronted by the former miner at his drop ship's landing site.

"That is Major Rodrig, Colonel," Rodrig replied calmly, "and I am a member of a clandestine group trying to resolve this situation without unnecessary bloodshed. I am trying to ensure that your team and the civilians are safe."

"My team will look after itself, Major," Black sneered, "and my plan should result in only minimal civilian casualties. I deem them to be an acceptable number. I've not heard of any clandestine force in this theatre of operations. I have my orders and I'm ordering you to clear the space."

"You haven't heard of us because we are a *secret* organisation, Colonel," Rodrig replied with cracks appearing in her calm mien. "We've been in this area for some time now and have a clear understanding of the train of events and what is likely to happen. In fact, we have a plan in place to take the occupants of the building without significant casualties."

"Not interested, Major," Black declared. "Your operation is superseded, if one even existed. We don't need any help with this. It's what we are trained to do and we'll do it quickly and efficiently."

With that, Black turned away and joined his troop. Rodrig watched, frustrated, as her plan turned to dust. She noted that the Marines had older style military armour, more bulky than their own and much heavier. Their weapons were also much heavier and varied from team member to team member. The fire power on display was very impressive, however.

Rodrig returned to her own quarters where the rest of the Warriors awaited her. She explained the position quickly and concisely, anger and frustration causing her to clip her words and let go a string of curses before taking a breath and pausing. The rest exchanged appreciative glances, having learned some new swear words, and wondering what was coming next.

"Our mission now," Rodrig said as calmly as she could, "is to protect as many of the non-combatants as we can, and to be ready to take a hand. Kresta and Randall, you hold the militia back as much as you can. Jasper, you take the rest of the team and see if you can clear the likely battle zone. Take part only if you must or if I task you to do so. I'll stay here and maintain a watch. Justine has isolated the Guild's signal and the General managed to break its encryption in no time at all, somehow.

"The Marines have older style armour but they're well armed. I imagine they're going to go for a frontal assault after clearing any obstacles. Be aware they expect civilian casualties so they won't be too careful about avoiding them."

"The Guild have some serious firepower themselves," Jasper replied. "There's been some activity over there for the last couple of hours. According to some reports, there has been a lot of construction work around the main square fronting the Council headquarters. I checked it out and I'm sure I saw some fixed gun emplacements in adjacent buildings. The reflective glass on all of the buildings hides it but I could see through open doors. The Guild may have had more people than we thought on Helios. Maybe warn the Marines about it?"

"It's been made clear that they won't listen to us. Can you pinpoint where you think these emplacements are?"

"It's on the map already," Jasper replied. "We've been updating it from the latest intel. Each of the buildings around the square. Couldn't see what the guns were. My best guess is some sort of heavy blaster, likely at least a pair. If they're Empire-sourced units then they will have some real stopping power. All of the Empire ones do. If they're Union-sourced then it depends on the model. I would guess they will be heavy though."

"Okay," Rodrig nodded. "We go full armour on this one, standard load out. The new stuff from the General. My bet is that it's better than the Marines' older gear, especially the armour. We have no insignias so there's no link to the Warriors. The militia wears mismatched armour anyway, so hopefully it won't stand out too much. Kresta, just explain that you were allowed to keep your own on discharge. Hopefully the militia won't know any better."

An hour later Kresta and Randall arrived at the designated meeting place. The Helios militia were sitting on a few benches or standing in small groups of two or three. Fear was the overarching emotion on show. Several showed signs of recent tears. Others obviously had sought liquid fortitude, or other substances. Most held their weapons without any real confidence. None looked comfortable in their armour, which mostly was comprised of a mixture of older second-hand and cheaply made newer elements that combined for a mottled finish. The gathered militia stared when Kresta and Randall opened the duffels they carried and started to assemble their body armour.

"Where did you get that?" Ritter asked as he watched Kresta step into the armour's legs, eyes wide as the legs self-sealed.

"This is our regulation armour from our last deployment," Kresta replied matter-of-fact. "It's designed for us so when we left we were allowed to take it with us. Part of the reserve system."

Ritter nodded, watching enviously as the Warriors unrolled the single piece, flexible breast and back sections and slip them on over their heads, followed by lower torso segments that they stepped into. The legs self-attached to the torso, which in turn attached itself to the chest and back section. Arms followed, after which they extracted gloves and clipped them to points on the armour's flanks. Boots that looked more like soft shoes were next. The real party piece was the helmet, as Kresta knew, and he kept that off for now.

The militia were armed with old multi-shot super-velocity pellet carbines, which were excellent in their long-ago day but were old and slow now. One or two had their own pieces but Randall was sure they could not be used with precision. Indeed, his contact with the militia members had convinced him some time before that, if there was a serious firefight, they would be of little use other than being targets. In that, he surmised, he had reached the same conclusion as the Guild planners - the militia were to be scapegoats and would be sacrificed for the Guild to escape. The Warriors could not just sacrifice them, however. The Warriors would have to run cover for them.

It was only after he had started to extract his weapons and clip or strap them in place that Randall realised total quiet had fallen on the assembled militia. All were staring at him. Or rather, they stared at his weapons. Distracted by thinking about how he and Kresta would have to shield the militia, Randall had geared up as he always would. A wicked double edged knife was checked for blemishes and then clipped across his chest. His personal handgun, a heavy percussion pistol that fired hardened ceramic pellets, was clipped to his right thigh, where his hand fell on it easily. A second handgun, firing energy pulses and inevitably called a blaster by all and sundry, was hung from a stud on his left hip and strapped down. Next came a pulse rifle which Randall swung around and slung over his back, where a mild magnetic field secured it but still allowed it to be grasped and brought into play readily. This was complemented by a bandoleer of grenades that could be fired from the launcher mounted beneath the pulse-rifle's main barrel. This he settled across his chest such that it did not impede his knife. Randall looked around in the silence and then glanced to Kresta.

The latter had continued to kit up also. The armour was identical but Kresta carried a blaster on each hip and an odd kind of power-assisted cross-bow arrangement slung over his left shoulder. He also carried a knife, this one slender and razor-edged, more like a short sword, and carried in a scabbard strapped down his right leg. A second scabbard held incendiary-tipped quarrels for the cross-bow and was slung across his right shoulder. Kresta checked Randall briefly, received a similar check in return, and turned to face the room.

Ritter stood open-mouthed, while Jukking was thin-lipped.

"Did they let you keep all of that too?" Ritter asked Kresta.

"No," Kresta replied shortly. "Our weapons we acquired ourselves. No questions about where."

"Um, okay," Ritter replied faintly.

"So if we were to fight against you, with our current training, weapons and armour, who would win?" Jukking demanded from across the room.

"We would," Kresta replied. "You're inexperienced, with less capable armour and poorer weaponry. In a pitched battle you wouldn't survive against us. Our old squad would have made mince out of you."

Randall nodded in agreement, although of course there was no old squad, at least not one that held both him and Kresta. Still, the reality of the situation could not be denied. The militia was poorly trained - untrained, in fact - and badly equipped. This would be ugly.

"Now," Kresta said sharply, "gather around. We've been told that a contingent of marines is coming in to try to deal with the Guild." He glanced around the even more worried expressions, verging on panic. "I'm not sure how that'll go but they won't worry too much about collateral damage. Neither will the Guild. So, we'll hold back a little and see how that goes. I have a feeling we'll get to play a role at the death of this action, but there's no point getting mixed up in the heavy stuff."

"But we've been told to be there, now!" Ritter said in a high-pitched voice.

"Stay calm," Kresta replied evenly. "We won't put you in harm's way for no purpose but remember why you're here. You joined a conspiracy by Empire agents to overthrow the legitimate government of a Union planet. This is to make it clear that you were dupes and your allegiance is, in fact, to that government and the Union. There will be some danger involved. You have no choice."

"And," Randall continued, "as we did before, your participation has been recorded but if any of you cut and run that also will be recorded. Those who stay the course will be exonerated."

"How can we be sure of that?" Jukking demanded angrily, perhaps confirming that she had intended to be one who cut and ran.

"You can't," Kresta said bluntly. "Just like you couldn't know if you should believe what Oreal and Ventix told you. I can tell you that they were setting you up to take the blame and probably all of you would have ended up dead. At least we don't have that intention."

"You said you would bring others to help us, too," Jukking retorted.

"And we have, but they're not coming here. At the moment they're keeping an eye on the marines that have just landed. They're trying to get civilians out of the way. They'll join in at the right time."

Kresta and Randall split the militia into two groups, making sure that Jukking and Ritter were kept apart. Kresta led the group of twelve with Jukking, while Randall led the remaining eleven that included Ritter. The short quick-walk to the back of the Council complex exposed the lack of fitness of most of the militia. The few civilians who saw the armed groups stared and then moved rapidly away from the area, which Kresta appreciated. It made the job of clearing civilians that much easier.

Meanwhile, Rodrig monitored the drone and fixed camera footage of the marines from her quarters. She kept an open channel to the team members, describing what she was seeing. The whole contingent of marines marched from their landing site down the centre of the main thoroughfare to the square that fronted the Council complex. They stopped in a line across the main entrance to the complex, making an impressive display in their gunmetal-coloured combat armour, standing tall and quite still. Colonel Black strode forward confidently. Rodrig was unable to make out what he said when he reached the security station but she could guess.

"Black just demanded that Oreal, his cronies and the Guild members surrender without delay or face the consequences," Justine reported from where she had positioned herself diagonally across from the same security station, confirming Rodrig's assumption.

"Stay out of sight, Justine," Rodrig directed. "Jasper, update on the civilian situation?"

"We've managed to get most of them out of the immediate area," Jasper reported. "Luckily there's a fair amount of space around the Council buildings, so if they manage to keep this localised the spillover might be low. A few refused to hear us, some opted to stay anyway. Others are spectating. Expect lots of personal devices to be videoing this."

"Understood," Rodrig replied. "Kresta, Randall, see if you can get into the complex from the back and take the militia to the holding area we discussed. If you can stay there during the marines' action then do so. Otherwise, act at your discretion. Justine, make sure all of this is recorded. Jasper, Anders, Orest, Ulfis, see if you can identify Guild positions. Don't ignore the other buildings where we think there may be weapons. I don't trust the quiet. Be ready to step in when I say."

She received a series of short replies as each acknowledged the message. Thoughtfully, Rodrig keyed a separate transmitter channel.

"General, I have a feeling we'll be facing something more than we thought," Rodrig said while maintaining a close watch on the screen.

"Do you have anything specific?" the General responded immediately. "I can see your feed and things look calm."

"Remember all that work being done on adjacent buildings over the last week? And the work that we were told was done a while ago? I think they expected some form of military action and have built emplacements in other buildings. Maybe as a safeguard. It's what I'd do. I have four of the team trying to find out if that's the case."

"I will contact the sector commander," Marjorie replied. "*Kaiser* has a full complement of marines and the standby squad can be deployed at short notice. I will make sure it is very short notice."

"Thank you, General," Rodrig said. "I'll leave it to you to make that call based on what happens down here."

Colonel Black, meanwhile, was through with the waiting. He ordered the main gates to the Council compound to be breached and stood back as three of his squad ran to the massive gates and placed micro-charges in several places. The three returned to their places in the line and waited. On a further signal the three each detonated their charges. The large gates were smashed as the military-grade explosives met the ornamental, though substantial in weight terms, construction. The gates crashed to the pavement, into the square. The line of marines advanced across the wide approach to the tighter gate opening, each hefting their weapons of choice. As they reached the narrower opening events took a turn for the worse.

"Weapons signatures!" Anders reported urgently. "Multiple weapons. Just came up. Buildings east, west and north of the Council compound. It's a trap!"

"Anders, Orest, Ulfis," Rodrig snapped without delay, selecting the three former special forces soldiers, "locate and destroy those weapons. Justine, stay in place. I need eyes on those other buildings and I need all of this recorded."

As the three Warriors leapt from their places of concealment, the front of the main Council building fell forward, revealing three heavy blasters. At the same time panels fell from the base of the three other buildings facing each side of the Council Square. Three more heavy blasters were exposed, one in each building. The marines' response was instantaneous. Before the first blaster had fired every marine had opened fire, all the while moving into different positions and seeking whatever cover they could find. At the same time, the three Warriors charged towards the the surrounding buildings, each taking a different path to avoid angles of fire.

The marines were exposed from every side. The open nature of the square on which the Council compound had been built, combined with the walls of the compound itself that formed the only cover while simultaneously pinning the marines against the large stones of the wall, created a killing ground. Black, standing in front of his marines, was targeted specifically and was struck by multiple blasts. He stood no chance and was dead within the first moments. However, by being the focus of the initial shots, he gave some time for the other marines to take whatever evasive actions they could. Most found that they now were subject to the bombardment, and they stood little chance. The Guild gunners mercilessly pumped blast after blast into the marines' positions. Most of them were torn apart, their armour standing little chance against the heavy weapons. Swathes of the square's paving were scored and melted at the same time.

Ulfis reached his objective first. His active armour allowed him to leap to a balcony at the rear of the building that faced the left side of the Council square. He used a tiny breaching charge to blow a solid door open. Once inside, he raced along a service passage to a likely corridor, stormed straight through a plate plexiglass door located a short distance along the corridor and then charged across what proved to be a mezzanine level which overlooked the lower level. Plexiglass splinters crunched under his armour boots, adding a counterpoint to the echoing blaster shots from below. The wide staircase leading to the lower level was guarded by a single Guild soldier who spun as the plexiglass door shattered. Ulfis flicked the firing selector of his ultra-carbine to semi-automatic and fired repeatedly. The high velocity pellets peppered the chest plate of the Guild soldier's armour before he could bring his own older-style blaster to bear. The first two ultra-velocity kinetic pellets pushed him back and staggered him, while the third and fourth cracked the armour in several places. The fifth and sixth shattered the armour's chest plate and tore through flesh and bone. The seventh and eight added to the damage but the soldier was already dead. Ulfis charged past the Guild soldier as his body slumped to the floor.

The staircase leading down to the ground level stretched ahead of Ulfis. The Warrior took in the position at a glance. There appeared to be no more than five Guild soldiers operating or protecting the heavy gun. Seated behind the gun was one soldier, while two others were fiddling with what seemed to be targeting scanners. The remaining two were already turning to face Ulfis. The Warrior ripped a clip of five explosive rounds from his harness and slapped it into the lower magazine of his carbine. He fired from the hip, sending all five charges to different target zones. Two he aimed at the scanners, one at a point between the two soldiers turning to engage him and the last two at the gun's firing seat and its occupant. The results were rather more than he expected.

The scanner operators tried to jump away from their positions while the other two soldiers darted sideways even while spraying bursts from their energy carbines without effect. Ulfis' rounds detonated like a rolling wave of sound. The targeting scanner operators had only just managed to disengage from their scanners and were flung like rag dolls. The two soldiers were spared some of the blast force as they had flung themselves to the floor. Still, the concussion of the blast punched them in a tangle of arms and legs across what had been a wide, pseudo-marble floored foyer. The emplaced gun, however, provided the most impressive result. The first round hit the lower gun barrel itself and exploded, destroying the adjacent gunner's seat and its occupant. The second hit the energy reserve. The design proved that this was an Empire design, for the Union heavy artillery had no such reserve storage and, if they did, it would not have been adjacent to the gun.

Ulfis' eyes opened saucer-wide as he realised where his last round was heading. Ignoring the ragged and unaimed carbine bursts, he turned to run back along the corridor. Three steps into his dash his explosive round hit. A moment later the energy store overloaded in spectacular fashion. The foyer erupted in a loud pyrotechnic display. A huge burst of light spewed from the front of the foyer along with a wave of super-heated air travelling just ahead of a thunderous crash. The remaining plexiglass of the foyer's external walls exploded out-wards, sending shards into the square. Ulfis, still on the mezzanine level, was picked up and thrown along the corridor that he had used for entry. He had the presence of mind to hunch as small as possible. Through the already shattered plate plexiglass door he was blown only to crash into the far wall. Ulfis was pinned face-first against the wall while the heat blast raged from the exploding energy store, only to slump to his knees once it had died away. Stunned, amazed to be alive and seemingly uninjured, Ulfis twisted to stare back at the dam-age he had caused, which he could see clearly now because the mezza-nine floor had collapsed up to the point where the corridor started. A gaping hole was all that was left of the foyer. The gun had been flung outward and rested on its side in the square with a twisted gun barrel.

Ulfis tested arms and legs and then checked the heads up display in his helmet. Both tests were successful so he carefully stood. The ringing in his ears from the concussion subsided so that he could hear that the fight continued in the Council Square. The chronometer on his helmet display showed that barely more than a minute had passed since he breached the building. He had experienced the time dilation of combat before and knew the effects would pass. He stood straight, stretched a few kinks from back and neck, then squared his shoulders in a conscious effort to reset himself. Only then did he make his way to the rear balcony once again.

Ulfis' spectacular result had served the other Warriors well. The enormous blast as the gun in the left-most building exploded and was launched into the square served both to mask the approach of Anders and Jasper and also to stun the Guild soldiers in the other two buildings. Anders decided that Ulfis had provided a clear example and fired two full clips of explosive charges into the foyer of the right-most building. No aim was required, just a spread of charges fired as fast as he could hit the trigger stud and change clips. The results were nowhere near as remarkable as Ulfis' but were almost as effective. The Guild soldiers who manned the gun and aiming units were cut down where they sat. The two remaining Guild soldiers were stunned but tried to fight back, only to fall to the charges from Anders' second clip.

Amidst the sounds of the ongoing fight across the square, Anders picked his way into the foyer, carefully scanning to left and right as he did so. The foyer of the right-hand building was a replica of the left-hand building, and the Guild had placed their forces in similar manner in both of them. Anders only became aware of the guard on the mezzanine level when the first slug struck him a hammer blow to his right shoulder, followed a split second later by a second to the same area. He was spun around and allowed himself to be carried by momentum in a spiral to the floor. The slug was followed by a series of shots that peppered his location. Shards of floor tiles spattered him where he lay but no more shots scored on him. His helmet display provided the helpful information that he had been hit, which he knew, and also that he had a broken clavicle, which he had not known. Even as the pain started, a combined painkiller and stimulant was applied that brought the pain down to a bearable level rapidly.

Anders was in trouble. He struggled to bring his carbine into use, holding it in his left hand while his right was virtually useless, with pain relief or without it. Anders glanced down to his shoulder. The armour held, with nothing more than small scuff marks where the slugs had hit. A few more shots from the older carbine of the Guild soldier followed, one of which plinked off Anders' leg armour. More floor tiles shattered and sprayed shards of ceramic composite across the foyer. Anders could hear the Guild soldier moving carefully down the heavily damaged stairs. He followed the progress with his ears, straining to hear every tentative step. The background of the continuing battle in the square, even with two of the big guns silent, made the task difficult. Anders knew that his situation would be known by Rodrig and that she would take measures to assist, but that could be too late. He maintained radio silence even when injured, trusting to his gear to do its job and transmit the details of his injury. A tentative move of his right arm to support the carbine held in his left hand caused a stab of pain that overwhelmed the benefits of the painkiller and he quickly allowed it to drop again. So, he was one handed with a two handed carbine.

Carefully, Anders placed his carbine on the floor beside him and reached across his body to where he had his hand gun strapped. Like many of the special forces soldiers of the time, his personal hand gun was an older modular type, modified to use the newer carbon-ceramic pellets packaged with an advanced propellant. He gasped as his right arm was moved from its rest position but he was able to grasp his pistol and extract it from its holster. Only then did he notice that he could no longer hear the Guild soldier moving and that the noises of battle seemed to have faded somewhat. With a frown, Anders thumbed the safety off his pistol, holding it by his side. A slight scuff came from his left side, the one more exposed. Sure enough, the Guild soldier was standing quite still, his older helmet faced toward Anders and his carbine already coming up to aim. Advanced or not, Anders' newer armour would not withstand a sustained pummelling from that older carbine. Desperately, Anders raised his pistol from his side and fired twice in a single motion, but he missed both times. The Guild soldier ignored the rounds passing and deliberately took aim while Anders tried to settle his aim through the pain of his shoulder wound.

Suddenly, the Guild soldier shook violently and his chest armour split under the impact of successive ultra-high powered pellets. As the Guild soldier collapsed, Anders relaxed with a sigh and waited. Justine moved into view, scanning the foyer for threats before glancing to where Anders lay. Justine pressed a stud and her helmet visor became fully transparent. She raised her eyebrows to Anders, who responded with a weak back and forth tilt of his left hand, the generally understood signal for "I'm not going so well", before resting his head against the wall behind him.

Two buildings secured, but that left two to go.

17

Mission End

Orest made his way to the building directly facing the Council building across the square. The emplaced gun in that building had a lesser effect once the surviving Marines had scattered to find cover, but it had caused great damage in the opening salvo. Now the Guild soldiers were seeking out their targets and delivering well-placed and damaging bursts from the heavy energy weapon. The shots were spaced apart as targets were sought out. Orest pressed himself against the right wall, with the shattered plexiglass front wall of the foyer spread out in a wide arc of debris before him. He took a deep breath before making his move. It was at that moment that Ulfis hit the energy store with his explosive rounds. The huge flash of light and stupendous *crash* that accompanied it caused nearly all attention to be drawn to the left-most building momentarily. Orest took advantage of the confusion to dart unseen around the corner of the building and step into the foyer. He moved quickly to a service counter and crouched behind it. A few seconds later, the gun started its slow rhythm once again.

Orest was the odd one out of the former special forces Warriors. Where his fellow special forces veterans were from the tradition of rapid movement and hard strikes, his speciality had been quiet infiltration. He had built a strong reputation as one who could make his way into an enemy position using stealth rather than force, guile instead of violence, precision instead of broad-based destruction. However, once he was in a position where violence was required, he was the opposite to stealthy and quiet, although he was precise still.

Orest carefully reached up from where he crouched below the counter and placed a tiny three-sixty degree camera on the counter top. He leaned against the counter and tapped the relevant wrist-pad controls to allow his helmet to pair with the camera. Using his eye-tracking controls, he narrowed the image to ignore the wall behind him and some distance to each side, leaving a slightly bug-eyed view of around two hundred and fifty degrees. Experience enabled him to look through the distortion and accurately identify the locations of the Guild soldiers. Unlike the other two buildings, this one had only a single level to worry about. There were three Guild soldiers guarding the two target operators and the gun operator. The three were stationed roughly equally apart, with one standing slightly higher than the other two, probably on a step or small stool. The heavy gun was located in the foyer's centre, with the target operators on each side staring at monitors. Orest calculated the angles, rehearsing his actions in his head a couple of times. Carefully, he retracted his helmet and reached into a belt pouch. His questing fingers found what he was seeking and he pulled out and popped into his mouth a stick of gum. A couple of good chews and the flavour released. Bacon with maple syrup. Perfect!

Orest stretched his neck left and right, loosened his shoulders in preparation and carefully checked that his ultra-carbine was powered and cocked for action. This he swung over his shoulder and made sure that it quietly snapped into place on a back-mounted magnetic point. He loosened and then checked his two personal handguns in their holsters. Like an old-fashioned gunslinger, Orest's handguns were strapped to his thighs. The two were mismatched, oddly. The right side gun was a custom twelve shot pistol with an oversized grip to suit his large hand, reworked with a lengthened and strengthened barrel. The sighting system had been removed. His ammunition was also custom. Orest's gun fired large calibre pellets from cartridges that carried fifty percent more propellant than normal. He liked to stop what he hit. He switched the safety off. The second was a needler, a derivation of an Empire design that had been obtained some time ago that emitted extremely narrow beams of energy. Once again, he had customised the needler to provide a larger battery than normal which provided greater energy or more shots. He advanced the energy level. He smiled briefly as he recalled the General's appraisal, her almost feral grin and nod when she first saw him kitted out.

He stood from his place behind the counter. He realised that the gun in the second building had fallen silent as he stood and smiled grimly. His turn! He had not been seen, as the guards' attention had switched momentarily to the now silent second gun. He could almost see their unease at losing two guns, and the realisation that they probably were the third in line. The guard who stood on the step was the first to see him, standing easily by the counter with both hands by his sides. The guard shouted and pointed before swinging his carbine towards Orest. Too slow! Far too slow! With practised ease, Orest smoothly drew both handguns. He fired one pellet from the right gun at the first guard, followed by two from the needler. The extra punch of the oversized pellets crunched through the guard's torso armour, while the energy beams sliced through his helmet. Before the first guard finished slumping to the floor, Orest swung to the other two and fired, both arms forward, stepping towards them left and right, sharing the damage evenly. Both guards were dead even as they became aware that they faced an opponent.

Orest turned to the gun operator and targeting team. Child's play! Each took one shot from the right handgun, with a check shot from the left. The action had taken twelve seconds. Orest walked over to the emplaced gun, pushed the operator from the seat and examined it. It was an old design, an Empire one for sure, but altered for human physiology. The aiming mechanism had been jury-rigged which, Orest surmised, was the reason they needed to have an external targeting unit. Orest looked through the optical sights and found he could see all the way across the square. An idea occurred to him and, after a moment's thought, he broke radio silence.

"Two-three, asset available on request," he broadcast over the team channel.

Rodrig frowned at the breach of mission protocols and then realised what it meant. She hoped Kresta and Randall did likewise. They did.

"Our time," Kresta declared. "Let's go. Remember," he continued, glancing around the assembled militia, "you come with us or you get charged. Your call."

Without waiting for any reaction, Kresta left the meeting room, followed by Randall. The two Warriors shared a tense smile as they heard the rest shuffling out after them. Swiftly, he led the reluctant group to the back entrance of the Council building. Once there he gestured for Jukking to move forward. When she did, tentatively, he hammered on the closed door with his armoured fist. Randall pushed Jukking towards the door. She was to act as spokesperson for the group.

The door slid open and one of the Guild soldiers glared suspiciously at the assembled group before focusing on Jukking.

"What do you want?" he asked brusquely.

"We, er, we were told to be here," Jukking replied hesitantly.

The Guild soldier narrowed his eyes as he glanced over the group again. Kresta and Randall had moved to the back of the group and kept their helmets retracted. The soldier's eyes skipped over them without noting anything odd.

"Wait here!" he ordered, and gestured for two other Guild soldiers who were standing behind him to move forward while he turned away.

The two stared at the group with hard eyes, which were visible through their open helmets. Kresta glanced to Randall with one eyebrow raised at the lapse of operational readiness. The latter gave a very short nod to show he understood. Thirty seconds later the first guard re-appeared.

"You're to join the chiefs up the front," he snarled. "Make sure you're ready to fight. Come on, quickly."

He started to turn away. Kresta and Randall stepped forward with handguns ready. Both fired twice. Two Guild soldiers went down from a single head shot each, but the third was targeted by both Warriors. The result was not pretty. Randall shrugged as he looked at Kresta.

"Wasn't sure you had him," he said conversationally.

Kresta merely nodded before turning to the assembled group. Shock was etched on almost every face.

"Safeties off!" Kresta ordered. "Helmets on! When we get in there I'll give the signal and you start firing at the Guild agents. All of them. No quarter or you will die. Randall, take the rear. No stragglers," he finished with obvious intent.

The two Warriors extended their helmets, which rose from their collars and enveloped their heads, concealing their features and presenting an intimidating sight. Confidently, Kresta led the group forward. The Warrior of the Light was followed by twenty-four would-be self-serving revolutionaries wearing mismatched armour and carrying outmatched weapons, followed in their turn by the second watchful Warrior.

The front of the building proved to have a room that stretched across the whole building. It was less of a foyer and more an open gathering space. Or it had been. Two Empire-designed heavy guns were emplaced side by side. Their stubby barrels extended over the top of a small courtyard that usually led from the square to the auto-opening doors and was a popular location for citizens to meet. Now nothing more than shards of plexiglass occupied that courtyard.

"Two-three, target centre, left one, right one," Kresta said onto the team channel.

"Two-three, target is set, program is set," Orest replied a moment later. "Full charge. Set for full depletion. Thirty-seven seconds duration."

"Light 'em up, then evacuate," Kresta directed, holding his right fist up to hold the militia from entering the front room.

Three seconds later Orest pressed the firing stud on the gun directly across the square from the Council building and departed at a run. A full bracket of automated shots hammered into the front room. Shouts rang out along with commands to target the gun in the opposite building. The besieged marines were forgotten for the moment as self-preservation took over. At a rate of almost one shot per second Orest's program sent twenty-eight blasts into the confined space that was the headquarters for Oreal and the Guild soldiers while Kresta held the militia back. The impact of the blasts was devastating to the more exposed Guild soldiers, but not to the guns. Both large guns were targeted against Orest's captured weapon and started to return fire as Orest's thirty-seven seconds came to an end. Almost half of the Guild soldiers were down, Kresta estimated when he cautiously stuck his wrist camera around the corner and panned left and right. The shots had gone slightly too far left and right, so that while the guns were spared the nests of Guild soldiers were not.

"Up," Kresta commanded, turning and physically dragging Jukking to her feet. "Stay aware of your team mates. Be aware we may have marines coming into the zone. Do not shoot the marines. Otherwise, shoot anything that moves."

The rest of the militia slowly stood. Several had cowered at the near continuous reports of the guns' energy blasts. As the heavy weapon fire stopped, it was replaced by kinetic pellet rounds fired from outside the building, probably by the few remaining marines. At least there were some still alive. Kresta detached his wrist camera and pressed its adhesive pad against the wall where it could record the action. He knew the amount of information it gathered would be useless in this situation, but the militia amateurs would not know that.

"Remember, you fight or you get charged. We'll know who," he said, gesturing to the camera. "Let's go!"

Randall moved up alongside Kresta and then moved across the wide corridor to the opposite wall. At a nod from Kresta both Warriors walked into the mayhem. Kresta targeted the gun aimers seated at their consoles. The first fell without being aware of the attack, but the second called out a warning before Kresta turned his way. The third and fourth leapt from their seats and grabbed their carbines. Kresta took down the second operator before he reached cover. Randall merely sought targets of opportunity. Any Guild soldier who stuck their head up was such a target and Randall used his ultra-carbine with ruthless efficiency. The first few seconds allowed the two Warriors to deal with five of the Guild soldiers - Kresta's two aimers and Randall's three victims. Then the Guild fought back.

Kresta estimated that around fifteen Guild soldiers remained active in the fight. Most of the others would be dead following Orest's action. He had yet to see Oreal or his lieutenants, Ventix and Bredic. They would be a priority for the Warriors. Behind him Kresta heard the militia firing their carbines. The much older models that the Guild recruiters had provided to them had far less stopping power, but they at least caused uncertainty amongst the Guild. Into the mix came the boom of a large calibre gun and Kresta stole a quick look over his shoulder. One of the militia had brought what may have been his own weapon to the fight, a large handgun that took two hands to aim and fire. Kresta smiled grimly. That may cause even more confusion if he could aim it well enough.

Randall heard a gurgle behind him and spun to see one of the militia collapse, blood spilling from a throat wound. He had been protected from the front. That meant there was some sort of flanking move happening. Randall tapped three times on his throat mike as a signal to Kresta that he was moving. He had already worked out where the likely angle of attack was and fast-crawled towards the back of the room in which the firefight was occurring. Pellets flew above his head and he recognised the peculiar whistle that came from the type of rifled pellets many marines used. It seemed the marines had joined the fight in earnest. Towards the back of the room there was a round column, decorative rather than functional. Randall crawled to it and moved to a crouch on its lee side. He attached his wrist camera to the muzzle of his carbine and gently pushed it around the column's girth. There! Three Guild soldiers were creeping around the side of the room, using the heavy, solidly built furniture that ringed the walls as cover. Randall considered. The solid furniture seemed to be strong enough to stop the hardened ceramic pellets of the militia, from what he could see, which meant they might act as a containment barrier.

Randall switched his carbine to the lower barrel and inserted a clip of five explosive rounds into the magazine. Standing, he aimed just above the furniture so that the charges would explode against the wall slightly below that level. Without pause he fired the whole clip, spacing the shots out to impact in a line along the wall. The charges exploded away from the wall but the force was reflected again by the solid furniture. The three soldiers were caught in the concussive wash and backwash. After a few moments, Randall turned to other targets. It was likely the three were dead or, if not, would be out of commission for some time.

On the other side of the room Jukking was terrified. She was hiding behind a large planter while hardened ceramic pellets zipped and spun past her. This was not what she had intended at all when she agreed to help Oreal take over the government. She had been promised that it would be easy. Her own payoff would be considerable, of course, even before the mines started to pay off. How did it come to this? Could it be that she had made a mistake and had, in fact, been duped by Oreal and Ventix? The very idea galled but it was possible. Now she was involved in a deadly battle and she had no idea what to do. She was certain that Kresta would follow through on his threat to have her charged if she ran away - she paid no heed to what problems her actions may have caused to any others.

A scuffing sound came from the direction of the wall and Jukking turned to look, eyes wide, turning her carbine in the same direction reflexively. A Guild soldier was shuffling along the wall. Jukking's startled reaction brought the soldier's attention to her. Immediately he swung his rifle to align on her. Frantically, Jukking looked left and right but could find no way out. She moaned in fear even as the soldier fired. The pellet struck the planter alongside her head, spraying her helmet with planter chips. Panic-stricken, Jukking closed her eyes and tightened her grip on her carbine, inadvertently pressing and holding the trigger stud. The carbine fired the entire magazine of hardened ceramic pellets in a continuous burst, striking the Guild soldier in the chest and working up. The first shots staggered the soldier and caused him to miss his next shot. The line of pellets struck the neckline, the continuous hammer of the shots cracking the thinner overlapping helmet armour at the neck. The pellets worked up the chin and jaw. The helmet cracked again and the soldier staggered again. Finally, the weight of hits caused the helmet to crack open and Jukking's last two shots penetrated the helmet, striking the exposed forehead, penetrating the skull and exiting in a spray of blood and brain matter.

Jukking opened her eyes when she heard no more shots coming her wy and shared open-mouthed at what she had done. Her carbine clicked repeatedly as she still held the trigger stud down. Dumbfounded, she looked from the downed soldier to her carbine, looking up to see a second Guild soldier aiming at her. He fired two shots that took her in the throat.

Ritter saw the end of Jukking. It was Ritter who had brought his father's old pistol, one that he had been taught to handle as a teen when he and his father still had a working relationship. Now, wide-eyed, he stared at Jukking's inert body while the Guild soldier deliberately aimed and placed two more slugs into the helmet. Ritter and Jukking had never been friends, coming to the militia from self-interest more than any belief. But she, like him, was a child of the founders and Ritter was surprised to find that that meant something. So it was that he raised his father's old heavy calibre pistol, aimed at the soldier who had killed Jukking and fired three shots. The soldier's armour held for the first two heavy slugs but failed for the third. Ritter watched stone-faced as the soldier died.

Kresta took stock. The Guild were losing numbers but so was he. The militia were suffering losses. Their near non-existent training, sub-standard equipment and old armour proved to be no match for the better weaponry and training of the Guild. The guns continued to fire but were less effective without their aimers, so the remaining marines were not so easily targeted. Still, the blasts continued even as the battle raged around the guns, adding noise and vibration to the confusion. Randall finally managed to clear the gunner from one of the guns, and the cessation of half the noise came as a surprise.

"One-one," Kresta muttered onto the team channel. "Need those marines in here asap."

"Copy," came the reply from Rodrig. "They're starting to move in now the second gun has gone silent."

Kresta acknowledged with a single click on his mike. Where was Oreal? That was the key to the operation. Kresta looked around carefully, firing intermittently if a target presented itself. The Guild was down to a much smaller number of soldiers now so, unless he had been killed, Oreal must be keeping low. Kresta noticed Ritter moving steadily across the room, taking advantage of cover where he could, although inexpertly. He looked determined, like a man with a target, which was very unlike Ritter in Kresta's experience with the man. Ritter was staring at a point across the room that Kresta was unable to see clearly.

"One-two, eyes on Ritter," Kresta called.

Randall swivelled his head to locate Ritter and saw the man making his way across the room. Randall followed Ritter's stare and saw a small well, like a sunken seating area surrounded by plants, that had two or three people cowering in it. The lower level would have offered some additional protection from the slugs flying around, and probably from the effects of Orest's blaster shots. As Randall's gaze fell on the sunken space, one of the occupants carefully rose to look over the room. Ventix! So, where Ventix was then, reasonably, they could expect Oreal to be also.

"One-one, I may have the target location in sight. Sunken seating area close to the back corner." Randall paused. "Sighted Ventix but he's the only one I could see. Ritter is heading towards that area. Not sure why. I'll provide cover."

Kresta acknowledged with a muttered "copy" while continuing to survey the battle zone. With the marines moving in, the time for the Warriors to leave was fast approaching. Somehow they needed to wrap this up. He could use Orest's firepower right now. One gun still gave sporadic fire but that would not last. There were no aimers now so the gunner was shooting by visual targeting, which was little more than guesswork for that type of gun. In a smooth sequence of movements Kresta switched to the lower barrel, stripped a clip of five explosive rounds from his vest webbing and inserted it into the lower magazine, stood and fired the whole clip at the remaining gun. Amazingly, none of the remaining Guild soldiers took a shot at him. The action took no more than five seconds. His shots were true, mostly. The gun disappeared in a cloud of smoke and a shower of debris, largely comprised of shrapnel from the charges and floor tile shards.

The smoke also provided an opportunity. Ventix darted from the sunken seats, firing a carbine in full automatic. He sprayed the pellets as he stopped and signalled. Behind him came Oreal and Bredic, the former security chief, in crouching runs. Oreal held a large handgun while Bredic wielded a small version of a crew-fired automatic weapon. Even as Kresta decided that Bredic's weapon might be the main danger, he saw Ritter walk into view, aim deliberately with the ancient pistol and fire four shots into Oreal. The deputy premier shuddered violently. His face registered shock before he collapsed to the floor. Bredic spun to face Ritter, who was calmly reloading the pistol from a belt pouch. Kresta saw Ventix spinning around as Randall fired at almost point blank into his torso before both Warriors directed their fire on Bredic. Too late! Even as Kresta joined Randall in shooting at the former security chief he fired at Ritter, stitching a line of heavy duty slugs across his armour. Ritter was thrown against the nearby furniture, which twisted him away from the remainder of the slugs. The firing stopped as Bredic fell, his old armour shattered in multiple places.

Kresta and Randall carefully looked around on a scene of carnage. All firing had ceased. The distinctive Guild armour was joined by the mismatched militia armour in scattered heaps, some of them still moving. Moans and groans replaced the gunfire.

"Need multiple medics here," Kresta reported tersely.

"On their way," Rodrig replied. "Do what you can and then get out of there."

Kresta replied with a single click of his mike.

"Check out the militia," Kresta said to Randall.

The latter nodded and turned away. Kresta walked over to where Oreal lay face up and spreadeagled in a spreading pool of blood. The Empire agent was not wearing any body armour, strangely, and Ritter's heavy slugs had torn through him. Stony-faced, Kresta moved to Ventix, noting the twin pattern of hits on the chest and helmet. Randall, quietly-spoken and introspective, had been meticulous in his attack on Ventix, producing maximum damage with the minimum of effort. He did not bother checking Bredic, as the man's armour had been destroyed and there was no chance of him being alive. Slowly, Kresta moved around the Guild soldiers. He removed carbines, handguns and various knives from bodies as he went. Of the estimated forty-five soldiers that he checked, he found only three alive, two of them being the aimers who had been blown away from their gun when it was destroyed, and the third gasping for breath and bleeding from multiple wounds.

"Hold," a hard voice said from behind Kresta.

He turned slowly to see two marines, carbines lined up on him. Kresta reached up, slowly again, and pressed the stud to retract his helmet. The two marines stared as the helmet retracted fully into the collar attached to his armour.

"That's hold, captain," Kresta replied evenly, giving himself a rank he thought would be enough to cause them to think before doing anything.

"Captain of what?" the marine said. "You have no unit insignia or rank showing."

"That's correct, I don't. Nor does my fellow captain over there," Kresta replied, gesturing to where Randall was crouched over Ritter.

"That's not for you to worry about, corporal," he continued with the glare he had used as a team sergeant. "Did your colonel survive?"

"No, sir," the marine replied as he lowered his carbine, apparently deciding to take Kresta on face value, followed reluctantly by the second marine.

"Who's ranking?"

"Not sure, sir," the marine replied.

"Right, then you," Kresta nodded to the second marine, "find out who's senior and have whoever it is report to me in here. You," he continued looking at the first marine as the second hurried off, "find your communications equipment and make sure your command is aware of the situation and that you need medics and reinforcements. I'm sure my commander has already made the call, but better to be sure. Then I want a perimeter established on the square to hold back anyone who is not a marine or a military or civilian medic. There will be dead and possibly injured in the other buildings to be dealt with, too, but you probably don't have enough personnel to deal with those, so maybe just have one of your troop circle around them and make sure weapons are gathered and sight-seers are kept clear."

"Aye, sir," the first marine replied, turning away.

Kresta walked over to Randall. He had dragged seven of the militia to a point close to Ritter and was ministering to them from his med-kit. Randall looked up and nodded.

"Jukking is shot to pieces," Randall said, "but I think Ritter will make it. He took four rounds but I can't see that any of them hit anything major." He shook his head. "Amazing! All of the survivors have wounds, mostly slug burns and breaks where that cheap armour stopped a slug the hard way. But we lost about fifteen, I think."

"Okay. I've got the marines starting to get things organised, then we go. Oh," he said, stopping and looking back as he turned away, "and we're both captains."

"Congratulations," Randall replied with a grin, turning back to his work. "I'll be using all of the pain relief I have, but they'll be okay for the local medics from there."

Kresta nodded. He unhooked his own medkit and tossed it to the floor alongside Randall and then turned back to see a marine with sergeant's stripes navigating through the damaged furniture. One arm was held awkwardly and there was a pronounced limp.

"Captain, Sergeant Blakish," the marine non-com said, sketching a vague salute as she surveyed Randall and the injured. "I have six able enough to form the perimeter you ordered and reinforcements are already inbound. Your major called them in. Medics, too. Just the two of you did this?"

"Good work, Sergeant," Kresta replied. "No, there are more than two but you'll never see the others. And these are the local militia. They were instrumental in us winning this fight and lost most of their number. Treat them with due care. There are at least two and maybe three of the Guild soldiers over there" - he pointed to where the unconscious aimers lay - "to be taken into custody. Meanwhile, the captain and I will leave this to you to finish up. And sergeant, we never had this conversation and we were never here. Understood?"

"No, sir," Blakish replied as she surveyed Kresta's advanced armour and weapons. "But if you're ever recruiting, please look me up. I'm betting the locals didn't do as much as you make out."

"I'll keep you in mind," Kresta replied with a slight smile, all but confirming Blakish's assessment.

"Ready," Randall said as he stood. "They'll be okay until the medics get here. Thought we would have civilian medical here by now, but apparently not."

Kresta nodded. He looked over the destroyed building entry and shook his head. The two Warriors picked their way to the back door.

Rodrig watched warily as General Selvis entered the briefing room. The team had been ordered to meet with the general even before they could debrief among themselves. It was only thirty minutes since the Warriors had been lifted off Helios and mere minutes since they had reached the orbiting cruiser. As Selvis walked across the conference room to where the team waited as a unit Rodrig found it hard to read the expression worn by the founder of the Warriors.

Rodrig reflected on the mission just completed. The objective had been to determine whether the movement on Helios to leave the Union was valid, and they had proved that it was not. In doing so, they had validated the use of such a unit using non-military methods. The second objective then, having discovered that the movement was caused by Empire agents, was to nullify them. True, the firefight that brought the end to the mission was not part of the original plan but, having determined that a confrontation was almost assured, the team had moved to use their military skills. The Guild soldiers were all but completely destroyed. Too many members of the militia had been killed, unfortunately, and Rodrig was hurting about the casualties. However, the Warriors had been able to maintain a stealthy presence and withdraw after the fight without being identified, at least publicly, as a Union unit. Their only casualty had been the injury to Anders which had been field dressed - that would heal quickly. But what would General Selvis think? Would the Warriors continue?

The team turned as one to Selvis, subtly shifting to form a tighter group. It was not lost on Selvis and she was forced to stifle the grin that came.

The general was proud of what her team had achieved. She had discussed the mission and its bloody outcome in a video with Admiral Lester and the Chair of the Union Council while the team was en route to the ship. The former was elated with the result. The latter was pleased at the resolution but not so much about the casualty count. Selvis had expressed to both of them her satisfaction with the team for its first mission. She did not fail to note the gleam in Lester's eye as he confirmed that the Warriors would be allowed additional time to prove themselves further.

She already had some ideas for improvement. The mission demonstrated that military skills were needed, but it also confirmed that the intelligence side would be vital. A better relationship with the formal military organisation would be a priority for those times when the situation called for force. That was something that she had discussed when the Warriors were first mooted, and that also had been proven by this mission.

"I have discussed the mission and its outcome with the relevant Union authorities. The media is reporting on how the militia intervened to assist the Union marines to quell a cell of Empire agents that sought to undermine Helios' government. There may be some suspicion that others were involved but so far there have been no reports to that effect. So, I have been authorised to pass on to you all that it has been a job well done."

The team exchanged glances. It was far from a ringing endorsement of the outcome and all awaited the next statement.

"There remains the question of casualties," General Selvis continued evenly. "The Guild had more than fifty personnel, excluding Oreal and his inner circle. There were only three survivors. The so-called militia, who were quite prepared to remove the legal government to assist Oreal, lost seventeen of their twenty-nine members with a further nine severely injured. In addition, the marines lost twelve of their number, including their commanding colonel, and all survivors were injured to some extent. The politicians are worried about that, although the Marines' losses have been put down to their colonel's actions."

The team stared at the general as her dead-pan expression dissolved and the familiar feral grin appeared, causing the tension to dissipate.

"I have no such concerns. Now, we need to use this experience to make us better."

part three

AGENT EXPOSED

380 years before the events described in Children of Ennaris

| 18 |

Drummel Penetrated

"Ansel Mellivar is here to see you," the assistant said into her communicator button.

"Thank you," the CEO of Drummel Industrial replied. "Please escort her to the conference room. And make sure the executive team is assembled."

Max Grellix took a deep breath and stood. He stepped from behind his desk and checked in a mirror hanging beside the door. Everything was in place. This would be a test, he knew, and he was not sure how it would go. Ansel Mellivar had established herself as a significant expert on many aspects of ship design, propulsion, communications and deep space living. She had consulted for the Union Fleet and was responsible for ship design changes that were being implemented across the Fleet to ensure personnel would be able to live in space for lengthy periods, something that was becoming more necessary.

Drummel Industrial had suffered in recent times. The plans left by the original Mellivar, who was a legend in both Drummel Industrial and the Union Fleet, had all been expended. They had led to rapid advances in ship design and, when combined with the work done by two of Mellivar's collaborators, Besnil Barjen and Jamison Dart, had allowed Drummel Industrial to lead the Union in military and, increasingly, civilian vessels designed for both near and deep space. Besnil had retired over a hundred years ago, and Dart not much after that. Drummel, himself, of course, had died well before then. It was only in more recent times that it had become evident just how brilliant that small group had been. Drummel Industrial had introduced no new ships or significantly enhanced capabilities for more than thirty years now. Their competitors were closing rapidly as, ironically, several batches of brilliant young designers and engineers had come to the fore in those competitor companies and were using Mellivar's designs and principles to make their own advances.

And now this one of Mellivar's descendants had descended on Drummel Industrial. The company was very well known across the reach of Union space, of course, and the executives of Drummel Industrial were actively sought for various discussion panels or for expert opinion on a large range of topics. Several were actively involved in Union planning, especially military planning. What most people did not know, Fleet Security aside, was that Drummel Industrial was mostly owned by Ansel Mellivar and a couple of distant relations. On his death, and given that he had no family living by then, Drummel had bequeathed his entire share of the ownership of Drummel Industrial to Mellivar and her descendants in the same proportion as their holdings inherited from Mellivar herself. Famously private, the Mellivar family were the silent power behind the Union Fleet's growth in capability. Rumour also said that one member of the Mellivar family had also been instrumental in establishing the shadowy Warriors of the Light.

Grellix squared his shoulders as he entered the conference room. It was situated atop the main administrative hub for the Drummel shipyard. From its wide window set into the wall opposite the door, one could see the shipyard stretching into the distance on both left and right. Various manufacturing facilities were scattered through the shipyard's expanse, seemingly at random. In reality, they were placed to ensure that components were manufactured as near as could be to the point where they would be used. Standing at the window and looking at the view was a tall woman. She turned as Grellix entered.

He was taken aback by the fierce expression on her face which she quickly replaced with a neutral smile of greeting. Dark hair was brushed back and fell down her back, held at the nape of her neck by a simple clasp. She wore a red tunic that was so dark it approached black, extending just below her hips over tight-fitting black trousers that covered the top of soft black boots. Dark grey eyes set in a lean face bored into Grellix as he approached her. He had the distinct and uncomfortable feeling that he had been stripped bare of any secrets, scrutinised and catalogued in an instant. He took a deep breath to calm his suddenly racing heart and nodded a greeting. He reminded himself that he was CEO of one of the largest industrial companies in the Union, but still he felt unsettled.

"Ms Mellivar, I am very pleased to meet you," Grellix said, gesturing to the large round table that occupied approximately half of the room. "Please, take a seat. My executive team has been asked to join us shortly."

Ansel Mellivar nodded and walked unhurriedly to one of the chairs. Grellix sat in his accustomed place, where he could enjoy an unobstructed view of the shipyard. It had other, hidden benefits, too.

"Is there anything I can arrange for you? A drink, something to eat?"

"Coffee would be very welcome, Mr Grellix. Black, please."

Ansel Mellivar's voice was low and relaxed. She sat back in her chair but Grellix had the impression that she was ready to spring up at any time. He pressed a stud in front of him and asked for two coffees.

"I am impressed by the shipyard," Mellivar said. "I must admit I had not expected something quite so extensive."

"We have the largest shipyard in the sector," Grellix replied, with a nod. "In fact, for several sectors around. Given that we manufacture some of the larger ships here, but also bring several ships at a time in for refits, the size is necessary. And, of course, it has grown in stages. When your … um, ancestor was with Drummel Industrial the shipyard would have been no more than a quarter of the size."

Mellivar nodded politely. "And there were not so many discrete manufacturing units at the time, were there? These units are placed to allow something like a production line to function?"

"Yes, that's right. We take a new ship through several stations, drawing them along the line. Each station does its part in building the ship. The final fit-out sometimes takes place elsewhere but we have the ability to do so here for most of the ships we produce." Grellix considered his next words. "I must admit, I was surprised to hear from you, given that none of Mellivar's descendants have taken that much interest in Drummel over the years since she left."

"Oh, we have taken an interest, Mr Grellix," Mellivar replied in her low, controlled voice. "We have had representatives monitoring what occurs, and we have retained many contacts within the Fleet hierarchy also. I feel I am well informed of the current position of Drummel Industrial."

"Ah," Grellix started to speak and then stopped as two women and a man entered the conference room, followed by a steward carrying a silver tray bearing two fine porcelain cups and a coffee flask. The steward placed the tray on the table between Grellix and Mellivar and then retreated. The door whispered closed.

"Ms Mellivar, I would like to introduce you to my executive team," Grellix said, standing to introduce the newcomers. "This is Millis VanZis, head of design and research, Grevil Hansel, head of materials manufacture, and Ursa Jilbani, our shipyard director."

Mellivar nodded politely to each as they were introduced. Millis VanZis was a woman of average height, with pale brown hair cut short, pale blue eyes and pale coloured face and hands. She nodded politely as she took a seat beside Grellix. Grevil Hansel was a tall, strongly built man, with dark, sharp features, almost jet black hair that framed his long face and an intense expression. He also nodded in greeting, a short, sharp action, and took a chair on the other side of Grellix. Ursa Jilbani was the second woman. She was short and lean with hair the colour of pale straw falling to just below her shoulders. She smiled a greeting to Mellivar and then deliberately moved to take a chair alongside her.

"I'll sit over here, if you don't mind," Jilbani said in a mild voice with a slight accent that Mellivar could not place. "Otherwise it looks like a panel interview, and I doubt that's why you're here."

"I must admit I have been intrigued at why you are here," VanZis said. "I have never known a member of your family to take much of an interest in Drummel."

"Ms Mellivar was just telling me that she and her family have, in fact, maintained a keen interest in Drummel for quite some time," Grellix commented. "Why is it that such interest has not been satisfied by direct contact with myself or my predecessors."

"Oh, some of your predecessors were aware of us," Mellivar said with a smile. "Especially when things were not quite where they needed to be. And we have been kept informed of progress on a regular basis. As I said, we have had resources within Drummel for the entire time, and many in Fleet who have kept us apprised."

"That sounds rather like we have a security problem," Grellix said with a slight edge to his voice. "And I'm not sure I like having such information leaving my company without me being aware of it."

"Nor would I," Mellivar replied. "But let's be very clear, Mr Grellix. This is not your company. It is mine."

The blunt statement took the wind out of Grellix, and caused VanZis and Hansel to glance at each other, while Jilbani only smiled. Grellix hesitated for a moment and was about to speak again when the door hissed open and another man entered. This man was of middle height and slightly heavyset but did not give the impression of being over-weight.

"I apologise for being late," he said into the quiet following Mellivar's statement. "There was a problem I needed to deal with."

"This is Mark Harvik, our head of security," Grellix said in a tense voice. "Mark, Ms Mellivar was just telling us that she gets regular reports from someone in the employ of Drummel Industrial, as well as from Fleet."

"I did not say it was from someone in Drummel's employ, Mr Grellix," Mellivar said evenly. "I said we are kept informed and have agents that monitor events that occur here."

Harvik glanced from Grellix to Mellivar, and then nodded thoughtfully. He pulled out a chair and sat. He extracted a small datapad from his pocket and placed it on the desk in front of him, considered for a moment and then tapped out a short sequence. The datapad lit up. He tapped a few more times, examining what came up and then nodded.

"A monthly report, usually on the fifteenth of each month, via an encrypted packet that is routed through a series of anonymous nodes," Harvik said as he looked up from the datapad to Mellivar, eyebrows raised in mute query.

Mellivar smiled and nodded, while Grellix stared, stunned, and VanZis shook her head.

"Yes, the AI sends me an update of the most pertinent events each month," Mellivar said. "Very good. I was sure that was buried very deep."

"Oh, it was," Harvik agreed as he tapped a final sequence on his datapad and looked up at Mellivar. "But six months ago we had a glitch in one of our primary nodes, nothing significant but we took the opportunity to upgrade it significantly and all but a few routines had to be rebuilt. This was one of the few that didn't need it, and it was reset automatically, which made me curious. All the others had to have some form of redesign but this one was fully up to date without any intervention. So I traced into it a bit and finally found what it was doing. It's very clever," he concluded, nodding his approval.

Grellix turned to Harvik. "Can you delete or disable it?"

"Oh, you don't want to do that, Mr Grellix," Mellivar replied.

"Why not? I don't appreciate having everything I do spied on." Grellix almost snarled at Mellivar, his complete change in demeanour surprising the other executives.

"Because all of your systems would be wiped if you did," Mellivar said coolly, "after transferring the contents of certain systems to my own storage nodes, of course."

Grellix stared again while Harvik just nodded as though that was the most logical thing one would do. The others looked on nonplussed.

"Which brings me to the main reason for me being here," Mellivar replied. "I will be joining the company as CEO."

Grellix started and stood. His face was suffused with fury.

"You can't do that!" he shouted. "I was appointed by the Board of the company and you can't replace me at your whim."

"Oh, it's not my whim, Grellix, and in any event I *am* the Board," Mellivar said calmly. "I am doing that. You can't stop me."

"And you expect me to just walk out of here quietly?" Grellix shouted. "You have no idea how loud I can be. Your reputation will be nothing when I'm through with you."

"No, I don't expect you to just walk out of here," Mellivar said with an edge to her voice for the first time. "You will be in prison."

Harvik watched the scene impassively while both VanZis and Hansel looked stunned. Too much had happened in a short time for them to take in easily. Jilbani, once again, only wore a slight smile. Grellix, on the other hand, stood abruptly and stalked to a cabinet and flung open the door, reaching for what most in the room thought would be a liquor bottle, of which there were several. Instead, he pushed open a hidden compartment in the cabinet top and pulled out a small blaster.

"No, I don't think I'll be going to prison," Grellix sneered in triumph, "but you'll be dead and I'll be far away from here."

"No," Mellivar said. "Fleet security is already outside that door. You are going nowhere."

She pressed a stud on her collar and immediately the door swung open, revealing a man and a woman in the black uniform of Union Fleet security. The two officers walked into the room, drawing their own weapons when they saw Grellix holding one. With a snarl, Grellix backed to the wall of the room. He pushed his free hand against the wall panel. Nothing happened. Again he pressed, and a third time.

"Yes, your escape route has been disabled," Mellivar said. "And even if it were not, your escape vessel has been impounded."

Grellix turned the blaster on Mellivar and held down the trigger. Nothing happened.

"And security located your hidden blaster and disabled it, too."

"Ah, that would have been during that security review we had last week?" Harvik asked, seemingly unperturbed by what was occurring.

"Yes," Mellivar replied, gesturing to the two security people. "Captain Sanders here had been informed of the situation and she made sure the place was examined in fine detail during that inspection."

"I thought they had been here for a little too long," Harvik nodded.

"Max Grellix," Captain Sanders said in a low, confident voice. "We are arresting you for being an agent of the Empire. Put the weapon down, stand still and place your hands behind your back."

Grellix reached down and placed the useless blaster on the floor but, instead of standing still, he pulled a wicked-looking needle knife from a sheath in his boot and leapt at Mellivar. However, where she had been sitting calmly a few seconds earlier, now Mellivar was on her feet. She deflected Grellix's knife strike and with a blur of movement spun Grellix away and against the wall. He bounced off and staggered slightly. For a moment it looked like he might give up, but then he crouched and pulled out a second needle knife from his other boot. Mellivar sighed in resignation. He would not go easily and they needed him alive to find out if he was alone or if there was a full enemy cell in Drummel Industrial. She stood calmly, waiting for Grellix to make a move. Looking around briefly, she saw that the four Drummel executives had moved to huddle against the wall as far from the fight as they could be. Harvik stood in front of the other three as a shield. Mellivar nodded in approval as she turned back.

As she had hoped, Grellix assumed that she had been distracted and took the opportunity to attack. He swung into a complicated set of movements that saw the razor sharp knives weave a lethal barrier in front of Mellivar. Mellivar waited, stepping back cautiously and allowing Grellix to advance. Watching her opponent's hands closely, Mellivar chose her moment and dropped her hands from their defensive posture for a moment, as though tiring. Grellix's eyes blazed in triumph as he pressed harder, his hands moving at dazzling speed, the two needle knives appearing to leave faint traces as they cut the air. Mellivar continued to back away, drawing Grellix further from his apparent escape route. The seemingly one-sided fight had moved and was against the broad window, with the large conference table between the combatants and the others. The two Fleet security agents watched events, holding their own blasters in hand, but prepared to wait for the outcome, as they had been instructed.

Mellivar stopped retreating. In a single movement, she crouched and flung herself up, spinning above and behind Grellix, almost brushing the high ceiling, to land softly. Grellix spun and stopped abruptly. Mellivar now held two short sword hilts which she held as extensions to her arms, held at forty-five degrees from the straight line formed by her torso. As the watchers gasped, the two hilts flared into life and slender blades of energy extended from the hilts. Grellix snarled and leapt to attack, his knives once again weaving their pattern. Now, however, Mellivar moved to meet his advance. Her swords flashed in their own pattern, learnt millennia before. Needle knives met slender swords in a continuous series of clashes, too close together for individual sounds to be identified easily. The two stood almost toe to toe. Grellix went from feeling certain triumph to uncertainty as Mellivar blocked his every stroke and strike with apparent ease. Her expression was one of concentration but not fear. Rather, she expressed utter confidence. Uncertainty, however, did become fear for Grellix as Mellivar increased the speed of her movements. Grellix now had to defend as the twin swords moved inexorably faster, and it was he who started to back away. Desperation replaced fear.

Suddenly, Grellix stepped back half a pace and fell to one knee, lunging forward with both knives under the arc of Mellivar's swords.

One of the knives was jammed into Mellivar's thigh while the other struck her in the lower torso. Grellix's grin of victory over this most difficult of opponents was short lived. The first knife wound seemed to be ignored, and the second knife strike was deflected by some sort of shield. Grellix looked up into Mellivar's face to find it expressionless. Then he felt the pain. He looked back down to find both swords had pierced his own body up to their hilts. Mellivar stood quite still despite her blood running freely from the thigh wound. Grellix tried to stand but could not. Instead, Mellivar rolled him onto his side, deactivating the swords as she did. Blood welled from his wounds and pooled around him on the floor of the conference room. His last sight was of Mellivar standing over him with the stubby sword hilts extended at forty-five degrees once again.

Captain Sanders was already calling her team in as backup, while Harvik opened a small cabinet and extracted a medpack. He ripped it open and tossed the pack to the second of the Fleet Security agents. Mellivar slapped the sword hilts into thin sheaths that extended down the legs of her trousers. The swords and sheaths faded from sight. With a grimace Mellivar pulled the needle knife from her thigh and collapsed into a chair.

"These were new boots," she complained to Captain Sanders. "Now look at them."

"It's your fault for not finishing him earlier," Sanders said. "Hills, get that medpack on her."

Hills, the second security officer, pulled the bandage sachet from the medpack and slapped it over the wound. The sachet split open and the bandage arranged itself in a swathe of filaments that extended through the cut in Mellivar's trousers and into the wound. A fast-acting anaesthetic was released at the same time and Mellivar sighed as the pain retreated.

"The team will be here shortly," Sanders told Mellivar. "We already have Grellix's office sealed off and will start to examine it but I doubt we'll find anything there."

"Very well. I will leave that to you." Mellivar looked to where the four Drummel executives stood. All but Harvik still looked stunned by what had happened. "Harvik, would you find another conference room for us please? Then I want all four of you to wait there for me. Do not speak to anyone. It is time this company started to move forward again."

| 19 |

Superstar

"Is everyone clear about what will happen?" Ansel Mellivar asked. The key executives of Drummel Industrial and their immediate subordinates were all gathered in a hanger, which was part of the docking facilities below the conference room where Mellivar had confronted Grellix two weeks earlier. All were standing around a small low stage on which Mellivar stood. In front of her was a holographic table, and above it was a holograph showing several ships and components. There were many glum and dispirited faces in the crowd. She waited until finally there were nods all around.

"Some of you appear uncertain. To make it absolutely clear, I will repeat. Drummel Industrial has been infiltrated by Empire agents, with Max Grellix at the head of the cell. Fleet Security has identified a further five members of what we expect to be a fairly small number of Empire agents. As a result, security within Drummel will be stepped up. Also as a result, it is expected that several of the most secret developments of the last few years have been made available to the Empire. We can expect them to adapt their own ships and tactics to negate those developments." She waited a moment to make sure her repeated statements sank in. "Any questions so far?"

"Do you think the whole cell has been identified?" Harvik asked from one side.

"We can't be sure," Mellivar said, nodding to Harvik to acknowledge the right question being asked at the right time. "But Fleet Security has their best people working on it. If there are other agents, then they will have left some sort of trail and it will be found."

Of course, *Fendaristil* was also on the case. It was *Fendaristil* that had raised the alert in the first place, and then had used Drummel's internal security as the channel to Fleet Security.

Millis VanZis raised a hand to which Mellivar nodded.

"I guess one thing we all need to know is what changes will be made here," she said, gesturing at the group of people surrounding her. "Many of us have been at Drummel for years, but I'm guessing we're all stained by association with Grellix."

"You are correct," Mellivar replied, raising her hand at gasps of dismay. "However, the fact that you were taken in by an Empire agent is not your fault. In fact, it was a report from within Drummel that first alerted Fleet Security to the possibility of there being something wrong here. No, I won't tell you who it was, but I know the name and I am most grateful. So, what we're going to do is work to understand what has been exposed, and then make better ships, weapons, sensors."

Mellivar pointed at the holographic display and continued, "These are the designs we believe may have been compromised, based on research to date. I want to know if there are others. Harvik, I want you to coordinate with each department head to work out a plan to track down any form of unusual communication going out from Drummel. Except mine," she added with a small smile.

Harvik nodded.

"Next, we will assume these are compromised, which means the Union Fleet's capabilities may be damaged. So far, only seventeen of the revised Star-class cruisers have been delivered to the Union Fleet. After discussing the situation with the head of Fleet Logistics, we have decided to halt work on that design. Instead, we will use the same base design and evolve and upgrade it, including retro-fitting the existing Star-class ships."

Ursa Jilbani, the shipyard director, frowned. "We have seven hulls laid down and in various stages of completion. There are the seventeen current generation Star-class ships out there but we also have, ah" - she paused while tapping her datapad - "seventy-four earlier generations still in service, a few going back to the ones designed by Mellivar and Besnil." She shook her head as she realised she was speaking to another Mellivar. "I mean the first Mellivar. Anyway, they were to be rotated through to see which could be updated and which would be better being scrapped. Some of them have been in service for well over a hundred years."

"And that program won't stop," Mellivar said. "The hulls under development will be fitted with the new design components. Several of them may need to be modified or have some elements removed again, but most will be able to remain as they are while the new components go through testing and manufacture. Then the program of refits will continue."

"How long will that take, though, for the new designs to come through? We'll also need the yards to be ready for repairs and other ship modifications, so we risk creating a large backlog." Jilbani frowned again. "We probably need those uprated design in two weeks or less if possible."

Mellivar smiled and gestured to Millis VanZis.

"We - and by that I mean Ansel mostly - have the next generation design ready," VanZis said briskly and tapped a button on the holographic display table.

The display changed from the image of the compromised designs to a new one. The same basic Star-class ship was shown, but the experienced eyes of the Drummel Industrial team were drawn to a number of different features. Excited comments and gestures told the story.

"Is that a holographic projector on the bridge?"

"That looks like a redesigned power grid. Why do we need that?"

"Five, no, six key weapons turrets!"

"What's happening to the comms array, it looks like - oh my…"

"The engine bay is wider. What's that second drive assembly?"

VanZis allowed the excited comments to wind down.

"I'd like to take credit for some of this but almost all of this is from Mellivar," she said, gesturing to Mellivar while the assembled group looked from one to the other, "and the rest is based on what she brought with her also. The new Star-class generation will have an uprated primary drive, supported by an enhanced primary power grid. The secondary power grid will provide additional energy to the engines if necessary, but will be largely used to power the weapons arrays. Yes, we will have holographic displays for some of the bridge functions, but not all. The most critical bridge functions will retain traditional hardware controls but they will have ancillary functions via holographic extensions. Mellivar has been able to get the power requirements for the holographic emitters to be only slightly more than a normal panel display. That, in itself, will revolutionise several aspects of Union technology."

"Not to mention home theatres," someone interjected from the group, to general laughter.

Mellivar smiled as some of the tension was released. "Perhaps we can open a new division," she quipped.

VanZis continued as a few chuckles died out. "Weapons are up-graded. Pulse cannons are evolutions of the existing design, with more power per pulse available, greater range and greater accuracy thanks to better targeting systems. Recharge time is shorter, too. We will have hybrid torpedoes launched from four forward tubes but will be adding two tubes each to port and starboard. Each of the torpedo tubes will be part of a weapons cluster. They are those weapons tur-rets you saw, Herris," she said, nodding to the man who had com-mented on them. "There will be better defensive arrays able to fling more pellets into the defensive arc in faster time and some electronic counter-measures we will discuss in the detail sessions."

"Communications?" one of the women asked.

"Yep, a slightly different array," VanZis nodded. "We have the usual tri-band array for planetary and in-systems communications, and we also have an uprated sublight transmitter."

"But what's that third one?" the same woman asked, pointing to the communications arrays behind the bridge area that showed three distinct elements.

"Oh that," VanZis said as though it were of no consequence. She paused for a dramatic moment before continuing, "That's for the faster-than-light comms array."

There was a moment of quiet before the words sunk in. Then a hubbub erupted once again, quelled after a minute by VanZis raising her hand.

"Yes, an FTL array. That second engine mount is for an greatly up-rated FTL drive, and so we will need to have the ability to communicate to and from a ship in FTL."

"But the size of the ship! It's too big for sustained FTL," a shocked team member said into the sudden quiet.

"It was," VanZis replied. "Apparently Mellivar has been working on the design for this engine for some time."

"We have redesigned the FTL engine that is used for short jumps only so far. It now uses less power and generates a much more stable field that supports larger vessels," Mellivar said, stepping forward once again. "Much larger but it still supports our smaller ships. So, many of the current fleet of patrol and mid-size ships will be able to carry them. It allows sustained FTL flight. It has been tested and proven to work. That will, therefore, need better navigation arrays and sensors, systems upgrades to control them, and training programs. All things you will be doing."

VanZis nodded once again. "So, ship design, communications, sensors, weapons systems, even better plumbing and medical, as well as engine upgrades and control systems. And while we've been discussing the Star-class, most of these elements will be available for upgrading those smaller ships Mellivar mentioned, the non-Drummel ones. Even the shuttles will get upgrades from all of this. This will revolutionise the Union fleet."

Grevil Hansel stepped forward slightly and asked, "Is there anything for the materials side of things? It kind of feels like we're missing out on things."

There were a few disconsolate nods from several of the team members assembled. Mellivar nodded.

"I've not had the chance to speak with you, Grevil," Mellivar said, "but yes, there are changes required. We have a new composite for use on interior surfaces that will resist some of the forces that will be encountered under sustained FTL. And the exterior tolerances will have to be tightened again. We have a new nano-coating of the hull surfaces to withstand some of those pressures but also to protect the crew from radiation better than the current coating. The weapons will need a more refined alloy and there are one or two new materials to assist. And the sensors will need to have much finer components, with a further refinement of the sensors themselves."

Mellivar looked around the gathered people who represented the leaders of Drummel Industrial. These would be the people who would lead the next jump in capability.

"This is a whole of company effort. Everyone will be involved. I will take the CEO role for the immediate future. There will be greater security, as I mentioned, and we may uncover additional agents. This is going to be the jump in capability to take the Union up to and hopefully beyond the current abilities of the Empire ships. We will be licensing parts of the designs to other shipyards but we will be making most of the components under the tightest security and the strictest manufacturing methods you have ever seen. You don't mention any of this outside Drummel. Any breaches will be dealt with harshly, I am afraid." She smiled at the nods that were given by many of the group. "So, let's get to it."

The group dispersed with smiles instead of the glum and dejected expressions that had met Mellivar at the start of the meeting. There were excited, though whispered, conversations as the members of the group dispersed. The aura of hope and refreshed spirits that pervaded the group was pleasing to see. She hoped they could deliver.

Marjory entered the bridge and flopped into her chair.

"So," *Fendaristil* said. "How did it go?"

"As if you don't know," Marjory snorted. "I know you were listening in."

"Yes, but that's all I could do. That Harvik is good! He isolated the video feeds and has started on hardening the audio as well. I had to use one of the back-channels we set up to hear anything at all."

"Well, I think they all felt more engaged than they were at the start," Marjory said, rubbing a hand over her face. "I think they can do what is needed."

"Are you sure about handing over these designs?" *Fendaristil* queried. "They were to be held back for some time yet."

"Yes, but uncovering agents at the very top of Drummel was a shock," Marjory replied. "Likud has identified one of his key threats, it seems. It means that the Union may have to grow capability faster than planned. The main thing now will be to make sure that they don't decide to challenge Likud directly with their new strength. It will take some time for the Fleet to reach such a level so I have time to plan how to deal with that possibility."

"But the new ships, especially the biggest ones still to come, will almost be on a level with the last of the Ennari warships. I thought the idea was that we would be able to defeat them if we needed to do so."

Marjory nodded slowly. "That was the plan, yes. Plans change when they need to, and this one needs to adapt as we go along. I have been surprised that we managed to get this far with that plan largely intact."

"So, what's first?"

"As usual, we need to make sure the existing Fleet vessels can stand against the Empire ships. As they probably do have the designs for the shields and sensors, those are first things to upgrade. Engines come next but work on that must start immediately. It will take much longer because of the manufacturing changes needed. Fuel production needs to be altered slightly also, but that will be simple. Then weapons. And then we start with the next generation of ships."

"You have built in some safeguards, I gather?"

"Yes," Marjory replied with a faint smile. "We will lock the more advanced capabilities for the time being. The ship AIs all have base level commands to hand over control to an Ennari controller with the right command code. And I will be building that control capability into the new ships, as well as a full capability release. It will be inactive by default. The hard part will be hiding some of the newer components. That's why we also need to build more automation into the shipbuilding process. I don't want too many eyes seeing some parts of the builds."

Almost three years later, Mellivar stood at the large conference room window with Grevil Hansen, watching as the first panel of the new hull material rolled off the production line. Eight robotic thrusters grasped the huge expanse of armoured composite and slowly moved it towards the waiting shipyard. Partially revealed within the construction dock were the bones of a large ship, the first of the Stellar class battleships, almost akin to an old Ennari light cruiser. Slowly, carefully, the robots positioned the hull plate and came to a halt. Great arms extended from the surrounding gantries and the plate was gripped and gently positioned against the waiting spars. A swarm of construction robots sped into the yard and applied the advanced bonding agents to the plate and the spars to which it was to be joined. A dizzying dance ensued as the construction robots spun, dipped and darted from place to place, each with its own role to play. Four hours after the plate was hauled from the manufactory, the construction robots swarmed away again, back to their housings to await their next task. The new plate, which had looked so large when it moved past the watchers, appeared to be a tiny patch on the giant shell of what would be the largest ship ever built for the Union fleet.

"One down," Grevil Hansen said with satisfaction. "Lots more to go, but the first one is always the best to see done."

Mellivar nodded pensively as she watched the second plate being manoeuvred from the manufactory and start its journey to the shipyard. The nearly three years since she had assumed control of Drummel Industrial had been both pleasing and frustrating. It was pleasing because she could see her plan coming together. It was frustrating because Drummel Industrial had grown so large that managing it was both time-consuming and difficult. She itched to be back on Ennaris. By her count, Trabor would be revived now and her loss would be noted. It would not be long before Drewflin would be brought out of stasis to be confronted with her long absence. It was likely that he would have no alternative but to believe her to be dead. She shivered at the thought.

"Mellivar, are you alright?" Hansen asked with a frown of concern.

"Oh, yes," Mellivar replied, making the effort to shake off the weight of her thoughts. "And I agree that it is satisfying to see the start of a new ship. We have a long way to go yet, though."

"But the start is key," Hansen said, turning back to watch through the window. "Only once started can progress be made."

Progress there had been, Marjory mused, even as she nodded agreement. The first change had been to radically upgrade the sensors. She had held back only the most advanced technology that Ennaris had produced, plus an upgrade that she had designed but had never tested just before the rebellion started. Union vessels would have better short and long range sensors than any ships except the most advanced from Ennaris, and they no longer existed. In addition, they would be able to track disturbances in the strange dimensional space that allowed faster-than-light, or FTL, travel to occur. The disturbance was akin to the bow wave caused by a water-borne vessel and these sensors could identify and track them in the hands of an expert operator. The program to refit as many of the Union fleet as could take them would last many years but a start had been made.

The new uprated control systems had taken the Union segment of space by storm. The holographic controls had been tested extensively by several very sceptical Union spacers and been found to outperform the hardware versions. Still, there remained a core concern about holographic controls and decisions had been made to trial them but to maintain corresponding hardware versions. It was of little concern to Marjory, but the advance had put Drummel in the media spotlight. Strangely, the joke about home theatres had come true and prices for reduced-function holographic projectors were already falling into the realm of affordable for many people. Drummel had spun off a separate company to deal with the demand and licensed the technology to several trusted partners.

The communications array had been more problematic. The power distribution on the most recent group of over a hundred Union vessels was found to have been changed from the original designs of Mellivar and Besnil, which meant that it would not support the additional drain of the new array. The changes were subtle but clear once the new components were fitted. Closer examination showed that those ships stood a better than even chance of losing power without warning. Not only was the power grid on the ships insufficient, but several components had been manufactured to lower tolerances than designed. It was Grellix's influence without a doubt. It would be a program lasting well over ten years to refit those ships, and in the meanwhile their crews would have to be on guard against power failure every time they took them out. After three of the affected ships had failed at inopportune times and been destroyed with all hands, the Union Fleet decided to merely use them in controlled Union space. That reduced the Union's capabilities. Drummel's shipyards now had a permanent list of docked ships awaiting the refit.

Despite that setback, Drummel Industrial had moved to the fore of Union design once again. Its manufacturing processes were now so advanced that Marjory decided to start the final phase of shipbuilding earlier than she had planned. This would see the Union move to a position where its largest capital ships would outgun most of the Empire's largest vessels. She left the details of upgrading as many of the existing Fleet vessels as possible to VanZis and Jilbani, as well as the next generation of Drummel management, and concentrated on bringing to life the Superstar class of battleship. For these, she had special plans, for they would be the second last class of starship that she planned to build, and on these ships she believed the future of the Union would depend.

Marjory sighed softly, partly in satisfaction and partly in resignation. Seven years of design and planning had led to the moment that she now shared with Millis VanZis. They stood at the observation window in the conference room atop Drummel Industrial's headquarters, the same spot where she had stood with Grevil Hansen four years earlier. This time the occasion was that fitment of the first of the hull panels to the first Superstar-class ship, dubbed SS One by the design team but already named *Starmaster* by whoever in the Union Fleet came up with ridiculous names for starships.

This class of vessel would not be built in large volume. The quantity of material required to construct the ship was enormous, for the ship was huge when compared to the older Star-class vessels. Almost twice the length and half again as wide and tall, the Superstar ships were explicitly designed to combat and defeat the Empire's newest heavy capital ships.

First seen fifteen years before, these Empire ships were massive, very ugly to Marjory's eyes but more powerful than any vessel then in use in either Union or Empire space. Likud's hand was obvious to Marjory. There was nothing of grace about these ships. They were built to kill, purely and simply. The images gleaned from engagement reports showed what looked like a gigantic rectangular hull, long and flat, with squared bows and a huge superstructure riding above it towards the rear. The engines that pushed it were equally massive, extruding well behind the main hull as though the designers could not work out how to integrate the two elements which, Marjory surmised when she examined the images, was likely to be the case.

Weapons systems bristled from all parts of the ship. Stretching along the length of the flat sides were pods and blisters that held offensive and defensive weapons. On top and bottom of the flat hull were more of the weapons pods as well as enormous mounts, one on each of the top and bottom of the hull, with huge energy cannons that seemed to be able to swivel to fire in wide arcs. Torpedo or missile tubes were spread down both flanks facing fore and aft. Most intriguing, though, was a huge array of emitters of some sort. Marjory suspected that Likud had tried to build a planet buster and was using a staggering number of energy weapons to act in tandem. The power drain of the weapons systems would be enormous, which partly explained the massive size of the engines that spewed masses of spent fuel ions in a glowing trail behind the ship. It would not be fast off the mark or nimble, but the fire power was truly monumental. Marjory did not want to face the monstrosity in a one-on-one fight. This would have to be a fleet engagement.

Drummel Industrial's new Superstar class was designed to survive against Likud's latest behemoth, but in a very Ennari fashion. Sleek and clean lines were reminiscent of an Ennari killer leviathan, although only Marjory knew that, and played down its immense fire power. Marjory had brought to bear almost all of the technology that she planned to share with the Union. One or two pieces were held back for future developments but most were on display here. Or not on display, rather, for much was hidden. The most advanced long and short range sensors were installed, and every component on the ship that was needed to make it an effective fighting force was backed by triple redundancies. Physical torpedoes were gone for the first time in a Union vessel. Instead, plasma ejectors based on those in *Fendaristil* had been installed behind screens above and below the blunt-nosed bow, although Seema emitters remained off limits. Missile tubes ran down the length of the gracefully curved sides of the ship and the defensive cannon emplacements were flush to the hull but able to extend to better target incoming missiles or torpedoes. The capital weapons were four large cannons that could not be hidden but appeared to flow from the upper hull. They were not as massive as the two on top and bottom of the Empire ship's hull but Marjory suspected that they were equal to the energy output. Eye-catching as they were, though, those guns were not the only primary armament for this ship. A series of small railguns were mounted along the dorsal and ventral lines to supplement the energy-based defensive weapons, and a single large railgun was placed in the nose behind a hatch. This was much larger than any railgun known to date and was capable of longer and more rapid fire than any previous design. In this design, it still would run hot after a relatively small number of shots but it could fire a greater number of larger projectiles faster and further, and with greater energy and thus greater velocity, than any other railgun.

Equally important for the ship's survival was the most advanced shield system installed in a Union ship. While Marjory continued to refine her designs, the overlapping energy shields of this ship would stop or deflect anything that was known to be in the Empire's armoury. Whether its new monster had something new was yet to be tested, but Marjory believed that the Union would have a vessel capable of standing against the best the Empire could throw at them.

Finally, the engines were enormously powerful. They were not as massive as the Empire ship, but nor would they look like an afterthought being welded to the back of the ship. They were as advanced as any Ennari vessel that Marjory knew of, and had some additional refinements that Marjory adapted from the work Besnil had done, which had been adaptations of the original Ennaris design. The ship would accelerate rapidly at sub-light speed and could make the jump to FTL faster than any other Union ship to date.

So, Marjory mused as she watched panel after panel be drifted from the manufactory and fitted to the hull, this was almost the last of the advances she had planned for the main Union fleet. She was satisfied. It had taken less time than she had planned to get to this point. So far, the Union had not tried to overplay its hand and she was confident that the current leadership would be equally as smart in its dealings with member planets and those with whom it had dealings from other civilisations.

She had been out of stasis for thirty-five Earth years by now, and the last fifteen had been spent back at Drummel Industrial. It was time she left again. She would make sure this new ship worked as she thought it would, and then she and *Fendaristil* would find somewhere relatively close to hide.

| 20 |

Ambush

Well, Marjory thought to herself, the plan *had* been a good one. *Starmaster* had been launched with more pomp and ceremony than she was comfortable with, the inevitable teething issues had been ironed out, mostly before the launch, and the ship was in service. Drummel Industrial had a blend of the trusted old executives and new managers selected by Marjory, and the plan for the next thirty to fifty years had been laid down. A small number of improvements had been suggested by the design department which Marjory had approved and then promptly promoted the designer who had come up with them. Additional advances had been made in the construction of *Starmaster* to the control systems, holographic emitters and a range of conduit and circuit components, all intended to harden them against various forms of kinetic, energy and EMP attack. Again, the people who had come up with them were rewarded. The next generation were put into positions where they would take over Drummel Industrial inside ten years. More remained to be done but the main ships of the Union Fleet would be able to hold their own now.

So Marjory had made her exit once again. After informing Fleet Security that she was leaving - otherwise a major search would ensue - she called her staff together and announced the future vision and the fact that she would not lead it. She was surprised at the level of dismay her announcement had caused, even tears in some quarters. Marjory had made sure that her staff had been well supported, of course, because that was just good management, but she had never seen herself as a warm and friendly type. In fact, she saw herself as the opposite - at the weapons design centre at Escantil she was called *argenpellar*, although not to her face. That translated roughly into the Union Standard equivalent of Iron Heart. Battle Mages, as a rule, did not display significant emotional intelligence, or not openly at least. Apparently, though, some of her actions were seen by the more sentimental of the team as evidence of emotional attachment which, she thought as she brushed a hand across eyes that had become slightly misty for some reason, was ridiculous.

Now, however, having made her way out of the well-trafficked lanes of the Union, she had come across more evidence of Empire infiltration of the Union. It could only be that, she thought, and it could only be in Fleet Security, as she had provided a broad idea of her initial course to them and not to any at Drummel. How else to explain the three ships that had swept up on her in what she had to admit was quite a good display of piloting. They had been laying in wait across the most likely path for her course to take, which may mean that others were waiting on other potential paths. If that was the case, then there may be more of them arriving shortly. Of course, she had not been taken unawares.

"Battle Mage," *Fendaristil* had broken into her thoughts as she had mapped out a convoluted path to her intended place of temporary exile, "there are three vessels lurking in the asteroid field that we are approaching."

"Lurking?" Marjory queried as she reviewed the long range sensors and noted the ships' positions. "Have you been reading those dreadful Earth novels again?"

"Union Standard has some very useful words," *Fendaristil* replied without directly answering the question. "I particularly like 'lurking', though. It has a feel on your tongue that invokes dim light and dark clothes and people partially hiding behind lamp posts."

"You don't have a tongue," Marjory retorted, "and you have never seen an old Earth lamp post."

She brought up the schematics of the three vessels that *Fendaristil* had been examining as they moved towards the asteroid field. Two of the ships were heavily modified in-system shuttles and the third was a small freighter. All were fitted with older Drummel Industrial engines, but that was not something to be surprised about. Drummel's engines were used in many ships built by rival shipyards. What was a surprise were the two externally mounted missile tubes and the small railguns that each vessel carried as primary armament.

"Nevertheless," *Fendaristil* continued, "there are some words in Union Standard that we should bring back to Ennaris. The three ships are moving."

"I see them," Marjory said, fingers dancing over the holographic control interface as she and *Fendaristil* readied the ship. "And I am pretty sure that we have enough words that have similar meanings."

"Yes, but they don't sound as evocative," *Fendaristil* demurred while placing target reticules on each ship. "Do you want to evade, catch or kill, Battle Mage?"

"Catch, I think," Marjory replied. "Only Fleet Security knew we were coming this way. I am sure of that. And that means someone in Fleet Security gave that information away. Are the ships communicating to each other or anyone else?"

"Not that I can see," *Fendaristil* replied after an infinitesimal pause to run a further check. "There was a pulse before they started to move but nothing since."

"Probably just coordinating. But keep an eye out in case there are others covering other possible routes. That may have been a call for reinforcements."

"Nothing on long range sensors, but I will monitor for the usual indicators," *Fendaristil* said. "We are being scanned."

"Whose sensors?"

"It would appear they are using sensors licensed by Drummel Industrial to Jallas Space Technologies," *Fendaristil* said as specifications for the sensors popped onto the display screen in one corner.

"Very well. Make sure we don't look like anything other than a small yacht. When they get about half way here disable their sensors."

Marjory, as the first Mellivar, had made it a rule that any licensed technology was made to use Drummel Industrial firmware, which most licensees liked as they enjoyed similar capabilities to Drummel's equipment and were not put to the expense of writing their own control software. That rule had been enforced rigorously across the years, and had proven to be very profitable. What no-one, even in Drummel Industrial, had realised was that there was a control sequence that allowed someone with the right command codes to disable or take over the licensed tech, in this case the sensors. Marjory, and thus *Fendaristil*, was the someone who had the right codes.

"Coming within range," *Fendaristil* replied. "They are targeting us."

"Anything for us to worry about?" Marjory asked as the main screen showed the three vessels closing on *Fendaristil*.

"I doubt it. The missiles appear to use standard high yield explosive rather than nuclear or plasma warheads and the railguns are from Kenda Systems and likely propel light-weight pellets that we should be able to deflect. There is a shielded energy weapon somewhere in the converted freighter. The specifications suggest it will have to be in the cargo bay, as there is no other space large enough."

"How many people?"

"I am unable to get a firm fix yet," *Fendaristil* replied. "Standard crew for the shuttles would be pilot and co-pilot although each can carry six passengers on that class. The freighter crew complement would be five. However, the modifications for the shuttles to reach inter-stellar space are likely to mean the passenger compartment is less functional."

"Let me know when you get a count," Marjory said. "No hail yet?"

"Not yet. They are on an approach vector to encircle us, two from the front and one from the rear. Their weapons are powered and missiles have targeting solutions. I have screens ready to deploy. My weapons are powered but not yet deployed."

Fendaristil, Marjory knew, could deploy and fire the main weapons in an eye-blink, while the shields would stand up to enormous punishment. Marjory had continued to tinker with the shields for most of the time that she had been away from Ennaris. If nothing else it passed the time, but it was a key technology that protected rather than destroyed. Despite the fact that she had designed any number of ways to destroy things and people, and that she quite possibly was the most lethal person in the galaxy, she always came back to seeking ways to protect others. That did not necessarily include the ones about to attack her.

"The ships have small crew complements based on life sign scans," *Fendaristil* reported. "The freighter has three, one shuttle has two and the second shuttle has three. I am shutting down their sensors now."

The freighter was one of the two ships to approach from the front. There was a small wobble as the sensors shut down and the pilot found himself flying blind. At the same time the two shuttles slowed slightly but did not deviate from their course.

"Their sensors are down but their targeting systems are tracking us. They must be independent."

"Engage the cloak and move us above them," Marjory ordered.

Fendaristil disappeared from sensor view and gently moved above the plane of attack by the three ships. Marjory watched with interest as the converted freighter rotated and the cargo bay doors opened towards where *Fendaristil* had been.

"The shield has dropped from the energy weapon. It is a plasma cannon, power signature similar to Empire weapons."

"Could that hurt us with the shield modifications we have been making?" Marjory asked.

"Possibly," *Fendaristil* replied. "We have not tested the latest changes against such a weapon."

"Very well," Marjory shrugged to herself, resigned. "Target the two shuttles and then move us above the freighter."

Fendaristil made no reply. In moments its main energy cannon had been deployed and four energy bolts had been dispatched. The two shuttles disappeared in separate bursts, clearing to reveal clouds of debris swirling around the ships' shells. *Fendaristil* had already moved to a point above and slightly ahead of the freighter. Twin blaster bolts pierced the space where the cloaked ship had been.

"Two more ships are entering the system," *Fendaristil* reported.

"Probably they were watching another potential route," Marjory said, nodding as her earlier conjecture was confirmed. "What types of ships are they?"

"Both are converted shuttles," *Fendaristil* reported. "They are similar to the two that confronted us. The freighter is firing again!"

Fendaristil rocked suddenly, and again.

"The freighter has adopted a spread firing pattern. Two blaster shots impacted our shields. Shields are holding but our location has been identified. I am moving position."

Fendaristil shifted rapidly. Marjory had to lean suddenly to maintain balance. Almost as soon as *Fendaristil* had moved the freighter concentrated its fire on the location that had been revealed by the blasts impacting on shields. The freighter started to change position itself, orienting the open bay door in the direction of its fire.

"The freighter is preparing to fire the plasma cannon. We probably are out of its line of fire." *Fendaristil* sounded quite confident.

"Are you completely confident that is the case?" Marjory asked.

"No," *Fendaristil* answered shortly.

"Is there any chance of getting me on that freighter so I can ask a few questions?"

"Not at this time. If I drop the shields for you to exit the ship we risk being impacted by a blaster shot."

"Then we need them to come to us," Marjory said. "That's worked in the past."

"You have an idea?"

"Next time they bracket us stay in the same location. Can you vent some plasma or oxygen or both? That may look like a hull breach."

"I could ignite the plasma and make it look like we were struck. To make that look real we will have to reduce the shield depth. There may be actual damage caused as a result."

Marjory nodded. "The risk is worthwhile. It is important to find out who gave out our route. These vessels obviously have Empire technology in them and there would only be one way for that to be the case. So, as we have seen before, it is likely that someone in Fleet is a traitor."

"The freighter is firing again. It is a tighter pattern but is shifting." *Fendaristil* rocked again. "Impact. Reducing the shield depth." The ship rocked again. "And reducing again."

The ship rocked violently. Somewhere something fell. Marjory made a note to find that and fix it - it was unlike her to leave anything that could fall or, worse, fly around. There was another impact and *Fendaristil* rocked violently again.

"Dropping cloak. Shields holding. Venting plasma," the ship reported calmly. "Minor damage in the engine bay. I have commenced repairs. Firing plasma."

Fendaristil had appeared, seemingly from nowhere. The plasma released as a gaseous plume. A few moments later the plume erupted in a spectacular blaze that quickly diminished to nothing. *Fendaristil* maintained the protective shield but now appeared to be adrift.

"I have taken inertial dampers off line to simulate drift," the ship AI reported. "The freighter appears to have ceased firing. I am altering the shield frequencies so their sensors do not detect it."

"Assuming they take the bait, drop the sensor coverage over the cargo bay entry but hold it everywhere else. What about those other two ships?"

"Still approaching. I estimate between thirty and sixty minutes for them to arrive. They appear to be slowing."

"Let us hope we get this done by then. Maintain a firing solution to them. If they start anything don't wait for me. Destroy them," Marjory said as she stood from her chair, listing slightly as the ship drift had an effect.

"Yes, Battle Mage," *Fendaristil* replied formally.

"I will be in the cargo hold. Prepare the medical chamber in case I need to keep one of these alive."

Marjory made her way through the small ship to the cargo bay at the rear. *Fendaristil*, although often called a shuttle by those who knew no better, was more than three times the size of the shuttles that were attacking it. Almost a third of that space was the cargo bay. While designated on Ennaris as a pocket destroyer, the ship had also been designed as a rapid deployment vessel for the small teams of highly skilled experts that Ennaris had maintained to support its far flung colonisation missions, along with a wide array of equipment options. When empty, the bay was the ideal space for Marjory to exercise, maintain her incomparable skills and, in this case, entertain visitors.

As she had done once before, Marjory stood at the end of the bay, having closed and locked the access hatch. The bay doors were open, which Marjory hoped would not be seen as too abnormal. Gravity was maintained and the force barrier held the atmosphere inside.

"The freighter has deployed a small runabout," *Fendaristil* reported.

Marjory nodded to herself. So far, so good. She stood easily, waiting. Much of the life of a battle-trained Mage of Ennaris was waiting and the successful ones developed or already possessed a mindset that allowed them to remain patient as events unfolded. From her chosen site she could see a limited amount of space to the rear of the ship through the open hatch protected by the energy barrier.

"The runabout is paused to one side."

"Probably assessing," Marjory replied. "How many in the runabout?"

"Three, probably the entire complement of the ship," *Fendaristil* replied.

"Can you tap into the ship's systems?"

"Trying. This ship's systems have been hardened against intrusion. The sensors were easy because of the traps left for us to use."

"Keep trying," Marjory said. "I want to know where they came from. You may be able to find some communications that will help, too."

"The runabout is moving again. The freighter is orienting so that the plasma cannon is aimed at the cargo bay. I will extend the shield depth once they are aboard and close the shield gap."

Marjory did not reply. One advantage of having a truly advanced AI running the ship - effectively *being* the ship - was that it took logical decisions for its own protection. In the Ennari fleets, such AIs had near equal status to the ship's captain, but the captain had the final decision about offensive weapons deployment. After all, the logical way for a ship's AI to safeguard itself was to destroy everything around it, which was not a suitable outcome in many cases.

A small, blunt-nosed boat edged into view. It was little more than a capsule attached to a thrust motor, adequate for very short distances but very cramped for three people in environmental suits. Marjory wore an experimental Ennari device that would immediately deploy a smart suit if the atmosphere was compromised, but the Union and its member worlds, including the Warriors of the Light, still used relatively bulky suits worn over their regular garb. That was an area that Marjory had decided not to push onto the Union any harder than necessary. Her usual black tunic and close-fitting trousers stretching over pliable black boots made her difficult to see in the dim light of the cargo bay, although she expected they would have some sort of scanner that would find her easily. Her twin Mage swords were hidden in plain sight, as usual, sheathed on the outer thigh of each leg.

The runabout pushed through the energy barrier that hold the breathable atmosphere within the cargo bay and settled to the deck. A hatch opened upwards like a clamshell, to Marjory's approval, as it allowed the passengers an easy and fast exit. The three members of the freighter crew disembarked, each holding pulse rifles aimed and extended, swiftly sweeping the cargo bay before covering Marjory. All three wore advanced environment suits, with clear visors on close-fitting combat helmets.

Without a word all three opened fire on her. The pulses from their rifles met her Mage barrier and were repulsed. The three exchanged glances and the withering fire from the three rifles continued. Marjory's face set into a frown of concentration. The protective barrier was learnt by battle Mages early in their training. Usually, it was meant to provide short term protection in the event the Mage needed to refresh a weapon charge or retreat. There was some strain involved in maintaining it for more than a slow count to ten. Many Mages were unable to hold the barrier for any longer and were exposed when it collapsed. Other, stronger, Mages could hold the barrier for two or three times that duration. Marjory, the strongest of battle-trained Mages, could hold it for much longer than that.

However, she knew that the penalty for holding the barrier until she could do so no more was that she would have no resources available for anything else. It appeared that the pulse rifles being used to target her were capable of longer duration firing that a normal Union rifle. And Marjory disliked waiting. While battle-trained Mages were trained in patience, Marjory also had decided long ago that defensive tactics were best combined with aggressive intent.

She grasped the hilts of her twin swords and pulled them from the thin thigh sheaths. She saw the surprise on the faces of the three when their blaster fire was confronted by two handles with what looked like short and stubby knife blades. That surprise turned to consternation when the energy beams flared into life and the lengths of the Mage Swords extended from the hilts. Swords against pulse rifles? The volume of rifle fire increased.

At almost the same moment the ship shuddered. *Fendaristil* had fired missiles, which meant the oncoming ships must have launched an attack, or adopted a posture that represented a significant threat. A second shudder was followed by a third, each different to the first. Plasma and pulse cannons.

The centre-most of the trio attacking Marjory hesitated, glancing to the runabout. Receiving bad news, Marjory hoped. That caused him to lose his focus on Marjory for a moment, which was all she needed. She dropped the Mage barrier, launching herself towards the intruders while dropping and rolling diagonally. She deflected a pulse with her swords, and then grunted as a second pulse tagged her across the left shoulder. Pain flared but she held her focus. A second pulse clipped her above the right thigh. By then, she was close to the right-most of the three. The swords flashed. The rifle clattered to the deck, along with the rifle wielder's hand. Marjory stood behind the intruder.

The other two stared aghast at the energy blade of the Mage Sword that now extended through the body of their companion, emerging from the front. Marjory pulled back, allowing the blade to slide clear of the body, which collapsed to the deck. Marjory concentrated on holding herself upright. The pain of her two wounds made the effort difficult. She knew that she had limited time available to her. She had to finish this.

"*Fendaristil*, status," Marjory said aloud, so the two remaining intruders would hear.

"The two shuttles have been destroyed," *Fendaristil* reported, also aloud.

"You see," Marjory said to the two, stepping around the body of the third, "you have attacked the wrong ship."

The remaining two opened fire again, and Marjory threw herself *up*, pushing through the pain to spin across the cargo bay. The twin swords flashed as they deflected blast after blast. In a moment she had moved from one side of the conflict to the other, faster than the two could follow. A flick of a Mage Sword made a deep slash across the upper arm of the one who had been furthest away from her, causing the rifle to clatter to the deck. A second flick and a similar slash appeared on his leg, causing him to collapse. Marjory held her pain at bay, even while being aware of the blood running down her left arm and right leg. Still, she staggered slightly on landing, giving the remaining intruder the chance to attack. He charged at her, still firing his rifle. Marjory pivoted on the spot. The rifle blasts passed so close that she heard them fizz through the air in front of and behind her.

She had little endurance left now. Ideally she would take both alive, but that would be difficult.

The charging intruder continued to fire his rifle and Marjory had to raise her barrier hastily. She staggered under each blast. Then he was too close for the rifle to be an effective weapon. Marjory dropped the barrier at the same time that he dropped the rifle and made a strange gesture with his right hand. A tiny needle blaster swung from a holster strapped to his forearm into his gloved hand. Desperately, Marjory closed with him as he fired. She felt the thin beam of the needle blaster hit her as she drove one of the Mage Swords through his torso, angled up to pierce his heart and emerge between his shoulder blades. With a grimace of pain, she made the blade flicker out and the third intruder slumped to the deck.

Marjory breathed deeply. The needle beam had punched through her left thigh. Three hits in a single fight. That had never happened to her before. She had been over-confident. But the second intruder remained alive and she needed him to talk. Gritting her teeth, she staggered to where the second intruder lay, the pain from his two wounds having rendered him unconscious. Marjory wished that was an option for her. Gritting her teeth, she bent to release the helmet, grunting and almost falling as it came loose. She discarded the helmet, then grasped the intruder by the neck ring of his environmental suit and started to drag him back to the cargo bay door.

"*Fendaristil*, ready the medical bay for two, me and one of the intruders."

"The medical bay is ready. Do you require assistance?"

"Yes, I may not make it to the medical bay if I have to drag him too."

Marjory watched, bemused, as a maintenance bot detached from its niche in the cargo bay and sped across the short distance to Marjory. The bot extended a grasping claw and gripped the intruder's suit. With a sigh of relief Marjory let go. The bot backed through the cargo bay door towards the medical bay dragging the inert body behind it.

Marjory staggered after it, trailing blood across the formerly pristine deck.

| 21 |

Closure

It was the following day, ship time. Marjory felt much better, having spent the previous thirteen Earth hours in the recovery pod. Her wounds had been cleaned and treated with a gel laced with medical nanobots, one human advancement over the Ennaris treatment that she had introduced of which she thoroughly approved. The wounds were closed and new skin was grown. Now she could stand and move gingerly, if unsteadily. *Fendaristil* calmly informed her that the needle beam had missed one of her main arteries by less than a finger's breadth, but that no lasting damage had been done. Her Mage energy was rebuilding quickly, as it always had done, and she was ready to question the second intruder.

He had received similar treatment to Marjory. However, because his wounds had been lateral slashes that severed muscles and tendons, there was every chance that he would not regain full use of his arm or leg. Marjory instructed the medical bot to rouse him while leaving the pain largely blocked.

He regained a precarious consciousness. Marjory waited while he became aware of his surroundings. He glanced from her to the stubby domed cylinder that was the medical bot standing by his side. He was restrained and so had limited movement, but still he tested the strength of the arm and leg bonds that held him down. He subsided and looked once again at Marjory. She regarded him impassively.

"I won't tell you anything!" he declared defiantly.

Marjory nodded, as though expecting nothing less.

"Well, I will make an arrangement with you," she said after a short while. "I will release you once you tell me the name of your informant in Fleet Security."

He sneered in response.

"I will provide you with enough currency to make a fresh start," she continued, undeterred, "and drop you far enough away from the sector's Fleet facility to give you an even chance to escape. The alternative is that I deliver you to Fleet Security. I imagine that whoever your informant is will be senior enough to find out and take action to silence you. The choice is yours."

Marjory delivered the alternatives in a matter-of-fact way, her unemotional tone of voice made all the more chilling because she was regarding him steadily while she spoke.

"I will leave you to consider your course of action. You are the only survivor of your five vessels. I am sure that your masters will be pleased to hear that you have survived and will make their own arrangements should the Fleet informant not do so. I understand their methods are unpleasant."

Marjory stood smoothly, turned carefully and walked from the medical bay as though fully healed, holding herself fully upright by willpower alone. Once in the short corridor outside, she slumped against the wall to regain her physical strength. She made her unsteady way to her own cabin. Once there she considered eating a meal but, instead, she carefully lay on the bunk and practised one of the forms of meditation that she had been taught so long ago. She moved from there into a restful sleep, with the nanobots continuing to work on her recovery while she slept.

She awoke and lay still, unsure as to how long she had been asleep. Gingerly, she tested arms and legs, twisting her body from side to side. There were no tell-tale twinges of pain, so she pushed herself to a sitting position. Still no pain. She swung herself around so her legs hung to the floor and carefully stood. All was well so far.

"*Fendaristil*, how long was I asleep," Marjory asked.

"You slept for seventeen point three Earth hours," the ship's AI replied immediately. "During that time the medical nanobots completed their repairs of your injuries and deactivated. The injured intruder has been sedated once more. The deceased intruders have been removed from the cargo bay and placed in a holding stasis for your examination. We remain in the same location as we were when attacked, although I did take the liberty of moving out of the firing path of the plasma cannon. The freighter remains intact should you wish to examine it. The blood stains have been removed and I have started to effect repairs to the cargo bay where the blasters impacted."

"Oh, I apologise for that," Marjory said with a grimace. "I did try to absorb as many of them as I could."

"I understand, Battle Mage," *Fendaristil* replied. "The damage is relatively minor."

"Good." Marjory walked from her cabin towards the bridge. "I need some food and then I will examine the freighter. We may learn something useful about the Empire's - Likud's - weapons."

Two hours later Marjory piloted the captured runabout through the still open cargo bay door of the freighter. She regarded the object fixed to the deck of the cargo bay with interest. It was obviously the plasma cannon. A stubby barrel protruded from a broad but flat cylinder with a shallow dome on top. Various cables ran across the deck to receptacles in the bay walls. There was a space the right size for the runabout and Marjory gently swung the craft around the cannon and positioned it with the bow facing the bay door. There was no atmosphere in the cargo bay so Marjory activated her personal environment containment field - the one she finished developing after she left her life as the founder of the Warriors of the Light - and pressed the button to open the runabout hatch.

She walked carefully from the runabout to the cannon, for there was no artificial gravity in the bay. The construction of the gun was solid, very solid. Heavy metal plates were attached to the floor and the thick-walled cylinder rose from the plates. The stubby cannon was modern in style and Marjory examined the ejector carefully. In essence it was the same as the main plasma cannon on *Fendaristil*, although far more massive in design than that of *Fendaristil*. She suspected that it would draw enormous power, which explained the exposed cables running across the deck, but may not have as much impact as Fendaristil's more compact unit. There was no control panel visible and she did not want to experiment with it. So she turned and walked to the cargo bay door leading into the craft itself.

A simple control panel was fixed to the wall beside the door. There was a red light that she assumed indicated that the cargo bay door was open. She pressed the button beside the light and a tone sounded. The cargo bay door closed. The red light changed to green, and a second light, below the first, lit red. Air flooded into the cargo bay and the red light changed to green, but Marjory did not release the personal environment field. She pressed the button beside the light again and the hatch from the cargo bay to the vessel unlocked with a clang and swung open, into the bay. Carefully, Marjory stepped through the hatch, finding herself at the end of a short passageway. Artificial gravity was active here. Two doors branched off on one side and three on the other.

She made her way to the first door and pressed the single button. The door slid into the wall, revealing a small and untidy cabin, with an unmade bunk, clothing strewn around the floor, food wrappers mixed in with the clothes, a locker fixed to the deck beside the bunk and little else. The second room was another cabin the same size as the first, but this one was fastidiously tidy, with the bunk made up in military style and nothing out of place. Marjory pursed her lips in thought. Perhaps ex-Fleet? It may be one way they had of contacting people still in uniform.

The third cabin was slightly larger, allowing a small desk to be added to the bunk and locker. This cabin was neat also, but not to the extent of the second. Of more interest to Marjory was a small tablet that had been left on the desk. She picked up and pressed the tablet screen where custom demanded that the activation point would be found. Nothing! Shrugging, Marjory held the tablet and left the cabin.

On the other side of the passageway closest to the cargo bay were communal facilities, showing the effect of three males living in close proximity. Marjory wrinkled her nose and closed the sliding door again. The second door on that side revealed a small galley and eating area, with two tables able to seat six people. A small food preparation counter was at one end, complete with rehydrator and a protein synthesizer. The first would make dehydrated packets more edible, while the second would take various forms of source proteins and produce variously flavoured foodstuffs. Both were fairly standard for a freighter, and were in good condition. Below the counter were cupboards and what Marjory assumed was a refrigeration unit. She did not bother to look inside.

Marjory made her way from the galley to the end of the passageway where she expected that the closed door should lead to the bridge. It did. Three chairs were bolted to the deck, two closer to the front of the ship and one slightly behind them and centred. The latter would be the command chair. Each chair had a small screen attached to one arm, such that it could be swung in front of the seated person or operated to the side. Marjory seated herself in the command chair and swung the screen around. It activated automatically. Marjory shook her head in disbelief. The screen had not been locked and showed what probably was the last thing the ship's captain would have seen before leaving to board *Fendaristil*.

The screen showed the track that the freighter had taken and the last position that it had been able to determine for *Fendaristil* before the sensors were disabled. A second screen, also unlocked, showed a view of the sector, zoomed to the two systems that were shown as potential traversal points for Marjory and *Fendaristil*. Two ships were shown in the path that she did not take. There was no third option. So, all of the interceptor ships were accounted for. Marjory sat back and thought for a moment. It was unlikely, but perhaps someone as sloppy as this pirate - for it could not have been a proper military man who ran this ship - would have left traces of the person who gave them the information.

Marjory tapped the universal icon for communications and looked at the options. The list of recent messages reached back several weeks, well before she had announced that she would be leaving Drummel. There were rendezvous coordinates for previous missions as well as the latest one, and various interactions with anonymous agents scattered across the sector that Fleet Security would find interesting, but she could find nothing that gave her a name. Ship to ship communications showed nothing of note. The ship logs were minimal in nature, as she expected. Finally, Marjory tapped the icon for the face to face communications, which was only useful when the parties were a relatively short distance apart and almost never retained because of the volume of storage chewed up to hold copies. The list was short, going back two weeks. But there were two conversations recorded with someone named Lieutenant Gabriel Hruschel. Both sides of the conversation were available. Marjory selected the latest one and tapped the icon to play it back.

"Quinby, the shuttle has left Drummel," Hruschel said. "She's on her way. The last information she gave the Admiral is that she was heading towards the Kreillis sector. That probably means there are only two likely routes she would take. I suggest -"

"Leave your suggesting to me," Quinby, obviously the pirate captain, replied brusquely. "I know how to do this. No matter how tricky this one thinks she is I have it covered. We have some new upgrades that should make this easy. Ironically, they're from her own company."

"Don't take her lightly," Hruschel urged. "There's something odd about her. She doesn't seem to get old like everyone else, and her ship never gets serviced. And that ship has been recorded for hundreds of years now in that family."

"She's a business woman, nothing more," Quinby snorted, causing Marjory to smirk. "She won't know what hit her. Literally. I don't intend to give her any warning. We'll just blow her away."

Marjory stopped the playback.

"*Fendaristil*, did you copy the communication logs? All of them?" Marjory asked.

"Yes," the ship replied via Marjory's suit's inbuilt communication nub. "I have it stored."

"Bundle it up for me please. I will add a message and then we will send it to Admiral Lessor. She can take care of the traitors in her own midst. There will be more than one. And we have a passenger to deliver to the nearest Fleet Security base."

Three days later, *Fendaristil* received a message directed to Ansel Mellivar. Admiral Lessor, the deputy director of Fleet Security, looked directly into the lens of the recorder and smiling grimly.

"Ansel, you will be pleased to learn that you helped to uncover a major ring. Some of them we have been watching for some time, but you gave us the lead we needed to roll it up. Lieutenant Hruschel was arrested this morning, along with a senior attache in the Union President's office. Seven others have been positively identified as part of the cell and have been detained. Investigations are continuing. We sent the Third Fleet to recover the freighter that attacked you. That cannon will be examined in detail. If there was nothing else, that cannon would be enough for you to receive a major award. I know your family has always declined them, but just so you know." The Admiral looked away from the recorder for a moment, then looked back. "The Third Fleet also identified debris from what looked like a space battle. It seems there were four other vessels that had been destroyed in the near vicinity to that freighter. I don't suppose," she said drily, "that you have any idea about them? Well, take care of yourself, Ansel. We have taken a leap forward with your help over the last few years. I wish you had stayed, for I fear the Empire will continue to build their forces against us. I just hope that you and your family will be able to assist us in the future."

Marjory closed the message playback and sat back in her command chair with a brief smile. There was still some way to go, but the time was close. She hoped. Meanwhile, she had some work to do in preparation, and then she would settle herself in for a sleep.

| part four |

STINGER

300 years before the events described in <u>Children of Ennaris</u>

| **22** |

A Mellivar Proposal

"Admiral, you need fighters as your nimble attack craft. They need to be able to blast through the Empire's small attackers and deliver enough payload to damage the larger ships and possibly destroy the smaller ones."

"Mellivar, we've been over this before. Small fighters were left far in the past when we managed to get into space because they're not suited to the type of engagements we have. The smaller patrol ships have done the job for us and will continue to do so in the future."

"But the Empire has developed their own version of small attacking fighters specifically because of the success we have had in the last hundred years in holding the bigger ships at bay. The game has changed now." Mellivar pointed to the holoscreen showing an image of a small, blunt-nosed craft that had stubby, almost vestigial, wings protruding from a cylindrical body that, itself, ended in a large bulge where the engine was housed. "It may not be very manoeuvrable craft at the moment but it's fast enough to be hard to hit. This one was captured from a lucky shot. Usually when we have encountered them, we have suffered."

"Then we need to make sure our point defences are better," Admiral Bedis countered. "Fleet made a decision long ago that small fighters were not suitable for space engagements. That position hasn't changed. We don't have to have a fighter just because they do. In any event, they've had little impact in our run-ins with them so far."

"That is so far. They will improve. I believe the previous attempts were poorly defined and executed. I can do better. At least allow me to prototype the design I have," Flight-Colonel Mellivar replied. "I can have it built in complete secrecy at Drummel and we can see if it provides anything of benefit. I'll even fund it."

That caused the Admiral to pause and consider. The one constant through the last three centuries or so had been that a member of the Mellivar family would arrive on the scene and introduce some new advances in defensive or offensive equipment, as well as other technology that improved surprisingly many aspects of Union society. It was a sequence of interventions that he had found fascinating from the time that he realised that a pattern of sorts existed. It was one to which he had devoted some time, even writing his graduating thesis from the Academy on the impact that a single family could have if they stepped into the picture at the right time consistently. Perhaps, he mused, this was his time to witness it.

Flight-Colonel Mellivar had moved through the ranks rapidly in a short time. She was constantly described as an old head on young shoulders, and the description was apt. She had survived situations where many others had not. In one now-famous encounter with Empire-inspired rebels in Drefak, a human planet in the Twelfth Sector, the then Second Lieutenant Mellivar had taken command of her small patrol after the commander had been killed, infiltrated the rebels' headquarters and somehow killed or captured the rebel leader and his lieutenant. In doing so she had lost no more of her patrol and they had suffered minor injuries only. The rebellion had faltered and petered out thereafter. In what would prove to be a pattern repeated over the fifteen years since then, she had achieved a level of devotion among her subordinates that bordered on worship. Oddly, she never seemed to recognise the qualities she displayed that caused such an outcome.

Admiral Bedis did recognise those qualities, however. She had proven to be an exceptional tactician, an equally exceptional fighter in hand-to-hand combat, and uncannily proficient in a wide range of weapons. But, when she led her teams, she also showed great care and attention to their own well-being, refusing to place them in situations where they would be sacrificed, as so many young commanders did. She was renowned as a hard task-master, trained her charges more than any others and discarded no-one. Those who were unable to meet her demanding standards were retained and redeployed to suitable roles within her command. As she rose through the ranks, she had amassed a loyal and devoted cadre of Fleet followers.

And she was a Mellivar. At no time had she flaunted her obvious family wealth, but there was no denying that it existed. She played no day-to-day role in Drummel Industrial, her family's company and still the leading manufacturer of advanced capital ships, engines and weapons in the Union. However, that she maintained a keen interest in the workings of that company was clear. Her growing legend within the Fleet could have suffered because of her family's involvement with Drummel. Instead, she had managed to achieve the exact opposite when she had taken dramatic and drastic steps to remove the company's leadership several years earlier.

Bedis had been captain of the *Corona Fire*, an elderly Star-class ship, while Mellivar was a young first lieutenant on a smaller corvette, the *Sandworm*. Following the loss of three newer Star-class ships in what should have been survivable encounters with Empire cruisers, it had been found that the ships had been fitted with sub-specification conduit linkages and breakers. Simulations showed that failure under stress of those components were likely to be the cause of the ships' losses, as they would have been unable to maintain and sustain power to shields and weapons. Drummel Industrial was blamed for cutting corners. The story told in the mess rooms around the fleet was that the then Lieutenant Mellivar had stalked into her commanding officer's office and demanded a leave of absence to deal with urgent family business. The leave had been granted by a somewhat shaken commander - he told of looking into the hardest eyes he had ever seen as she had made the request - and then seemingly from nowhere a ship had raced to rendezvous with the *Sandworm* and Mellivar had departed.

A week later Mellivar descended on Drummel Industrial with the force of a category five ion storm. She was accompanied by a squad from Fleet Security. Almost all of the leadership of the company were replaced in a swirling maelstrom centred on Mellivar. Two of the executives were subsequently convicted of embezzlement of funds, proof of which came from Mellivar via a source that had never been revealed. None of the rest had found an executive role since. The faulty equipment was confirmed and Drummel had instigated a program of replacement at the company's cost, along with several other components that Mellivar decided were sub-standard. The fallout also claimed the careers of two senior officers of the Fleet's supply arm who had allowed the sub-standard components to be accepted. While she sought to keep her involvement as quiet as possible, it proved to be anything but. In the Fleet mess halls, Mellivar's star shone bright.

All of this raced through Bedis' mind as he considered the proposition. The Empire fighters were not as effective as they could be, but that would change, he knew. Fleet's doctrine was that small, single-occupant attack ships were redundant. It had been tested several times to his own knowledge and, each time, the powers among the Fleet confirmed that doctrine. However, at that time the Empire had not had anything of the type, either. Perhaps it would be better to have investigated and possibly even proven such a design in the event that it was required. And it would be led by a Mellivar, which almost guaranteed success. And Drummel would fund its design and development.

"How would you propose to house and supply such craft?" Bedis asked, seizing on the obvious flaw in most people's thinking about fighters. "A fighter won't carry fuel for long flights and would expend it quickly. And we have no ships capable of acting as supply vessels."

"No, we do not have any at the moment. There would have to be a new ship type designed for the purpose. I have one ready to be prototyped," Mellivar replied. "But the small ship would also be far more efficient at using its available fuel in most cases. The main problem for fighters is weapon load-outs. We need to provide enough punch in a small package. I have some thoughts on that also."

"You make it sound like you have experience with such craft, Flight Colonel," Bedis said with a smile.

"I have been working on the designs for some time, Admiral," Mellivar replied carefully. "In fact, several of my forebears had conducted some tests on various components that would make up an attacking or defensive fighter. And the basic design for such a craft was laid down some time ago. I have refined it and brought it up to date."

Bedis found that he was not surprised. Across the years, the Mellivar family had delivered exactly what was required at precisely the time when it was required. That advanced designs were available was not fortuitous in any way. It was a planned intervention by this family with an incredibly long and sustained plan of some nature. Bedis was sure that was the case. That they were dedicated to the cause of the Union he did not doubt. How that could be sustained across so many generations was a mystery to him.

"And a carrier of some sort?" Bedis asked, sure that he knew the answer.

"Yes, I have a design for that also. It is a modification of the Star-class medium cruiser," Mellivar replied, confirming his suspicion. "In fact, the existing design has several features built in that will allow us to add hangars readily. So have the designs for the Stellar and Super-star classes."

Again Bedis nodded. The Star-class ships were the mainstay of the Fleet's capital ships, while there were few Stellar-class and fewer still Superstar-class ships. That they were already designed to have hangars as options should have been a shock but hearing Mellivar say it did little more than add a nail to the Fleet doctrine's coffin. Bedis found himself nodding. Yes, this was his time to witness a Mellivar intervention.

"You have two years, Flight Colonel," he said. "And I want to be kept apprised of progress by you personally."

"Yes, Admiral," Mellivar agreed. "But we will have the first fighter well inside two years."

| **23** |

First Flight

Fifteen months later, Marjory stood with Sandel Moire, her hand-picked shipyard manager, at the huge panoramic window overlooking the Drummel shipyard. It was strange, she thought, for it seemed like it was only a short time before that she had stood at the same window in almost the exact same spot with Grevil Hansen as the first panels for the Stellar-class had rolled from the factory, and again with Millis VanZis for the first panels for the Superstar class capital ship. Those were huge ships and took a relatively long time to construct. The fighters were another thing altogether, with many prefabricated components already made, tested and proven.

The fighter frame was handed from robot to robot. Made from a very light - and newly formulated (for Earth) from a Mellivar specification - alloy that had incredible strength, it would be the mounting point for everything that made the fighter a deadly craft. At each stage, a fresh component was added to the frame, from the engine to the prepackaged control modules, light-weight test weapons, retractable landing skids and prefabricated, fully enclosed cockpit assembly. It was a symphony of parts becoming their own sections which became a whole craft. In almost no time, the assembly was complete, except for the outer skin.

Moire watched the components come together and reflected on the ships that Drummel had produced over the years. All had been incredible machines for their times and all had shunned the idea that form had no place or that function was the only factor in design. Drummel ships were always considered to be design masterpieces, even the larger Star-class and massive Superstar-class vessels. This fighter was no different. Moire had done some research, looking at ancient fighter designs from pre-space travel and the early efforts to translate those into space before it was decided quite quickly that they were not required. Those craft were designed to slip through air as efficiently as possible, and some of the design characteristics meant to do so gave many of them a sleek and, to his eye, an attractive shape, especially in flight. The first of Earth's space fighters did the opposite. They were ugly, unwieldy craft with few redeeming visual qualities.

This Mellivar-designed fighter harked back in some ways to those days when atmospheric requirements governed design. It was long for a craft that was little more than an engine and weapon platform with a pilot strapped to it. The engine dominated the tail, of course, with baffles and shields to direct emissions, heat and turbulence away from the ship itself. The body of the ship was a narrow and flattened oval-shaped cylinder in profile, with the cockpit mounted at the point where the tapered nose cone was attached. The nose of the fighter appeared to be a sharp point but was, in fact, very slightly blunted. A stubby fin stretched from behind the cockpit to an almost vestigial tail assembly that Mellivar asserted would allow atmospheric flight. On each side of the body shell were small wing mounts, with the wings able to be almost completely retracted when in space flight or extended for atmospheric use. Moire had doubts about how the craft would fly in atmosphere but Mellivar seemed to be confident.

Moire turned to Marjory, who was watching the final external components being fitted.

"Is it what you thought it would be?" he asked.

"It's almost as I remember it," Marjory replied before she realised what she had said. "From a model I saw as a young girl, of course," she added.

"You had models of these as a child?"

"Yes," Marjory answered, wondering how far she should take the conversation. "My family had investigated many designs over the years and models were always made first to test design principles."

"Did I tell you that I did some research into old fighter planes?" Moire asked, apparently satisfied.

"No. Did you find anything interesting?"

"The best examples always seemed to me to be quite beautiful machines," Moire mused aloud. "But I doubt any of them could hold a candle to the stinger."

"Stinger?" Marjory asked.

"That's what some of the Fleet people have taken to calling our fighter," Moire said with a grin. "They feel it will do little more than give a sting to anything they come across. My team have taken that on board and decided to make it work for them."

"Stinger," Marjory said with an answering, but far more feral, grin. "Yes, I like that. I think people need to remember that some stings can be deadly. Perhaps we can show them that in the near future."

"Well, we'll have a full flight of twelve craft ready for the demonstration," Moire said. "All of the tests have proven out. The weapons are the weak spot for the demonstration, though."

"They are running behind schedule slightly," Marjory nodded. "But this demonstration will be about flight characteristics more than weaponry. And I expect the new mini-cannons to be ready not long after. It may even be better to do this in two separate demonstrations anyway."

"There's a lot of space within the frame that we don't seem to be using," Moire said. "More when you see it than the design sometimes indicates. Is there a reason for that?"

"There is a reason," Marjory confirmed. "We will start to work on a new form of missile designed to be carried by these stingers. But that space can also be used by a variant to carry a second person. It can be useful for insertions."

"The Warriors may be interested in that," Moire replied, looking at the space behind the pilot's seat with new eyes. "Yes, I can see the potential for that. We may be able to come up with other uses, too."

"Moire," Marjory said seriously, "the primary purpose of this craft is as a fighter. Yes, you may come up with ideas but always remember that the primary mission is to attack the enemy or defend your own ship."

Moire nodded, drawn back to the present from thoughts of a range of stinger-based craft. First things first. There was a demonstration to get right.

"Admiral, please follow me," the attendant said to Bedis as she gestured towards the viewing area.

Bedis dutifully followed along, although he knew the way. This was the Fleet's testing range, an area of space distant to any travelled routes. It had been used routinely to test upgrades, refits and, occasionally, new equipment for over two hundred years. Such facilities were used more frequently when there was a Mellivar in the mix, he thought as he took his place in the viewing area.

There were only a few people present. Sandel Moire nodded politely to Bedis from his place towards one end of the platform. Moire looked nervous to Bedis, which did nothing to ease his own anxiety. Despite making it clear that the fighter was an experiment and was not guaranteed to be pushed into service, rumours had been swirling for some time about a new weapon to combat the Empire's fast attack craft.

Those craft, lambasted by many in the Union Fleet when they were introduced by the Empire, were being taken seriously now. Less than a year previously, well after Mellivar was given leave to start this project, a patrol ship had been jumped unexpectedly by a flight of six Empire small attack craft - the powers that be could not allow themselves to say *fighter* - and was seriously damaged. They survived, it was thought, because the attackers were a long way from their base or mother ship, and thus could not tarry long enough to see the job done to completion.

However, worse was to follow. In an engagement only three months previously, a Star-class cruiser had been destroyed when an Empire heavy cruiser commander, who as a group were usually so unimaginative in their tactics, used a combinatior. of heavy fire from the cruiser and its accompanying twin, and then brought the attack craft into the battle from behind the Union ship. It was fire from the small craft that caused the breach that allowed the *Sunbeam* to be destroyed. What was worse when the news became known, was that *Sunbeam* had released escape pods which were systematically hunted by the small craft and destroyed. All hands were lost from *Sunbeam*.

After that loss, the Fleet hierarchy suddenly realised that they faced a new problem, not something that could be joked about. Bedis, who had taken criticism at even allowing the fighter experiment to take place, found himself under pressure to deliver a means of protecting Fleet ships from these fighters but also delivering a counter-punch that would allow the Fleet to adopt similar tactics to the Empire. Without killing escape pods, Bedis mused. So, he hoped Mellivar would conform to the long history her family had of delivering the required weapons and ships at the time the Union needed them.

The viewing platform was a little more crowded now. Several more Fleet officers were in attendance, as were more of the executives from Drummel Industrial. Bedis was looking for Mellivar when the announcement was made.

"Please take your places. The demonstration will commence shortly. Today's demonstration will be of flight characteristics of the new craft, nicknamed the Stinger." There were a few nervous laughs at the originally disparaging name being adopted for the craft, and Bedis knew that it would be a Stinger no matter what official designation it was given. "The demonstration flight will be led by Flight-Colonel Mellivar."

Bedis started. Mellivar was leading it? But she had no training in these craft? Or did she? Who really knew what the Mellivar family had done? The fact that Mellivar had those designs ready to go, and openly acknowledged that they had been developed over the years by other generations of her family, suggested that some sort of experimentation may have occurred out of sight of any onlookers. Of course, no-one in the Fleet had experience with small fighter craft, for the Fleet had eschewed them for hundreds of years.

"Please look to your right," the announcer asked of the watchers.

Far in the distance to the right, a small set of spots appeared, rapidly growing larger. In a matter of moments, the spots had resolved into a formation of small craft. Moments later the six ships of the demonstration flight flashed past the viewing area. Over the speakers came the voice of Mellivar.

"Alpha flight, formation three."

As the assembled onlookers watched the flight split into two units of three, one unit going vertical to the plane on which they had been travelling, while the second did a tight loop and swung back towards the viewing platform. There followed fifteen minutes of different modes and speeds of flight, with the two units facing off against each other in mock dogfights or individually showing how the craft could manoeuvre, including a final demonstration of the six ships in unison coming to a halt in front of the viewing platform. They hovered and five of the craft slowly spun in different directions, an effective display of the handling, shape and styling of the ship which, Bedis had to admit, was quite a beautiful craft. He had seen models and design briefs over the last few months, but seeing the ship in its native element was something else. If it performed in combat as well as it looked then the Union may, indeed, have an effective counter.

Bedis looked around. The Fleet personnel were glued to the large window, alternately watching a large viewscreen that showed the relative positions of the ships to the viewing platform. The Drummel people seemed to be a little nervous, Bedis thought curiously. A murmur brought him back to the viewscreen. A new indicator had appeared. A large blob moved towards the demonstration area at speed. The Fleet people looked to Bedis who sought to evince calm, although he had no idea what was happening. To his knowledge, the demonstration was done. On the viewscreen the blob separated into one larger indicator surrounded by six small dots. It was coming from behind the viewing platform. Intrigued, Bedis turned to look out the main screen again. From above and behind the platform, the unmistakable shape of a Star-class ship swept into view. The sleek lines of the large craft rapidly filled the window as it charged forward. Around the ship six more Stingers acted as escort. Bedis smiled and nodded approval. At about one kilometre from the platform the ship swung into a turn, slowing as it did so.

Bedis gasped and he heard corresponding exclamations from the other Fleet officers. The bow of the ship had been hollowed out. A large flight bay, for it could be nothing else, opened beneath the nose of the ship, which had been redesigned for the purpose to be less a tapered point and more of a flat nose above a gaping mouth.

"Alpha flight, adopt designation Hammer flight," Mellivar's voice came over the speaker. "Attack formation."

The six ships that had been slowly rotating abruptly stopped and rocketed away from the platform, forming into a sharp three-dimensional arrowhead. As the watchers stood open-mouthed the six ships reached a point several kilometres from the Star-class ship and swung around.

"Hammer flight, attack," Mellivar ordered. "Shield flight, defensive formation. Engage."

The six fighters of the newly designated Hammer flight darted forward while the six ships of Shield flight moved ahead of the newly-created carrier and spread into a formation - like a shield, Bedis mused. The two sets of ships moved towards each other and another set of dogfights ensued. One ship stood out as it swung and swooped, jinked and dived and spun. Bedis, watching as amazed as the others, knew that was Mellivar. Finally, Mellivar called a halt.

"Hammer and Shield flights, break off."

The ships separated from their various engagements and formed into their two flights, circling the Star-class ship in tandem.

"*Stargazer*, prepare to receive fighters," Mellivar ordered. "Hammer flight, return to base."

On the Star-class ship, *Stargazer*, the flight bay suddenly blazed with light. The six ships of Hammer flight formed into two elements of three abreast. The first flight charged towards the flight bay. Bedis found himself holding his breath. A carrier landing had not been attempted in who knew how many years. The ships decelerated when close to the mouth of the flight bay and smoothly entered the bay, followed closely by the second element of Hammer flight.

"Shield flight, return to base."

Shield flight followed Hammer into the flight bay. Moments later the lights of the bay flicked off, leaving a gaping black opening again. Bedis took a deep breath, allowing the excited chatter of those other onlookers to wash over him. He noticed Moire looking much more relaxed. So, she had done it. No weapons yet but, as a demonstration went, it had been impressive. Outside the viewing platform, *Stargazer*, which would be the first carrier of the Union fleet, accelerated away, swinging around and behind the platform.

| **24** |

Preparations

"Weapons are a little behind schedule," Marjory said to Bedis a short while later as they sat over coffee in a small lounge. "We have them in prototype and they are proving out. There are a couple of minor changes I want to make and then we will mount them and see how they perform. There will be a small railgun to fire kinetic rounds and a blaster cannon to fire energy bursts. The primary defensive weapon will be the energy cannons. They will be the main weapon in dogfights, too. They will be easier to target and fire. We have a missile load being prepared also, but they are further away. The missiles themselves are ready. The guidance system needs more work, though, to be able to switch from attack to defence. We want to be able to target the Empire's ships and fighters and use the missiles as a stand-off weapon."

"It was an impressive demonstration," Bedis conceded. "I wasn't expecting to see a carrier."

"Well, Drummel had an old Star-class that we pushed back into shape. It was designed for the purpose, although I have some other ideas that we will try out. I also have a design for a new specialist carrier that has the flight bays at the sides rather than the front. It looks a little unwieldy but reduces the risk to the carrier from a poor landing, which will happen at some point."

"How do we integrate a carrier into the Fleet?"

"The best way is to have two carriers to a main fleet," Marjory said. "Most of the time the fleets are split up and patrolling different parts of their sector, so having two carriers allows for some flexibility."

"And how many fighters will each carrier have?" Bedis asked.

"Two squadrons is the optimal complement," Marjory replied. "I have designated them Hammer and Shield. Hammer is the attack squadron. Shield is the defensive squadron. The weapons loads would be different, although each could perform the defensive role. In some engagements, in fact, both squadrons may fly attack."

Bedis nodded, impressed at the thought that had gone into tactics already.

"And you seemed to be quite at home in that cockpit," Bedis said. "I have to admit that I was surprised when I found you leading the demonstration."

"I always test my designs, Admiral," Marjory replied smoothly. "I have done so for a long time now. And I have some experience in craft of this type."

"Your family's prototypes?"

"Something like that, yes," Marjory said.

"Well, for now we need to push hard to get the fighters into a usable force. What sort of training time do we need? How many can we produce? And when can we get them deployed?"

"We have a few more tests, but if we push *Stargazer* into active service we could have two full squadrons ready in a month. But the pilots will not be ready for several months after that. I could have destroyed every one of the pilots I flew with today," Marjory said in a matter of fact voice. "We can't afford to put these out there and have them all die in their first fight. Some of them will, there is no doubt," she said unemotionally, "but the fewer the better. So, a complete training program will have to be put in place. I have the details already laid out." She tapped an icon on her tablet. "That has been sent to your secure store. As for how many we can produce, again Drummel and licensees can roll them out faster than we can train pilots. Carriers are a different thing. We could pull Star-class or Superstar-class ships back and refit them, but we don't have any that we can spare at the moment. I will start to put the carrier design into production but we will have to deal with the inevitable real world design problems. Say another year to get the first set of three or four done."

"No chance we can bring that in faster?"

"Unlikely, Admiral, but we will try. Once the designs are completed for manufacture then we can accelerate. The first ships will be where our simulations get their true tests. As I said, there will be real world problems that simulators do not detect." Marjory thought. "At a pinch, we could deploy *Stargazer* with the demonstration stingers once the weapons are ready for real use. And the pilots are better trained."

Bedis nodded thoughtfully. He looked through the window of the lounge into the distance of space for a moment. Finally, he turned back to Marjory.

"We may have to do that," he said at last. "We have intelligence that the Empire is building up for something. We feel it's likely to be some sort of large-scale attack. Where, we don't know. Nor when. But if history is anything to go by, it will be in force."

"Yes," Marjory agreed. "Likud does like massed power."

"Well, this Likud does, any way."

"This Likud?" Marjory asked quizzically?

"There were no reported sightings of the Likud for some time, leading us to speculate that there was a change of leadership. We think the old Likud may have stepped down or been forcibly removed. A new Likud seems to have taken his place. And he appears to have stepped up preparations for whatever he is planning."

Marjory merely nodded. There was no point challenging such theories. There was only one Likud. He would not have been replaced, but he may indeed have something planned. Unimaginative though he was, and vicious as well, he *was* partly battle trained and had reasonable knowledge of Ennari techniques and tactics, as well as ships and weaponry. The Empire fighters were crude, very crude, but Marjory recognised Ennari characteristics in them. The capital ships were typically Likud. They were large, heavily armoured, heavily armed, and fought in sufficient numbers to overwhelm opposition. Union ships had been reporting that they were attacked by three and four cruisers in recent times rather than the pair that had been the norm in the past. The Union may have seen that as proof that a new Likud occupied the Emperor's throne. Marjory was sure that it was Likud finally responding to the changes that had occurred over the last two hundred or so years.

"Well, we will do the best we can do," Marjory replied. "I will step up the training of the demonstration team so they are as ready as they can be, and get the recruits' training accelerated. And we will fit out *Stargazer* with the full weapon load for a Star-class ship. Some of it needs to be altered to accommodate the fighters' flight deck, but it will be a fighting ship still."

"Very well," Bedis nodded. "I'll take care of commissioning *Stargazer* as the first carrier for the Union Fleet. I have a feeling, Mellivar, that you may have delivered exactly what we need at this time when we need it."

Again, Bedis thought. A Mellivar delivered what was needed when it was needed, again.

| **25** |

Stinger Action

"Admiral on the bridge!"

The bridge crew came to attention as Bedis walked through the bulkhead door leading from the transport tubes to the bridge. He waved them back into position.

"As you were," Bedis said, making his way to the command chair.

"Sir," the communications officer called, "Flight-Colonel Mellivar is on approach. She reports a full complement of stingers."

"Very well. Hangar bay to prepare to receive fighters," Bedis ordered, finding that order to be surreal given his own position around the orthodoxy of fighters in space only three years before.

"Hangar bay reports ready, sir."

Only ten minutes later the communications officer relayed that the fighter squadrons were both on board. Bedis nodded and checked his command tablet. All stations reported green.

"Set the coordinates as provided, please," Bedis ordered. "Signal the fleet to accelerate to point two light. All ships to prepare for FTL transition."

Bedis sat back as the orders were passed throughout the ships that comprised the Sixth Fleet. He watched the command team go about their business efficiently. He could have chosen any ship to carry his flag as newly minted admiral of the Sixth Fleet, but he chose *Stargazer* for two key reasons. First, the whole reason for this reduced fleet to be in existence was to get the carrier into what was expected to be a difficult fight. Second, he was intrigued at seeing what Mellivar would produce in terms of tactics and team dynamics.

Reports coming from the training centre that had been established for the first fighter pilots were that she displayed a grasp of fighter tactics and methods that were astonishingly advanced. It was true that she was a formidable pilot in her own right, but that had been on capital ships, patrols boats and shuttles. There was no ability to become trained in fighter tactics before now because there had been no fighters. There was no history to draw on beyond early attempts long ago that went nowhere. Before them, one had to go back to atmospheric fighter forces on Earth. No planets had sought to build such machines, relying instead on the Union Fleet for air security, and the Union had consistently refused to countenance the use of small fighter craft.

There was just something that did not ring true, but Bedis could not put his finger on it. He had absolutely no doubts about Mellivar's dedication to the Union and its principles. Nor did he doubt the commitment of those of her family in the past. But where did she get such a grasp of those tactics? The situation was one that he turned over in his mind from time to time. His musing was interrupted by Mellivar's arrival on the bridge.

"Admiral," Mellivar acknowledged as she took the seat that had been added to the usual bridge complement for the commander air group, a very old term that had been resuscitated only recently.

"Flight-Colonel," Bedis replied with an answering nod. "No problems, I take it?"

"One of the ships is running a little rough but we will have that rectified shortly. Otherwise, all stingers are accounted for. Capture by the damping field worked as expected."

"Admiral," communications reported. "All ships are at point two and report ready for FTL."

"Very well, set the mark and jump."

Which technically was incorrect, of course, Marjory mused. A long history of popular fiction and entertainment genres had popularised the idea of a jump to FTL and some sort of space below space.

In reality, it was more of a transition to a quasi-quantum dimensional state using the speed of light as a reference point and then … Jump was good enough, she thought.

Time in FTL seemed to pass quickly. Union ships all set their clocks to Earth Standard Time for ease when in the depths of space, so duration could be measured accurately. In this case, the Sixth Fleet would have to travel twelve light years, which meant something like fifteen days in the jump. During that time there could be no extra-ship activities, for the forces that FTL entailed would tear apart anyone leaving the ship. Part of the advanced design that Marjory had brought to the Union in the past was what allowed the ships to transit FTL space. There were accidents still, usually when entering or exiting FTL too close to stars, or when a ship travelled into uncharted territory and ran into something. However, the right sensors could track approaching FTL streams, while ships in FTL were unable to sense anyone awaiting them, which made the exit from FTL a tense time. She had plans to address those concerns, using research that had been underway on Ennaris before the rebellion.

"Flight-Colonel Mellivar, you have the bridge," Bedis said as he stood and stretched.

Marjory nodded as the admiral left the bridge. Unless they tried to go through a star, FTL travel was the most boring form of space travel ever, and Marjory was very familiar with it. Of course that had been when she commanded an Ennari fleet, but she had introduced FTL travel to the Union some years ago and so had experienced it anew in this new age. It was boring still.

Fourteen days, nine hours and sixteen minutes later, Marjory was taking her turn as bridge officer again. She looked up as a chime sounded. They were about to exit FTL.

"Admiral to the bridge," Marjory directed. "Sensors to maximum, shields to maximum, all weapons hot but anyone who fires without orders will be outside cleaning the windows without a suit," Marjory continued to chuckles around the bridge.

Two minutes later Bedis arrived on the bridge and took his usual seat.

"We exit FTL in another nine minutes, admiral," Marjory said. "Sensors and shields are at maximum, weapons are on line and held. Permission to leave the bridge?"

"Granted," Bedis said, glancing to Marjory. "Give 'em hell, Mellivar."

"Aye, sir," Marjory replied evenly.

Four minutes later, Marjory walked into the ready room of the fighter force. All of the pilots stood from their seats as she entered, and she waved them back to their seats.

"We exit FTL in four or five minutes," she said. "Some of you have combat experience on other platforms. None of you have faced combat in a stinger. Trust in your training and your ships. Our stingers are the equal to anything the Empire can throw at us, and probably better. Shield squadron will hold and protect *Stargazer* and her fleet. Hammer squadron will form on me. We will hold above and behind *Stargazer* after launch. With luck, the Empire commanders will not see us until we start our attack run. Let's go."

Without further ceremony, Marjory led the pilots from the ready room. Situated just behind the hangar, it took the pilots very little time to reach their designated ships. The klaxon sounded to indicate that transition from FTL was about to occur, but the pilots took little notice. There was no noticeable change or effect to worry about, after all. Three minutes later, strapped into her ship, Marjory saw the green status signal light on her stinger's display.

"Bridge, Hammer and Shield are ready to deploy," she reported.

"Understood, Flight-Colonel," came Bedis' voice. "We have exited FTL a little further from the action than expected. It seems the Empire decided to make this fight happen closer to Grelsax than was anticipated. It will take us a further seventeen minutes to get there. First and Fourth Fleets are engaged and taking losses. We have six Empire heavy cruisers breaking off to take us on."

"Admiral, recommend the stingers launch in five minutes and take position behind Stargazer. We may give them a surprise," Marjory said.

"Agreed," Bedis said after a pause, then left the channel open while he turned to his bridge crew. "All weapons hot. Independent action is approved. Mind the stingers when they get out there."

"Admiral, we have a saying in my … er … family," Mellivar said to the open channel. "May the hunting be good and the enemy worthy, and the victory sweet."

"Good hunting, Flight-Colonel," Bedis replied.

"Shield squadron, launch," came the controller's voice over the ship to ship communication a few minutes later.

Marjory watched her screen as the defensive squadron launched. She could not see them of course, for the fighters launched via tubes that catapulted them into space. There was nothing she could do for them now, although once she launched she would have the chance to give them some forms of encouragement. These stingers were not as capable as the Ennari craft with which she was most familiar, but they were close. There was one advantage she had that none of the others had, though.

"Hammer One, authorise Marjory nar Drewflin," Marjory said as she waited to launch.

"Hammer One, recognise Marjory nar Drewflin," she ship's AI replied.

"Reconfigure to Ogun," Marjory directed, invoking the Ennari Guardian to whom all Battle Mages looked for inspiration.

The ship's AI changed tone in reply. "Battle Mage, Hammer One on line. Battle map displayed. Weapons are nominal."

"Hammer squadron, launch," came over the ship channel.

"Hammer squadron, form on me after launch," Marjory directed. "May the Guardians protect you."

Across the other twenty four members of the squadron there were quizzical looks, shrugged off in the tense time of launch.

The twenty-five members of Hammer squadron launched moments later, flung through the tubes to emerge in the blackness of space. In the distance were six Empire heavy cruisers, while further in the distance were the First and the Fourth Fleets, unseen from this distance but displayed on long range sensors relayed from *Stargazer*. The two squadrons were being harassed by tiny specs that represented the Empire attackers. The stingers swung in a tight arc to the rear of their home carrier, forming up in a textbook V-flight formation behind Marjory.

Sixth Fleet moved to engage the six Empire heavy cruisers. Three Star-class cruisers surged ahead of *Stargazer*, spreading out to take the attention away from the carriers. Six corvettes charged, three to each side, to act as the two arms of a pincer. Small patrol ships swung in behind the Star-class cruisers, using them as protection until they were within range for their own weapons to have any chance of being impactful. Hammer squadron held station as *Stargazer* followed in the wake of the cruisers.

The Empire ships closed rapidly. Abruptly, well before Marjory would have done so, all six opened fire with heavy blasters. The Union ships avoided or deflected the blasts with ease and held fire. Marjory waited. Shield squadron spread in their defensive formation around *Stargazer*.

"Shield squadron, weapons free," Marjory called moments later. "Hammer squadron, on me. *Stargazer*, Hammer is go."

Marjory pushed the throttle control to the limit. The thrust of the ship's acceleration pushed her back in the cockpit. Marjory's eyes narrowed and the familiar feral grin curled her lips. She, the preeminent warrior, had missed this. Around her, Hammer squadron followed her trajectory. The twenty-five ships surged forward.

"Hammer One, identify optimal attack configuration, plot squadron routes," Marjory ordered to her ship AI.

Her screen reconfigured to show multiple tracks, two of them in blue and the rest in shades of red. Icons identifying stingers flashed above the blue paths. Marjory took in the display at a glance.

"Hammer, divide into two elements," Marjory directed without hesitation. "Routes are coming on your screens. Hammer Two, take the lead of element two."

She touched a stud to send the routes to her squadron members. The ships split into two elements. On *Stargazer,* Bedis stared in astonishment as the paths of the two squadron elements diverged. Each element charged at small gaps that had opened in the Empire formation. The Empire ships continued on their plotted paths. The Sixth Fleet ships opened fire, being careful to direct their fire away from the speeding stingers. The Empire ships laid down a withering defensive fire, while their main blaster cannons continued to pump energy blasts at the Sixth Fleet ships moving to meet them.

A flash to Marjory's right told of a stinger being destroyed. Her display showed a red icon, followed by a second and then a third. Her force was being destroyed before they were in range. Their formation was near perfect - and so was predictable.

"Hammer squadron, break formation. Independent tracks. Weapons free."

The twenty-two remaining ships scattered. All maintained their tracks towards the Empire vessels, but via wildly differing paths. Jinking, diving, swooping and twisting, Hammer squadron darted forward. The Empire ships' screens were absorbing the energy blasts from the Sixth Fleet, all the while keeping up a steady fire of their own.

"Battle Mage, weakness identified in the shield of Empire Five," Hammer One reported.

"Hammer Two, Empire Five's shields are weakening. Concentrate element two there," Marjory directed. "*Stargazer,* concentrated fire on Empire Five."

On *Stargazer,* Bedis merely nodded at the glance from the communications officer, who relayed the directive. Two corvettes immediately switched all their fire power to Empire Five, supported intermittently by two of the Star-class cruisers. The shields of Empire Five took blast after blast. Finally, one of the blasts broke through the weakened shield and crashed against the hull, destroying point defence cannons and shield emitters. Debris swirled around the strike zone. The hull could take blast after blast from energy weapons before the massively thick armour gave way, but there was now a hole in the ship's defensive coverage and each subsequent hit would extend it. The corvettes maintained a withering fire with their energy weapons on that now vulnerable area even while evading the blasts aimed at them.

Hammer Two led ten ships of the second element through the gap at speed. One stinger flew into the path of a remaining point defence cannon and was destroyed. Another missed the gap in the shields and met a similar fate against the cruiser's shield. The remaining nine reached their designated firing points. Bay doors opened beneath each of the sleek fighters. What had been the empty bay behind the pilot for the demonstration now held an array of weapons designed to attack the armoured Empire cruisers. Six stingers fired two missiles each before jinking around inside the shield radius and strafing the skin of the vessel. Three stingers fired two torpedoes each before following suit. More and more shield emitters and defensive emplacements were destroyed, allowing the fire from the Union corvettes and capital ships to take more effect. The nine stingers made a single strafing run before turning and running back through the expanding shield gap. Once outside the shield radius they followed a pre-planned route that would take them behind the Empire ships.

All of the missiles were targeted at the same point. Each accelerated within moments of being dropped. There was almost nothing to stop them, as the remaining defences were being destroyed progressively by the stingers until they sped away. The small target area was hit repeatedly by the stingers, finally opening a fracture in the thick armour. The six torpedoes were targeted at the same zone and would arrive almost simultaneously. As the last stinger exited the target zone, the first torpedo hit. These torpedoes were greatly uprated version of an old design. Each torpedo was a delivery vehicle for a second missile. As they approached their target, the outer casing of each torpedo was ejected and the inner weapons fired. A solid head designed for striking through armour was accelerated even more by a second stage rocket motor which destroyed its host torpedo as it ignited. The solid head would dig deep into the armour and then explode with enormous force. The goal was to tear open the skin of the ship. The first torpedo hit and exploded, tearing the small gash further. The second hit near it and extended the gash. The third did the same, but the gash now penetrated most of the way through the heavy armour that had been weakened by concentrated energy weapons fire before the stingers attacked. The fourth completed the job. The explosion tore open the armoured skin to leave a gaping wound. Atmosphere spewed forth, carrying with it objects of all shapes. The fifth and sixth torpedoes flew through the wound almost immediately and exploded seconds later, deep within the ship.

With the stingers away from the target zone, the Union ships concentrated their fire on the torn area of armour. Blast after blast tore away more and more of the skin until, finally, they also penetrated the ship. Internal bulkheads did little to hold back the devastating power of those energy blasts in the confined spaces within the hull. Blast after blast destroyed the inner workings of the ship. Stores of missiles near the forward launch tubes exploded, as did energy stores for the defensive cannons, both of which added to the carnage. Finally, Empire Five appeared to shimmer and dance sideways before cracking open in a massive explosion. The ship split apart in a dramatic plume of flame and smoke that was quickly doused by the vacuum of space. Huge pieces of the ship were flung away by the force of the explosion and now became dangerous additions to the battle zone.

Empire Five became the first victim of the Union stingers.

Marjory, meanwhile, led her stingers in a weaving path towards what she felt was the next most vulnerable ship. This had been tagged as Empire One, and was the left-most vessel of the line of cruisers. By attacking this ship, they would offer less opportunity to be caught in the cross-fire of multiple ships. Of course, once the capital ships came within broadside range any such consideration was moot. That was not yet the case.

The stingers closed on their target rapidly. Empire One laid down a defensive barrage that claimed a further two stingers. As they had done during training, the remaining stingers released their own barrage. Railgun bullets and energy blasts rained on the selected zone of Empire One's shield with the intention of overwhelming it in one spot. The stingers were aided by the continuing blasts from the corvettes that had closed the gap to the Empire's capital ships faster than the Union's larger vessels and were now engaged in deadly and fast-moving short range duels with their foes. The Union ships flitted above and below the main field of battle. Their weapons maintained a constant fire while the stingers evaded the heavy weapon blasts of the Empire cannons. The Empire ships were huge and powerful, while the Union corvettes, the successors to the gunboats of the past like *Sandpiper*, were fast and nimble but lacked those very heavy weapons.

Marjory's tactic worked. As the corvettes swung around the edges of the battle zone, one after the other directed its fire on the selected shield zone. On Hammer One the ship AI passed orders in Marjory's name to the remaining stingers, pinpointing where to strike. Each of the nine remaining stingers released six missiles, holding two each in reserve. Fifty-four missiles streaked towards Empire One. The stingers each jinked and moved out of a direct line of approach. Empire One's close-in defences picked off the missiles one by one until more than half had been destroyed and they remained hundreds of metres away.

Then, in a feat of flying that would be discussed for many years, the Union corvette *Sellis* swung across the line of the missiles, absorbing the defensive fire and allowing the twenty-three remaining missiles to run unimpeded for a short while. *Sellis* also provided cover for the Hammer stingers that swung into the shadow offered by the seriously damaged, but still fighting, corvette. Covering fire from Empire Two had dropped as it was targeted by four of the Union corvettes and the missiles closed the gap to Empire One rapidly. The missiles were further helped when, at the further end of the line, Empire Five exploded, flinging huge pieces of armour plate into the battle zone. Empire Three was forced to change course abruptly to avoid being struck, which caused Empire Two to slow slightly to avoid a collision with Empire Three. As *Sellis* cleared the field, venting atmosphere from multiple points where her own shields had failed to stop the barrage of short-range energy and kinetic hits, the missiles entered their targeting range. Each oriented on the designated point and lit their final stage rockets, flinging themselves at Empire One.

In a matter of moments, five of the missiles were destroyed, but the rest struck Empire One's shield at the target point. The cruiser's shield was overwhelmed and failed in that area. Immediately, Marjory directed her nine remaining Hammer stingers to reform into a wedge. They sped through the gap in the shields with railguns and energy weapons blasting at the shield emitters and close-in defensive cannons in a fast strafing run. Hammer One directed and coordinated the missile release points. All remaining missiles were released, after which all Hammer ships swung around and shot back through the shield gap and scattered to make defensive targeting more difficult.

"What did you use for targets?" Marjory asked as she swung on an erratic course away from Empire One.

"I identified what appear to be lines of access portals along the sides of the ship," Hammer One's AI reported. "I directed three missiles to each of five of the access portals, with staggered impacts. The remaining three missiles were directed to the defensive cannons nearest to most of the targets."

Marjory nodded. "Let's hope that works. Well done!"

"Thank you, Battle Mage," Hammer One replied. "Impacts will commence in five seconds."

Explosions rippled along the side of Empire One as the missiles hit. The first three missiles destroyed a swathe of defensive cannons, allowing the rest to swing onto target. One was hit by a cannon round but rather than being destroyed it was knocked off course and hit a nest of kinetic cannons, further depleting the defensive resources.

The five portals were hit by the remaining missiles in quick succession. Slightly weaker than the armour surrounding them, the tiny access portals that had been identified by Hammer One buckled and burst inwards as the first missiles hit. They were followed by the second set of missiles which breached the armour through the small gaps that now existed. The third missile wave, targeted against only four of the five targets, pushed into the ship and exploded in the narrow confines, causing massive damage. Empire One listed and swung away from the battle zone, exposing its damaged side to *Sellis*, which had stayed nearby and now swung around and made an erratic pass with its still active main guns targeting the damage zone. Further explosions lit the dark interior of Empire One. The cruiser's main cannon fell silent and the defensive fire became sporadic and untargeted.

Empire One pulled further away from the battle zone and the line of the Empire ships.

Marjory looked to her screen. She had seven ships of Hammer's first element left, none with missiles or torpedoes. Element two had nine ships with a small collection of missiles and torpedoes.

"Hammer Two, reform on me five kilometres above Empire One," Marjory ordered.

She led her remaining stingers in a loop, using the badly damaged Empire One as a shield. The cruiser's defensive cannons still fired occasional random bolts and two of the stingers had to avoid them, but all made the rendezvous unscathed. Marjory watched with approval as Hammer Two smoothly disengaged her remaining fighters and swung wide. Moments later, Hammer Two joined to the left of Hammer One. Marjory looked out over the battle zone for targets. There were four Empire cruisers still in action.

| 26 |

A Step On the Journey

Empire Five was still being attacked mercilessly when Bedis was hailed by his sensor operator.

"Admiral, Empire Three has launched fighters. They appear to be aimed at us. I make it ten ships."

"Only ten? Very well, keep a watch in case there are more," Bedis acknowledged. "Shield squadron, be advised we have ten fighters inbound from Empire Three."

The ten Empire fighters swung in a shallow arc to pass above the area of concentrated energy weapon fire. *Stargazer* produced a wave of defensive fire from its topmost turrets that reached out towards the attacking fighters. Four torpedoes were dropped from each ship and they darted forward.

"*Stargazer*, Shield One. Confirm these are the only enemy fighters," Major Ansellis called.

"Confirmed, Shield One. Maintaining a watch for any others," *Stargazer's* communications officer replied.

"Shield flights Alpha and Beta, with me," Ansellis directed. "Shield Two, hold position with Gamma and Delta."

Shield squadron divided into two elements, as Hammer had done. The first element, led by Ansellis, surged forward while the second held station by *Stargazer*.

"Admiral, forty torpedoes inbound," the communications officer reported. "Point defences are tracking. Shield is moving out of the line of fire."

"Okay," Bedis nodded. "Shield Two, point defences will be firing. Feel free to join in. Launch the interceptors."

"Affirmative," Lieutenant Hills in Shield Two replied. "Gamma and Delta flights, weapons free. Target those torpedoes."

Stargazer launched ten interceptor missiles and then a short time later the defensive energy cannons burst into life, interspersed by point defence railgun bullets. The twelve stingers added their own energy fire, although to little effect given how far away the torpedoes were still. Three torpedoes were destroyed at long range by *Stargazer's* missiles. A further twelve were destroyed shortly after as they moved into the furthest edge of the main defensive envelop. The torpedoes started to move slightly in their track course as they approached *Stargazer*, weaving and swooping slightly to make their track less predictable. As they moved closer, however, they also came closer to Shield's twelve ships, arrayed around and well outside the expected defensive cone of fire.

A whoop came over the communication channel as a stinger destroyed a torpedo. *Stargazer* fired more interceptor missiles even as the point defences accounted for torpedo after torpedo. Eight more had been accounted for, but sixteen remained tracking for *Stargazer*. Interceptors took two out.

"Admiral, the railguns are overheating," Bedis was informed. "Fire control expects them to fail any time."

"Pull them off line one by one for the minimum time needed," Bedis said. "If some of them freeze we should still have others available. Concentrate fire on the closest of the torpedoes. Shield Two, we'll need your help."

"Affirmative," Hills replied again. "Gamma, with me. Delta, remain in place."

Gamma flight charged towards the approaching torpedoes, firing their main guns constantly. As they came closer, the stingers switched to their small railguns. Three more torpedoes were destroyed. Gamma's stingers blew past the incoming torpedoes in a blur. *Stargazer's* defences concentrated on the remaining eleven, and a further seven were accounted for. Now only four remained.

Shield Ten, leading Delta flight, took note as *Stargazer's* railguns went offline one after the other. The energy weapons were not as effective as the kinetic weapons at stopping the torpedoes, and struggled to maintain a track. Making his decision, Shield Ten opened his communications channel.

"*Stargazer*, Delta flight engaging. We'll take the three to the right."

Delta flight darted forward, into the maelstrom of defensive energy fire. Using their railguns only, the six stingers swung into the path of the four torpedoes. Two stingers targeted each of the three right-most torpedoes, leaving one for *Stargazer* to deal with. The three were destroyed, the last only when it was almost on top of the stingers. Debris from the torpedo tore into the stubby wings and tail of Shield Fifteen before it could move away, although the pilot's shell remained intact. Shield Fifteen spun away from the fighting zone.

"Admiral, impact amidships in nine seconds," the weapons officer announced. "Railguns firing again."

The cannons continued to target the sole remaining torpedo. Many missed entirely. A small number of the railguns rejoined the battle. Finally, two seconds from impact the last torpedo was destroyed by the railguns and the defensive guns went silent. A ragged cheer went up from the bridge crew. Bedis sighed in relief.

"Alright people, we're still in a fight here," the admiral reminded his bridge crew. "We have a damaged stinger to recover and more in the battle. Status."

The Union corvette *Sellis* was extensively damaged and drifting after its heroic assistance to Hammer squadron, although its main cannons were online and continued to fire. The corvettes *Hester* and *Junis* were damaged beyond repair and escape pods were ejecting from both ships. Three patrol boats no longer registered and one of the Star-class cruisers was venting atmosphere. All ships reported that their shields were badly depleted from the bombardment of the Empire ships. Four Empire cruisers continued to fight, although two of them displayed significant damage.

The twelve stingers of Shield flights Alpha and Beta had been reduced to seven following their short but intense dogfight with the Empire fighters. The ten fighters had been destroyed, however, and the remaining Shield members were moving back into formation with the members of Gamma and Delta.

"*Stargazer*, Shield is in place, eighteen stingers available," Ansellis reported. "Weapons down to a handful of missiles and railguns. Most of the railguns are running short on ammunition. Request permission to cycle ships through the hanger deck for reload."

"Granted, and well done Shield," Bedis replied immediately. "Hanger deck, prepare to receive stingers. Combat load out. Sensors, find Hammer."

"Okay, how do we end this?" Marjory asked.

"Analysis indicates there are weaknesses in the extended engine exhaust nozzles of the Empire cruisers," Hammer One's AI reported. "Specifically, their configuration. The available sensor readings are limited, but it appears that the cruisers' shields don't cover the engine exhaust nozzles entirely, and they seem to interfere with the shield, too. I am putting a potential firing solution on screen. This ship is slightly behind the others so the overlapping rear defences may be reduced."

Marjory's screen changed to show one of the Empire cruisers from the rear, with targeting information for a zone in the centre of the four great engine exhausts. The Empire cruisers had their oversized engine nozzles stacked in two pairs of two. In the exact centre of the four nozzles was a tiny area that appeared not to be covered by the shields. Further, it appeared that there were no defensive weapons in the immediate vicinity, likely due to the effects of the out-sized engines, Marjory thought. She thought they would cause problems. However, approaches to the zone were covered by overlapping zones of fire and, of course, the emissions from the engines themselves were effective defensively to some extent. A target location was indicated by a red diamond, pulsing gently. Marjory considered what she as seeing, and made her decision.

"Hammer squadron, target is coming on your screens. We will be attacking Empire Three from the rear. Hammer Two has the lead. You will target your remaining missiles and torpedoes at this location. We only need one to get through. First element will fly cover. When you have released your load, join with first element in providing cover."

On *Stargazer,* the communications officer watched the icons of Hammer move rapidly away from the battle and frowned.

"Admiral, Hammer appears to be disengaging," she reported.

Bedis snorted. "Mellivar disengaging? Don't bet on it. Keep an eye on them. Let me know which of the Empire ships they target."

The communications officer divided her time between the battle underway and watching the icons as they moved into a cluster a hundred kilometres behind the Empire ships. With a thrill, she saw them turn in a three dimensional arrow head formation and start a run. She reported the start of the run to Bedis and then stared, dumbfounded at what she saw.

"Hammer squadron, prepare for the attack run," Marjory called. "Flank speed on my mark. Mark!"

All seventeen ships of Hammer squadron accelerated and kept accelerating, the massive engines of the stingers pushing them to speeds faster than anything else in the battle. They sped back towards the Empire ships, closing the distance rapidly.

Bedis shifted his position to look at the screen showing Hammer's position. He nodded to himself. Typical Mellivar, he thought, going for the throat.

"All ships to target Empire Three with half of their weapons," Bedis ordered. "I want that ship blanketed from every direction."

The extended melee of the battle changed shape. Two of the six Empire ships were out of the fight but four were fighting at close to full capacity. The Union forces had suffered significantly. All wore battle scars from where shields had degraded or kinetic strikes had caused damage. The ships had swung past each other during the intense battle, and were now turning to engage once again. The Union ships now began to target Empire Three with the majority of their firepower, all while maintaining alternate fire at the Empire vessels closest to them. The remaining corvettes darted through the now shrinking gap between the fleets so that Empire Three received fire from all sides except the rear.

Into the mix sped Hammer squadron. The stingers without missiles or torpedoes spread and maintained continuous energy fire on the relatively few weapons pods that protected the rear quarters of the vessel. Despite attempts to target the stingers from the other Empire ships' rear weapons, Hammer was moving too fast for them to maintain target locks. As they closed, Hammer's pilots changed to firing their railguns. Many of the kinetic rounds smashed through the lighter shielding at the rear of Empire Three and the defensive fire died out. Four missiles and two torpedoes were launched by the stingers of what had been element two. Hammer sped down the flanks of Empire Three, strafing the sides and targeting shield emitters and defensive pods.

In unison, Hammer swung around and sped back towards the rear, spreading their formation as they did so. The first of the missiles struck the now completely unprotected rear target zone and exploded against the heavy plating. Empire Three shuddered visibly from the combined strikes of the following missiles. One of the engines flamed out and the ship yawed gently. Hammer sped past the zone moments later, just as the first torpedo struck. The torpedo hit the centre of the target and penetrated through the damaged panel to deliver its secondary warhead between the four engines. The second was slightly behind the first and fired from a wider offset. Empire Three's yaw shifted the target zone and the torpedo could not compensate in time. Instead, it flew directly into the flamed out engine, driving far into the extended exhaust channel before hitting the engine itself. Its secondary weapon then fired and pushed the warhead deeper into the engine space, rupturing the huge fuel containment store that fed all four engines. The effect as the warhead exploded was devastating.

From ten kilometres behind Empire Three, Marjory watched as she readied Hammer for another foray. Empire Three seemed to skid to the right even before the force of the explosion was seen. That explosion was huge. The fuel store detonated with enormous force. The rear of Empire Three disintegrated and secondary explosions rippled through the ship. Short-lived flames spurted through destroyed hatches all along its length. Marjory could only speculate that the ships were designed with some sort of connected conduits for fuel and weaponry, although that was illogical. Nonetheless, something had caused Empire Three to blow apart in spectacular fashion. Muted cheers came over the ship to ship channel, which Marjory ignored. She still had a fight to end, and there were a handful of missiles and one torpedo remaining.

"Hammer, form on me," Marjory ordered. "*Stargazer*, focus on Empire Two."

On *Stargazer* the communications officer did not even look to Bedis for confirmation before relaying the order, which amused the admiral. He went back to fighting his ship. When he did get a glance from her, he merely nodded affirmation.

Empire Three had caused major disruption to the line of the remaining three Empire ships. To avoid collision with the tumbling wreck of the bulk of the ship, the three remaining ships had to move further out of their line of attack, giving the Union ships momentary respite. Bedis took the opportunity to pull his ships into a markedly different formation. *Stargazer* and two corvettes moved above the fight plane and directed most of their fire at Empire Two, while dividing the remainder of the fleet between Empire Four and Empire Six. The remaining Star-class ships moved below the plane and split their fire between the latter two Empire ships, while the remaining corvettes moved back and forth, shifting targets as they did so.

The concentrated fire told the captain of Empire Two that his ship was the next target. All defensive weapons on Empire Two swung to face the rear and the ship started to weave slightly to allow the guns and cannons the opportunity to cover the approaches. Marjory swung Hammer above the plane of attack. Four of the stingers had available stand-off weapons, with five missiles and a single torpedo between them. As she started the attack run, Bedis ordered *Stargazer* to close with Empire Two.

"Hammer One, swing in behind *Stargazer*. We'll fly interference. But don't be late," he added drily.

Stargazer moved into the path that would be taken by Hammer as they swung from high above the plane on which Empire Two operated to reach their attack vectors. Immediately, the carrier faced Empire Two's weapons load. *Stargazer's* shields suffered immediately. Luckily, with only Empire Two to worry about, Bedis could direct power to bolster the shields facing the enemy ship. *Stargazer* rocked continuously as Empire Two directed its considerable firepower at the Union ship. Crew members were tossed against walls or consoles and injuries mounted. A sequence of blasts managed to get past a weakening shield emitter and *Stargazer* suffered a hull breach. Those crew unfortunate enough to be in the vicinity were sucked into the vacuum of space even as bulkheads slammed shut. *Stargazer* staggered at the impact.

"*Stargazer*, disengage," Marjory directed.

"Hammer One, Shield is back on line," Ansellis transmitted. "Full combat loads. Think they'll be useful?"

Anyone who had battled against Marjory, Battle Mage of Ennaris, would have recognised the feral grin that spread across her face, and they would have quaked.

"Shield One, take the lead and target Empire Four. Throw everything at them," Marjory directed.

"Shield One," Ansellis acknowledged as he led the remainder of Shield away from Hammer's track.

Back into the fray charged Hammer. The squadron darted from behind the shelter of *Stargazer* as the carrier rolled to protect the newly vulnerable hull breach zone and accelerated away from Empire Two. The Empire cruiser continued to pour energy fire at *Stargazer*, seemingly having lost sight of Hammer. Too late, the defensive weapons swung back as Hammer's ships sped along the flanks from behind, firing continuous energy blasts and expending the last of their railgun ammunition. At the rear, the five remaining missiles and the single torpedo were fired. The four stingers that had fired them sped forward to contribute their own railgun fire to the mayhem. Many of the defensive weapons emplacements were destroyed but the main guns continued to fire.

Marjory directed Hammer away from Empire Two as the five missiles impacted the zone between the massive engines, followed moments later by the sole torpedo. The weakened panels between the engines' exhaust nozzles buckled at the onslaught and the torpedo slammed through, releasing its secondary charge that blasted forward and penetrated the engine room before exploding. Empire Two bulged at the rear before the hull ruptured for half its length. There was no single explosion visible to external watchers, but the ship's skin split in several places. Atmosphere vented along much of its length. Power died and Empire Two went dark with the exception of several pin-pricks of emergency lighting that showed on the superstructure.

The damage to Hammer had been severe. Only six stingers had sped away from Empire Two, and two of them were limping. However, as she switched her monitor to view the wider scene, Marjory realised that the battle was over. Empire Six was accelerating away from the engagement zone, while Empire One was adrift. Empire Five, Empire Three and Empire Two were destroyed, while Empire Four also drifted following Shield's successful attack that Marjory had missed in the chaos of her own action. Only nine stingers remained of Shield. The remaining ships of the Sixth Fleet were scattered. One of the Star-class cruisers had been all but destroyed, and three of the corvettes were limping and venting atmosphere. All of the Union vessels were damaged to some extent. *Sellis* was adrift.

As Marjory surveyed the scene, Empire One exploded, followed by Empire Four.

Perplexed at the cause of their destruction, Marjory looked further afield. It appeared the larger battle that had been waged by the combined First and Fourth Fleets was also ended, but who had emerged victorious she could not guess. Her screen showed many damaged or destroyed Union and Empire ships, with several Empire ships speeding away.

"Hammer and Shield," Marjory called, "recover to *Stargazer*."

The battle was over. It was time to deal with the aftermath. And she had letters to write.

"It looks like the two Empire ships self-destructed," Bedis replied to Marjory's query, as they sat over coffee in the wardroom. "The same happened to those ships badly damaged but not destroyed in the main battle zone. It would appear the choice in the Empire is win or die."

Marjory nodded. That would fit with Likud's own philosophy, as long as it was not him doing the dying.

"We're calling it a draw," Bedis continued. "First Fleet lost all of its corvettes and lighter ships, and all but two of the Star-class ships were destroyed or damaged enough that they won't fight again, including the flagship. The Fleet is all but gone. Fourth Fleet fared a little better but also lost most of its ships. Sixth Fleet still has a fighting capability, although we took quite a few losses also. The Empire had fourteen heavy cruisers and seven light cruisers. They lost eight of the heavies. We accounted for five of those, which has raised a few eyebrows. They also lost five of the light cruisers."

Marjory nodded thoughtfully. "The stingers may have been a factor," she mused carefully.

"Ha!" Bedis snorted before smiling ruefully. "Don't try to be subtle, Mellivar, it's not you. The stingers *were* the difference, and I've made that point very clearly. I was completely wrong about that and you were right. We'll have to increase the training and may need to look at better integration between the Fleet and the fighters, but I think this engagement will drive both the use of the stingers and that better integration. I already have Admiral Greppis from Third Fleet wanting to discuss it and I've been ordered to brief the Union joint chiefs when we return. I want you with me there."

"Yes, Admiral," Marjory replied, as her thoughts turned inward.

This had been another part of the journey and one that she had thought may not be successful. But it was, although they had been lucky and the Empire commanders had been taken by surprise.

Still, the time was coming closer to when she could leave the Union and return to Ennaris.

part five

HORNSBY

*175 years before the events described
in <u>Children of Ennaris</u>*

| **27** |

Fresh Design

"**L**ieutenant, *Grevis* has been lost!"

Lieutenant Tellis Mellivar cursed. One minute into what had always looked like being a disaster and the small Union patrol had lost one-third of its firepower. Her own vessel, the Union patrol ship *Athena*, was evading the large energy pulses being fired by the two attacking Empire medium cruisers.

"Survivors?" Mellivar rapped out.

"None. *Grevis* just exploded. She flew into one of the pulse blasts directly," Ensign Kelvin reported.

"And *Belvoir*?" Mellivar asked, referring to the third patrol ship.

"Evading," Kelvin replied.

"Third Empire cruiser," Weapons Sergeant William called out. "Just in sensor range, moving towards us."

"Look for the other," Mellivar ordered. "There will be a fourth. They travel in pairs."

"Aye, Lieutenant," William replied.

"Get me a line to *Belvoir*," Mellivar ordered. "It's time we left."

"Mellivar? How do we handle this?" Lieutenant Frasor, commanding *Belvoir*, asked.

Mellivar was pleased that there was no quaver in Frasor's voice. But there was no mistaking the anxiety her fellow ship commander was experiencing.

"We run," Mellivar replied, working her navigation computer. "We will feint towards Mentis and then swing back into the Patch."

"That's further from home," Frasor warned, ending his words with a grunt as *Belvoir* suffered a near miss. "That was close. If we're going, we need to go. They're about in range where they won't miss."

"Steer three seven nine dash eight nine, put all power to your rear shield and angle it at seventy-three degrees. We will come up beside you and do the reverse. On my mark."

"Ready," Frasor replied. "Hope you know what you're doing."

"We will see," Mellivar replied. "Two, one, mark!"

Smoothly, *Belvoir* swept in a tight turn, straightening on course for the Mentis Anomaly, an odd region of space where ships' navigation equipment gave strange readings. Behind her came *Athena*, moving faster to come up alongside.

"Shields, now!" Mellivar rapped out.

"*Belvoir* shields are as you ordered, Lieutenant," William called out. "Our shields are lining up with them, reverse angle."

"Very well. *Belvoir*, we will stay in this formation. Make sure you do not drift. I will mesh the shields," Mellivar said, wincing as the two Empire cruisers that had jumped them effectively bracketed the fleeing patrol ships.

"Mesh the shields!" Frasor exclaimed. "How do you do that?"

"Like this," Mellivar replied, making the last adjustments to the command pad and executing the instruction.

The shields of the two vessels joined to form a single shield, shown on the ships' screens as two angled planes with a common edge like a reverse V. The joined edge pointed towards the oncoming Empire cruisers. Inside the arms of the V were the two patrol ships. Bridge crew on both ships exchanged incredulous expressions at the near impossible move that was done so easily by Mellivar.

"Flank speed on my mark," Mellivar directed. "Two, one, mark!"

The two ships leapt forward, towards the anomaly. After a moment, the Empire cruisers matched and surpassed their speed, gaining on them inexorably.

"*Belvoir*, we will swing around the Anomaly and put it between ourselves and the Empire ships," Mellivar said.

"Lieutenant, the other two Empire cruisers are moving to cut off our path back to base," Ensign Kelvin reported.

"Understood," Mellivar nodded. "So we will not go that way. Keep an eye on them, though. William, make sure *Belvoir* stays in formation and monitor the shield. We can take one hit but probably not two."

"We'll be very close to the Anomaly on this course," William said. "Is that wise given that we don't know what it is?"

"It will be fine," Mellivar replied. "Stay on task."

The Anomaly was as intriguing to Union spacers as it was annoying. It had been located more than fifty years earlier and mapped. Strangely, it had remained exactly in the same position for that time, and remained a mystery no matter how many investigations were conducted. Mellivar, however, knew exactly what it was. She donned her headset. The small microphone swung into place as she adjusted the channel settings.

"Farstation Two-One-Seven, recognise Marjory nar Drewflin," Mellivar muttered quietly. "Hold stealth mode."

The Ennari farstation AI received the signal on the archaic transmission type used by the Union ships, took a fraction of a moment to match the voice to its records and replied.

"Farstation Two-One-Seven, recognise Battle Mage Marjory nar Drewflin."

"Farstation Two-One-Seven, designate Ordoreth vessels *Belvoir* and *Athena* as friendly."

"*Belvoir* and *Athena* recognised as friendly," the farstation AI confirmed.

"Farstation Two-One-Seven, designate Andorethi vessels as hostile."

"Designated."

"Farstation Two-One-Seven, all weapons free. Clear to engage Andorethi vessels once *Belvoir* and *Athena* have flown by."

"Affirmative, Battle Mage," the farstation AI replied.

The two patrol ships were rocked as a blast from one of the closing Empire cruisers struck the joined shields and was deflected.

"Taking fire," William reported. "Shield join is fluctuating."

"*Belvoir*, I'm dropping the shield join. Angle your rear shield to present a flat plane," Mellivar ordered.

She entered the commands into the command pad. The rear shields of the two patrol ships separated once again and both oriented to present a flat barrier. Another blast from the pursuing cruisers clipped the edge of *Belvoir's* shield.

"*Belvoir's* shield is weakening. I think that last one must have affected one of the generators," William said. "Approaching the Anomaly."

Mellivar nodded as yet another blast buffeted *Athena*. The small ship staggered sideways before being caught by Mellivar and the course re-established.

"Our shields are failing, too," William called out.

The two ships swung in unison around the region known as the Mentis Anomaly and set their noses towards another region known as the Patch. This was a region of shifting magnetic fields and uncertain asteroids where navigation was perilous and sensor returns were poor and patchy. But it was an ideal place to lose chasers.

The Empire cruisers followed the course set by the two smaller Union ships, moving to sweep around the Anomaly. Farstation Two-One-Seven's AI acquired them on its targeting scanner and released the weapons safeguards that were usually maintained. As the second cruiser swung past it, the farstation issued twin plasma bursts followed by a spread of eight missiles. True to Empire designs, the two cruisers had minimal shields facing aft. The plasma bursts hit the rear shields and overloaded them as the first of the missiles arrived. These, of course, were Ennari missiles, not the less capable ones manufactured so far for the Union. Each cruiser took the brunt of four missiles, targeted at the same locations, selected by the farstation AI after analysis of the vessels.

Both cruisers were destroyed at the same time. The first missiles fired at each ship breached the rear containment of the oversized engines that jutted out behind all Empire cruisers. That took both ships out of the pursuit as the massive power units flamed out. Worse, though, was that the following missiles flew through the same breach and exploded deep inside the engine compartments, destroying fuel lines and energy containment fields. The rear of each ship disintegrated as the fuel store exploded.

On *Athena*, Mellivar noted that destruction of the pursuers with satisfaction, while for the other members of the two Union crews it caused confusion.

"Lieutenant, the two cruisers just blew up!" Weapons Sergeant William exclaimed. "There was no indication. Both just blew. It was like something targeted them from behind, but there's nothing there."

"Well," Mellivar remarked, "let's make the most of whatever it was. Start whatever repairs we can manage on the shield generators and we'll see what other damage was done. With luck we can hide in the Patch for a while."

The unexpected loss of the two cruisers gave the ship commanders of the other two Empire cruisers pause. Their sensors may have shown some type of energy pulse but, at the time, the cruisers were preparing to intercept the Union ships when they started their return to their own space, and the farstation shields had hidden the missile launches. After running a search for unknown Union vessels, and with their prey now hidden in the Patch, the two Empire cruisers returned to their own patrol.

The immediate consequence of the action that saw Mellivar extricate two of the three patrol ships from what many considered to have been an impossible situation, was the she was promoted to Lieutenant-Commander. Despite making it clear that the two Empire cruisers had not been destroyed by her actions, the review board agreed unanimously that her tactics were the best that could have been devised. In addition, this was the first engagement for a very long time where any of the now seriously outmoded patrol ships had escaped from an Empire ambush.

"And she's a Mellivar," one review board member, Admiral Jarris, had growled. "They always produce surprises. I want to see what this one can do. Let's give her something bigger to play with."

The tactic of joining the shields together was examined from all angles and, finally, was deemed by a range of experts to be a sign of genius. Mellivar was made to demonstrate how it was done multiple times, after which the tactic, and Mellivar's method, was added to the learning resources for Fleet ship captains. Experienced hands marvelled at the intricate calculations that were needed and marvelled again at the thought that it was done under fire. The extensive lore surrounding the members of clan Mellivar grew again.

A second consequence was that she was appointed to the command of the Centaur-class destroyer *Hornsby*. The Centaur-class ships had been in service for well over a hundred years. There were very few left in service and they were considered to be far inferior to designs by Drummel Industrial and its several competitors. Spare parts were difficult to find and usually needed to be custom-made. However, in a period of budget constraints and increasing Empire aggression, every ship was needed and so the remaining Centaurs remained active.

Hornsby was not a pretty ship. There were no flowing lines as were found on a Star-class cruiser by Drummel Industrial, nor were there the aggressively sculptured bow and flaring sides of the heavily armoured Moon-class vessels from Bellis Corporation. Rather, *Hornsby* had a utilitarian and seemingly unbalanced design, with a sharply pointed bow, narrow flanks, a flat keel and a raised superstructure that held the bridge and living quarters for most of its relatively large complement of spacers. The below decks area seemed to be too small for the superstructure that sat atop it. Its weapons load was considered to be poor by Fleet standards for a ship of its size. Past efforts to improve that situation had run into power problems. The ship was operating at the limits of its power generation capabilities. It was never a good design and its myriad flaws were on display.

Mellivar's introduction to her new command was far from auspicious. *Hornsby* had been operating as part of the Third Fleet on the fringe of one of the contested areas between the Union and the Empire. A difficult patrol had ended in a pitched battle with four pirates, during which *Hornsby* had sustained significant damage, including the loss of its main command staff when the prominent bridge had been subject to sustained blaster and missile fire from the pirates. The pirates had made their escape while *Hornsby* had limped back to base, bloodied and battered, under the command of a junior Lieutenant from the night watch.

It had been touch and go as to whether *Hornsby* would be scrapped, but the loss of two other destroyers in an Empire ambush meant the ship was given a reprieve. However, the repairs required were enormous, especially as parts were unavailable and so would have to be manufactured.

"I'm sorry, Mellivar," Admiral Hinkson, commander of the Union shipyard at Millig Base, said as the two sat over coffee. "I know you've just arrived here, but I'm afraid there's no good news for you about *Hornsby*."

"How bad?" Mellivar asked.

"The structural damage is reparable, that's the good news, but the fittings are almost impossible to obtain. We'll have to fabricate almost everything, and that takes time with all of our other work. Our best guess is two months to get the structural work back in shape, and then maybe another six months to get it all complete."

The two officers sat, contemplating the position in which they found themselves. For Marjory, as another Mellivar in this time, the news was a set-back, but perhaps not a total one. Her main self-appointed task this time was to fill in at least one gap that she and *Fendaristil* had identified in the Fleet armament. She had one final capital ship she planned to deliver in the future but, for now, the goal was something much more nimble but with heavy fire-power. A Centaur-class ship was not her ideal subject for this work, but it was what she had. Could she turn this to her advantage?

"Admiral," Marjory said as though she had a sudden thought. "I have a proposition for you. Let me redesign parts of *Hornsby* and make your repair job easier. I have some ideas that we could try out."

"I can't just turn the design of one of our ships over to you," Hinkson said with a short laugh. "My career would be toast."

"What if I obtained Fleet approval?" Marjory asked. "I don't want to put you in a difficult position in this regard, but I am confident that I can obtain permission."

Hinkson turned the idea over. Almost any other officer would be scorned for believing that they could improve a Centaur-class vessel. In most people's eyes, the best improvement would be complete and total destruction. The person making this proposal, however, was a Mellivar and in Fleet ship design circles it had become a mantra that if a Mellivar turned up and asked to build something then the best policy was to let them.

"And would this work be done by your family's facilities?" Hinkson asked.

"No, Admiral," Marjory replied with a smile. "Drummel Industrial has enough on its plate with recent upgrades to the Star-class design and stinger improvements. I believe Millig Base has the tools and skills needed. However, I will have Drummel manufacture some parts if necessary."

"Well, Commander, if you can get clearance then I'll clear a dock for you to use, somehow. How long will you need?"

"With your permission, I will pay a visit to Fleet, but I need to get some designs in place first."

"I'll have the Centaur-class specs delivered to your inbox," Hinkson said.

"Thank you, Admiral," Marjory replied.

There was no need for that, as *Fendaristil* had obtained detailed plans and specifications once Marjory's posting to *Hornsby* was known. However, Marjory had Hinkson on her side for the moment, so any offering to assist would be accepted to deepen the commitment.

| 28 |

A Mellivar Ship

The meeting with Fleet Logistics was a strange one for Marjory. She had had her share of battles with the bureaucratically-minded leaders of the Union Fleet's Logistics arm over her long time assisting the Union, and expected to be met with opposition that she would have to batter down. Instead she was met with a warm welcome such as a celebrity might receive.

Her request for a meeting with the senior admiral for Logistics for the sector had been agreed promptly, as had been her request to discuss the disposition of *Hornsby* with Fleet Admiral Bensin, Third Fleet's commanding officer. That was unusual enough, for senior admirals did not have swathes of free time in their calendars to be allocated to relatively junior officers on request.

Even more strange was the reception received when *Fendaristil* dropped out of FTL just over a million kilometres away from the Fleet sector headquarters. The usual challenge was made as expected, but *Fendaristil's* identification codes in response produced a flurry of communications and a priority passage through the approach channels. On arrival at her assigned dock, Marjory was met by a security escort and whisked through the arrival procedures and then to the Fleet Adjutant's office.

"Lieutenant-Commander Mellivar, welcome," the ensign on reception said as Mellivar was deposited by her escort. "Captain Vensing will be with you shortly."

"Thank you, ensign," Marjory replied, before making her way to the inevitable hard chairs ranged along the facing wall.

Around the reception room were several schematics and pictures of old Fleet ships, including an early Star-class medium cruiser. 2D images, she thought, rather than holographs. Interesting. One caught her eye and she stood to examine it further. Yes, as she thought, it was an image of *Sandpiper*, the small gunboat that had been the first Fleet vessel that she had encountered. She was staring at the image, remembering, when the door opened and a middle-aged officer emerged.

"An old Redoubt-class gunboat," he said as he walked over to join Marjory. "*Sandpiper*. This was the first one to survive an encounter with two enemy cruisers. Amazing! They were virtual death-traps for the people who flew them. But I assume you have some familiarity with that ship's story."

"Yes, one of my forebears worked with Fleet and *Sandpiper* was one of the ships used to prove her designs," Marjory replied. "She was a good ship, flown by good people."

"Well, your family has had a lot to do with the changes that have occurred since then," Captain Vensing nodded. "Please, come into my office and we can discuss what you need. Admiral Bensin will be available shortly."

A short time later, with coffee served, Marjory gave Vensing a quizzical look.

"Captain, I am a little surprised at what I can only call an unusually quick agreement to this meeting and an unusually warm welcome," she said, watching Vensing's reaction. "My request may be out of the ordinary, but not enough to warrant such priority."

"Yes, it's unusual," Vensing replied, "but when Admiral Hinkson informed Admiral Bensin that a member of the Mellivar family wanted to discuss changes, well, let's say that it created some interest."

"I am not even sure my ideas will work," Marjory objected.

"Commander, every design your predecessors delivered has worked flawlessly, so history is firmly on your side."

"Not all," Marjory responded. "There have been problems and losses."

"Yes, but mostly by those who sought to damage the Union. In other cases, of course, early designs were surpassed by later Empire ships that were built in reaction. Each time, however, a fresh Mellivar design was received to update older vessels or to create new ones. Or new weaponry. Or new tactics. Or other technologies." Vensing regarded Marjory over the rim of his coffee mug. "When Fleet Logistics hears the name Mellivar, our hopes are raised."

Marjory nodded, thinking about how she had had to fight for her designs to be built in the past. While this level of support was odd, she hoped that it would allow her some additional freedom to do what she felt was needed.

"Well," she said as the office door opened and an older man entered the room, "I hope you will not be disappointed."

"I find that unlikely," the newcomer said as Marjory stood. "I'm Vlad Bensin, Commander. I'm very pleased to welcome you to Huy-si Base."

"Admiral," Marjory acknowledged, saluting.

"Please sit, and tell me why you wanted to see me."

Marjory considered which of the several pre-prepared approaches she would use. Like most senior military people, Bensin was direct and to the point. He had to be to get things done. He would be pressed for time, undoubtedly. Direct it would be.

"Admiral, I believe we have a growing problem. We are being picked off by Empire ships, especially our smaller vessels. For whatever reason, the Empire ships are ignoring our capital ships. That may be because our capital ships and stingers combined have a better chance of defeating them. Those capital ships usually travel with support vessels, of course, so Empire vessels travelling in their usual pairs are vulnerable.

"We still patrol with our smaller ships, however, to deal with pirates and other problems, and they are the ones being hunted now. I believe we need to improve the capabilities of the smaller ships. In fact, what I have in mind is like a return to the days of *Sandpiper*. I propose to convert *Hornsby* into a modern-day gunship."

"And you think an old Centaur-class can do that?" Bensin asked, sceptically. "*Hornsby* is being repaired because we need all of the hulls available. In other times she would be scrap."

"I understand," Marjory replied. "*Hornsby* is under-powered, under-gunned and is out of proportion for the mission. However, she is a sound ship in other respects. And our production facilities are running at capacity, so awaiting a new custom-built ship is not possible."

"And you believe we can give *Hornsby* new life?"

"I do. In many ways *Hornsby* is the best opportunity to try these changes. She requires so many repairs to be space-worthy again, and so many parts must be manufactured for the purpose, that we can treat her like a blank canvas of sorts. In fact, I propose to almost completely rebuild her, but without needing to start completely."

Bensin gazed at Marjory for a moment, receiving a direct, confident gaze in response. Both held the pose for a few seconds before Bensin gave a small smile and nodded.

"Very well," he said. "Show us what you've got. You're half-way there with your family reputation, but only half-way. Take us the rest of the way."

Three weeks later, Marjory returned to Millig Base with Admiral Bensin's approval to do what she could do to, in his words, "bring that derelict back from the dead."

She was met by Admiral Hinkson and the two spent the afternoon period in an office set aside for the purpose, reviewing designs and making plans. A constant stream of design and engineering staff entered the office and exited with varying expressions ranging from surprised to amazed. The rumour mill kicked into over-drive when the news spread that the Lieutenant-Commander was one of *those* Mellivars. Marjory took to spending her sleep periods on *Fendaristil* rather then in the quarters assigned to her, as much to avoid the stares and pointing fingers as to continue to work with her ship's far more advanced AI on refining the design.

Hornsby was moved from a standard refitting dock to one designated for primary construction. A larger than normal number of the shipyard's construction bots were assigned to the project. A huge opaque net was hung around the ship, and security was stepped up in her vicinity.

For almost a month, watchers were treated to the sight of barge after barge of material being carried way from *Hornsby*. Shattered pieces of ablative sheeting told the story of the old, nearly destroyed superstructure being cut away, while huge quantities of old power and data cables told of an unexpected depth of renovation. When the single large engine was removed - it could be nothing else, despite efforts to shield it from view - eyebrows were raised. Finally, an oddly eclectic mix of cabin furniture and fittings, machinery and assorted external fittings including sensors, mounting points, laser cannons and very old point defence railguns were carted away. Speculation mounted.

Activity appeared to slow after that, surprising observers. The frantic pace that had been in evidence as demolition progressed was missing. Large sheets of oddly curved and angled composite plate were shipped behind the shrouds, along with huge spools of new cabling and modern power conduits. Work was progressing, therefore. However, there was an air of waiting for something. Speculation ran wild.

That speculation came to an end, to some extent, at least, when an enormous Superstar—class ship arrived. The viewing windows were crowded when the cargo ship *Besnil* emerged from the blackness of space, with the Drummel Industrial logo lit by massive spotlights. Very few of the staff of the shipyard had seen a Superstar-class vessel, for while it was now an old design that had been maintained and uprated, very few had been built and even fewer remained in service. Even for those who had seen one, the massive size of the Union's largest vessel took their breath away. The ship hove to across the end of Hornsby's dock and enormous doors opened in its side where the hanger bay was situated on ships of the line. Excitement mounted, only to be dashed when the dock shroud was extended across the gap to *Besnil,* blocking the door and any activities from view.

Besnil remained in place for more than a week. Her surprisingly small crew rotated through the station, resisting any and all attempts to get them to give any indications as to what was happening. The rumour machine kicked off anew when it was realised that the ship's complement included senior members of Drummel's engine and ship-fitting staff. The Drummel staff were entertained by Marjory and Admiral Hinkson while they visited, but otherwise were closeted away behind the shrouds.

After nine days, *Besnil* departed, gliding away from the dock more gracefully than a ship her size was thought to be able to do. Her fluid, almost organic lines gave the appearance of a gargantuan sea creature in its natural element. The shroud was reset to block any view again.

The pace of work stepped up once more. Cabin fittings were installed, but not in the quantity expected. Was the crew size to reduce? That expectation grew when the ship's galley equipment also proved to be less than was usual for a Centaur-class ship, which usually needed a large crew complement to deal with the inefficient equipment of those ships.

Finally, almost five months after work had started on *Hornsby*, the shrouds were rolled up and the shipyard personnel gathered wherever they could to see what had been created of the old ship. Jaws dropped as the ship was manoeuvred from the construction dock to the usual crew boarding gantries.

Gone was the oddly proportioned ship with the ungainly superstructure and sharply pointed bow. The raised superstructure had been removed completely and the newly flowing lines ran from the bow to the stern on all sides, which meant that the command and living quarters must have been moved inside the ship's hull, like most Drummel ships' designs. The formerly pointed bow was blunted and rounded, and the lines running to the keel were far less sharp. In fact, twin parallel bulges running from below and behind the bow gave it a more rounded front cross-section and hinted at enhancements that several onlookers speculated were weapons turrets. Given the smooth-skinned design on Mellivar craft of the past, with external weapons, sensors and communication arrays deployed only as needed, that was agreed to be the most likely answer.

At the rear, the ship flared out to both sides, rather than tapering as the old *Hornsby* had done. That seemed odd to most watchers, given that the old single engine had barely filled the space left by the Centaur's odd design. What's more, the ship seemed to be shorter by several metres. The changed appearance, it was agreed, made *Hornsby* a prettier ship than she had been, but the stern seemed to be too large for the engine. Conversation died away and returned with a rush, however, as the ship was pulled into its bay and sharp-eyed observers realised that they were looking at twin engines. What's more, they were two *big* engines. One engineer, standing at one of the observation windows, silenced everyone.

"Damn," he said in awe, "they're twin Mark Nines."

Necks swivelled to see who had made the statement. Captain Hambeth was a very well credentialed engine maintenance engineer, with a long record of working on almost every engine in the Union fleet for forty years and an encyclopedic knowledge of his field. If Hambeth said they were Mark Nines, then they were Drummel Industrial Mark Nines. And as the implications of putting two such huge, and hugely powerful, engines into a ship the size of *Hornsby* sank in, the collective breath was taken away.

Then there were the smooth sides of the ship. The old *Hornsby* had been encrusted with sensor pods, point defence pods, communication pods and any number of protuberances that made it look like an old sailing ship suffering from a barnacle infestation. This version had none of that. There were pods but they blended with the curves from the side bulges that started quite large at the bow and tapered to merge into the stern.

The keel was no longer a flat expanse. Rather, a third bulge had been added, running the whole length of the keel. Weapons were not on view, so perhaps that addition was a weapons platform? Offensive or defensive? Speculation continued.

"She's beautiful," someone said, and received general agreement.

How such a plain, utilitarian and tired ship could be transformed into the fresh, attractive vessel they now saw was a puzzle for so many. The thought processes that could see this beauty buried in the Centaur lines could not be fathomed. It was, however, put into context by a final breathless comment.

"It's a Mellivar ship."

| 29 |

A Trial Passed

"Well, Commander, your *Hornsby* has become the talk of the town," Admiral Hinkson commented with a wry smile as he and Marjory sat over coffee the evening after the reveal. "I don't think I've ever been quite so pleased to be proven wrong. I was sure *Hornsby* couldn't be resuscitated before you came along."

"It was a lot of work, Admiral, so in many ways it is not the same ship that we started with."

"Almost eighty percent of the old lower hull remains intact," Hinkson said, "so it remains the old Centaur underneath."

"But it is ten metres shorter, has had all of the upper hull, almost all external surfaces and interiors replaced, new command systems, new sensors and communications, uprated weapons systems, and vastly upgraded engines. It also has the control system from the latest Star-class ship. It will only need half the number of crew, and will not have the same mission. The old *Hornsby's* lower hull is there but I am afraid the ship's spirit may have been damaged."

Marjory paused, considering the changes she had wrought on the old, unloved *Hornsby*.

"That's an oddly philosophical view," Hinkson said, surprised.

"Where I am from, in my ... er ... extended family, we take the ship's spirit seriously," Marjory replied pensively. "I can only hope it remains intact. I hope it can forgive me."

Silence fell as Admiral and Commander fell into their own reveries.

"Well," Hinkson said into the silence, "Vlad and his team will be here in a few weeks for the shakedown. There's a lot of interest in your work. We already have a question about *Hornsby's* mission. How would you describe it? You designed this for a clear purpose, after all."

"Yes," Marjory nodded. "Our weakness at the moment is that we have nothing smaller than a Star-class carrier or cruiser that can stand against the Empire's current tactics. *Hornsby* is designed to deceive the Empire ships' commanders. It will look small and vulnerable, but it will be able to charge into the fight faster than anyone expects and has fire-power far above the norm for a vessel of the size. It will be able to hunt down the Empire ships and it will be able to destroy them. And it will be able to defend itself and other ships. We will lose the element of surprise once the tactic has been used a few times, but even then the use of small, fast, hard hitting ships has merit."

"Hmmm," Hinkson mused, "I've been thinking about that and did some research. Long ago, before we made it to space, Earth's ocean fleets had underwater war vessels, submarines. One of the types of submarines had a similar mission profile. They were called hunter-killers."

"Hunter-killer," Marjory repeated, and a strange, almost feral gleam came to her eyes. "Yes, that describes our mission perfectly."

"Admiral on the bridge," Ensign Baldry called as Admiral Bensin strode through the bulkhead door.

The bridge crew came to attention.

"As you were," Bensin said, turning to Ensign Baldry. "Ensign, this is a working warship, not the academy. We don't bother with those formalities out here. Now," he said, twisting back to where Marjory had re-seated herself in the command chair, "let's see what she can do."

"Yes, Admiral," Marjory replied. "As you know we have been testing *Hornsby* extensively for the last four weeks. There have been a few teething problems but nothing out of the ordinary and all have been fixed. All equipment checks out. All systems are working correctly. So, we thought we would make this a slightly longer trial run."

"Excellent," Bensin said. "It's been a while since I've been on a real patrol. We've allowed a few days for this, so I want to see what she can do."

Marjory merely nodded. This would be a good test, but she was confident in what had been produced. After all, *Hornsby*, now, was something of a bigger cousin to *Fendaristil*. Marjory's personal ship had been designed to be a small, deceptively fast and surprisingly potent warship in the guise of a large shuttle-like vessel. The same design philosophy had been applied to *Hornsby*.

"We have reports of pirates raiding out near Scyllas," Marjory said. "We'll jump out there and see if we can find them. If we can, then we will stop them. If we cannot find them, then we will find other ways to demonstrate *Hornsby's* abilities."

"Pirates, eh?" Bensin growled. "I hate pirates, always have done. Skyllas is an important waypoint for many civilian vessels and our Fleet ships. It's a good mission. I like it. You're clear to proceed, Commander."

"Yes, sir," Marjory replied. "Ensign, clear the boarding tubes and release the docking clamps. Helm, when that has been done move us away from the bay, positioning thrusters only until we are clear then one-quarter power to the outer marker."

Hornsby drifted sideways until she was a hundred metres from the docking bay. Baldry double-checked that the boarding tubes were clear.

"Clear of the bay, Captain," he reported.

On cue, the two huge engines were moved to one-quarter power and *Hornsby* accelerated away from the station, reaching the outer marker for the station's security sensors thirty minutes later.

"Set course for Skyllas," Marjory ordered. "Jump when ready."

Hornsby oriented on a course for the large rock named Skyllas and accelerated to jump velocity. The engines switched mode from sublight to faster-than-light and she jumped.

Eight hours later, *Hornsby* emerged from the jump. Smoothly, the bridge crew commenced the usual checks to make sure that the jump had been completed correctly and, because this was a shake-down cruise, that the test criteria had been met.

"Captain, we're on target," Lieutenant Chandi on the helm reported. "The jump brought us out within standard margins. Skyllas is eight hundred thousand kilometres off the port bow. Full sensor sweeps in operation. Reading two vessels partly hidden behind Skyllas. Tugs or large shuttle size, based on their returns."

Fifteen minutes later all test results had been received. There were no errors reported. The main viewscreen now showed a crystal clear view of Skyllas with the tails of two ships jutting from behind the large space rock. Marjory exchanged satisfied glances with Bensin.

"Very well," Marjory replied. "Set course …"

"Captain, a third vessel has jumped into the system," Lieutenant Brescia, the navigation officer called. "ID shows it's a civilian merchant vessel. I'd guess it's using Skyllas as a nav point."

"The two vessels have started to move towards the merchant," Baldry reported.

"Sound battle stations," Marjory ordered. "All weapons online but leave the doors closed. I want a comms solution for those ships, please."

"Channel open, Captain," Baldry reported.

"This is Commander Tellis Mellivar, commanding the Union patrol vessel *Hornsby*, to the vessels hiding behind Skyllas," Marjory said. "Stand down and prepare to be boarded. This is your first and only warning."

The broadcast message produced several actions. The merchant vessel started an immediate turn away from Skyllas towards *Hornsby*.

At the same time, the two suspected pirates accelerated out of their hiding place and started after the merchant ship.

"Captain, the pirates have out-sized engine signatures and show stronger shields than normal," Brescia reported. "They'll catch the merchant before it can reach us."

"Then we'd better do what we came here to do," Marjory replied. "Engines to flank speed. Open all weapons bays. All weapons hot but hold for orders. Bow shields to full."

Hornsby leapt forward, rapidly decreasing the distance to the merchant vessel. In response, the pirates swung to face *Hornsby* and moved slightly closer together. The merchant vessel veered away from what obviously would be a fight.

Hornsby revealed an array of armaments that would have left the observers of the ship reveal speechless. The two pods behind the bow split open to reveal two railguns, one on each side, that were far over-sized for a ship of *Hornsby's* displacement. On the keel the third pod retracted its doors to display a large energy cannon, which extended on a pylon and swung around to point towards the oncoming ships. On the sides, pods split apart to reveal point defence blasters, lasers and small railguns, while missile racks rose from bays on the top surface. In a blink of time, *Hornsby* had changed character from a smooth-skinned mid-size ship to one bristling with weaponry.

"Designate pirate one on the left, pirate two on the right," Lieutenant Brescia said as the plot on the viewscreen changed to show the two vessels in exquisite detail. "Secondary power grid online. Confirm pirate one is a tug. Pirate two seems to be a converted freighter."

A flash from pirate one told of an energy weapon being fired.

"Weapons fire," Brescia reported. "Evading."

"Far too far away for that size gun," Marjory commented calmly as *Hornsby* swung in a shallow arc so the energy blast missed.

"Captain, both vessels show railguns powering up. Small to medium size, low rate of fire. They should have no effect on us."

"Very well. I did give them a single warning that they have opted not to hear. Weapons, fire two slugs at each, standard spread, followed by forward main cannon shots, two each in succession," Marjory ordered calmly. "Fire!"

"Weapons fire incoming," Brescia reported. "One railgun slug each. Energy weapons powering up. *Hornsby* firing."

Hornsby's two larger railguns fired twice each, with each slug being offset slightly to catch unwary opponents. It was unlikely that the slugs would catch an agile ship, but the main blaster had a much better chance of causing damage.

Pirate one jinked sharply, causing the railgun slugs to miss. Pirate two, however, maintained course. It fired a second railgun slug, but almost immediately the first of *Hornsby's* larger slugs arrived. It punched through the thin skin of the converted freighter, and its momentum carried the larger pellet through internal bulkheads before exiting the ship diagonally to where it entered. The old freighter vented atmosphere explosively, causing the ship to tilt and skew, even while it continued on its path.

Pirate one straightened back on its course towards *Hornsby* as the Union ship's energy cannon fired the first of its four blasts. The old tug tried to evade again but the first energy blast clipped its tail. The pirate ship was pushed sideways. It suffered damage but, still, its pilot fought to bring it back on course. The second energy blast, however, impacted the stricken pirate two and caused devastation. The powerful blast drove a hole through the flank of the vessel as it tumbled on its course.

The third blast was directed at pirate one again, and this time the impact was direct on the bow. The pilot had fought the ship back close to its course, but that put it directly in line with the cannon blast. The bow was engulfed in the blaster bolt. The tough old tug was staggered but pushed through the impact. However, the forward-placed bridge was heavily damaged. The fourth blast missed pirate two, but the damage was too much for the old freighter. The engines continued to run but the ship tumbled, uncontrolled.

"Hold all weapons," Marjory directed. "Lieutenant Brescia, I want one railgun targeted on each pirate ship. Lieutenant Chandi, hold us at five hundred metres from pirate one. Ensign Baldry, I want to know if any pirates survived. Use the sensors to search for heat signatures away from the engines."

"No heat signatures from either ship, Commander," Baldry announced a minute later.

"Pirate two's rate of tumble is increasing," Brescia reported. "Its engines are still running."

"That will be a hazard to someone," Marjory said. "Ensign Baldry, ready missile tubes. High yield. Tube one to target the freighter amidships. Fire when ready."

"Aye, Commander," Baldry replied. "Tube one loaded. Firing!"

The missile only had a short distance to travel. It impacted the old freighter nearly two-thirds of the distance from bow to stern. The explosion of the warhead seemed to cause little more than a puff of fire and smoke that cleared quickly, but the effect on the ship was catastrophic. The old freighter broke up, even as the engines, now starved of fuel, died. The tumble of the largest pieces slowed but the small cloud of debris continued on its trajectory. While still a danger, it would be less so than a whole ship tumbling erratically.

"I've never seen the effect of the ninth generation Blackbird missile," Admiral Bensin said to Marjory. "Effective!"

"Against a lightly armoured ship like this one, yes. Like its early torpedo cousin, the armoured tip punches through the thinner skins and then the warhead explodes half in and half out of the ship. For something like an Empire cruiser, though, the goal is multiple strikes in a single zone so we cut gouges in the plating. That's assuming the missiles get there, of course."

"Commander, pirate one remains stable," Lieutenant Chandi called. "Its engines are out and the bridge is gone. There was venting from a few places but that's ceased, so I'm guessing no atmosphere."

"Very well," Marjory said. "Close all weapons ports. Stay on station with pirate one. Admiral, may I have a word, please?"

Bensin nodded and rose to follow Marjory to the captain's cabin, located behind the bridge.

"A good exercise, and effective," Bensin said as he took one of the two seats in the room.

"Yes, although I think there is some room for improvement," Marjory nodded. "We're using too much energy for screens rather than the blasters, and we can turn the engines up once the shakedown is done."

"And you have something else in mind, right?'

"I am thinking of the tug, pirate one," Marjory replied. "It's old, very old would be my guess, and yet it was able to evade our railgun slugs. Only the blaster caused it problems, and that was because it had no shields worth anything. But the ship itself survived."

"I agree," Bensin replied with a slight smile as he watched Marjory focus on a far distant point, deep in thought. "And your point?"

"This is just a thought, and I would have to work it through, maybe with Drummel's designers. What if we took a more modern tug, gave it the largest engines and blasters we could fit, but no shields?"

"It would last a very short time in any engagement," Bensin replied.

"Agreed, but what if we paired it with another tug, with the same large engines and our strongest shields, capable of shielding itself and a second ship?"

Bensin considered, turning the concept over in his mind. The benefits could be significant, but the difficulties would be huge.

"You would have to have the two ships locked together in battle," he said to Marjory.

"Yes, almost like a single destroyer, the two acting as a single ship."

"The level of control required would be hard to attain."

"I agree, but we would be able to slave the navigation systems while allowing independent control of the rest of the ship. The AIs would do most of the flying. Good training takes care of the rest, assuming we can get the shields right."

"And how do you envisage them being used?" Bensin asked.

"The ships would have small crews," Marjory mused. "They may not even live on the ships long term. We would need as much room for weaponry as possible. They would need to be highly automated, even more than usual. I would see them being used as fast attack craft, able to take on ships much larger than they are as part of a battle. We probably could use them for patrols, but I feel they would be more effective as fleet vessels."

"And *Hornsby?*"

"I think the idea works and could be applied to bring old hulls out of retirement. The Centaur-class ships have a template now, but others would have to be redesigned. That is probably more expensive to do than revising tugs, and slower."

"You haven't gone up against an Empire ship, yet," Bensin pointed out. "The pirates were good for a shakedown, but it's not the same thing."

"*Hornsby* will have to join the fleet again so we can prove her out," Marjory agreed with a nod. "Meanwhile, if you agree I can look at plans to convert or build out a set of seventy-series tugs as paired attack ships?"

It took Bensin no time at all to agree. A second Mellivar design! *Hornsby* looked likely to produce the effect planned. How Lieutenant-Commander Mellivar had seen that capability in the unloved Centaur-class still was a mystery to him. He was intrigued at what she might be able to do with the more modern, stronger-bodied space tugs, which already were little more than large engines with pushing and towing gear attached.

| 30 |

First Test

"Admiral Hinkson on three," Ensign Baldry reported.

Marjory selected channel three on her command pad and directed the comm channel to her earpiece.

"Admiral, Lieutenant-Commander Mellivar."

"Mellivar, I've been going over your plans with some of the designers at Millig. They're excited at what you have but one of them has suggested some changes. She thinks we could get performance improvements to the shielding tug by putting emitters on small outriggers along the length of the ship."

Marjory thought for a moment. Outriggers would work, but only if they were far enough away from the main hull, where emitters usually were mounted.

"How big would the outriggers be?" Marjory asked.

"They would not be large themselves, but they would be extended when the ships go into battle. She believes we would get almost ten percent more power than a hull-mounted array."

"I think she may be right," Marjory replied. "That's a good idea and worth trying. Has she been able to simulate it?"

"Yes. It's waiting for you to review when you have a chance."

"Thank you, Admiral. The Third Fleet will be returning to port in a couple of days. I will review them when we have docked. Your designer deserves a commendation."

Two days later, Marjory sat back from her work console. On her screen was the design proposal by Hinkson's designer, and Marjory had just spend an hour examining it and trying to pick holes in it.

"Not bad," she said. "That would work."

"I estimate an improvement in shield efficiency of eleven point three percent," *Fendaristil* replied. "However, I believe that a further improvement of five point one percent could be achieved if the out-riggers were assisted by extending emitter stalks across the hull."

The display changed. The schematic of a tug was shown with long out-rigger extensions extending at forty-five degrees from each side of the lower hull. Overlaid on the schematic were concentric arcs showing the shield emitter forces. Now, they were joined by a series of stalks that jutted out from points on the hull. With the stalks, the boundaries became thicker, the forces more layered. The shield edge's energy rating increased.

"Oh, very good!" Marjory nodded. "Will it be stable?"

"It will be stable," *Fendaristil* stated. "There are obvious compromises because the one set of emitters will have to shield two ships, but shield strength is good and steady."

"I will send this to the Admiral. This may be the advantage these ships need."

"Sixteen percent?" Hinkson repeated, astounded. "That's incredible."

"It was very good work by your designer, and we were able to extend it a little."

"We?"

"My design AI always takes part in my design efforts. It allows me to evaluate many more possibilities, including some outside the box," Marjory replied.

"Is your AI any more advanced that our own?" Hinkson asked, eyeing Marjory askance.

"That's a family secret, sir," Marjory replied with a smile. "But we have always used AIs to assist us in our work."

"And by 'we' this time you mean?"

"The Mellivar ship designers," Marjory answered, which was not strictly speaking a lie, although it referred to herself alone.

"Well, it seems to work. Our sims agreed with yours. I have my staff trying to locate two tugs that are not required. That's a tall order, of course, but we'll find them." Hinkson stood from the coffee table and stretched. "Do you plan on overseeing the fit-out?"

"I believe I have a Fleet admiral who expects me to be on *Hornsby* when he sails next," Marjory replied with a smile. "Besides, you have the same crew that worked on *Hornsby* so they will understand what to do."

"And we have new engines and uprated sensors, shield emitters and weapons arriving in three weeks from Drummel Industrial. They will make a difference."

Almost a year later, *Hornsby* was on its third cruise and it had yet to face an Empire ship. As Marjory had promised Bensin, *Hornsby's* power plants had proven to be robust and strong and were able to be pushed hard. That gave additional power for the blaster cannon, and meant the improved railguns could operate for longer before needing to recharge. Some minor improvements had been made to the targeting systems, and the weapons systems had received some additional tuning. The ship was as ready for battle as it could be.

Two weeks into a completely uneventful cruise, Marjory had just stood from her command chair to fetch a coffee when Ensign Baldry raised a hand. All activity on the bridge ceased while he listened to the Fleet channel.

"Commander, *Bella* reports contact," Ensign Baldry reported. "Long range. Two ships, estimated to be medium cruisers."

Marjory sat again, waiting for orders that would have to be coming. She was not disappointed. The voice of Captain Emsig, Third Fleet's operations officer on the flagship *Starbright*, came over the bridge speaker.

"*Hornsby*, hold for Admiral Bensin. Prepare for tasking."

"Sound battle stations," Marjory directed.

"Mellivar, time to prove that old cow can do what you said it could do," said Admiral Bensin a few moments later in his usual calm and dry voice.

"Aye sir," Marjory replied with a smile. "This old cow is ready to fight."

"Ha, good to hear. We have two Empire cruisers at extreme sensor range. We believe they haven't seen us yet. I'm detaching *Starmist* and *Darkridge* with a few support ships to see if we can get them in a pincer. The rest of the Fleet will move back and stay out of their sensor range. You, however, get to play innocent decoy."

"Understood, sir," Marjory replied. "Do we get to show our teeth?"

"When you're in range you are weapons clear," Bensin replied. "But I need you to take it slow so the pincer can get in place."

"Aye sir, we will take it slow and steady."

"Good hunting, *Hornsby*. Bensin out."

"Helm, reduce speed by one third, stay on this course," Marjory ordered.

"*Starmist* and *Darkridge* have jumped away," Lieutenant Brescia reported. "The rest of Third Fleet have started to reverse course. We're on our own."

Four minutes later Brescia reported again.

"I think we've been spotted," she said. "The two cruisers have changed course. They're heading directly towards us."

"Very well," Marjory ordered. "Check that all systems are online."

"Missile tubes report loaded," Lieutenant Chandi reported. "Engineering reports engines are ready for full power. Shields are at thirty percent. Railguns are powered but the doors are closed. The main blaster is powering, now at eighty percent. Blaster doors are closed also. Point defence systems are ready to be deployed."

"Thank you," Marjory said, her voice calm. "Steady on course. We will play the unsuspecting rabbit stepping into the trap."

Another ten minutes passed. The gap between the Empire ships and *Hornsby* had dwindled.

"We're within their range," Brescia reported.

"Steady," Marjory ordered, sensing the stress levels rising on the bridge. "No false moves."

"They've started to separate," Brescia said.

"Engineering, be ready for flank speed," Marjory said in response.

"Engineering, aye," came the phlegmatic reply, causing Marjory to smile slightly.

"Designate Empire One on the left, Empire Two on the right," Weapons-Sergeant Biri said into the quiet. "Standard separation. Commander, they'll fire in a few seconds."

"Empire One, blaster fire. Missiles in flight," Brescia reported in a strained voice. "Empire Two, blaster fire."

"Engineering, flank speed," Marjory ordered, and *Hornsby* leapt forward. "Go evasive. Shields to full. Open all weapon bay doors, weapons clear. Target four railgun shots at Empire One, spread pattern seven. Main blaster, target Empire Two, sustained fire. Missiles one through four, target Empire One. Missiles five to eight, target Empire Two. Fire!"

Hornsby was closing the gap to the two Empire ships in a shallow concave arc, dipping below the oncoming railgun slugs and the blaster fire as the weapon bay doors slid open and the weapons extended. The two railguns oriented on Empire One and fired two large hardened pellets each, while the main forward-facing blaster cannon fired blast after blast at Empire Two. The missile battery ejected eight missiles. Within moments the sleepy, unaware lamb had become a wolf with very large teeth.

"Railguns, four more at Empire One, spread pattern two. Main blaster, target Empire One, sustained fire. Railguns, target Empire Two, four shots, spread pattern five," Marjory ordered rapid-fire.

"Railguns to forty percent," Biri reported as Hornsby shuddered slightly under the weight of its own weapons fire.

"Let's use it," Marjory replied. "Target Empire One, ten shots, spread pattern five."

"Incoming blaster shots," Brescia called. "I think we took them by surprise."

"They're about to get another one," Chandi said. "*Starmist* and *Darkridge* jumping in in three, two, one."

Flashes told of the two capital ships arrival from jump-space, along with their support ships, within attacking range. They opened fire immediately.

"Empire One hit," Biri called. "Two railgun slugs. Empire Two took a blaster burst near the tail as it evaded. Engines are damaged."

"*Starbright* inbound," Brescia reported. "Third Fleet fully engaged. Stingers have been launched."

"Take us below the plane," Marjory ordered. "Roll *Hornsby* through one eighty degrees. Engineering, whatever you have left. Railguns, as many shots to each ship as you can while we go past. Main blaster, target the engines of Empire Two, sustained fire as long as you can."

Hornsby swept below the line of flight and rolled to present its belly to the underside of the Empire ships. As it passed beneath the massive cruisers the twin railguns opened up, chewing through their munitions with abandon. The large slugs walked along the underside of the two cruisers, ripping through any mountings and puncturing the thick plating in several places. Point defences peppered *Hornsby* as she passed, but the strengthened shields withheld the energy blasts and deflected the small railgun pellets. In turn, *Hornsby's* own point defence weapons added their own impact, although most of *Hornsby's* systems were to the top and sides of the hull. As *Hornsby* reached the rear quarter the main blaster swung around and opened up, targeting the damaged engine of Empire Two.

On *Starbright*, Admiral Bensin watched his screen, spellbound, as his fleet pounded the two cruisers, but most of his attention was on the formerly near-derelict *Hornsby*. The old warship reached the back of the two cruisers but the main blaster cannon merely swivelled to face the rear and maintained its rate of fire. Empire cruisers were notorious for having weak shields at their sterns and Empire Two proved to be no different. *Hornsby's* blaster fire finally found a vulnerable spot and Empire Two's engines flamed out. The last two shots of the blaster sailed into one of the engine exhaust nozzle and decimated the huge engine assembly.

The rear quarter of Empire Two buckled as explosions tore through the engine compartment. The second weakness of the Empire cruisers - the near proximity of the fuel store to the engines - proved to hold true still as the blasts ignited the fuel store. Empire Two's stern was blown off the ship. The fleet's attention was directed to Empire One now, which continued to fight. The result was, however, a foregone conclusion. Within a few minutes more, Empire One was a wreck, with a cloud of debris being pushed aside by venting gasses.

Several of the fleet ships moved closer to the stricken vessels when Marjory, with hundreds of years of experience fighting against the Empire ships, called over the fleet band.

"All ships, move away from the Empire vessels. Self-destruction is imminent. I repeat, move away from the Empire vessels."

That caused the Union ships to beat a retreat, just in time. Both Empire cruisers exploded in twin clouds of shrapnel. Two of the Union ships took impacts from large pieces of hull panels that caused damage but the rest were able to evade the larger debris or absorb the impacts of smaller pieces.

On *Hornsby*, Marjory nodded to her small crew.

"Well done, everyone. Stand down battle stations. I want a damage assessment done before we close the weapons bay doors. Lieutenant Brescia, map those larger pieces of debris and let me know if they will cause problems to shipping lanes. Weapons-Sergeant Biri, secure all weapons. Start a check on the performance of the railguns and blaster, reload the missile rack. Lieutenant Chandi, take us back into position to shield *Starbright* if necessary. Full sensor sweep as far as we can go. Let's make sure there were only two. Engineering, I want a report on the state of the engines in ten minutes."

The bridge staff jumped into action. Marjory smiled in satisfaction. The crew would have to review their part in the action, and absorb what they had achieved. However, Marjory had shown what a pocket warship design could do and her fertile mind already had some ideas to strengthen the tugs as they were uprated.

| 31 |

Jack and Jill

Bensin called his ship commanders to a conference the following day. Every ship had some form of damage, although only the two that suffered impact damage were of concern. Still, damage repair parties were hard at work.

"Mellivar, that was inspired," Bensin said once greetings were exchanged between the attendees. "Any scepticism I had about refitting *Hornsby* is gone. She performed exactly as we wanted. Exactly as you promised, in fact."

"Thank you, Admiral," Marjory replied as collective nods were given by the attendees. "The element of surprise helped greatly, but *Hornsby* would not have survived if we were a sole ship, even with stronger shields. It was only *Starmist* and *Darkridge* jumping in at the right time that took the pressure off us. Then, when *Starbright* and the rest of the fleet arrived, we had free rein."

"We'll review that, but I think you're right there. We will have to change tactics to make the best use of *Hornsby* and any others like her. However, the advantage of having ships like that in the fleets will outweigh any concern about tactical changes."

Marjory nodded and the post-action conference continued to review the battle. It was a good outcome. It was better than she would have expected, in fact. The Union had another usable weapon, with the tugs concept still to come.

Six months later, the twin tugs joined Third Fleet. The *John Steere* and *Jillabi*, immediately dubbed *Jack* and *Jill* by some Fleet jokers, were not pretty craft. The boxy, utilitarian design of a heavy duty Fleet tug offered few aesthetic features. When the already over-large engines were replaced by even larger and more powerful ones, and with *Jack* laden with an enormous array of weaponry in place of its heavy hauling equipment, and *Jill* sprouting sensor and shield stalks that were distributed across almost all parts of the hull, the twin ships looked like nothing anyone had seen before.

Bensin was bemused by the ships' appearance, even though he had been privy to their design and construction progress. He and Marjory had discussed the best way to use these odd ships and had decided that the direct approach was best. That had always been Marjory's intent, in any case. These ships offered little in the way of finesse so they would just be pointed at an enemy ship and let off their leash.

Bensin reviewed the specifications with Marjory over coffee. He shook his head in amazement at the list of weapons mounted on and within *Jack*, and then again at the size of the munitions store that the ship carried.

"I don't think I've ever seen so many weapons in a single vessel below Star class," he said, gazing at Marjory. "How did you manage to fit all of that into a tug?"

"Mainly by not having anything much of a crew," Marjory replied. "The crew quarters are tiny on both ships, mainly for in-mission use. Otherwise the off-duty crews will live on another ship. We have automated almost everything. That also allowed us to cut down on such spaces as meal rooms. The tug is quite a tight space anyway, but these are even tighter."

"We'll have to find very special people to fly these," Bensin mused. "Most Fleet crew would find them too confined. They'll either be very brave or crazy."

"Brave I think. For these two ships, we have volunteers from an old Honshu-class frigate that was in for decommissioning," Marjory replied, "so they have some experience in cramped quarters. And they all understand the risks involved."

"Have we finalised the command structure? As we discussed, two ships working so close together will have to be under a unified command."

"Yes. Each ship will have two shifts, maybe three if we find two does not work. There will only be three on the bridge at any time. The commander will be on *Jack* and the XO on *Jill*. Second shift will have the same relative seniority structure. They will also be the pilots, which limits the candidates for those positions, although the ships' AIs will take a lot of the load. Each ship will have an engineer on the bridge, while *Jack* will have weapons specialists and *Jill* will have sensor and shield specialists. We plan on two shifts. Time will tell how well that works."

"At least this first crew know each other," Bensin nodded. "Are you sure about these shields?"

"Yes. They will have to travel very close together, belly to belly almost, when in combat. The outriggers on Jill will almost seem to wrap around Jack. The control systems will deal with much of that. The shield emitters will cover both ships easily. They may well be the strongest shields in all of our fleets. It will take something hugely powerful to get through them."

"We'll find out soon enough," Bensin replied. "Third Fleet will be patrolling the Corridor for the next few months and we can expect to find some enemies out there."

The Corridor was a moderately-sized section of space that was in dispute between the Union and the Empire. It was a confined space, with a series of intense magnetic anomalies stretching along one side of the Corridor and a dense asteroid belt acting as a second wall. Any vessel drifting too far out of the Corridor on the third side risked running into the small Bor Nebula, which had its own navigation obstacles, while the fourth side faced Union space.

There were several promising planetary systems along the Corridor that would need very little terraforming to be human-supporting, and the Union had included it in the Ninth Sector for almost a hundred years. For the last thirty years, however, the Empire had decided that it would contest this region. There had been several battles, with losses on each side. The Union and Empire had increased their patrol sizes until the Corridor was patrolled by small fleets.

The Union usually assigned part of a main battle fleet to patrol the Corridor. Third Fleet, however, was rebuilding after almost being destroyed twenty-two years previously. With *Jack* and *Jill*, the fleet comprised eighteen ships. The struggle to get suitable ships built at the time meant that its complement of vessels was only fifty percent complete. In effect, Third Fleet was no more than half a fleet at this time.

The fleet dropped from FTL into normal space half a million kilometres inside the Corridor, which was close to the minimum safe limit. The three capital ships formed an arrowhead pointing down the length of the Corridor, with *Starbright* in the lead. *Hornsby* was positioned above and behind *Starbright*, while *Jack* and *Jill* were below and behind the flagship. The remaining ships formed a screen. Sensors were extended to their maximum ranges in search of threats. None were found.

The Corridor would take months to traverse at sub-light speeds, so the usual tactic was to jump from known patrol point to known patrol point and remain in each location for two or three days. In the meanwhile, the Fleet would conduct training exercises while pickets maintained a watch for Empire activity.

At the third patrol location Marjory was sitting relaxed in her command chair on *Hornsby*, watching the ships manoeuvre on her viewscreen. The picket ships were out searching for risks and various exercises were underway. One of the exercises held Marjory's attention, for it was *Jack* and *Jill* acting as a paired assault force.

The two ships moved from their assigned positions to join forces, with *Jill* rotating as they met so that the two ships appeared to form near mirror images. As one, the two ships leapt forward, charging towards the corvette *Jarlis,* which acted as target for the exercise. The twin ships sped past *Jarlis* much sooner than Marjory expected, before separating and circling back to their starting positions at a far more sedate speed. That augured well for their ability to get into battle. Of course, they had to survive the battle, too, which was harder to test without live fire, which Admiral Bensin refused to countenance.

Twice more *Jack* and *Jill* ran simulated attacks, with slight differences in their attack profiles. Each time the process to pair the ships appeared to be quicker, as the crews became more confident in their ships and the control systems. They had repeated the same exercise multiple times at each patrol location, so it was now a well-understood process, but Marjory found it pleasing to see the improved performance.

At the fifth patrol location, five days later, Third Fleet secured from the jump and, almost immediately, long range sensors identified multiple Empire ships. The ships jumped at general quarters while on patrol, so the call for battle stations did little more than raise tension levels. The Empire ships moved towards the Third Fleet.

"Five capital ships, medium or heavy cruisers, with ten larger support ships, destroyer size, and a further ten smaller ones, like our frigates or gunships," Lieutenant Brescia reported. "Two mid-size ships are falling towards the back, probably supply ships. Estimate we will be within engagement range in about three hours. No other enemy ships in the vicinity."

"Very well," Marjory replied. "Keep an eye on them in case they accelerate. Five is unusual, so stay alert. Secure from battle stations. Rotate the crew through a short rest period, but I want everyone back at battle stations in two hours."

| 32 |

Battle Mage

Almost two hours passed without incident. *Hornsby's* crew was at battle stations while the two fleets moved inexorably towards their confrontation. The tension grew, but where on other ships it might result in arguments and fights, on *Hornsby* it took the form of closer scrutiny of sensor readings or redundant checks of weapons or defensive systems. All looked to Marjory, sitting calmly in her command chair, allowing the time to run down, and were calmed themselves.

"*Starbright* has extended her hangar pods," Ensign Baldry reported. "*Starmist* and *Darkridge* are creating separation."

"Very well," Marjory replied calmly. "All weapons hot but keep the bay doors closed. Engineering, prepare for full power running on primary and secondary grids. Forward shields at maximum, rear shields at fifty percent."

"We've been tasked with one of the cruisers, designated C3," Lieutenant Brescia reported. "The capital ships will take C1, C2 and C4. *Jack* and *Jill* have been tasked with C5."

"That's being thrown in at the deep end," Lieutenant Chandi said as her fingers danced across her command pad.

"Stingers launched," Brescia said. "Hammer and Shield squadrons have been tasked with the smaller ships. Enemy fighters have launched, but only about thirty of them."

"The Emperor has never really understood the value of the single-seat fighter," Marjory said, thinking of Likud's disdain for anything smaller than a capital vessel, "even though the Empire had them before us. Let's hope he never does."

"Enemy ships are within range of our main cannon," Weapons-Sergeant Biri reported. "I've got slammers loaded into all missile tubes, Commander. I assumed you'd want to get in close."

Marjory nodded to Biri, with the smile that once sent shivers down the backs of her training opponents at the Resgalar Academy on Ennaris.

"Thank you, Weapons-Sergeant. We will go head to head, I think. All shields to full. We will be targeted by the smaller ships as we go in. Let's give them a headache before they are ready. Ensign Baldry, inform *Starbright* that we are starting our run, as planned. Lieutenant Chandi, flank speed on my mark. Biri, do not open the bays until we are within two thousand kilometres, then you are weapons free. Chandi, go!"

Hornsby swept out of her assigned position. The twin Mark Nine engines flared like mini suns and pushed the rebuilt ship to its maximum rated sub-light speed within moments, and then beyond. The Empire ships fired blasters but almost all missed, as *Hornsby's* speed took them by surprise. Chandi maintained an undulating, ever changing path towards C3 rather than a predictable direct path.

"*Jack* and *Jill* are engaging," Brescia reported. "We're taking fire. Shields holding."

Hornsby shuddered as the Empire vessels adjusted their targeting and started to score hits, although many missed still. The reinforced shields held, flaring and coruscating as energy blasts were dissipated.

"All ships engaged," Brescia said. "Main cannon fire from *Starbright*, *Starmist* and *Darkridge*. Destroyers have entered the pattern, Corvettes have gone above and below."

This was a tactic worked out by Admiral Bensin and his tactical team. Understanding from long experience that the Empire captains worked from a fixed plan of attack, the Union commanders often tried different tactics to force them away from the plan. It appeared that the Empire captains could not adapt their tactics quickly, and at times not at all, which had allowed the Union ships to win fights or to escape from engagements where they should have been beaten. So, the nimble corvettes had been tasked with both distracting the Empire commanders and destroying as many of the smaller support ship as possible.

"Five thousand kilometres," Chandi reported.

"Stingers have blown through the Empire fighters," Brescia reported. "Three stingers lost. Twelve of the Empire fighters were destroyed. *Anderlist's* shields have failed, taking heavy damage. Escape pods ejecting. *Jack* and *Jill* are being targeted by C5. So far, so good."

"Two thousand kilometres," Chandi called.

As Chandi spoke, Weapons-Sergeant Biri opened all weapons bays simultaneously. Almost before it had finished deploying, the huge main blaster cannon was firing, while the twin railguns were only a moment behind. Into the mix the point defences added their own unique sound and near constant vibration.

"Missiles inbound," Brescia said, continuing her stream of reports. "Three fighters have targeted us. C3's shields are fluctuating. Weak point identified."

"Increasing railgun rate of fire," Biri called. "That weak point should fail in a few seconds."

"All inbound missiles destroyed," Brescia continued. "*Starmist* reporting damage and slowing. Three corvettes - *Dormis*, *Amphor* and *Frendis* are disabled."

"C3's front shield has failed. Railgun impacts. Increasing blaster fire."

"Missiles," Marjory ordered.

"Missiles away," Biri reported. "Full spread of slammers, tracking true. Railgun hits are destroying their point defences. Slammers impact in five seconds. *Hornsby's* shields are holding at seventy-five percent. We're clear of C3. *Starbright* is venting from several decks.

Starmist and *Darkridge* have reached the enemy line and are taking hits."

"Take us around," Marjory said calmly. "All hands brace for combat turn. Reload slammers."

"Slammers have hit. Surface explosions on all missiles. Secondary explosions … now. All slammers show success. C3's skin should have ruptured."

"Reversing course," Chandi called, sending *Hornsby* into a skidding turn.

The great engines' exhaust funnels shifted on huge gimbals to direct thrust to assist the turn. On *Hornsby* the crew held on tight as the turn subjected them to forces beyond the ability of the ship's advanced systems to counter. But in a remarkably short time *Hornsby* was lined up for another run.

"C3's shields have failed. C3 is starting to turn, but slowly. C5's shields are fluctuating. C1 and C2 are taking damage. C4 has run through the line and is turning."

"Biri, two slammers into each engine of C3. Chandi, once the slammers are gone swing us along the line to C2 and then C1."

"Slammers away," Biri called. "Reloading."

"Turning, C2 in twenty seconds."

"Biri, same again," Marjory ordered.

"Slammers have impacted on C3," Brescia maintained her flow of information in a matter-of-fact voice. "C3 is breaking up."

No-one cheered at the victory. There were no celebrations of any kind. Hornsby careered along behind the line of Empire ships.

"Missiles away," Biri reported. "Loading bears into the empties."

Marjory nodded. The BER-5 missiles, formally known as Bell Engineering Revision-5 missiles, but colloquially known as "bears", were designed for close combat. They were the same size as the mid-range slammers but carried far less fuel and so had a reduced range. Where the missile warhead and fuel were almost balanced on other missiles, the bears had multiple advanced warheads with their own motors, designed to burn for a few seconds only.

"C1 in five," Chandi called.

"Last slammers away. Loading bears."

"Take us straight up," Marjory ordered. "Full power to the rear shields. Biri, status."

Hornsby pulled up, relative to the plane of most of the Empire ships. The ship charged away from the battle.

"Blaster is recharged. Railguns at ninety percent. All tubes loaded."

"C2 is badly damaged," Brescia reported. "C1 is drifting. Both are intact still. Neither has shields. Main weapons remain active on C1 but engines are down. *Starmist* has lost engine power and is drifting away from the fight. *Starbright* appears to be mobile but communications are down. Last report was that bulkheads were holding. *Darkridge* is fighting still, but has lost dorsal shields so is trying to orient to protect the upper surface."

"Stingers and enemy fighters?" Marjory asked, scanning the viewscreen.

"We're down to thirteen stingers in Hammer Squadron and nine in Shield. Enemy fighters have been destroyed. At least, I can't locate any signatures."

"Keep an eye out. What about the smaller ships?"

"Most of the smaller ships are damaged on both sides and largely out of action. *Jack* and *Jill* took a run through them and managed to even the score after the first run at C5. Two enemy gunships remain active and are converging on C4, which has completed its turn."

"Chandi, turn us around again, please," Marjory ordered. "Ensign Baldry, I want you to control point defences. Manual targeting at whatever you can hit. Biri, set launchers to auto-load bears. Set for manual targeting of the railguns."

"These will be the last of the short-range missiles, Commander," Biri reported.

"Understood. Brescia, direct the stingers to attack C1 and C2. Finish them off. Where's C5?"

"Stingers will regroup and then attack. C5 is under attack again by *Jack* and *Jill*. C5 is damaged but fighting still."

"Very well. Chandi, we're going to corkscrew them."

"Really?" Chandi asked, before catching herself. "I mean, aye Commander."

Marjory's answering grin told her story. This was her place, going into battle with her crew, adopting tactics that were out of the ordinary.

"Engineering, I am releasing the locks," Marjory said.

"Aye, Commander," came the instant response. "We'll keep an eye on her for you."

Marjory smiled and then tapped her command pad in a specific pattern, bringing a secondary display to life. She laid her hand palm down on the screen and waited as a scanner worked quickly from side to side. The display cleared and presented additional options. She tapped two icons in quick succession, releasing safety constraints from the power systems.

"Biri, you'll have a bit more power to the blaster but not for as long and recharge will take longer," Marjory called.

"Aye, Commander. Reading plus twenty."

"In range," Brescia called. "C4 is firing her main cannon. The two gunships are shadowing, one up, one down."

"Their standard configuration," Marjory nodded. "Chandi, corkscrew now. Biri and Baldry, take your shots."

Hornsby began a spiralling manoeuvre that avoided C4's blaster fire. The spiral took the ship in a continuous roll, with the dorsal hull always facing into the spiral. *Hornsby's* shields flared as blaster fire from the two gunships hit them. C4's main blaster cannon seemed to be unable to track *Hornsby*, however, so smaller point defence blasters and railguns joined the gunships' efforts. Biri held his fire, staring at his screen intently. Ensign Baldry was firing every small blaster and railgun that *Hornsby* had, peppering the gunships in return.

"Chandi, once I fire the missiles I need you to roll for the blaster to acquire C4," Biri called.

Without awaiting Chandi's response, Biri mashed the firing tab. *Hornsby* was in position so that the two gunships placed above and below C4 could both be targeted. All eight missiles tubes fired, with four bears aimed at each Empire gunship. Immediately, *Hornsby* rolled to allow the belly ordinance to be used. Biri stabbed the firing stud and held it down. A blast of energy reached from *Hornsby* across the small gap to C4, and kept coming. C4's shields absorbed and spread the energy blast for three seconds, longer than a normal blaster burst would last, before buckling. The last of *Hornsby's* blaster charge washed across the hull of C4, obliterating defensive positions and sensor blisters. At the same time he held the railguns' targeting reticule on C4's hull with his second hand and pressed the firing stud. The twin railguns fired round after round as Biri moved the reticule to follow the line of the hull as *Hornsby* swept long its length. The railguns fell silent as the blaster was discharged.

"Chandi, roll again," Biri commanded.

The ship rolled again and the missile tubes lined up once more. Biri stabbed the firing stud again and all eight tubes launched their loads.

"Missiles away," Biri reported. "Blaster and railguns recharging."

"The gunships have been destroyed," Brescia reported. "C4 taking hits. Eight good hits. We must have overtaxed the power grid, Commander. Our shields are fluctuating. C4 has taken heavy damage."

By now *Hornsby's* corkscrew had taken it beyond the enemy ships and Chandi straightened its course and commenced a turn.

"Status of the fleet," Marjory called.

"*Starbright* continues to vent from multiple decks and remains out of comms. *Starmist* is still adrift but power is coming back slowly. *Darkridge* has lost all shields and is running at reduced power on one engine only. We've lost three of the corvettes and one destroyer. The rest are all reporting damage. None can fight. *Jack* and *Jill* have finished C5 and can still fight. Stingers are recovering to *Starbright*, so the hangers are still working, but there are only twenty of them."

"Commander," Biri said into the quiet after Brescia's report.

"Mister Biri?"

"The enemy ships continue to drift. All are damaged enough so they can't fight."

"Yes, and?" Marjory asked before realisation struck. "But they haven't self-destructed! Brescia, scan for a sixth cruiser!"

"I thought five was an unusual number," Biri muttered. "They always travel in pairs."

"Nothing on screens, Commander," Brescia reported.

"Message to all ships. All ships are to move out of the battle zone and converge on *Starbright* if they can," Marjory directed. "If these ships do self-destruct there will be a lot of debris flying about."

"Message sent," Brescia reported. "Most of the ships are moving, although several are without power. *Starmist* continues to drift."

"Keep an eye on those that can't move," Marjory directed, then had a brain-wave. "See if *Jack* and *Jill* can help move them out. Nothing much of the old tug equipment remains on them but they have the power, even if they add a dent or two."

"*Jack* and *Jill* are moving to assist," Brescia reported.

"Vessel sighted at extreme sensor range," Baldry called. "Matches enemy cruiser configuration. Coming fast, estimate is one hour."

"That cruiser could just about destroy the fleet given the number of damaged ships," Biri commented.

"Send to all ships," Marjory directed. "Enemy cruiser inbound. *Hornsby* will engage as far away as possible. Mister Biri, weapons status."

"Blaster is charged, Commander, as are the railguns, but the slugs are in short supply. Missile tubes have been reloaded but they'll have to be standoffs, I'm afraid. We have no slammers or bears left. I'm not sure we have enough to take on another cruiser."

"Load whatever we have and target that ship. Send the plot to my screen, please."

"Shields continue to fluctuate, Commander," Baldry reported. "Trying to compensate, but it looks like we may lose at least one zone. I just don't know which one."

"Thank you Mister Baldry. Computer, note to log. Lieutenant-Commander Mellivar recommends the crew of *Hornsby* for citation for meritorious service. Send the log to any ship capable of receiving it. Engineering, engine status."

"Engines are online and running fine, Commander," came the reply. "She'll do you proud."

"Thank you, chief," Marjory replied. "I am transferring engineering control to my station."

"Commander?"

Biri turned to look at Marjory, who looked the grizzled veteran in the eye for a long moment.

"All hands, abandon ship," Marjory said, holding eye contact with Biri. "This is not a drill."

Brescia and Chandi looked aghast, while Baldry was confused. Brescia started to object but Marjory held up a hand abruptly.

"That was an order, not a request," Marjory said calmly. "To your stations."

Brescia, Chandi and Baldry stood from their stations and moved towards the door from the bridge. Biri remained seated for a few moments and then stood, facing Marjory in the command chair.

"Are you sure, Commander?" he asked. "Is there no other way?"

"I designed this ship and I know what it can do," Marjory replied. "I want this crew to live and I want the fleet to survive. It is a simple equation. And it was an order, Weapons Sergeant."

Biri was silent for a moment longer before moving. When he did it was to stand to attention and salute, holding it until Marjory returned it. Only then did Biri leave the bridge.

Marjory sighed. She checked that she had control of the systems she wanted, and watched the screens as the few escape pods launched, moving back towards the main fleet.

"Configure for silent mode," Marjory directed.

"Silent running," the ship computer replied.

"Activate protocol Ogun," Marjory said. "Authority Marjory nar Drewflin."

The ship's computer voice changed subtly.

"Protocol Ogun has been activated, Battle Mage. *Hornsby* AI activated in full. Ship systems are below optimum. I estimate that shields will fail in seven minutes. Main blast cannon is available. Railguns are available but low on ammunition. Full power is available."

"Direct all shield power to the bow shields. Configure as an umbrella."

"Shields configured. Six minute until the enemy vessel is in range."

"Very well," Marjory replied, remaining seated.

"Inbound vessel," *Hornsby's* AI reported. "Identified as Ennaris warship *Fendaristil*. Vessel is cloaked."

Marjory touched a tab on her screen and stood.

"*Fendaristil*, come alongside. *Hornsby*, transfer control to *Fendaristil*."

"Control transferred," *Hornsby* confirmed.

Marjory left the bridge, walking the short distance to the main hatch. The viewscreen beside the hatch showed an umbilical tube extending from *Hornsby*, apparently to nothing. She entered the code to open the hatch, waited while it swung open, and then pulled herself through into the weightlessness of the tube. The hatch swung shut again. Marjory pulled herself swiftly through the tube, arriving at *Fendaristil's* hatch in moments.

"I'm on board," Marjory said.

The main hatch swung closed. The umbilical tube was released at *Fendaristil's* end and retracted into its housing around *Hornsby's* main hatch, which also closed to leave the smooth lines of the pocket warship unblemished.

"As soon as the cruiser is in range fire *Hornsby's* missiles," Marjory said as she walked onto the bridge.

"They're unlikely to get through unassisted," *Fendaristil* commented.

"Then we will assist," Marjory replied. "Prepare a Seema burst to travel ahead of the missiles. Then *Hornsby's* railguns are to fire everything they have left. Point defence railguns are to fire whatever they have left, too. You are weapons free."

"Seema burst away," *Fendaristil* reported. "*Hornsby's* missiles are away. I am firing two high impact missiles. Plasma burst released."

Fendaristil swung away from *Hornsby*, which continued to speed towards the Empire cruiser.

"Railguns active, all slugs expended," *Fendaristil* reported. "Trajectory on screen."

The main viewscreen showed the track of *Hornsby* and the cruiser, with the Seema burst, missiles and small cloud of railgun slugs bridging the gap, while the plasma burst appeared to chase the missiles. Less than twenty seconds later the Seema burst met the cruiser, which had not deviated.

"The Seema burst has caused the front shields to fail. Two *Hornsby* missiles have been destroyed but six have impacted. High impact missiles have impacted. Plasma burst impact. Significant damage to the bow section. Railgun slugs have caused hull breaches."

"Fire the blaster. Keep firing as long as possible," Marjory ordered.

"Yes, Battle Mage," *Fendaristil* replied, as *Hornsby's* main blaster cannon fired the first burst of energy towards the cruiser. "Are you sure of this?"

"We need the cruiser destroyed or we risk losing Third Fleet and if that happens we probably lose the twin tugs concept. We are too close to achieving our goals for that to occur. This makes sure it won't."

Hornsby continued to send blast after blast across the dwindling space between itself and the cruiser. The first blast impacted and punched through the weakened bow of the huge vessel, which belatedly started to turn. That resulted in the following blasts marching along the cruiser's hull, destroying swathes of pods that littered the Empire ship's hull. The cruiser continued to fly, however, and its remaining defensive batteries came alive, sending blast after blast at the oncoming Union ship.

"Blaster has discharged. Shields will fail in seconds," *Fendaristil* noted. "*Hornsby* will reach the cruiser in one minute."

"Set the self-destruct to explode five seconds before impact," Marjory ordered.

"Set. Shields have failed. *Hornsby* is taking impacts from defensive systems. I am moving away."

Marjory watched with a steely gaze as *Hornsby* reached the damaged cruiser, which had been unable to complete a turn or evade the oncoming ship. The self-destruct mechanism was simple in principle. It caused a containment failure in the engines which initiated a run-away breach and resulted in a massive explosion as the remaining highly volatile fuel was ignited, all in three seconds. During the first two seconds, a series of charges erupted along the top, bottom and four sides of the hull, destroying hull integrity. *Hornsby* blew apart, the explosive fireball engulfing the enemy cruiser while large sections of the weakened *Hornsby* hull were blasted into the hull, superstructure and tail assembly of the cruiser, causing huge damage.

The impacts caused the Empire cruiser's engines to fail catastrophically, in turn igniting its own fuel stores. The cruiser emerged from *Hornsby's* fireball as it dissipated in the vacuum of space, continuing to speed on its course, only to have explosions tear through the length of its weakened hull. Finally, two massive explosions tore the ship apart, flinging large pieces of debris in all directions.

"Set a course for Farstation Nine-Three-Seven," Marjory directed evenly. "We will reset the plan there and I will enter stasis."

On *Starbright*, Admiral Bensin was in shock. The loss of *Hornsby* was disappointing but ships were lost during battles and he had experienced that enough times to understand it. The loss of good officers often followed, and Bensin had experienced that enough to understand it also. But this loss included Lieutenant-Commander Mellivar, a member of perhaps the most important family in the Union and one who had just delivered yet another innovation to help the Union stand against the Empire. In his time with Mellivar he had come to realise that she was the consummate warrior, one for whom surrender was not an option. That she fought her ship to the end was not a surprise. That her action probably saved the Third Fleet was not a surprise. The sense of personal loss that he felt was the surprise.

Across the Third Fleet reactions varied. Most stared at viewscreens that showed *Hornsby's* final moments open-mouthed, astounded at what the last desperate action had achieved, before returning to their rescue and repair work. On the bridge of *Jill*, the sensor operator was trying to make sense of strange readings that seemed to indicate additional weapons fire had been involved in the action, including what looked like odd energy pulses. He could find no explanation.

Hornsby's escape pods were retrieved and the final actions were replayed to the former crew. Standing around a viewscreen the two shifts of crew tried to understand what they watched. The chatter outside the group revolved around the tactics used and the loss of the Commander. One of the group made an observation with which all agreed.

"I don't understand how she got so close and was able to cause so much damage before the self-destruct went off," Flight-Sergeant Walmer said, with wonder in her voice.

While everyone pondered that, Weapons-Sergeant Biri gave his answer.

"She was a Mellivar ship."

| part six |

SUNBURST

*10 years before the events described
in <u>Children of Ennaris</u>*

| 33 |

New Tactics

"XO, the Admiral is dead!"

The entire crew of the reserve bridge, with the executive officer in command and the second shift on duty following heavy damage to the main bridge, stopped what they were doing and turned as one to the giver of the message, and then to the receiver. Even as the ship rocked heavily once again, and sparks were flung from a damaged console, they held their breath and watched. The moment stretched.

"Very well, Lieutenant," Commander Mavin Serra replied, sadly. "Ask the medical crew to place his body in the locker, please."

The locker, as it was known in the Union Fleet, was little more than a freezer. But it was a freezer used to hold the bodies of Fleet personnel who were killed during a patrol or battle, and so became something more. Usually, those placed in the locker were ship-based personnel, for the bodies of stinger or shuttle pilots who died in action often were unable to be recovered. Now it would hold the body of Fleet Admiral August Krillik, one of the most decorated of the Union's commanders. For many of the crew of *UCS Starwind*, flagship of the Union's second fleet, he was the only commanding admiral they had known or flown with.

"Back to stations," Serra ordered, and the bridge crew turned to their tasks once again.

The ship rocked again. Serra turned to the main viewscreen mounted at the front of the bridge. It was a quirk that even though there were no windows to see through and every part of the external environment and the ship's path through it was described by the vast array of sensors scattered throughout the vessel, the crew still pointed forward and the viewscreen was mounted as though it was a window. Marjory, in the guise of Mavin Serra, youngest ever executive officer of a Union fleet flagship, pushed the thought away as her weapons officer turned to her.

"XO, the Empire fleet is breaking away," he said with a frown.

"Is that not good news, Lieutenant?" Marjory asked, raising a single eyebrow.

"Yes, of course," the weapons officer replied, 'but they've broken off when they probably could have destroyed several of our ships with little real damage to themselves. We're outgunned in this engagement, and out of position. They could have picked off several ships and then jumped away."

Marjory nodded. Lieutenant Sanden, slated to move up a rank in the coming promotion reviews, had given a succinct explanation of a puzzle. The Second Fleet was scattered over a larger area of space than was wise, and the Empire's Drell Fleet could have ground down many of the fleet's ships had they wanted to do so, one at a time. Admiral Krillik had made a tactical blunder in this engagement, one that proved to be deadly for many of the Fleet's personnel, including himself.

"Let's puzzle over that when we have the chance," Marjory replied. "I think you are correct, but for now we need to get away ourselves. This could be a feint. Recall the stingers," Marjory ordered, "and get the remaining ships into a proper screen around *Starwind*. How many have we lost?"

"*Justiniar*, *Hellis* and *Stimis* are lost with all hands, Captain," communications specialist Lieutenant Greersil replied, voicing for the first time that Marjory - as Commander Mavin Serra - was now in command of the ship. "*Starlight* and *Starmist* show major damage and heavy casualties. Captain Freelim was listed as missing when *Starlight*'s hull was breached, along with many of the command crew.

Second Lieutenant Bard has taken command from the engine room. That's resourceful," Greersil noted with an approving nod. "Captain Cristis was injured during the battle and Commander Pectoz has assumed command of *Starmist*. *Crook* and *Trull* have hull breaches and are effecting repairs. *Starwind* has hull breaches in the aft quarter and we have crews attending to the repairs. Casualty lists are being prepared. Twenty-nine stingers lost from *Starwind's* complement and all forty from *Starlight* and *Starmist*."

Marjory listened to the litany of lost ships and lost personnel bitterly. Three of the six fast attack corvettes were gone and two more damaged, and the two heavy cruisers badly damaged. Most of the senior officers of the second fleet were dead or incapacitated. Which meant ...

"Captain, that makes you senior officer for the fleet," Lieutenant Sanden said, mirroring Marjory's thought.

"Very well, inform all remaining ships of Admiral Krillik's passing and that I have assumed command of the fleet. I want the remaining stingers refuelled and re-armed and half of them to launch as extended cover, with the other half on stand-by. I want them out on the limits of our sensor spread so they act as early warning. Switch them out at two hour intervals. *Crook* and *Trull* are to move closer to *Starwind*. Any spare repair crews we have are to assist them to get the ships ready for a jump. All other ships are to make repairs sufficient to ensure safe jumps. Navigation, plot a course for Wentis Base. Greersil, will six hours give us enough time to get enough repairs done? Yes? Good. Jumps will initiate in six hours."

Marjory looked around the bridge staff, all of them veterans of multiple battles. All looked rattled to varying degrees. This battle had been a disaster for the Union.

"Lieutenant Sanden, I am promoting you to Lieutenant-Commander. You are now my executive officer. I cannot guarantee that will remain the case once we return to base." She glanced to Sanden, who nodded his understanding and stood to move from his console. "Second Lieutenant Freslop will assume duties as weapons officer.

Sanden, I want updates from all ships every hour, repairs and casualties. I want a complete list of available ordinance and weapons status. Schedule a senior officers' conference for two hours' time. Communications, prepare a message to Fleet informing them of the fleet's status, casualties and our exit plan. I want that ready for my review in fifteen minutes."

All eyes were on Marjory as she rattled off the immediate needs. She realised that she had slipped out of the role of the youngest ever Commander but shrugged it off. It may just become part of the growing legend of Mavin Serra. She had the feeling that she was now running out of time and there was something about the change of Empire tactics that seemed … targeted. Marjory thought through that path to logical conclusions, recalling Likud's tactics. Her eyes opened wide.

"Communications, flash message to Fleet. I want to know if the other fleets have suffered similar attacks and what have been the results if they have."

Sanden stared at her, mouth opening as realisation struck.

"A targeted attack?" he asked.

Marjory nodded.

"It is a guess, but would be in keeping," she replied tensely. "Look at the ships we lost or that were badly damaged. All of them had senior and experienced captains. All three of our Star-class ships had their bridges targeted. All three were commanded by highly experienced veterans. Maybe it was an attack on the command structure."

"Captain, Fleet is requesting a reason for the request," Greersil said into the sudden quiet following Marjory's statement. "I have replied that it is a Fleet security matter and that the acting admiral will contact Fleet command shortly."

Marjory nodded her approbation and then turned to her screens again. She had to get the fleet ready to jump back to base and then there would have to be a full rebuild. She had one card left to play but was afraid she may have left it too late.

"Captain, Fleet reports that Third, Fifth and Sixth fleets have also been attacked. Capital ships were targeted." Greersil paused. "High casualties," he finished.

Marjory grimaced, her mouth dry suddenly. Likud was making a move.

"Do we know where First and Fourth fleets are?"

Sanden nodded. "Yes, we have enough of an idea that we can contact them."

"Send a Fleet emergency message to Fleet Admirals Porter and Maesil. Prepare for targeted attacks by overwhelming force. Target is senior, experienced command officers. Sign it Serra, second fleet, acting Admiral." He glanced to Greersil who had eyebrows raised in mute query and shrugged. "I know, but saying 'Acting Admiral' tells them that Admiral Krillik is dead or incapacitated. It will get their attention faster."

Greersil nodded and turned back to his console. Marjory glanced to the main viewscreen, showing that the remaining ships of Second Fleet were moving into position with the injured ones closing on *Starwind*. There was another thought that intruded, though, and caused another moment of dry mouth. How did the Empire know where they all were? One or even two fleets being found and attacked could be bad luck or coincidence but not four fleets, and not when the Empire fleets obviously had been reinforced for the purpose.

The Union had a security leak. Another one. But this one might be the worst.

The news was no better once the remnants of Second Fleet finally made their way to Wentis Base. First Fleet had suffered badly and Fourth Fleet was almost wiped out. While each had accounted for several Empire heavy cruisers in the process, the Union had suffered its worst setback in centuries of conflict with the Empire, and all in the space of a week. Most of the Union's capital ships had been destroyed or suffered significant damage. Worse, many of the senior Fleet commanders had been killed, the leadership ranks decimated.

The Union leaders recognised that it was not coincidental and intensive investigations were started, but with little confidence that the traitors would be uncovered quickly.

Marjory seethed at the inaction that she saw in response. She found herself installed as acting Admiral of the Second Fleet, but was given to understand that the appointment was unlikely to be made permanent. She *was* promoted to full Captain, however, and found herself in the odd position of being one of the youngest and yet most senior of the fleet commanders. If they only knew, she mused as she awaited a call with the Union Fleet headquarters. Her primary concern, as it had been for almost five hundred Earth years now, was how to conclude her mission.

She had been so close! From the first set of sensors and shields that she had loaded to *Sandpiper*, the small patrol gunboat, to the Stellar and Superstar class heavy cruisers that had not been built in anywhere near the number required, she had taken the Union on a rapid military uplift journey. She knew that she should be proud of her achievements. Not only did the Union have ships of equal capability to those of the Empire, but in many respects they were more advanced. The Warriors of the Light, one of her most cherished initiatives, had proven themselves to be invaluable in fighting off the influence of the Empire agents, of which there were many. In fact, the difference was the Empire's extensive use of subversive agents, seeking to undermine everything from the military chain of command, supply chains, and medical advances to the political and social fabrics of the numerous worlds that comprised the Union. Agents had been uncovered with monotonous regularity, some by Marjory herself over the years, in all parts of the Union.

Those agents continued to be a major cause of damage. After all this time, and with her experiences from her own home planet of Ennaris to this current mission, Marjory still could not understand how so many people could be taken in by promises of personal gain that, usually, proved to be ephemeral. There had been the few agents who had been blackmailed into performing acts of espionage or terrorism, but most agents were recruited for prestige, money or personal power. The motivations were so alien to her that she constantly found herself being surprised when a senior Fleet officer or political figure was exposed. She knew that she had been singled out from an early age for her unique skills and thus had been guaranteed a life that would want for nothing, but she was certain that she would not have succumbed to the temptations on offer even had she not had those advantages.

Now, she waited for an interview with the Fleet Directorate, an arm of the Union that had been established to bring together the various elements that controlled the logistics of the Fleet. In her various guises down the years, Marjory had been involved with the various logistics and supply arms that had existed, some of whom had been poor at their roles and some that had been exceptional. Her involvement with the Directorate had been limited in this iteration of her mission. As always, a bureaucracy tended to build itself first, and the Directorate had become one of the largest arms of the Fleet, with very senior officers who had never seen combat or who would not have the first understanding of how to fight a warship. Marjory could only speculate on why she had been tasked with attending this interview. Perhaps, she mused with a snort, they wanted her opinion on the wallpaper to be installed in the officers' messes.

It was depressing. Marjory had been preparing to return to her life on Ennaris and prepare for the events that must be imminent. There, she would stand with Drewflin and lead the fight against Goroth to remove the threat he posed to her home world, at least as far as the Prophecy said existed, and then they would rebuild their planet to be a power in this new galaxy. This identity was planned to be the last she would need, in fact. That may not be the case now. She had heard nothing from Fernis or Dharmoney, and so was making some assumptions that may be wrong. She pushed away the impulse to sigh and instead straightened herself in her chair. If she had to stay for a further time then so be it. She would do so and she would continue to drive the Union to where they could stand against the Empire. And in doing so, they would be able to assist Ennaris.

Marjory started as the door to the interview room slid open and three people entered. Two of them she recognised but had never met. They were the most senior admirals of the Directorate - the Director and her deputy - but neither, she knew, had seen active service since they had been ensigns. They conspicuously wore an array of ribbons attached to their crisply pressed uniform blouses, in contract to Marjory's habit of wearing none of her various awards and the more utilitarian garb of a working Fleet spacer. The third person was a civilian, or was dressed in civilian attire, and she did not recognise him. Marjory stood.

"Captain, thank you for coming," the civilian said as he advanced towards her, hand extended in greeting.

Marjory nodded and shook the offered hand, then gave salutes to the Fleet officers. Both returned them with accompanying nods.

"Please, let's be seated," the civilian continued. "I am assuming you know Admirals Hillis and Yenq. Yes? Good. You probably don't recognise me though. My name is Brectil Infis. I am the liaison between the Union Defence Secretary and the Fleet. The Secretary was meant to be here today but has been delayed. He asked me to meet with you in his absence."

Marjory inclined her head in greeting but said nothing. Silence, she had learnt long ago, often was the best method of getting others to say more than they meant to do.

"Well, I have asked for refreshments to be served, and they will be here shortly," Brectil Infis said. "For now, let me congratulate you on your promotion to captain, the youngest ever in the Union Fleet, and on your successful escape from the Empire Fleet."

Marjory snorted, to a disapproving glare from Admiral Yenq, the Deputy Director.

"We did not escape, Mister Infis," Marjory replied with an edge to her voice. "They left. There is a very big difference."

"Yes, well that's correct, of course, but I understand from the bridge officers' reports that you assumed command and were effective immediately. Very effective. Frankly, I'm not surprised. It's part of the reason the Secretary asked for you to come and meet with us."

"I did what had to be done, and as we are trained to do," Marjory replied evenly, wondering where this was going.

"But not everyone does so, even if trained. You did. I hazard a guess that not many would have been as competent in that situation, with heavy losses and damaged ships to get back to base. I also understand that it was you who first realised that the Empire was staging a co-ordinated attack on our most senior commanders and our capital assets."

"It was a guess," Marjory said. "I would prefer to have been wrong."

"As would we all," Infis agreed. "And now we need to deal with what has been left behind, and the reason we asked for you to meet with us."

Marjory waited, glancing to the two admirals who sat stony faced. *So, not a Fleet decision but a political one*, Marjory thought. *Interesting.*

"And what would that reason be, Mister Infis? I have a ship to have repaired and a crew to keep busy. They have been through a traumatic experience and even the best trained of them is suffering loss. It is not a good time for their commanding officer to be away from them."

"It is your family history, Captain Serra, that draws us to you as much as your behaviour under extreme stress. We are hoping you and your family can assist us once again." Infis sat back and watched Marjory.

Marjory sat opposite Infis and kept her face still. She believed that she still had one card to play in this mission. Was the chance to play it being handed to her like this?

"You refer to the fact that I am a member of the Mellivar clan," Marjory said evenly.

The two admirals started in unison, glancing one to the other. Infis ignored them but Marjory found their reaction to be interesting. Something to be pondered later.

"I am, Captain," Infis replied. "Your ancestors played an enormous part in the history of the Union, and the Union Fleet in particular. At every juncture when we were facing dire times, a Mellivar arrived with a new advance of some nature. I've made a particular study of those events. With each advance the Union was able to stave off another danger. With each Mellivar came new ships, or an upgraded suite of components, or an advanced method of using them that our experts had not considered feasible."

Marjory considered mentioning that it was the same "clan" that had established the Warriors of the Light, but decided against it. Infis appeared to have done his homework. Perhaps this was her opening. Admirals Hillis and Yenq obviously had been unaware of the information Infis had just provided but she felt that they had been aware of the reason for the meeting.

"I come from a family that has made some contributions," Marjory replied, deciding to dangle a baited hook. "At the moment my own contribution is to captain a ship of the line."

"Not any longer, I'm afraid," Infis replied smoothly, taking the bait readily. "I have gone over your record. You scored the highest ranking for your engineering and design courses at the Fleet Academy, which I expected. You also scored the highest ranking in tactics and strategy. You completed your academy training in half the usual time and your instructors reported that you probably could have graduated even earlier. The Academy has never seen a student such as yourself."

Marjory was aware of all of that. She had very deliberately pushed herself forward this time around, seeking to make exactly the impression that she was the brightest star of the Union. With *Fendaristil's* assistance she had driven through the course work easily. As for her command of Fleet tactics and strategy, well she had been doing all of this before Earth's inhabitants had left their hunter gatherer phase. What she needed to do was to get herself into a position to put the final puzzle-piece on the board as quickly as possible. Perhaps this was it.

"Why no longer?" she asked, glancing to the admirals with a raised eyebrow. Neither of them gave any sort of response but both were obviously displeased.

"Captain, you have been assigned to the Fleet Directorate with immediate effect. *Starwind* will have a new captain assigned - already has had, in fact - and your effects have been removed from your cabin and placed in storage for you. Your job will be to find a way to defeat the Empire's heavy cruisers. To date we have been able to defend effectively but their change of tactics is troubling and defence is not the answer. We need something that can stand against them and fight back."

"One of my ancestors provided you with the Superstar class heavy cruiser and carriers," Marjory replied. "Only a few of the Superstars were ever made, and they were not to the correct specification. Why not go back to that design and build it."

"That is an option we are considering," Infis replied. "However, we are hoping that you have a little something in your family's design vault that can be added to the mix. In return, you will be promoted to an old rank, not often used today, of Commodore. When you return to active service, assuming success in this endeavour, you will be promoted again to Admiral."

"You must be desperate to make this request," Marjory said to Infis, ignoring the admirals. "You realise that I will have to have complete control over the process. No interference. I will need a minimum of five years, and I will build my own team, with staff selected by me. And I select my ship when I return to active duty."

Hillis and Yenq looked as though they had been served a dish of Hendari meal worms, the sour ones. Marjory's demand would sideline them completely, although she knew from long experience that she would have to fight against the Directorate. The bureaucracy had many ways to stall or deflect effort that they did not want made.

"It's not a request, Captain," Infis said immediately. "However, yes, we are desperate. Yes, we expected you to demand complete control. And yes, you will have your choice of ships when you return to line command." He paused, a shadow of uncertainty crossing his face before he took a deep breath and let it out slowly. "But I must ask this question. Do you have anything that could be used or adapted to bring us to parity with the Empire?"

Marjory let the moment play out. She reviewed the potential improvements that could be made to the Union fleet that would provide equality or better with the Empire ships. It would be a constant race with Likud, of course, but she knew he would go bigger and more powerful as his first impulse, where she would go better. Perhaps it was time to play his game, but with her own twist.

"Yes, Mr Infis," Marjory said, nodding slowly as she continued to sort her thoughts. "I have some ideas that may work."

Infis closed his eyes briefly, allowing the tension he felt to be seen. He took another deep breath, locked eyes with Marjory and nodded. Finally, he smiled slightly.

"Well then, Commodore Serra. Best to get to work."

| 34 |

Supernova Class

The next year passed in a cloud of hard effort. Determination to provide a counterweight to Likud's changed tactics gave Marjory the only motivation she required. For the team that she built, though, there needed to be something else. To them, she offered hope that the Union could not only stand against the Empire, but could prevail. All of the women and men who she gathered under her banner had known nothing other than warfare with the Empire. Indeed, that had been a constant for generations of Union citizens. For them, the continued attrition was a source of concern. In the civilian sphere, occasional bouts of panic had become more frequent. Those in the military arms noted with growing alarm the despondency of their leadership. It was this decay in spirit that she sought to reverse even as she hoped that her time with the Union was close to its end.

She felt confident that she had succeeded in her task. The Union Fleet remained the bulwark behind which the growing number of worlds that comprised the Union sheltered. The Warriors of the Light had become an important arm of the Fleet, a semi-independent unit that was deployed where situations were most dire. The change from its original complete separation from the military had been foreseen and was a logical development. The Warriors had grown significantly in number since their origination so long ago, but they remained a relatively small ultra-elite force. Several recent scandals had rocked their ranks, however, as they had rocked the ranks of the

Union military and political spheres. But to Marjory, who had seen the same repeatedly over the centuries that she dwelt with her human cousins, these were merely the visible part of what she knew was a deeper problem.

Greed, self-interest, desire for power over others, feelings of injustice centred on themselves - all had been shown to be motives for Union citizens to work to undermine their own society. Others had been blackmailed into working for the enemy, whose agents had shown themselves to be adept at seeking out misdeeds, crimes or merely ethical failures and exploiting them. Marjory doubted that Likud would provide many, if any, of the promised boons for those willing to betray their own. In fact, despite the fact that he had done the same thing during his own service for Ennaris, she doubted that he would have any regard for traitors at all. He would, however, use them to the fullest extent that he could.

To combat the potential influence of Likud's agents, Marjory made sure that her work was conducted only by those she trusted, those who she had selected herself. The work was done in a remote and highly secure facility. When the admirals of the Fleet Directorate sought to block her work, as she had expected them to do, she left them to be dealt with by the politicians and turned once again to Drummel Industrial, which was still the powerhouse of the Union's heavy space defence industry. She had no need to repeat any of the extreme measures that had been necessary in the past, for Drummel's current management was only too prepared to work with this scion of the owning family when she made discrete enquiries. In particular, Drummel Industrial had a small cohort of very gifted ship designers. These Marjory co-opted as part of her team. She then drafted into the group several of the most promising young officers of the Union Fleet, leaving several commanders grinding their teeth.

Among the Union officers who she drew into her sphere was the experienced Lieutenant Melton Bard, now promoted to First Lieutenant, who had shown such resilience and poise during the disastrous battle that almost decimated the Second Fleet. In something of a shock, Marjory found that Bard's small family became almost a second one for her, with the young Denton Bard worshipping the young-seeming Commodore.

With her latest team in place, Marjory began to put her ideas into practice. She started the Drummel designers on a complete review of the key components that were holding back the Union's ships. Nothing was out of scope. No ideas were too fanciful to be considered, although many were rejected. Some formed the basis of future research and design work. The Advanced Research Unit, as the team was called, came up with small and large advances in everything from astral navigation to waste disposal, from long range communication to molecular scanning. In some of these projects Marjory oversaw work that took the Union beyond what Ennaris' scientists had been able to accomplish, which brought a satisfied smile to her face. For brief moments, she could imagine herself back on Ennaris or at Escantil, the moon base.

However, while these advances were important to the overall efficiency and effectiveness of the Union women and men, it was the new ships that absorbed most of the time of the research and design units. The time came when Marjory called the design unit together and presented to them her ideas for the new design.

"You have all worked with the Star class cruiser, one of the oldest Drummel designs in the Fleet and still a potent ship," Marjory said to the group standing around the holotable. "It has been developed further from the original design, but essentially remains the same ship. The current StarCarrier class is based on this ship, as is the StarTransport heavy support ship. Several other designs are in the fleet also, but all are based more or less on the old Star class. Most of you have also seen the design of the Stellar and Superstar classes, which were never built in volume. This shows the difference between these classes."

The holotable displayed the familiar profile of a Star class cruiser. Beside it a larger Stellar class ship and the even larger Superstar class profile emerged into the image. While the Stellar class ship was larger than the Star class, the Superstar class was half again as long as the

Star class and nearly twice across the beam. Along the length of the ships' images were spots of different coloured lights that showed the weapon emplacements, red for point defences, blue for main energy weapons and green for the railguns, one of which could be seen on the Star class and two on the Stellar and Superstar classes. Missile batteries were shown as tubes running back into the ships.

"We're going to use the Superstar as a base for a new class of ship that will be able to take the fight to the Empire heavy cruisers. Many of the improvements to power grids and control systems that we have on the planning table will be incorporated in this ship first. We will add additional weapons, better sensors and shield emitters. And every ship will carry a complement of stingers."

"Commodore, that's a lot to fit into a Superstar class. It's big but can we alter its carrying capacity like that? We can probably add some of the additional weapons and any upgrades will help, but ..." Lieutenant Hollis shrugged as she finished speaking to indicate how little she could envisage this transformation occurring.

"I agree," Marjory replied, "so we will make it larger. But not larger for no reason. This will be the most potent ship on either side."

Beneath the Superstar class cruiser on the holotable a new image emerged, stretching half as long again but only slightly wider. This vessel retained the signature fluid lines of the Star, Stellar and Superstar class ships. Its clean lines glowed with myriad point defence emplacements, comprising both lasers and railguns, and the main energy weapons were spread across the upper and lower hull, four facing forward and two facing rearward. Missile batteries ran along both sides of the hull Starting from a point around one-third of the distance from the stylish bow and extending much of the way to the blunt stern. Below the missiles on each side were the retractable hanger bays. At the rear the ship bulged and then narrowed slightly so that the engine exhaust nozzles barely emerged from the hull. All of these features were eclipsed by the single railgun placed as a main weapon on the upper hull. Marjory smiled slightly and touched a stud. The myriad raised weaponry that marred the smooth lines of the holographic hull folded into the hull, leaving the expanse of hull looking largely unbroken. The team stared. Silence reigned for almost a minute as they examined the ship.

"She's beautiful," Lieutenant Bard said softly.

"This is the Supernova class," Marjory said into the silence. "It has a larger overall strike capability, carries two full squadrons of stingers, is massive enough to give the Empire heavy cruiser commanders pause given they equate size with capability, and will be faster than anything the Union has at the moment. We will be upgrading its power output and its shields to a newer form that will provide greater protection."

"There appears to be lots of unused space within the hull," Lieutenant Hollis ventured.

"That is room for future extension," Marjory said smoothly. "This ship will be built in small numbers, perhaps one per fleet, and it will form the basis for the Union's largest vessels for many years to come. The first Star class ship design was delivered over five hundred years ago and that design remains in production and is the mainstay of the fleet. Oh, it has been modified and upgraded significantly over that time, of course, and now is longer and broader, but essentially it is the same design. The Superstar class is about three hundred and fifty years old. There have been far fewer of them built than were expected. The Star class grew to be not that much smaller than the Stellar class and upgrades to both over the years gave them relatively similar performance. It made sense for the Star class to continue to be the main ship design, although I believe that the Stellar should have been built more, like the Superstar. All of those ships were designed to be as much defensive as offensive. The Union does not go on the attack, as a rule. It has been that way for most of its existence. This ship is different. This ship will project power. It will take the fight to the Empire. Its greater size will allow us to add the defensive and offensive capabilities it needs to win one on one with the Empire's newest heavy cruisers. Perhaps even one on two."

There were nods around the holotable as the team continued to examine the design.

"The main railgun," Weapons Sergeant Sertis said, pointing to the now hidden gun. "Its size would indicate the need for much more power, not to mention lots of storage for munitions. I can see large storage compartments beneath the emplacement. The engines appear to be larger, a lot larger actually. Will they provide that additional power for long enough?"

"Yes, we believe so," Marjory replied with a nod of approval to the question. "Of course, it is up to us to make sure of that. The goal will be to fire the main railgun independently of the other guns, and maintain a constant rate of fire for several minutes."

Sertis pursed his lips as he thought.

"That will need a large energy store, then," he said thoughtfully. "And it will need a dedicated channel for recharges. It's magnetic rather than kinetic, I assume?" He paused to await Marjory's smile and nod before continuing. "So, no real recoil to worry about. Angle of attack is limited to the upper front quadrant so it's a front-on weapon." He smiled and nodded to himself. "So, it's deployed while we charge them."

"Charge them?" Ensign Ashist asked.

"Yes, charge them," Sertis replied as he glanced to Ashist. "The ship accelerates towards its target, firing the main guns. At the right time she swings away, a missile barrage is fired and the main energy weapons top and bottom are brought to bear as the angle changes. We have everything firing at once. Commodore," Sertis looked to Marjory as he spoke, "request permission to be on that ship."

"We have to build it first, Sergeant," Marjory replied with a conspiratorial grin, "but we can talk about that."

| **35** |

The Reveal

It took four years to build the first Supernova prototype. There were many smaller or partial test ships built to examine and allow redesign of components, and most of them were destroyed in various ways as testing proceeded. What became clear was that the Supernova class of ship would be a hard sell to the Fleet Directorate, whose opposition to the project continued unabated. At one stage Marjory threatened to resign, a message that immediately brought Infis to a meeting and resulted in a directive to Fleet Directorate that Marjory's team was not to be impeded. To make the situation even clearer Admiral Yenq was re-assigned to a front line posting. Rumour was that Admiral Hillis retired to her suite and stayed there for a week on receiving that news.

In the meantime, the Advanced Design Unit made several breakthroughs, some of them prompted by Marjory and *Fendaristil*, drawing on some of the last of the Ennari designs that Marjory was prepared to use. The power plants in the long-standing Star class design shrank in size and increased in output, which caused great excitement in the fleet as it allowed the same class of ship to have greater range and more available power. Defensive shields also were improved, using some of that available power, and finally matched the last of the Ennari ships in passive defensive capability. Missiles became much smarter as the limited AI capabilities built into them were improved with uprated heuristic abilities, although they remained below the Ennari missiles used by the farstations. *Fendaristil,* in particular, expressed satisfaction with that improvement, even though the AIs would be activated and destroyed within minutes as they performed their tasks.

Some of the improvements, however, were breakthroughs brought about by hard work, brilliant minds applying themselves to problems and belief that an idea had merit and should be pursued. This resulted in advances beyond the Ennari designs, as had been the case long ago when Besnil had applied her own unique way of thinking alongside Marjory as the original Mellivar. The advanced sensors were made even better, with far better recognition algorithms that produced crystal clear images of the surrounding space to a distance of half a million kilometres, and only slightly fuzzy but mostly recognisable images for a further three million kilometres. The long range scanners benefited from these advances and others to stretch to nine million kilometres, while the FTL sensors were able to identify disturbances caused by FTL travel with much greater fidelity. Many of these advances could be retrofitted to existing designs.

One advance brought especial joy to Marjory. Sitting in a prototype ship that was essentially a bridge surrounded by spars and conduits that led to the single engine that was being tested, along with a range of sensors, power couplings and communication arrays upgrades, Marjory was presented with a steaming mug of coffee. Watching expectantly, her staff waited as she nodded absently and took an experimental sip. Marjory had long ago fallen in love with coffee. As a rule, however, for some strange reason that was to do with atmospheric pressures or the effects of shipboard climatic controls, ship brewed coffee could not be considered in any way to be as good as that available on the Union's planets or the larger stations. As a result, she tended to tolerate rather than enjoy coffee while in flight. Even *Fendaristil* could not suggest improvements there.

With the first sip, Marjory's attention changed dramatically. The coffee she tasted was rich and strong, as she liked it, the bitterness balanced by the crema floating on top that added the creaminess that she so often found lacking when on a ship. She looked up in astonishment to find her crew watching her and smiling broadly at her reaction.

"Where did you get this?" Marjory asked as one of the team laughed.

"Bard had a few ideas about how to keep the food on board fresher and longer lasting," Lieutenant Ashist replied from her monitoring station. "They worked. One of the methods was to have micro-climates created within the food storage chambers. And then he decided to do the same thing to the coffee held in the coffee machine. This is the result."

"Mr Bard," Marjory said as she took another appreciative sip, "if you keep this up you will make Admiral before me."

The team laughed before returning to their various tasks, the brief interlude over. Marjory glanced around the makeshift bridge at her team, once again absorbed in their work, and smiled with satisfaction.

The prototype review was brief by Fleet standards. Infis arrived with the Secretary of Defence and a retinue of assistants and aides. The Union Fleet was represented by only two members of the Home Fleet, Captain Hens Thengis and his assistant, Lieutenant Marlis Prema. Thengis was the most senior member of the Fleet design review team, although Fleet had been deeply involved in most aspects of construction. Little time was wasted. The usual shroud was in place stretching into space for over two kilometres from the furthest, space-ward, end of the test facility to where the party entered closer to the station hub. After introductions and small talk Marjory led the way through a hatch and into an airlock, then through a short passageway to a wide corridor.

The corridor was long, with discrete bulkheads spaced at regular intervals. Walls and floor were both white extrusions. As the party proceeded along the corridor Marjory noticed Captain Thengis examining the bulkheads, walls and markings with keen interest, his eyes poring over as many elements as he could see. At one stage, she caught his eye and smiled at his shocked expression before turning back to the Secretary of Defence as they approached a closed hatch.

"Commodore, this is quite a long walk and we are on a tight schedule. When are we going to reach this ship?" the Secretary asked with a frown.

"I'm sure we'll be there momentarily, sir," Infis said quickly, to which Thengis snorted.

The whole party stopped as Infis stared at the Fleet Captain.

"You have something to say, Captain?" Infis asked tightly. "Is there something funny about wanting to reach the ship?"

"Only that we've been on the ship for the last fifteen minutes," Thengis replied with a grin to Marjory.

Everyone turned to Marjory whose mouth twitched in a smile. She turned back and walked to the next hatch. She placed a hand flat on a security device. The group gasped as her hand seemed to sink into the device and a blue light ran across the surface. She pulled her hand from the device and the hatch split in two and slid open, revealing the large bridge of the ship.

Marjory strode onto the bridge, followed by the Secretary and Infis, then the aides and finally the two Fleet personnel. Thengis looked around the bridge and nodded appreciatively. Marjory's key staffers were in their places at the consoles that spread in a circle around a centre well. None of them took any notice of the new arrivals. At the far end, a large viewscreen took the place of a window, stretching from wall to wall and curving back as though to wrap around the viewers. The screen showed the space around the station, with every Union ship indicated and tagged, along with the moon around which the station orbited and an asteroid belt at the edge of the screen's display range.

"Full sensor display?" Thengis asked.

Marjory nodded.

"*Sunburst* has short and long range sensors arrayed along the dorsal and keel, as well at the bow and down both port and starboard flanks.

There are additional sensors at the stern and the screen can reconfigure to show the rearward view in full or as a window."

"*Sunburst?*" Infis asked.

"A space capable ship is always named, Mr Infis," Marjory stated. "The Supernova class is derived from the Superstar which in turn is derived from the Star class. Even though this is a prototype, it is space capable. In fact, it is in a state that it could be commissioned with little additional effort. However, at this stage it is a test bed."

"A limited prototype is hardly what we expected to see, Commodore," the Secretary of Defence said.

"I understand that, Mr Secretary," Marjory replied smoothly.

"So why have you decided to show us one?"

"I have not, Mr Secretary," Marjory said. "*Sunburst* left dock immediately we boarded. We are …" and she looked to the navigation console where Ashist held up five fingers "… five kilometres from the station."

"I felt nothing," Lieutenant Prema said as her eyes opened wide. "Nothing at all!"

"We used docking thrusters to move away from the dock and then minimal power to move from the station. *Sunburst* is a large ship and it takes a lot to make it stagger." Marjory indicated the viewscreen which now showed their location. "For the test we will jump to a location five light years away to demonstrate this ship's weapons and flight abilities. We will return to the station for a debrief in two hours."

"I'm not sure I'm comfortable with taking a prototype that far," Infis said. "Is it safe? We do have the Secretary with us."

Marjory gave him a withering glare.

"I am of clan Mellivar, Mr Infis, which is one of the reasons you wanted me to lead this effort. Our prototypes do not fail."

Infis' lips pursed, but there was nothing that could be said to that, although Marjory glanced to Thengis, who was smiling broadly, and winked.

"Set course," Marjory ordered. "Execute!"

"We have in front of us an asteroid field. We will be using asteroid X-9873, which is shown on the screen." Marjory pointed to the screen where the asteroid field was shown in vivid detail, and where one asteroid was highlighted. "*Sunburst* will target the asteroid with its various weapons systems in sequence. We will make four passes."

"What weapons complement does this prototype have, Commodore?" Infis asked, emphasising 'prototype'.

Marjory ignored the tone of voice to respond to the question.

"The first pass will be using the main energy weapons. This will be followed by railguns and then a missile barrage."

"That's only three weapons, Commodore," Captain Thengis observed mildly.

"I will decide what the fourth run will be when I see what remains of the asteroid," Marjory said, nodding. "We have several options available."

Thengis raised an eyebrow but said nothing else. The Secretary merely watched proceedings, dividing his attention between the viewscreen and the crew as they went about their various tasks.

"All sections report ready, Commodore," Lieutenant Bard reported from the weapons control station. "Main weapons are on line, squadrons are deployed."

"Squadrons?" Infis queried with a frown.

"Hammer and Shield squadrons launched immediately we arrived on station, Mr Infis," Marjory replied. "They have assumed a defensive position around *Sunburst*."

"I was not aware this ship carried a complement of stingers," Infis said. "Nor was I aware you had an active squadron on board."

"These are also prototypes, Mr Infis, but they are fully armed and combat ready also," Marjory said in response. "A Supernova class ship will always carry at least two full squadrons of stingers. *Sunburst*, as configured, has capacity for an additional squadron, or that many replacement stingers. The stingers we carry are of a new revision, using the original design and upgraded. Several of the changes made by other designers since inception have been removed as they were serving no useful purpose but added extra weight and compromised manoeuvrability. Then we added upgrades that *are* useful. These stingers have additional range, better stand-off weapons, better defensive shields, and are faster." Marjory smiled as she thought about what she could have added to these ships but thought it advisable to hold back still.

"Options, Commodore?" Thengis asked with a wry smile.

"Options, Captain," Marjory confirmed with an acknowledging nod.

Thengis appeared to be enjoying himself thoroughly. At least there is one ally in Fleet, Marjory thought. She had never met Thengis, although by reputation he was a hard charging ship commander. He had been one of those who had stepped up when the senior commanders were decimated several years before, taking command of the remainder of the Fifth Fleet when the capital ships were destroyed and the Empire heavy cruisers had sped away, much as they had done with the Second Fleet. Thengis had managed to pull the remnants of the fleet back to base without losing any others, and had been given rapid promotion as a result.

Sunburst's huge engines flared brightly as the ship accelerated towards the asteroid, still two million kilometres distant. The viewscreen showed the asteroid growing larger. At the bottom right of the screen a diagram of *Sunburst* appeared, with the four forward facing and two rear facing energy weapons shown.

"Deploy the main cannons," Marjory ordered.

The diagram of *Sunburst* showed the six main cannons deploying. Hatches opened and the cannons rose into place. Each cannon went through a series of rotation tests and then settled facing forward or rearward.

"Target the asteroid."

The four forward facing cannons twitched slightly as they aligned with the target.

"Target acquired, Commodore," Bard noted calmly.

"Fire in sequence, Mr Bard," Marjory ordered. "Five rounds each."

One by one each of the forward facing cannons fired an energy burst that sped towards the asteroid until each cannon had fired five times. Each cannon emplacement was highlighted on the viewscreen as it fired. *Sunburst* followed the energy bursts for a short distance before swinging away to reverse course, allowing the rear-facing cannons to acquire the targets and release their own five-shot barrages. *Sunburst* sped away from the asteroid even as the viewscreen showed the impacts of the energy weapons striking it, the first twenty shots from the forward cannons raising a cloud of debris into which the ten shots from the rear-facing cannons disappeared.

Slowly the debris field cleared enough to see that the asteroid remained intact, although chunks had been blown off it and tumbled deeper into the asteroid field.

"Mr Hollis, map those larger chunks and see if any of them are likely to cause trouble, please. Add them to the charts. Mr Bard, status of the main energy weapons?" Marjory asked crisply.

"All cannons report fully operational, Commodore," Bard replied. "Temperatures are stable, energy patterns nominal."

"Very well, second pass then. Take us back in, Commander," Marjory ordered, the last order to the helm station operator, Commander Frelsmith.

Sunburst swung back into line.

"Mr Bard, all guns are to fire simultaneously, five shots each, rapid fire," Marjory ordered for the benefit of the observers, as Bard was well aware of the agenda.

"All at once?" Thengis asked.

"Why? Is that a problem," Infis asked as he watched the slowly expanding debris field.

"Our ships don't have sufficient power to maintain rapid fire of multiple main energy cannons," Thengis replied. "We risk the power conduits overloading but more often the guns just can't fire because they can't get enough juice."

"*Sunburst* has uprated power plants also," Marjory answered Thengis. "You cannot just fire everything for ever but there is more power available for longer."

Sunburst approached the firing point again. On the viewscreen all of the forward cannons flashed repeatedly. For an observer watching the demonstration from outside the ship it would have appeared as though *Sunburst's* bow had disappeared in a blaze of light, only to reappear again as the cannons ceased firing. Once again *Sunburst* swung away from the attacking line and the rear-facing cannons picked up the attack with their own smaller version of the light show. A short time later the debris field was supplemented as the asteroid endured a further pummelling. All energy bursts from the forward cannons struck the huge space rock within moments of each other, followed by the rearward cannons' shots. This time the asteroid was noticeably reduced in size.

"Mr Bard?"

"Cannons report operational and nominal again, Commodore. Energy store is down to forty percent. Recharging."

Thengis nodded, impressed. He and Lieutenant Prema exchanged glances, the latter smiling broadly as she watched the asteroid debris swirl into space. Just being able to sustain fire would be a huge boon.

"Very well, then. Retract the energy cannons. Deploy the railgun."

Marjory watched the diagram of *Sunburst* as the cannons were hidden behind their hatches and the massive railgun rose into place. Thengis frowned as five other ghost images of railguns appeared for a moment placed equidistant around the bow but then, he reasoned, the software remained under development also and so he concentrated on the railgun being brought into view. It was enormous, easily the largest he had ever seen. The visible rail assembly, itself, was quite short but the size of the muzzle suggested that it threw large projectiles.

"This single railgun has a rate of fire more than twice that of our regular model," Marjory said to the observers. "The projectile can be up to twenty centimetres in diameter. The projectile velocity is rated at one hundred kilometres per second but we expect that to improve quickly. *Sunburst* can sustain fire for ten minutes with its current power rating, while also employing point defences, including the defensive railguns. For this demonstration we will fire five kinetic rounds but the gun can use a range of projectile types."

Thengis nodded, impressed once again. Railguns had been around for centuries, of course, but they had always fallen short in two key areas. First, the amount of power required to launch the projectile was huge, which resulted in lengthy recharge cycles. Anything more than a second or two was lengthy when in battle, and the normal main railgun would take up to thirty seconds to recharge after only a few shots, depending on other power draws. Second, the gun itself was bulky. The turrets usually were mounted permanently on the upper hull because of their size, which limited their angle of fire to narrow arcs. This model appeared to be much smaller and thus could be mounted in different locations, with a wider field of fire.

Sunburst swung back towards the chosen asteroid. This time, Marjory ordered the gun to fire from much further out from the target. The observers felt nothing as the gun spat five solid rounds from its square muzzle. The gun was retracting even as the first round struck the asteroid, followed in moments by the four following rounds.

The asteroid disappeared. A cloud of dust and debris was ejected once again. On *Sunburst's* main screen, the former location of the asteroid was now marked with a red circle. The asteroid was gone.

"Those rounds were merely solid metal composite," Marjory said into the silence that followed. "This model can also fire explosive rounds, but we are experimenting with small versions of the standard torpedoes with an armour piercing first stage and high explosive second stage. They will have to be greatly reduced in size and the muzzle expanded in size, so it is a laboratory exercise at the moment. However, it shows promise." She looked from the Secretary of Defence to Infis and finally to Thengis and Prema. "Is there anything extra that you wish to see?" she asked, to shakes of the head all round. "Then I suggest we move to the captain's lounge where we can discuss the project further. We will return to base once the fragments of asteroid are mapped and recorded."

| 36 |

A Trap Baited

It was eight months since the demonstration of the Supernova-class ship's capabilities. *Sunburst* had been formally commissioned, even though it remained a test bed as systems and weapons were enhanced. The bridge of *Sunburst* was quiet as Marjory made her entrance.

"Admiral on the bridge," Lieutenant Bard called.

The bridge crew came to attention as one. Marjory glanced around and nodded in acknowledgement.

"As you were," she said crisply. "XO, take her out."

"Aye, Admiral," Captain Thengis, newly appointed ship captain of *Sunburst* and executive officer of the reconstituted First Fleet, replied. "Mr Bard, prepare to separate from the dock."

Marjory left Thengis to his job and sat back to review the situation. The Empire had made its expected move, one in keeping with Likud's style. A large formation of heavy cruisers had been observed by a small group of Warriors who had infiltrated Empire space, and it was obviously being prepared for battle. Most of the Warriors had been lost in bringing their news from deep inside enemy lines. One, however, had stolen an experimental fighter and made his way to Union space. The news had startled and dismayed the Union leaders, although it had come as no real surprise to Marjory.

With so many senior officers having been killed, and so many capital ships seriously damaged or destroyed, Marjory had been called back to active duty sooner than expected. She retained command of her special projects team but, as promised, she had been promoted to Admiral and given her choice of ship. She had chosen *Sunburst*, to initial derision from some colleagues who could not understand why she would choose a test bed, but complete understanding from those who were aware of the advances made by her unit. When Thengis, a highly regarded career officer, specifically requested to join her, notice was taken. Finally, when she was given command of First Fleet, objections came thick and fast. All were quashed by a combination of political leadership and Fleet executive.

And then *Sunburst* had arrived at Wentis Station.

Thengis recounted to Marjory over the inevitable coffee how *Sunburst's* arrival had stopped everyone, everywhere, on the station. Viewscreens across the station were tuned to show new arrivals as they ended their approach and swung into their berths. When three berths were cleared of existing ships for *Sunburst* there was some confusion. But then the screens picked up the approaching Supernova-class ship. Jaws dropped. Conversations ceased. *Sunburst* was accompanied by two Star class cruisers, one Star class carrier, two Superstar class cruisers and a gaggle of destroyers, corvettes and support vessels. The relative size of *Sunburst* against what had been the largest ships in the fleet was mind-boggling. Attention quickly moved from the sheer size of the behemoth to the ship's smooth, elegant lines. It was unmistakably of the same design family as the now smaller capital ships but with different, more eye-pleasing, proportions that suggested that those earlier generations of ships had been built using the same design cues and then down-sized to fit their specification. Which they had been. The apparent lack of main weapons elicited discussion once tongues were found again. Stylised images of a sun bursting with light had been applied to both sides of the hull and on the stubby dorsal section and they veritably glowed as spotlights were trained on them from the hull, drawing even more excited commentary. Such a display of a ship logo had never been done before on a Fleet vessel.

Sunburst's screening ships swung away and into their own berths. Marjory moved *Sunburst* into the centre of the three berths that had been cleared. The ship faced into the station, its blunt bow on display for all to see via the enormous viewing windows, and the sheer bulk became even more obvious. The umbilicals extended from the docking points and latched onto the standard mountings along the front quarter, but none were able to reach the hard points further back. The designers had been aware that this would be the case, however, and allowed for it, but from above it gave the impression of a Hengarian sucker fish with its head firmly embedded in its prey and its long tail the only visible part.

The sensation lasted for days and Fleet personnel would spend off-duty time just staring at *Sunburst* from the observation points. Every senior officer requested a tour and Marjory assigned several of her research team to do the honours, after *Fendaristil*, safely stored in *Sunburst's* hangar bay, vetted each requester. Inevitably, the tours ended with those officers departing with slightly dazed expressions.

There was, however, work to do. *Sunburst* was fully fuelled and fully armed with ordinance for its many rail guns of all sizes and its multitude of missile launchers. A second, albeit smaller, sensation occurred when the two squadrons of stingers carried by *Sunburst* took their turn flying combat cover over the station. The reason for three berths being reserved became obvious as the hangar bays extended from the ship's sides, so *Sunburst* now completely occupied the space allotted to it. Hammer and Shield squadrons did a combat launch from the hangars rather than using the launch tubes, on the basis that one always took the opportunities to practice and train, and the speed of the stingers as they darted away from the station raised eyebrows once again. Thengis now found himself the object of envy rather than amusement at his choice of ship and the fact that he had been accepted.

Briefings occupied Marjory for most of every day. The estimated size of the Empire fleet being put together was a major concern. Fifteen heavy cruisers and a further ten medium cruisers - the Empire had no equivalent to light cruisers any more - combined with a relatively small number of more nimble ships was enough to decimate any single Union fleet. That had not been the case for hundreds of years. Union and Empire fleets had been close to parity for a long time, but this represented a return to the days when the Empire greatly outmassed the Union ships.

Wentis had three fleets docked or arrayed in holding stations around it, and the Fleet strategists were unable to shed light on whether they would be enough. New Star-class vessels had been built and launched in a rush, and there was concern about their resilience. Their captains had reported a litany of problems in what were essentially shake-down cruises for them, and the engineering teams were overworked as they attempted to resolve those problems while also readying the fleets for deployment. Each of the Empire ships was given a designation. Specifications were guessed at for several of them, as some were of a newer, slightly more massive type.

Marjory, examining the images closely, recognised that Likud had done little more than add even more armour and armaments to the same sized or slightly stretched versions of the older cruisers. That was not a surprise, given Likud's lack of imagination and skill when it came to ship or weapon designs. The ships appeared to have the same engines, still looking like they were tacked onto the backs of the ships. Perhaps they had the same weaknesses? Time would tell.

What was new was the ability of half of the ships to launch fighters, where previously that was limited to very few Empire ships. Hangar bays had been hung beneath several cruisers in what looked to be an afterthought, but Marjory suspected that they would be sound structurally and would likely carry significant numbers of the small craft. Intelligence suggested that this refit of fighter capabilities was the reason for the Empire not following up immediately on their victories of several years previously. It added a different dimension to what would be a very dangerous battle indeed.

When the same briefings had been made for a third time, and it was obvious that nothing new was becoming known, attention turned to preparing for the fleets to take their leave of Wentis Station. Third Fleet would be the first to depart, followed by Fifth Fleet. First Fleet would follow a day behind the others. Rendezvous points were finalised, tactics were agreed in the full knowledge that the agreed actions would not happen exactly as planned, and final preparations were made. Tension mounted. Station personnel fretted that this major outpost of the Union would be left unprotected, which fears were allayed somewhat when it was announced that the still rebuilding Fourth Fleet would arrive soon after First Fleet left, and would remain to act as rear guard.

Known enemy agents had been fed information about the location of a secret gathering for an exercise of the Third and Fifth Fleets, which were reputed to comprise the cream of the remaining Union ships. Final discussions revolved around what would happen if the Empire did not take this bait that had been dangled in front of them. Marjory, with her knowledge of Likud, was confident that it would be taken but could not make that known and could only express confidence in the plan. Knowledge of First Fleet, and especially *Sunburst*, had been tightly held and, despite the sensation caused when the latter had arrived at Wentis Station, there was confidence that its existence was not known by the Empire. Still, plans were made in case the plan failed.

Finally, Third Fleet left Wentis Station, followed half a day later by Fifth Fleet. Then it was First Fleet's turn. Marjory watched her team perform their jobs calmly and competently. All of the bridge crew were combat veterans, many from the disaster that saw the Union fleets decimated. All knew that they flew in the most advanced vessel ever built by the Union. All had confidence in the skill and judgement of Marjory, known to them as Admiral Mavin Serra. All knew that in combat many things could go wrong, however, and many of the Union ships had never fought before. Failure would be disastrous for the Union, but Likud's plan had to fail.

| **37** |

Sunburst

"Coming to our station, Admiral," Hollis reported. "Thirty minutes out."

"Very well, Mr Hollis. Captain Thengis, please inform the fleet. Sound general quarters. Weapons-Sergeant, point defences on line and prepare to deploy the main cannons as soon as we exit jump space. Shields to full. All missile tubes to be armed. Shield squadron to prepare to deploy as defence. Hammer to deploy on designated targets. Sensors, full sweep long range and short range, and I want jump space scanning at all times."

Marjory rattled off the list of orders and the bridge crew burst into action. The huge main viewscreen reconfigured to show multiple windows around the edge of the main image, which was a tactical plot of the space where they would emerge. Status displays showed everything from weapons readiness, ship status, long and short range sensor maps, and more. On the main screen several stars were shown, two of them with planetary systems. An asteroid belt became visible running across the top left quarter of the screen as the image zoomed in to show a smaller area, while all but one of the stars moved off the edges of the screen. The single remaining star was placed to the bottom left, with its three rocky planets shown with their projected orbits. The right side of the screen was empty.

"We should be two hours ahead of Third and Fifth Fleets, Admiral," Hollis said. "Jump space is quiet in detectable range. Long range sensors have no contacts. Short range sensors likewise. Exiting jump space in ten minutes. Projected exit point is on screen."

A blue circle appeared in the screen, between the orbits of the first and second planets. First Fleet would hide itself, as far as they could, amongst the seven moons of the second planet. Hopefully, by hugging those orbiting bodies and keeping the star of the system between themselves and the expected system entry point of the Empire ships, the fleet would be missed. It was a long shot but any advantage would help.

An hour later, *Sunburst* was parked as close as it could be to the largest of the seven moons. The capital ships all had their own moons and did likewise, trying as far as possible to keep the bulk of the moons between themselves and the expected Empire entry vector. The corvettes moved into the open. It was hoped that they would be seen as little more than a distant protective screen once the Third and Fifth Fleets entered the area of space that would form the battle ground. The support ships would jump to a point near the asteroid belt, away from the battle itself.

"Jump space disturbance, Admiral," Hollis reported from the sensor station. "Heading matches the approach vector of Third Fleet."

"They're early," Marjory said with a grimace.

The plans were set with very tight tolerances, so early arrival indicated a problem of some sort. If the Empire was monitoring the sector then the early arrival may cause them to arrive early and throw the plan into disarray. Of course, they may have seen First Fleet arrive and made their early entrance also, and that had not happened.

The screen lit up as Third Fleet arrived, emerging from jump space in a tight series of energy bursts. Led by *Justiciar II*, a Superstar class cruiser, the fleet consisted of three Star class cruisers, two destroyer class and 3 corvette class ships, plus one set of twinned tugs and a single heavily armoured tug. First Fleet's support ships had been left at an intermediate jump point, as had Fifth Fleet's. Third Fleet deployed in a standard spread for a frontal engagement.

"Another jump space disturbance," Hollis reported. "A big one. Not Fifth Fleet." Hollis looked to Marjory. "Coming from Empire space, Admiral."

Marjory nodded. Third Fleet's early arrival may mean they would have to engage without the support of Fifth Fleet. In turn, that may require First Fleet to intervene early. The plan called for the battle to be under way before First Fleet and *Sunburst* intervened.

"Twelve minutes," Hollis said, referring to the arrival time of the Empire ships. "And a third disturbance, Fifth Fleet. Fifteen minutes away, estimated arrival time."

"Very well," Marjory said. "Battle stations please. First Fleet is to hold station. Silent running."

Sunburst's bridge was quiet. Battle stations saw alert indicators move from amber to red, but there was no alarm, no blaring tones. The bridge crew watched the screen intently but calm reigned. Marjory and Thengis exchanged a glance. The former nodded. Whilst most of the bridge crew had been with her in the Special Projects unit, it had been Thengis who, in a short time, had integrated the older members of the team with those who had joined more recently.

"Empire fleet about to emerge, Admiral," Hollis said into the quiet twelve minutes later.

The main screen flickered as the Empire ships appeared, seemingly from nothing. Fifteen icons appeared on the screen, followed moments later by another ten and eight more immediately after. The Empire fleet moved immediately to confront Third Fleet.

"Two minutes," Hollis said tensely.

Third Fleet would have to hold their own for that time before Fifth Fleet would emerge from jump space. The Empire fleet opened fire from long range, the capital ships spitting energy blast after energy blast that formed a seemingly solid curtain. Marjory nodded as the Empire ships accelerated behind the energy screen that they had created. The heavy cruisers led the way. Fifteen huge, top heavy ships formed a cone-shaped arrow head, with the ten medium cruisers following in their wakes. The eight smaller vessels swung back and forth behind their larger cousins.

Third Fleet held their fire. *Justiciar II* and the Star class cruisers absorbed the long range fire, running interference for the smaller ships. The strategy for the battle called for the two Union fleets to present a unified front. With Fifth Fleet still on approach, that strategy appeared to be in tatters.

"Fifth Fleet emerging from jump space," Hollis reported.

The whole bridge crew watched the screen. Fortuitously, Fifth Fleet emerged from jump space above and at a forty-five degree angle to the charging Empire fleet. It took the Fifth fleet commander a moment to realise that the battle had started without him, but then the five Star class ships launched a full spread of missiles, while the eight corvettes of the Fifth Fleet darted forward, targeting the smaller Empire ships. Marjory breathed a sigh of relief. At least the plan could be brought back on track.

The Empire fleet divided in two. Ten of the heavy cruisers targeted Third Fleet while the remaining five heavy cruisers plus the smaller vessels targeted Fifth Fleet. *Justiciar II* led Third Fleet into the fray as the two fleets charged toward each other. The volume of energy fire increased and the shields of both sets of ships flared and glowed. At almost the last minute, the Union ships ducked below the line of attack, whilst maintaining near continuous fire from their main energy weapons. The three tugs, squat and ugly but equipped with enormous engines that could produce huge power, did the opposite and swung above the line of Empire attack. The single tug was equipped with a single main energy weapon, out-sized for the ship's mass, and a raft of torpedoes, while the twinned tugs, successors to *Jack* and *Jill*, had all of that and more, and advanced shields. The tugs' main guns opened fire, targeting the bridges of the Empire cruisers that stood high above the main hull. However, the ten Empire ships massed much larger than the Union ships and the volume of energy fire directed at the Union ships was massive.

"Admiral, estimate the first element of the Empire ships will have to turn in two minutes," Hollis said into the quiet of the bridge.

"Very well," Marjory replied, watching Third and Fifth Fleets' ships suffer under the battering of the Empire cruisers. "First Fleet prepare for a micro-jump. Set the target location. Designate targets for each ship. All ships to open fire immediately."

"Jump in one minute," Hollis reported. "Targets locked in."

A gasp came from Lieutenant Bard. On the main screen, two of the Star class ships were trailing vapour, indicating hull breaches. Both continued to fight but were falling behind the line of attack. One of the corvettes drifted, powerless. All three ships now took the brunt of the Empire attack. The corvette broke up even as escape pods were being ejected. Most were caught in the explosion that followed, while several were flung away from the site of the ship's demise.

"Track those pods," Thengis ordered. "Power to the main guns, deploy the main railgun, all defensive batteries online. I want a mix of high impact missiles and torpedoes in the shafts. Deploy hangar bays."

"Jump in five," Hollis reported.

The Empire vessels started their turn after charging through the Union lines, even while maintaining heavy fire. *Starshine* and *Starlift*, the two damaged Union cruisers, both switched shields to the rear. Their shields glowed red hot from the energy they sought to absorb or deflect.

"Now," Marjory ordered.

The last thing Marjory saw before the jump was *Starshine* start to tumble. All Union ships continued to exchange fire with the Empire cruisers.

"Jump," Hollis called.

The jump took three seconds. A hundred kilometres away from the turning Empire ships' flanks space rippled and First Fleet appeared. Immediately, all ships launched their missile and torpedo barrages. From *Sunburst's* hangar bays Hammer and Shield squadrons launched. Directly behind the last Shield ship, a single small cloaked ship darted from the hangar, having directed the sensors to ignore it.

Sunburst's main energy weapons opened fire, blast after blast targeting the two centre-most Empire ships. Interspersing each pair of energy blasts, the main railgun fired its hundred kilogram projectiles, every fifth one carrying a high explosive warhead. The line of First Fleet ships added their considerable weight to the mix.

The Empire ships were taken by surprise. As Marjory had noted during the briefings, the Empire commanders shifted their shields as they fought an action. At the moment, as they had almost completed their turn in preparation to take a second pass at the battered Union Third Fleet, their shields were largely directed forward, with light shielding at the rear. *Sunburst's* energy bolts blasted through the thin rear shielding and seared away the emitters from the hulls of its two targets. Bolt after bolt hit before the ship commander could react. Seeing the effect of the more powerful *Sunburst* energy cannons, Weapons-Sergeant Sertis shifted aim to cycle the main energy weapon through six of the Empire ships, two shots to each. Meanwhile, the railgun slugs arrived at the target ships.

The heavy armour of the Empire cruiser stood up to the challenge of the kinetic rounds, although they sustained increasing damage with each hit. The explosive rounds, however, created pits and cracks across the hulls of the ships that the energy blasts exploited as they found them. The heavy cruisers barely rocked at each explosion, but the damage was recorded by *Fendaristil* and relayed to Marjory on *Sunburst*. Marjory smiled thinly and directed the stingers to attack those specific locations on the Empire ships, several of which were now turning to meet this new threat.

Hammer squadron launched their torpedoes from long range before swinging wide and above the line of battle. These were the version of torpedoes developed by the Advanced Weapons Unit. They were faster and carried a much greater punch than their predecessors. The still limited but much improved AI capabilities of the torpedoes allowed them to dodge and weave to completely different patterns to their predecessors, confusing the targeting systems of the cruisers. Of the hundred and twenty torpedoes launched, five from each of the stingers, less than a fifth were destroyed. Most of the rest hit approximately where they were meant to. Five of the Empire ships suffered extensive damage as the torpedoes cracked open the weakened hulls to allow others access to the ship interiors.

Third Fleet rejoined the fray as they completed their turns. *Starshine* continued to tumble out of the battle zone, while *Starlift* proved to be unable to make the turn with its fellows and maintained its previous heading. *Justiciar II* was streaming vapour from multiple hull breaches and the remaining capital ships, *Starbelt* and *Starfish*, were scarred and blackened where the Empire's heavy energy weapons had scored hits. Two of the corvettes stayed with the stricken *Starshine* and *Starlift*, while the others sped above or below the line of battle to find different angles of attack.

"Take us in, Captain," Marjory ordered. "Between those two Empire ships."

Thengis looked at her quizzically.

"Full broadside," Marjory said.

A slow grin spread across Thengis's face, and he nodded.

"Aye, Admiral. Navigation, plot a course below and between the two enemy ships at the starboard end of the line. All First Fleet ships are to concentrate on the damaged cruisers or the two at the other end. Shield squadron to fall in behind *Sunburst*. Third Fleet ships are to direct their fire to the same ships. Mr Hollis, flank speed. Mr Bard, all missile tubes prepare to fire. Weapons-Sergeant, stow the main energy weapons, defensive weapons to full autonomous fire, main railgun to fire to port, high explosive rounds only. Ready? Go!"

Sunburst sped ahead of the ships of First Fleet. The two Empire ships at *Sunburst's* starboard continued to lay down fire on Third Fleet, but were undamaged and travelling no more than ten kilometres apart. *Sunburst* closed on them quickly and slid between them, although slightly below relative to the plane of travel. The Empire ships' energy cannons belatedly swivelled to face *Sunburst* and opened fire. Shields flared orange and red, and *Sunburst* rocked slightly to each hit, but the massive ship continued to charge between the two enemy ships. The huge railgun was firing to good effect, almost continuous fire that was unheard of in any ship from the Union or Empire.

"*Fendaristil*, plasma bursts on the main weapons of the Empire ships," Marjory directed quietly.

The small shielded ship stationed outside the battle zone swooped in. Its twin plasma nozzles had been upgraded by Marjory over the many years since leaving Ennaris, and the plasma generator had been improved likewise. From seemingly empty space above the two Empire ships four small but expanding gouts of plasma appeared, travelling on collision courses towards the Empire ships. Both ships sought to evade but were too late. The plasma washed over the main gun emplacements on the upper hulls. When the blast residue washed away both guns were twisted and blackened.

"Admiral, some sort of strange plasma energy just damaged the two ships," Bard reported. "No idea where it came from."

"Captain, now!" Marjory ordered. "Thank you Mr Bard. Please let me know if anything else appears," she continued, even as Thengis gave his orders.

"Missile tubes one to sixty, ripple fire. Fire!"

Hatches slid open in a moment and along the forward flanks of *Sunburst* missiles and torpedoes burst forth. They only had five kilometres to travel on each side and they made that in moments, thirty travelling to port and thirty to starboard. Almost all of them struck in a continuous line along the hulls of the two Empire ships. The damage was immense, even through the massive armour. Most of the defensive batteries went silent.

"Shield, take out their engines," Marjory ordered. "Hammer, finish them and then re-arm."

From far behind *Sunburst*, Shield squadron darted forward, dividing into two elements. Each ship fired a single torpedo at the known weak spot between the engine exhaust nozzles of the Empire cruisers that, for some reason that Marjory still could not fathom, had never been fixed. Perhaps Likud did not know how to fix them. Shield squadron attacked without opposition with the defensive systems down. The torpedoes sped to their targets and impacted only a few seconds apart. The Empire ships died hard and identically. Their engines exploded in short-lived blazes as fuel detonated. Remaining power went out throughout the ships. Both ships started to tumble and roll. *Sunburst* dropped further below them quickly and swung away with Shield squadron in its wake. Hammer dropped from its holding position and each ship launched their remaining torpedoes from twenty kilometres distance before speeding after *Sunburst.*

The two Empire ships shuddered as the torpedoes compounded the already heavy damage along the length of their hulls. Huge vents were ripped open in the hulls. Several torpedoes sped through the gaps and their high explosive blasts devastated the interior spaces. There were no escape pods launched.

The combined forces of First and Third Fleets had taken significant damage but had successfully overcome the remaining two Empire ships. *Justiciar II* was little more than a wreck, somehow still under power but heavily damaged and spilling escape pods. *Starbelt* had one of its two huge engines offline but appeared to be intact while *Starfish* was venting atmosphere from multiple gaping wounds but continued to fire its main energy cannon at the drifting Empire cruiser nearest to it.

"Fifth Fleet reports heavy damage, but the remaining enemy cruisers have retreated," Lieutenant Bard reported. "No other Empire vessels were destroyed but all are heavily damaged. *Meteor* is operational but has heavy casualties, and two of its three engines are damaged. It's venting atmosphere from eight decks. *Starsea* has been all but destroyed, also heavy casualties. Escape pods are non-functional. I've directed *Starsill* and *Gresham* to assist both ships. All other ships are damaged but functional and can take care of their own casualties. Two of the corvettes may have to be abandoned, however."

"Very well," Marjory said with a grimace. "Captain, make sure of *Sunburst's* status and any casualties. All stingers to be refuelled and rearmed for defence. Mr Bard, status of the two Admirals?"

"Admiral Hurlis is injured and unconscious but is expected to survive. Her bridge area took multiple strikes and sustained considerable damage when *Justiciar* shielded the smaller ships. Many of the bridge crew are among the casualties. Admiral Simpkin is reported missing. *Meteor's* bridge was also targeted and repair crews are yet to reach it. *Meteor* is being flown from engineering."

"Inform Third and Fifth Fleets that I am assuming overall command of the task force. Bring as many casualties onto *Sunburst* as you can. We have better medical facilities. Alert the Chief Medical Officer. Use whatever space you need to use. Ships that are too damaged to get back to Wentis will be destroyed after all personnel are accounted for." Marjory paused as she looked over the chart of the space around the battle zone that was displayed on the main viewscreen. "Hammer and Shield are to rotate flying cover until further notice. I want the ships of Third and Fifth Fleets to be brought into the command net of First Fleet. For now we will be a combined force. Casualties and repairs are the priorities." She looked around the bridge. "You all did well, but we have lots to do. Let's get started. Captain, you have the bridge. I will be in my quarters composing a report for Fleet."

"You've managed to save the Union with this one battle," President Jancis of the Union Congress said as she and Marjory sat over coffee. "There is some thought that the Empire may not survive this disaster. That the Emperor may be toppled."

It was after a special session of the Union Congress, called to honour those who had died during what had become known as the Battle of the Dreadnoughts. It also had installed Marjory, now the most decorated Admiral of the Union Fleet, as Grand Admiral, a rank that had not been used for centuries and an elevation that Marjory had almost refused. Now she snorted, imagining Likud allowing anyone else to take over.

"Unlikely," Marjory said evenly. "What we will see, if we have anyone able to monitor events, will be the disappearance of anyone who may remotely challenge Likud."

"You sound as though you know this Likud," Jancis replied. "He is the latest of many to carry that name or title. Why is he any different?"

Marjory thought for a moment. How best to respond? Because they had no experience with people able to lead extremely long lives based on accidents of genetics, there was a general inability to even consider that Likud may be the same person through all of the time that his name had been known. It stood to reason, then, that Likud was a title, hereditary or otherwise. Marjory knew better, but also knew better than to say that.

"I have studied history," she replied instead. "And a constant has been that those in positions of great power seek to do anything to hold onto it. It is why we have the checks and balances for your own position, Madam President, not for you alone but for all those who may be tempted to hold power beyond the time allotted. Imagine you have total power and wish to hold it. You would do whatever it took to do so. Consider also that the Empire ships do not have working escape pods. Consider that failed commanders are executed, along with their families. Consider that it is Likud who makes all key decisions, from what we know. Now take that ruthless attitude and apply it to maintaining his own position of power. How far would he go to do that? I imagine as far as he felt he needed to go."

"Well, your plan and your actions, with those of the other fleet commanders and crews, have ensured security for the Union for a long time to come," Jancis replied. "Our intelligence estimates it may take fifty years or more. And for that we owe you a great vote of thanks."

"The Empire will rebuild," Marjory replied, with a wry shoulder shrug, "and much faster than that. It will not take as long as it would take us to do the same, and the Union will be forced to deal with enemies from within as well. That will be the first stage of Likud's rebuild, to try to weaken the Union from the inside. And then he will seek to take his revenge."

"Your advice, then Grand Admiral?"

"We stay prepared, Madam President, and vigilant," Marjory replied. "We continue to stand behind the women and men who act as the barrier between the Union and those who may wish to harm it. We continue to seek out allies to work with."

"Allies? We have yet to find any other people able to provide any support against the Empire. It's as though we are the only two civilisations capable of such technological advances."

"You never know," Marjory smiled. "You just never know."

Epilogue

1 year before the events described in
<u>*Children of Ennaris*</u>

Marjory strolled up the ramp and onto *Fendaristil*. The pocket destroyer was securely berthed in the enormous flight deck of the First Fleet's flagship, *Sunburst*. Marjory was in an introspective mood. Increasingly of late, she had taken to spending time in the confines of her old ship.

It had been well over five hundred years - almost the same number of cycles in Ennari time - since she had left Ennaris and the duty that she had taken on with Drewflin, and the few other remaining Mages. Over five hundred years since Fernis had sought her out and given her the task of raising the humans of Earth to be a fit opponent to Likud's Empire. Not to save the human planet and confederation, or at least not just for that, but because of the expectation that it would be from the humans, lifted to civilisation by Ennaris' colonisation teams over many millennia, that the Children would come.

Marjory hoped that was the case. In many ways, she felt that her job was done, or very close to it. The Union now had the ability to, at worst, hold their own against the Empire. It had suitably trained people to operate that equipment and a philosophy that ensured that it would not be used for ill towards others. As the Battle of the Dreadnoughts had shown, it could also defeat the Empire with the right people in the right positions.

The continued infiltration by Empire agents, and the preparedness of some to forsake their fellow humans by becoming Empire agents, continued to bedevil Marjory, though. Over the centuries she had been responsible for uncovering and dealing with several cells, usually because they were attacking her in one of the guises she had worn at those times. Other cells had been revealed to be operating within the ranks of the Union Fleet, the Union's political framework or the leadership of individual planets. That made sense, of course. If one wished to undermine any sort of organisation or structure, then it was always most effective to do so from within.

The problem for Marjory was that she could not see *how* one could be prepared to destroy one's own civilisation for limited personal gain. For that was what these betrayals were about. The Union of Earth and its companion human and non-human worlds and peoples would be destroyed. Likud had not a shred of forgiveness in him. Impetuous and wild, wilful and unruly as he was, he also bore a ruthless and vicious streak that had been held in check only by more powerful figures around him. The results when he broke out of those strictures was literally catastrophic, as Marjory had experienced on Ennaris. Forgiving a civilisation that had met and ultimately grown to challenge his own Empire was not in his nature. The Union and its member nations would be destroyed utterly, if he had his way.

Marjory had dealt with miscreants before, some from within the ranks of the Ennari Mage community and others from within the large and wide-spread Ennari population, as it had been before the fall. Some of those came from the colonial missions, when members or whole teams decided to set themselves up as god-like figures over the people they were sworn to help. It was from one of those episodes that Goroth's rebellion, that led to Ennaris' near total destruction, had sprung.

Marjory sighed as she settled into her favourite flight couch. The incredibly hardy material was showing the first signs of wear. That it was well over five hundred years - cycles - old also was testament to the materials that Ennaris had developed and used as a matter of course. But it had been a long time since she and her ship had left Ennaris' moon base. *Fendaristil*, of course, never complained. The ship, and the almost self-aware AI that resided within its hugely complex matrices, was the most advanced ship ever produced by Ennaris. In itself that was merely evolution, as *Fendaristil* was also the last ship produced by Ennaris' once mighty ship-building complex. But *Fendaristil* had been designed, by Marjory and others who were long gone, in such a way as to hide its capabilities. And Marjory had continued to improve its capabilities since.

In fact, Marjory mused as she cradled a fresh coffee, it had been *Fendaristil* as much as her own efforts that had made this mission succeed as well as it had, assuming that it ended up as a success. The capabilities of *Fendaristil,* the ship, so far in advance of either the Union or Empire ships when Marjory had left Ennaris and still more advanced in some ways than any of them, had provided Marjory with the comfortable and secure base of operations. And *Fendaristil,* the AI, had expanded its own abilities, had learnt so much more than it may have in its original role as a pocket destroyer converted to the Battle Mage's personal vessel, that it had become a trusted companion, helping Marjory to develop strategies and tactics. *Fendaristil* had even assisted to incorporate some new design elements into itself from advances that Marjory and a small number of brilliant human scientists and designers had made as they adapted Ennari designs and technologies for human use.

Now, however, with her primary goals achieved, Marjory felt ... restless. It was something new, as though some new change was in the air. The fact that she had gone for decades in stasis between the episodes during which she had introduced new technology, techniques or tactics did not take away the fact that she had been away from Ennaris for a very long time. She sighed and took a sip of her coffee, one of the things that she would miss when she finally did head back home.

Whether it was serendipity, coincidence or the Guardians' own luck, at that moment a sensor noted that Ennaris' planetary cloak had dropped. A sequence of transmissions between pre-prepared stations followed. Finally, the last transmission executed. As Marjory took a second sip of her coffee a small, discrete light embedded in her console started to flash. Marjory stared at the flashing light for a long moment before realisation dawned, even as *Fendaristil* came to life around her in reaction to the signal.

She sat straight on the flight couch as her scattered thoughts were dragged together. At last! At long last! The signal that she had arranged so long ago had been activated. Her mission to the Union was almost at an end. Soon she could return to Ennaris.

It was time to put the final elements into play. It was time to locate and gather the Children. It was time to prepare for the final confrontation with Goroth, for she had no illusions that he would refuse a peaceful resolution. It was time to rejoin Drewflin, her one and only heart. It was time to fight once again for Ennaris, for her lost son, for Drewflin, for the people of Ennaris.

It was time!

About the Author

James K. McVey is an author living on the New South Wales Central Coast, in Australia. The four novels that comprise *Children of Ennaris* were his first published works.

Visit www.jameskmcvey.com.au for further information and updates on these and other works.